**Praise for *New York Times* bestselling author
Heather Graham**

"Heather Graham knows what readers want."
—*Publishers Weekly*

"An incredible storyteller."
—*Los Angeles Daily News*

"Graham is a master at world building and her latest is a thrilling, dark, and deadly tale of romantic suspense."
—*Booklist*, starred review, on *Haunted Destiny*

**Praise for *USA TODAY* bestselling author
Delores Fossen**

"Clear off space on your keeper shelf, Fossen has arrived."
—*New York Times* bestselling author Lori Wilde

"This is a thrilling and twist-filled read that will keep you guessing till the end."
—*RT Book Reviews* on *Lone Wolf Lawman*

New York Times and *USA TODAY* bestselling author **Heather Graham** has written more than a hundred novels. She's a winner of the Romance Writers of America's Lifetime Achievement Award, a Thriller Writers' Silver Bullet and, in 2016, the Thriller Master Award from ITS. She is an active member of International Thriller Writers and Mystery Writers of America, and is the founder of The Slush Pile Players, an author band and theatrical group. An avid scuba diver, ballroom dancer and mother of five, she still enjoys her South Florida home, but also loves to travel. For more information, check out her website, theoriginalheathergraham.com, or find Heather on Facebook.

Delores Fossen, a *USA TODAY* bestselling author, has sold over fifty novels with millions of copies of her books in print worldwide. She's received the Booksellers' Best Award and the RT Reviewers' Choice Best Book Award, and she was a finalist for a prestigious RITA® Award. You can contact the author through her webpage at deloresfossen.com.

New York Times Bestselling Author

HEATHER GRAHAM

HURRICANE BAY

HARLEQUIN®BESTSELLING AUTHOR COLLECTION

ISBN-13: 978-1-335-50240-7

Hurricane Bay

Copyright © 2018 by Harlequin Books S.A.

The publisher acknowledges the copyright holders of the individual works as follows:

Hurricane Bay
Copyright © 2002 by Heather Graham Pozzessere

A Man Worth Remembering
Copyright © 2002 by Delores Fossen

Recycling programs for this product may not exist in your area.

This edition published by arrangement with Harlequin Books S.A.

For questions and comments about the quality of this book, please contact us at CustomerService@Harlequin.com.

® and TM are trademarks of Harlequin Enterprises Limited or its corporate affiliates. Trademarks indicated with ® are registered in the United States Patent and Trademark Office, the Canadian Intellectual Property Office and in other countries.

HARLEQUIN®

www.Harlequin.com

Printed in U.S.A.

CONTENTS

Visit the Author Profile page
at Harlequin.com for more titles.

HURRICANE BAY

Heather Graham

This book is dedicated with the deepest gratitude to many people.

First and foremost, Choly Zequeira. You are a saint.

Sonia Fraser, Kettia Gaspard and Fay C. Watson. Thanks for so much.

The incredible folks at St. Philip's Episcopal Church, Reverends Eric Kahl and Jennie Lou Reid, David Karcher, Joyce and Glenn Downing, Vida Welborne, Ron Theobald, Sylviane Sacasa, George and Myrtice Hektner, Patrice Fike, Judy King, Julie McCready, Ellen Sessions, Lee Turner, the Right Reverend and Holly Richards, Manny and Laverne Diaz, John Dickason and Kris Charlton.

For the Southeast group—especially Doris McManus, Audrey Fetscher and Rocco.

Sincere thanks also to Dr. Antonio Ucar, Max Sanchez and Omar Garcia.

And with the greatest respect and appreciation to three special Metro-Dade policemen— Sergeant Greenberg and Officers Mallon and Szolis of the Kendall division.

Prologue

Web loved the Florida Keys.

In fact, his old nickname, Web, had been born there. So few people knew that name. It was special and unique, to a time as well as a place, just like the islands themselves.

Like pearls cast against the ocean, the Keys meandered down from Miami in a southwest string of dazzling and opalescent beauty. The water lay on both sides of the many islands, shimmering in shades of aqua, blue, green, ever varying with the different depths. There were two ways to leave the mainland behind, Card Sound Bridge and US1, and once those routes were touched, the magic began. There was nothing in the world like sunrise on the Keys, the sun arcing into the sky in shades of crimson ecstasy, the heavens flaring with sudden light, golds as brilliant as the reds, pas-

tels streaking from the bright colors with a soft beauty
that seemed to caress the soul. Sunsets were even more
heavenly, when the fiery globe of day began to fall in
slow majesty, creating a new realm of color, magenta
stretching fiery fingers out to the horizon, fading to
threads of yellow-tinged pink and mauve, until silver
and gray began to seep in and finally the orb of the
sun disappeared with a last gasp of steaming gold and
darkness fell.

There were few other places where darkness could
be so complete.

Not, of course, on the beaten path. Not where the
clubs stayed open, and the hotels and motels offered
streaming lights for their clientele, and not where the
laid-back Tiki bars still sent out soft beacons of welcoming, come-hither brightness. But away from civilization, where nature still prevailed, the darkness could
be as complete as a stygian hole, as fearsome as a hell
crawling with tiny demons, ready to eat away flesh and
go deep enough to consume a human soul.

Ah, darkness. It could offer so much. Sweet secrets
and sins, a place in which to hide...

And so it was at night, in the darkness, that Web
waited, reflecting on the mystery, beauty and romance
in the solitude of night and nature. And the task at hand.

There was an element of danger, of course.

A small element...but enough to give a little edge
to the thrill.

There were those who thought of Key West as the
main draw. But Web found the upper keys far more
welcoming and natural. Close to the heady civilization
of Miami, far enough away to offer the reefs, the sun-
rises and sunsets...

Not to mention shadow and darkness. An aura of mystery in which to meet *her* tonight. A surprise, of course, since she would have no idea of all he'd planned, the night, the breeze, the salty-sweet scent of the air, the beach…

Eternity.

She was so beautiful. Even more so when caught in shimmering rays of light…and shadow.

Web had planned tonight's event meticulously. Everything before her arrival had been set, and everything to follow was arranged to a *T*.

Almost.

The day had fallen into place perfectly, but now, as Web waited, the timing began to go awry. All the magic would be lost if she did not arrive soon. And this had to be the night, the night when so much would be solved, when reckoning would be met.

Web's watch ticked away the time. Minutes passed, then more minutes. Frustration, nervousness, set in.

Leave it to Sheila to be late.

It gave him time to reflect…

Every move she had ever made touched Web's heart and soul.

She had to come. And soon. Or all the detailed plans, the ebony mystique of the night, the brilliant ecstasy of dawn, would be lost.

And then…a sound.

Her car on the road.

Web switched on the portable floodlight.

The bright beam blinded her. It was like the wrath of God. Her car veering, she braked to an abrupt halt. Web calmly walked to the driver's side.

She shielded her eyes with a hand.

It might all have gone badly then. She might have had the window closed and the air on; it was cooler at night, but they were into the dead heat of summer.

But she had been driving with her windows open, luckily. It was a nice night. The air touched with coolness, a forerunner of the storm that would come in during the next day or two. The storm, of course, was part of the perfect plan.

"Who...what the *hell*?"

She had seen Web, of course.

"What in the world are you doing?"

"You agreed to meet me," he reminded her politely.

"For a minute, only a minute. And I never said I'd meet you *here*, in the frigging middle of nowhere."

She was angry and impatient at having her time taken up. Actually she was frequently impatient with anyone who wasn't in her favor at any given moment.

"It's so lovely here. I wanted you here with me, to see and appreciate just how beautiful it is here. I wanted to give you the night." Web sighed. "I take it you're not glad to see me?"

"Look, I just saw you earlier today. And I said I'd see you again, so we can talk then. *Briefly*." Her voice had a husky growl to it that meant she was getting really aggravated. "But I never expected you to half blind me on this godforsaken road. And you are an idiot. I could have hit you."

"But you didn't."

"You could have been killed."

"Interesting thought. But to see you, and alone, it was worth the gamble."

Suddenly she actually saw Web. "Are you wearing gloves?" she asked incredulously. "It's summer."

Being Sheila, she didn't have a clue.

"It's not so hot tonight. There's a storm coming in. They haven't named it. It's not a hurricane, a tropical storm, or even a depression yet. But you can feel it. Soon rain will pound. Lightning will soar across the heavens. Thunder will sound like drums."

"Great," she said, bored. "Poetry. That really explains the gloves."

"Oh…they're just diving gloves."

"Diving gloves? With a storm coming in? You're going diving *now*?"

Web ignored her question. "I told you, I really wanted to see you. Alone."

"Great." She tossed her silky hair and looked straight ahead at the road. "You've seen me. But we aren't going to be alone. I didn't agree to any of this ridiculousness. I have to go. I haven't got time for your games."

"You're so wrong. You're going to make time. To spend the night on the beach. To watch the sunrise. To…appreciate. You have all the time in the world."

"I don't!" She frowned, growing wary.

"Yes, you do."

Her frown deepened. "You have a camera."

"For taking pictures on the beach."

"We're not taking pictures on the beach. Look, I mean it, I have to go. I don't want to run over your feet, so get out of my way."

"No, no, you don't understand. There's so much that's worth experiencing, especially before a storm. The colors…you've got to see them. You never really see what's right in front of your face. You never saw…me."

She was staring at Web, completely confused and dismissive.

"Look—"

"Sheila, you *are* going to see the sunrise."

Web tossed the floodlight into her car, then reached for her. Real alarm rose in her eyes as she read something in his.

Web meant business.

She tried to hit the button to roll up the window. Too late.

"Let go! I'm leaving—now."

She hadn't expected the strength in the hands that curled around her wrists. She gunned the engine, but she'd put the car in Park.

"Dammit, what is the matter with you? You can't make me—"

"Oh, yes, I can. And guess what, Sheila? I'm going to."

Web got the door open and forced his way in, shoving her aside.

She started to scream.

But there was no one there to hear.

No one except for the mosquitoes that buzzed so annoyingly in the darkness, the night owl, the mangroves, the stars cast in the velvet sky and the sea breeze that drifted over the island.

And Web. But he didn't care. He just smiled, and within seconds, he had her silenced.

He was determined that they would share the coming of dawn.

Eventually the sun rose against the morning sky, the colors brilliant, despite the billowing clouds of the coming storm. Soon, soon…the rains would begin.

"See how absolutely beautiful?" Web asked.

Her eyes were fixed on the horizon.

"Really quite glorious," Web continued.

For once, she didn't argue. She just stared.

"You are as beautiful as the sunrise, Sheila," Web told her. "And I won't take long. I just want a picture or two."

Aim, focus, shoot…

The camera was a Polaroid. Instant gratification. He only had a few minutes to linger…to see the light, the shadows, the colors of this world.

The time had come. The scene had been set. The plan had been meticulously made.

But there was more to do, and he had to take care. The task must be completed, nothing left undone.

And so Web began.

Later the sun was full up, and Sheila…had moved on.

Anticipation filled Web's soul. Delight, glee, that each detail of the night and the dawn had come to such perfect fruition.

Now…

Patience. Web had to practice patience.

There was nothing left to do but wait…and watch as the plan unfolded.

Chapter 1

Kelsey Cunningham walked into the Sea Shanty like a diminutive whirlwind.

Dane Whitelaw was stretched out on one of the lounge chairs beneath the palm-covered roof of the back patio when he saw her walk through the rows of crude wooden tables toward him.

He'd been sitting there downing draft Budweiser as if it were water, and it still hadn't dulled the brutal dilemma that pounded through his mind like a storm surge.

He'd come here, far off the main road, to sit in the breeze and watch the boats out on the gulf because it was something he often did. The norm for him. Usually, though, he didn't inhale his beer.

If he'd expected something to happen after his recent discovery, it sure as hell wasn't *her*.

The minute his eyes fell on her, he knew she just meant more trouble.

She wore designer shades, a straw hat, sandals and a brief white halter dress. She was tanned, and her hair was a light honey shade, not the kind of color caused by endless days in the sun but a natural amber. She had dressed the part for a lazy, laid-back place like this one—she was even carrying some kind of fruity, umbrella-laden drink in a plastic cup. She looked like a tourist, which maybe she was now.

She knew him right away. Well, naturally. He hadn't changed much. She, on the other hand, *had* changed. Despite that, he had known her the minute she entered his vision. And a single word had come into his mind.

Fuck.

What the hell was Kelsey doing here now?

She made straight for him with long, no-nonsense strides and stopped right next to his chair.

Even with the heat, she managed to smell like some kind of expensive perfume. She was well-built, smooth and sleek, nice cleavage displayed above the bodice of the casual white dress that still managed to maintain a strange look of elegance on her form. She had gained an edge of sophistication in the years that yawned between them. And she didn't seem to remember him with any affection, or that they might once have been considered friends. Still, Kelsey was a beauty. Always had been, always would be. And a torpedo of pure determination.

And, long ago now, she had determined to keep herself far away.

So what the hell was she doing here now? Today, of all damned times?

She didn't give him a chance to ask, didn't even start off with so much as a simple "Hello."

"Where's Sheila?" she asked, a sharp note of demand in her voice.

His heart slammed. The name hit him like a blow to the head.

"Sheila?" he said, forcing a quizzical frown to his lips.

"Yes, Dane, where's Sheila?"

He studied her for a long moment. "Hmm. Not, 'Hi, Dane, how are you?' Or, 'Long time no see. How are you?'"

"Don't get funny. And don't pretend you don't know what I'm talking about."

"Kid, I'm not pretending anything."

"Don't call me 'kid,' Dane."

"Sorry. You *are* still Joe's kid sister, aren't you?"

"Dane, where is Sheila? And don't tell me you haven't seen her. There are witnesses, you know."

"Witnesses to what?"

"No one has seen Sheila in a week. The last time she was seen was here, with you. And you're going to tell me exactly where she is."

He was glad of his own sunglasses. And though there were few times in his current life when he was glad of his past, this was one of them. He kept his face totally impassive.

Because he did know what had happened to Sheila Warren, even if he didn't know exactly where she was. And in the last two hours, the one driving purpose in his own life had become finding the exact *whereabouts of Sheila.*

Of all the damned things he didn't need, it was

Kelsey Cunningham coming here now, accosting him. Looking for Sheila. As far as he knew, the two women hadn't seen each other in years.

"Sorry, kid. So she was here with me. She's here a lot. With a lot of different people. Why in God's name would I know where she is now…honey?" he asked, his voice a slow, lazy drawl, the tone purposefully insinuating. Why not? They weren't kids anymore. And the time when they'd been bonded together in sorrow was eons ago now. The last time they had met, she had been far more than cool. In fact, she'd been as frigid and brittle as ice.

Kelsey the compassionate. Sincere, earnest, a daredevil at times. Quick with laughter, swift to challenge. Full of empathy for any underdog; a pit bull against any evil, real or imagined. Once upon a time, Joe's darling of a sweet little sister.

Times changed.

"Dane, dammit, she talked to you. You were seeing her again."

Irrelevantly he noticed that she had grown into her effortless grace. And she had gained the ability to appear as cool and remote as a goddess.

He almost sat up, but didn't. He forced himself to shrug casually. "Seeing her? Well, yeah, honey, I was seeing her. In a way. Me and half the men in the southern half of the state, not to mention nearly every tourist in pants who set foot on the island."

"You asshole," she said. Her tone didn't rise, but something in her words conveyed the extent of her contempt.

"Yeah, honey, I'm an asshole. But before you go off in a tizzy about Sheila Warren, you need to accept the fact that she'd changed over the years. In fact, you pretty much need to accept the fact that she was damn close to being a prostitute."

She was silent for a moment. She didn't move, but it didn't matter. The fury she was feeling seemed to emanate from her like heat waves off black pavement.

"She was…a free spirit. But I know she was with you again and now she's missing. Someone knows something. If it's anyone, it has to be you. You talked to her, and she talked to you."

"Yes, she talked to me. And I talked to her."

"So talk to me."

He slid his glasses down his nose for a moment, studying her. "*She* talked to me nicely," he said.

"This isn't a social call."

"Right. So leave me alone."

"Since you don't seem to want to talk to me, I'll have to see to it that you talk to the police."

"Fine. The police are usually polite and courteous." He pushed his sunglasses back up his nose and folded his arms over his chest.

She was still staring down at him. He sighed and looked up at her impatiently.

"So what is it now? I can't help you. Can't you leave me alone anyway? See something you like? Hey, kid, have you changed, too? Just like Sheila? Do you want to…catch up on old times?"

Her composure was amazing. She took her time answering him.

"Do I see something I like? No, not at all. In fact, I'm amazed by how much I see I *dis*like."

"Well, then, you *have* changed, honey. So…you're not into the muscle-bound beach type anymore, huh?"

"I'm just not into assholes like you. Available? You must be joking."

He looked up at her blandly. "Is that all?"

"All? No, not quite."

She spoke softly, and, with an economy of motion, she twisted her wrist. The fruity drink fell over his chest like a rain of sticky slime. He almost jumped up to grab her. Instinct again.

He managed to keep his place on the lounge chair. It was important that she keep thinking of him as an asshole.

Strange, he hadn't seen her in years. But still…she was a Keys kid from way back. Joe's little sister.

No, Kelsey was a hell of a lot more than that, he reminded himself. But any fleeting memory of what might have been an inescapable bond in the past was quickly doused by the lethal trauma of the present.

Even more than he had feared when he first saw her, he realized that she was trouble. Real trouble.

And he sure as hell didn't want her…

Dear God, he didn't want her going the route Sheila had gone.

Still staring down at him, she shook her head with revulsion. "An asshole and a drunk," she said. "You're covered in liquor and you don't even move."

"I imagine it's good booze. I'll just lick myself all over," he said. "Want to help?"

With one last look of disgust, she turned on her perfect little sandal-heels and started to walk away.

"Kelsey!"

Despite himself, he got to his feet, every muscle in his body quickening with tension.

"Go to the cops, Kelsey, then get the hell out of the

Keys, do you hear? Go back to your hot job and your condo on the bay. Do you understand?"

She paused for a moment, then told him what he could do with himself.

"Whatever you want, Kelsey. But I mean it. Tell the cops anything you think they ought to know. Then go home."

"This *is* my home—as much as it's yours."

"The hell it is. Your home now is a cute little condo in a ritzy section of Miami, with a gate and a security guard. Now go away."

"Who the hell do you think you are?" she asked. She didn't expect an answer, but he gave her one anyway.

"I'm the man telling you that you don't belong here anymore," he said. *Especially not running around asking questions about Sheila.*

"Like I said, Dane. This *is* my home just as much as it's yours. And I *will* find Sheila."

She started walking away again, taking a circuitous route past the tables. He was tempted to go after her, shake her, tell her to get her nose out of the entire thing. FedEx her back to Miami.

Except that he would wind up getting arrested if he tried that. He was certain that if he so much as put a hand on her, she would call the cops for sure.

So he watched as she walked away through the back door of the Sea Shanty. He had to convince her to go back to Miami and get her the hell out of this. How, he wasn't sure yet.

But he would. He swore to himself with a vengeance that he would get her out of here if it was the last thing he did.

When she was gone, he clenched his teeth and shook

his head, suddenly glad the beer hadn't kicked in. He walked down the sand- and shrub-covered path to the small spit of salt beach off the back of the Sea Shanty and just kept going until he was immersed. It was the quickest way he could think of to remove the drink she'd spilled on him. And the cool water was good for his head.

He'd wanted to behave completely normally after what had happened. But Kelsey arriving like a cyclone had changed all that.

Now the police were about to get involved, and sooner or later they would find Sheila Warren.

Jesus.

He had to find her first.

Kelsey walked into the right side of the duplex just off US1 in absolute disgust. She threw her purse across the small living room, watched as it landed in a wicker chair, then indulged in a moment's delicious relief as the air-conditioning surrounded her. Sea breezes be damned. It was hot as hell outside.

Pausing by the door for a moment, she let out a breath of aggravation.

"Well, that went well," she said, murmuring wryly aloud to herself. Her fault, maybe. Okay, her fault definitely. She could have started out with a, Hi, Dane, how are you? Wow, it's been ages…

But he had looked like such a beach bum lying there. And Nate, the owner of the Sea Shanty who she was actually married to for a very brief time when they were young, had said he had been drinking all afternoon. And that he'd been seeing Sheila. That they had argued. And that Dane had been strange ever since he'd moved back down from St. Augustine. That he'd taken on a case up there and someone had died strangely and... Nate hadn't really known all the particulars because Dane hadn't wanted to talk about them. So something not great had happened, and he'd come home to drink himself to death. Sheila had told her, too, that Dane had been strange. Like a guy ready to throw his life away.

When they were kids, Dane had been like the Rock of Gibraltar. He and Joe had been the leaders of the pack. Even when she had wanted to run away from life and—more than anything in the world—from Dane, she had wanted things to go well for him. It had been upsetting to hear that he had fallen into being little more than a beach bum, with no care for the world, no ambition, no concern for anyone at all—even old friends.

Sheila had been concerned about him.

But it seemed that Dane didn't give a damn about her.

Kelsey kicked off her shoes and walked into the kitchen. She opened the refrigerator door, thanking God that she'd taken the time that morning to do a little shopping for herself. Juice, soda, beer and wine. She had a choice.

The heat she'd come from made her opt for a beer. She hesitated, her fingers curling around a bottle, remembering that she'd found Dane swilling the stuff. She moved her hand, choosing a bottle of cranberry-raspberry cocktail instead. No. She wanted a beer, and the fact that Dane had turned into a slug who drank the stuff lying on a lounge chair in the shade shouldn't keep her from what she wanted.

Why the hell had he made her so mad? Right from the get-go. Okay, she'd been disturbed from the minute she'd talked to Nate, maybe unreasonably angry with Dane before she'd even headed out to speak to him. Why?

Uh-uh, she argued with herself. She wasn't going to delve into the psychiatry of that one. She hadn't seen him in years. And still, today…damn, she'd blown it, that was all. She'd meant to talk to him, get information. Everyone knew he'd been seeing Sheila again. Maybe they hadn't become a twosome, the way they had been when they were young, but apparently they'd still been close. Even Larry Miller, another friend from the early days who she worked with *and* Sheila's ex, had apparently known that, because he'd mentioned something about Sheila saying she was seeing Dane again when Kelsey had told him she was heading to Key Largo for her vacation, to spend time with Sheila.

Nate had told her that Dane and Sheila argued the last time he'd seen her. Cindy Greeley, one of her and Sheila's best friends growing up, had told her the same.

She pulled out the Michelob, twisted off the cap, took a long swig and looked around the kitchen. "Sheila… am I crazy? Are you just being a careless and inconsiderate bitch, the way everyone seems to think? Where the hell are you?"

The air conditioner hummed in reply. No answer there. In the quiet of the early evening, the sound seemed absurdly loud.

She walked to the rear of the living room and opened the glass doors to the patio at the back of the duplex, separated by a small privacy wall from the neighboring side. Beyond stretched the standard-size pool that belonged to both occupants, surrounded by flowering plants and shrubs. The entire yard was surrounded by a rustic wood privacy fence. The backyard was beautiful and peaceful, the high point of the duplex. And actually, on the patio, she could feel a sweet, salt-touched breeze. She was startled to feel suddenly that it was good to be home. And it *was* still her home, no matter what anyone said—especially Dane.

Not that she had gone so very far. Her section of Miami was only an hour to an hour and a half away, depending on traffic. But life there seemed as different as night and day, even if the temperatures in both places were almost identical and the same flowers bloomed. A short walk from this duplex could bring her to the Atlantic, and she could look straight out from her condo patio and see the waters of Biscayne Bay, heading into the Atlantic, as well. And still, this was so different. She had felt it today at the Sea Shanty, the small-town warmth, the laid-back ease, even with the place crawling with tourists and the main objective among most of the populace being to make money off those tourists. There were other people, as well, retirees, Northerners sick of the snow, and weekenders who had fallen in love with their weekends and made Key Largo their home. She'd always wanted to see more of the world, and she'd gotten to see a lot of it now. Maybe that was why it seemed so good to feel as if she had really come home.

Once upon a time, home had been the pretty white-painted wooden house south on US1 on the ocean side of the island. No more. Her parents had sold the place years ago. They didn't come back here anymore. In fact, the house no longer existed; it had been torn down to make way for the tennis courts for one of the new hotels. It had bothered her deeply when she'd started driving around today, so much so that she wished she had told her parents she wanted the house when they offered it to her before moving to Orlando.

Too late now.

Like them, at the time she had just wanted to get out of Key Largo.

She knew, of course, that when she'd left, she'd been running away. There had been far too much of Joe here then, and she had needed a new environment. Time could do good things. Now she liked it because there was still a lot of Joe here. Just as she had liked seeing Nate at the Sea Shanty, feeling the sun and the breeze at the Tiki hut bar, knowing that a short walk in bare feet would bring her to the little patch of private beach.

The Sea Shanty was like a bastion of memory. Nate's dad had run it when they were kids. Now the place was Nate's. And when she walked in, she really had felt that sense of coming home, of memory, nostalgia and mostly good things. She had felt a sense of poignant pleasure, being there. But then she had spoken with Nate and mentioned how worried she was about Sheila. Nate had started talking, and then she had seen Dane Whitelaw, plastered and vegetating in the sun, sunglasses in place, beer at his side, the picture of total inertia.

Dane Whitelaw, of all people.

Wasting his life. She'd seen it so many times. People who used this little corner of Eden to escape all responsibility, to drown themselves in beer and couch potato themselves into early graves.

And he was lying, to boot. He had seen Sheila, talked to her...done a lot more than talked, by his own admission. Why not? They'd been off and on for years. The worst of it was that he should care, be concerned. Even Larry, whom Sheila had hurt, had been concerned, in-

sisting that she call him if she needed anything, if Sheila
needed anything, if there was anything he could do...
Sheila wouldn't even need to see him. If she needed
money, he would be happy to help her out. Nate had
been concerned, too, shaking his head and telling her
that they all worried about Sheila, but hell, what could
they do? She was a grown-up.

Nate had told her, too, that Sheila often made dates
with her friends—lunch, dinner, drinks, coffee, breakfast, whatever—and forgot to appear. She always had
an apology, of course. Even so, Nate had seemed concerned, even as he tried to tell Kelsey that she shouldn't
be. He hadn't seen Sheila in a week, and she never
stayed away from the Sea Shanty that long.

Only Dane seemed indifferent. Crude. It appeared
that he had come home just to drink himself into oblivion, and he didn't give a damn about Sheila or anything else.

And, of course, there was that last page in Sheila's
diary, which she had found beneath the pillow on Sheila's bed. At first she had shoved the book back under
the pillow, surprised that Sheila had kept a diary, then
determined that a diary was private and she had no
right to read it. But when Sheila hadn't appeared, she
had skimmed through, and then gone to the last page.

Have to see Dane tonight. Tell him I'm afraid.

Private or not, she was going to read every page in
the diary. Maybe she should have mentioned it to the
police.

No. Not yet, anyway. Not until she knew what was
in it herself. She wasn't airing Sheila's life to anyone,
unless it became absolutely necessary.

There was a knock at the door. For a moment she

clenched her teeth, wondering if Dane had decided to follow her back from the Sea Shanty. A man wouldn't need to be a P.I. to find out where she was staying.

And he undoubtedly knew the way to Sheila's place.

She marched barefoot to the front door, grateful that the owners of the duplex had done away with the old-time jalousie and put in solid wood doors. She looked through the peephole. Cindy Greeley, now her official next-door neighbor in the duplex where she herself was an unofficial guest, was standing on the porch with a tray of something in her hands.

Kelsey opened the door.

"Did you find out anything?" Cindy asked her.

Kelsey stepped back, letting Cindy enter. Even in her bare feet, she was almost a head taller than the other woman, five-nine compared with Cindy's petite five-two. The smaller woman was compact, with sun-bleached hair, huge blue eyes and a tiny frame. She looked as if she should be heading off to high school, but she'd always had a terrific head on her shoulders, had made it nicely through college, and now owned eighteen T-shirt and shell shops throughout the Keys that might one day make her rich.

"Did I find out anything?" Kelsey said, her tone both musing and slightly bitter. "Nope. Nothing."

"I told you," Cindy said.

"Well, wait a minute. Maybe not exactly 'nothing.' I did find out that everyone saw Sheila arguing with Dane, but no one knows where she is now. Except, of course, I'm sure someone is lying. Want to come in and have something to drink?"

Cindy gave her a quizzical look for a moment. "Kind of early for you, isn't it? You're the kid who never had anything to drink during the day. And I thought you just came from the Sea Shanty?"

"It's after five. Isn't that cocktail hour?"

"Yeah, I guess. Sorry. I didn't realize how late it was. Daylight Saving Time, you know. Seems it stays light so late. But hey, I told you to try one of those Wind-Runners over there. That should have knocked you for a loop. Didn't you get one?"

"I ordered one. But I didn't drink it."

"Why not? They're delicious."

"It spilled," Kelsey said. "Are you coming in?"

"Oh, yeah, sure. I just made quiche. Thought you might like some."

"Good, you supply the food, I've got the beer."

They walked on into the kitchen together. "I went down to the sheriff's department. Sergeant Hanson let me fill out a missing persons report, though he wasn't real thrilled about it. He didn't seem to think there was anything odd about Sheila being gone for a week. Usually all you need is forty-eight hours. Here, your remains could be mummified and everyone still thinks you'll show up when you feel like it."

"Kelsey, that's not true. It's just that..."

"That what?"

"Sheila was living...a certain lifestyle," Cindy said.

"Still, a missing persons report is important," Kelsey told Cindy. She looked pointedly at her friend. "And it's something no one else thought to do."

"Kelsey," Cindy said, taking a seat on one of the three bar stools at the kitchen counter, "I'm not sure what to say to make you feel better. You've got to realize, Sheila is always going off and not telling anyone."

"I'm worried because she was supposed to meet me. Here. We made plans. I took my vacation time."

Cindy shrugged, accepting a bottle of Michelob. "Kelsey, you haven't seen a lot of Sheila in the last few years."

"I haven't seen her at all for at least two years," Kelsey said.

Cindy spoke slowly. "So you just have to realize— you don't really know her anymore."

Kelsey shrugged, feeling the guilt that had plagued her lately over that very fact.

They'd all been friends, growing up. Slightly different in age, but friends because they were islanders, and the area had been pretty darn small back when they'd been kids. She was the youngest, Cindy was one year her senior, Sheila and Nate were the same age, two years older than Cindy. Of their little group, her brother, Joe, had been the oldest—with Dane Whitelaw just one month younger. Then there was Larry, who had been about the same age as Dane and Joe, but he had been a weekender, so he hadn't really been in the same tight-knit group. Sometimes there had been other kids in the group, as well, guys like Jorge Marti, and even Izzy Garcia.

They'd all grown so far apart over the years.

Well, except for the fact that she worked with Larry, who had been instrumental in getting her into Sherman and Cutty, the advertising and promotions firm where she worked in the conceptual design department. Then, of course, Cindy and Nate were still close friends. And maybe she hadn't really been that far away, because she had kept up with Cindy. And Nate. Despite the fact that she and Nate had been married and divorced in the blink of an eye. Oddly enough, though totally unsuited to be husband and wife, she and Nate had made it as friends. When she thought back, she was angry with herself for what she had done, marrying him. Of course, she had felt empty then, hurt and very alone. The void in her life had seemed like a bottomless pit. There had been nothing she wanted more then than to get away. And Nate…Nate had never been going anywhere. He'd loved Key Largo and known he was going to stay from the time he'd been a boy. Maybe she had thought of marriage as a means to run away. Whatever her thinking, it had been wrong, and she had done nothing but hurt Nate. Still, it seemed he had forgiven her. And he was happy. He loved his Sea Shanty. Loved fishing, diving, boating and just being in the sun. He had never talked about anything other than living his life right here.

Just as Sheila and Dane had talked about nothing but moving on.

She understood why with Sheila. And with Dane… maybe she understood him, too.

But they'd both come back.

And now she was back here, as well, especially to see Sheila. Except that Sheila had invited her down, sent her the key to the duplex and never appeared herself.

"Have you been out to see Sheila's stepfather yet?" Cindy asked cautiously.

Kelsey experienced a slight and involuntary shudder. "No," she said, her admission rueful.

"Well, neither have I," Cindy murmured. "And he's actually the man we should be asking about her."

"I'm surprised she keeps in any kind of contact with him."

"She has to. They're connected by her mother's trust fund."

"You know what?" Kelsey said, suddenly decisive. "I'm going out there right now."

"Wait a minute! Why?" Cindy asked. "We're going to have beer and quiche. Kelsey, you have to eat, you know. You can go out and see Andy Latham anytime. Go tomorrow in the daylight."

"It's still daylight now," Kelsey said. She was already at the door, slipping her sandals back on. "I suppose I really should have gone out there to see him first."

"Why? Sheila hated him, you know that. If she had plans, she'd never have shared them with him. Not that she really made too many long-term plans. I lived in the other half of the same building, and I never knew what she was doing."

"You just said she had to keep in contact with him because of her mom's trust fund. He still might know something," Kelsey said.

Cindy sighed. "Kelsey, her car is gone, so she obviously drove somewhere. Maybe you should start by looking for the car instead of with her stepdad. Though I still think you're making a mountain out of a molehill."

"Cindy, she knew I could only take so much time off. And she really wanted to see me. She was worried about something."

Cindy was silent, which made Kelsey aggravated—with herself and with everyone else. Maybe they were right. She hadn't seen Sheila in forever. A sense of guilt had brought her here, but the fact that she was feeling guilty didn't mean that Sheila had suddenly become responsible, or that she wouldn't forget her plans with Kelsey the same way she forgot plans with anyone else.

Sheila might have talked to her, sounding desperate, then forgotten the plans they'd made just a few minutes later.

"Want to come with me?" she asked Cindy.

"No," Cindy said with a shudder. "And I really don't think you should go out there, either. You should wait. Get Nate or someone to go out with you. Dane would go. Dane has actually opened an investigations firm here. This is the kind of thing he does for a living. If anyone can find Sheila, it should be him. Make him go see Andy Latham with you."

Kelsey shook her head, still feeling the burn of her encounter with Dane. "Hire one drunk to go see another?"

"You don't understand about Dane," Cindy said.

"Cindy, you'd champion Dane if he'd just robbed the National Bank."

"Not true. He's just…I don't really know the story, but one of his clients was killed in St. Augustine."

"Murdered?"

"Not exactly. According to the police, it was accidental manslaughter, or something like that."

"All right, so something bad happened," Kelsey said. "Bad things happen in the world. It shouldn't have changed Dane into a vegetable. Anyway, I certainly don't want his help now. He was like a slug this afternoon. I'll be fine by myself. Andy Latham is just scuzzy, not dangerous. I'll be back soon. Throw some quiche in the refrigerator and I'll microwave it when I get back." She was at the door.

"Great dinner companion you turned out to be," Cindy called.

"Sorry."

Kelsey, glad to feel that there was something she

could actually do rather than sit around and wait for Sheila, let the door close behind her and headed quickly for her car.

She was startled when the door opened in her wake and Cindy came out. "Hey!"

Kelsey paused. "Yeah?"

"Kelsey…he might have been drinking this afternoon at Nate's, but…why did you call Dane a drunk?"

"Let me see…Nate says he comes every afternoon. He'd had half a dozen beers by the time I got there. He was just sprawled out on a lounge chair when I arrived, looking like his mind had been fried for years. Nate said he's been back here for several months, and that he's opened a business so he can *look* like a solid citizen, but that his heart isn't really in it."

"That doesn't make him a drunk."

"He sure looked like one today."

"He goes to Nate's and drinks club soda most afternoons," Cindy said.

"Trust me, he was reeking of beer."

Cindy shrugged. "Okay, maybe he was drinking today. I've been known to have a few too many myself on occasion. Whatever. If you want to think he's a drunk, fine, think he's a drunk. I still think you'd be better off bringing a big drunk with military training out with you to see a scuzzbag."

"I'll be all right. I'll keep my distance."

"Honestly, Kelsey, you should wait," Cindy said.

But Kelsey was already on her way.

"Help me, Dane."

He could remember her words so clearly, and now,

with the lowering sun bringing the onset of evening, he found himself hearing their echo over and over again.

There were things he should be doing. But he had searched the beachfront over and over again, and he had found exactly what he had expected: nothing. The "near storm," as they were calling it, an exceptionally bad spate of weather that had never actually formed into a hurricane, had come through about a week ago before petering out when it moved north and west over Homestead and the Everglades. There had been no damage to the house, but palm fronds had come down with a vengeance, and the beach had been flooded for twenty-four hours before the water receded.

His first response upon examining the photo shoved under the door had been to search, regroup, search again, then think it all out and search for a third time.

No, his first response had been shock. Then sorrow. Deep, gut-wrenching sorrow.

Then had come the knowledge that he was being framed, and that no matter how hard he searched he wouldn't find fingerprints or proof of any kind that anyone but he had been on his private beach—with Sheila.

The time for emotion was past. No, maybe it could never be past. But he sure as hell didn't have time for the luxury of pity, self or otherwise. Nor could he fly off in anger.

Now it was time to spread out further, to figure out what the hell was going on and who the hell had hated Sheila viciously enough to kill her. Who was cunning, cruel and psychotic—and held such a deep and maniacal sense of vengeance against him?

With Kelsey in town, acting like the FBI, he was going to have to move more quickly than he'd imagined. Thankfully he had friends in the right places. But since he was withholding evidence, he'd also been aware that he would have to take everything very carefully. But now...

Now it was different.

He had an almost photographic memory, which was going to stand him in good stead right now. After the initial shock of seeing the photo, he had known just where to begin, starting on the most logical path to carry him in the direction of the truth. Except that, with what he did know, the path didn't make any sense. He shouldn't be wasting time, except that sitting here had never really been wasting time.

The water and the peace that could be found on a spit of dock on a little island called Hurricane Bay were always good for rational thinking and reasoning.

And remembering.

The long summer day was ending; at last the sun was beginning to set. This was the time when the world was most beautiful. He remembered, thinking as a kid, that his dad was just crazy. They'd had no air-conditioning, but his father had pointed out that the breeze always came through. The house had seemed a shack, but his dad had pointed out that they didn't need any art on the walls, because they had the most beautiful vista anyone could ever imagine, every night. All they had to do was sit on the rustic porch and watch the sun set, watch as colors came out over the Atlantic, pinks, reds, golds, yellows. Sometimes the skies would be clear and the blue would turn slowly to strange pastels, then indigo, and then night would fall. Sometimes there would be clouds in the sky, and they would become a billowy cobalt before turning into dancing shadows against the moon. When storms came, it was just as beautiful, if different. The lightning would strike the water like bolts cast down by a furious god, and the trees would whip and bend in the wind.

Everything his father had said was true. Now he knew. Just as he knew that no meal in the world was better than fresh fish, just pulled from the sea and thrown on the grill. Odd that he would come to love this place, Hurricane Bay, when he had been so blind to its charms as a kid. Back then, he'd had no idea how great it was to own a private island.

He was glad he'd had the time to let his dad know how much he appreciated the place and had come to love it.

Sitting on the wooden dock, staring out over the water, he closed his eyes and heard her voice again.

Chapter 2

"*Help me, Dane.*"

Sheila's voice was an echo in his head. A ghostly reproach.

He didn't need to keep hearing it. He'd already damned himself a hundred times over.

He'd been sitting here that night, just as he was now, the last time he'd seen Sheila arrive at Hurricane Bay.

But before that...

Would things have been different if he hadn't seen her in action just that day?

He'd been at the Sea Shanty just before she had come over. He'd been drinking soda water with lime, discussing surveillance cameras with Nate. Nothing big had happened. Nate thought that maybe one of his bartenders had decided he wasn't quite making it on tips and was helping himself to the till. Dane didn't intend to work for Nate, and he had no intention of charging for the advice he gave. Sheila had been there, too. She came almost every afternoon at about five.

She never bought her own drinks.

Maybe she hadn't known he was there. Maybe she had known and hadn't cared. Once upon a time, way back when, he and Sheila had been something of a two-some. But he had to admit, he'd never been in love with her. From the time he had been a little kid, he'd had a path in mind for himself, a plan for his life. A lot of that had come from Mr. Cunningham and Joe, but whatever the reason, his future had been the burning essence in his mind.

He hadn't wanted to wind up a fisherman in Key Largo, hoping for a catch, dodging the tourists, sucking up to the tourists, watching restaurant managers come and go.

If anything, he'd been determined he was going to own the restaurants.

And Sheila...

Well, at one time she might have loved him in her way. But she'd been just as intent on her own path. She'd wanted out. And getting out had meant more to Sheila than attaching herself to a man with no specific prospects, even if he had ambition. She'd spent her high school years sizing up the tourists and the weekenders—Floridians who usually lived fairly close to Key Largo, where they kept condos or vacation homes, and left their prestigious jobs in the city on Friday after work and returned Sunday night, ready to go back to work on Monday morning.

But he'd always thought he was her friend. They'd had their occasional thing together, even after their passionate breakup way back when. But not in the last few years. Not since he'd finished his military obligations, settled in the St. Augustine area, opened Whitelaw Investigations… and fallen in love with Kathy Malkovich.

He'd seen Sheila a few times since he'd retreated back home. Only with other friends, mostly, or sitting around the bar. She'd even shown up at his place once with Nate when they'd made a major dolphin fish haul a few weeks back and barbecued it on the grill at his place. Because of their past history, people were making more of it than it had been.

Nate had talked about Sheila's current activities, then cut himself off, remembering that she and Dane had once been more than friends. The usual guy talk had sounded too coarse, even for Nate.

So he should have known. Sheila had always been a flirt. And she was soundly of the opinion that most people fell out of love in life, and that some guys were good in bed and some guys weren't, so going to bed with a man because he could offer her something was in no way a sin. Look at the jerks most women slept with because they thought they were in love, or thought the guy was decent, she always said.

Sheila gave new meaning to the term "jaded."

That afternoon, though, just a week ago, he had really seen her in action for the first time. Seen her work her "magic" at the bar.

So he was a little jaded himself. Not exactly sunk in despair, but then again, not ready to go out and tackle the world. And when he had watched Sheila, he'd experienced some strange sensations. Relief, for one. He was thankful they'd never gotten serious or—God forbid—married each other. He felt sorrow, too, remembering the kid she had been. And he had also felt a bit of disgust, wondering what the hell she was doing. There she was, a beautiful woman, doing things she didn't need to do. She was young, with the world in front of her, and she had seemed to be on the path of self-destruction.

Her sole purpose was apparent from the minute she climbed on a bar stool next to a guy. First there had been the middle-aged Hispanic man sporting the loud jewelry. Heavy gold chains had hung around his neck, and his fingers had been bedecked with gold and diamonds. Sheila had crawled atop a chair with a cigarette, asking for a light. They'd started talking, and he'd bought her a drink, but he hadn't stayed long. There had been a woman waiting for him out on the patio. Before he'd left, however, Sheila had written something on a piece of paper and given it to him.

Then there had been the younger guy, maybe twenty-five. His cutoffs had carried a designer label, and his sandals were straight from the pages of *GQ*. His T-shirt had sported a label, as well—not just designer but *top* designer. Even if he ever got as rich as Croesus, Dane couldn't see spending that kind of money on a T-shirt.

Sheila had been studying her drink when the young guy had walked in. She must have had some kind of natural radar, because she'd turned around immediately, seen her new quarry, squashed out her cigarette and knocked another out of the pack in front of her.

They'd talked for a long time. And again Sheila had given him her number.

No one had appealed to Sheila after that. She'd noticed Dane at the back of the bar by then. She might have colored just a little, seeing him there. Then she'd tossed her long dark hair and come over.

"So…it's the long-lost home boy nursing his woes at the shanty bar, huh?"

"Hi, Sheila."

She'd lit her own cigarette then and tapped her matches on the bar.

"See, old flame, men do still find me attractive," she'd said softly.

"Sheila, you're beautiful, and you know it."

That had brought a smile to her lips. "But it isn't enough, is it?"

He remembered lifting his hands with a certain aggravation. "It depends on what you want. What the hell are you doing?"

She looked at him. "Do you remember when you liked me, Dane?"

"Sheila, I still like you. You're a friend."

That brought another smile. "You never loved me."

That seemed out of the blue. "*You* never loved *me*."

She looked ahead. "We both wanted to get out, and here we are again. You loved *her*, though, huh? That woman in St. Augustine."

He didn't answer because she didn't allow him to, rushing back in. "What's wrong with me, Dane?"

"Sheila, there's nothing wrong with you. We just didn't have the commitment, the shared interests, the right whatever."

She shook her head, staring ahead. "I couldn't stay with Larry, either. Why not? I should have. It's like I'm always looking for…I don't know." She stared at him. "Hey, want to sleep with me?"

"Sheila—"

"Oh, yeah. I heard. You're still in mourning. I wish you weren't. I'd feel…secure if I were with you."

"Sheila, feeling secure isn't a reason to sleep with a guy. Any more than money is."

She turned to look at him with amusement. "Money is as good a reason as any. Come on, Dane, aren't you feeling just a bit of the old magic?" She reached out beneath the bar, long delicate fingers light on his thigh, then zeroing in.

Actually it was the little jump of arousal he'd felt that had stirred his temper. He'd gripped her fingers, pushing her hand aside, and risen. "No," he told her angrily—and too loudly.

"Dane, don't leave me."

"Sheila, I can't leave you if I'm not with you."

He'd turned and left the bar. Nate had seen them, of course. He hadn't known what they were saying, but since he was at the end of the bar, he must have heard the anger in Dane's voice. And damn if Cindy Greeley hadn't been there, too, that day—he hadn't seen her until then, but there she was, with Nate at the end of the bar, showing him the new T-shirts she'd designed for his bar.

He'd said hi to Cindy and gone on.

That night Sheila had shown up at his house. She'd told him not to worry, she was just stopping by, seeing what he was up to. They were still friends, right?

"Friends, Sheila," he had told her, and let her in.

At first she had been so casual.

She'd asked him about what had brought him back. He'd told her it had just been time to come home. She hadn't believed him, but she had pretended to.

"I think, for you, everything changed with Joe."

He hadn't answered that. Instead he'd said, "Sheila, what the hell are you doing?"

"Getting by. I should marry some nice guy and settle down. Problem is, there aren't that many nice guys out there. Besides, you knew me when I was young and sweet and innocent. Okay, I was never innocent. But I *was* a little sweet."

"You were married to Larry Miller. There's a nice guy."

"A boring guy, I'm afraid. I like excitement. Or maybe every nice guy is a boring guy. I don't know. You know what, Dane? Men just don't come in the kind that I really want to keep. Actually, I may be a real voice for my sex."

"Oh?"

Sheila had laughed, and looked stunning. "Yeah. Guys are usually ratty to women. They fall in love… lust first, most of the time. They marry, they cheat."

"Not all of them. I'd say it's pretty even."

"Not on your life! Trust me. Men always seem to need someone to bolster their egos. Some guy told me once that it's just natural. You know, survival of the species. Long ago, guys had to sow their seed, just like lions, or some shit like that. Mate all they could so their DNA would go on and on. Instinctively they're still that way—except, of course, that they don't really want to procreate anymore, because on the not so instinctive side, something resembling brains kicks in and they don't want to pay child support. But some guys are innately bad, maybe not even in a way they can help. Look at all the old geezers looking for trophy wives. Sixty-, seventy-, even eighty-year-olds throwing out wives they've had for years, finding some beach bunny and patting themselves on the back for having a kid when they're members of AARP. Makes 'em macho."

"Sheila, you know, I have friends who have been left by their wives, taken to the cleaners big time by them."

"See, there you go. Defending your sex."

"I'm not trying to defend anyone. I just think that people in general aren't always so great to others. I've seen plenty of men behave like real assholes. I've seen some women who are just as cold and calculating."

"Different thing," Sheila said, waving a hand in the air. "Someone should do a study on it. As for me, well, I guess I'll just go on thinking that I'm standing up for my sex, using guys like paper cups, tossing them out as soon as they get a bit soggy." She'd looked at him then. "Dane…are you sure…I mean, sometimes, way back when, we'd get together when neither one of us had a steady thing going."

"Sheila, you've got to trust me here. I'm not what you're looking for. But I will give you a speech, which is what you need. You're beautiful. You deserve ten times more than you're giving yourself. Not to mention the fact that your lifestyle is dangerous. There are a bunch of assholes out there, not to mention the fact that these days the world is full of sexually transmitted diseases, some of which can kill you."

She'd laughed then. "Oh, great! You think I'm infectious. Dane, I'm careful as hell."

"No, you're not. If you were, you'd be looking for something more than money."

"It's not just money," she said softly.

"Then…?"

"I told you, I'm making up for all the assholes out there." She'd leaned against the pillows on the sofa then, watching him with a rueful smile. "I hear you're in deep mourning over something gone wrong. I can help. I can make you feel better. If only for a night."

He had to admit, the thought had been tempting. But Sheila couldn't really give him anything. And there was nothing he could give her.

"No good, Sheila," he had told her softly.

And still she'd stayed. They'd had some wine, played chess. She was a good player. Then they'd had some more wine. And finally it had been really, really late, and she still hadn't gotten up to go.

"I wish you'd want me, Dane."

"Sheila…"

"What's wrong with me?" she asked for the second time that night.

"Nothing. You're beautiful. It's what's wrong with me, and the fact that I don't think we're particularly good for each other."

Then that smile. "You know what? I don't sleep with that many guys. I string them along pretty far, but…I like gifts, good food, expensive bottles of wine. I swear, Dane, I'm not diseased or anything. I'm smart and I'm careful, and more selective than it might appear. And I always carry protection. Dane, dammit, I know you're hurting, but… don't you ever just get urges, need some kind of relief? I'm perfect for you. I know you don't love me, and I don't want anything from you except to be around sometimes… You can turn off the lights, drink yourself into a stupor, and I won't mind. And it's not like it's something you haven't done before, a place you haven't been before."

She'd made a move for him. Chess pieces had fallen to the floor. And he'd had a lot of wine, a lot of pain, a lot of guilt and self-recrimination, and a lot of longing. Sheila was beautiful. So overtly sexual she was impossible to ignore. Maybe men were nothing more than slightly evolved beasts. She hadn't been wearing a damn thing beneath her red dress, and she'd made a point of letting him know it.

"Sheila, I'm telling you, it just wouldn't be right." But there had been a guttural quality to his voice then.

"I don't care, Dane. I don't care. I just want to stay. For one night." She stood then. With definite talent, she let the red dress fall to the floor. "Call it a mercy fuck," she pleaded.

He wasn't sure he could throw her out naked. He wasn't sure he wanted to.

It hadn't occurred to him that she was scared of leaving. Chalk it up to arousal and maybe even a certain ego. Before he knew it, she was on her knees before him. Her eyes were pleading.

And Sheila was good at what she did.

They hadn't wound up in his bed, but right there, on the couch, where they'd played chess. He'd awakened feeling a dull throbbing in his head. Sex. Like eating food with no taste. Breathing in and out because the lungs did so without the commitment of the conscious mind. He didn't want to hurt Sheila. They'd both been banged up enough. He didn't want to talk, either.

Hadn't needed to.

Sheila had gotten right up, grabbed the red dress and walked to the door, pausing long enough only to look out to make sure it was light. "Thanks," she'd said, not turning back.

"Hey, my pleasure," he said lightly, hoping to make them both feel better.

Still, she hadn't looked back. That was when she had said it.

"Help me, Dane."

"I'm trying to help you, Sheila. You don't want to listen to me."

Then, still with her back to him, "You can't help it that you don't love me. I don't expect you to... I don't love you, either... Well, as much as anyone, but...I just..."

Then she'd turned for a minute.

"I need help."

"Sheila, we can get you some help—"

She'd laughed, cutting him off. "A psychologist for my nympho tendencies?" She shook her head. "You don't understand. And I can't...explain." She had stood in his doorway just a moment longer. In the soft pink light of dawn, he thought he saw a brief look of desperation cross her face.

"I look tough, but...I'm afraid."

"Jesus, Sheila, then you've got to change your lifestyle." His outburst had brought him to his feet. "Quit picking up strangers and going off with them. Settle down with a different goal in mind, rather than striking a blow against men for all women, or whatever it is you think you're doing."

A slow smile had crossed her face. "None of you have ever known just what it was like, being me. And... as for my crusade... Oh, Dane! You just don't know how fucked up men are."

And then she'd left.

God, she had *needed help! He hadn't seen, hadn't known, how much.*

It was the last time he had seen her.

Alive.

And now…suddenly, even his palms were sweating. What was the killer going to do next to implicate him?

He had to get to the truth.

Andy Latham lived on the Gulf side of the key.

It was something that had always pleased Kelsey, although she wasn't sure exactly why. Key Largo wasn't big enough for her to feel any advantage of distance just because he lived on the other side of US1. But she had never liked Andy Latham, and during all the years when they had been growing up, Sheila had hated her stepfather.

He fished for a living, as many people in Key Largo did. He lived off the main road on a little piece of property that tenaciously clung to the ability to be called land, off a small street that had once been little more than mangrove swamp but had been turned into viable land with fill from the dredging for a nearby hotel harbor that had been built in the late fifties.

It wasn't more than a ten-minute drive from the duplex to Andy Latham's house. Once upon a time it had been a pretty decent structure. Back in the fifties, contractors had known the full vengeance of storms. The home had been built well out of concrete block and stucco. It was a small house, two bedrooms, a kitchen, a living room and an open back porch that led straight to the dock and Andy's fishing boat. Kelsey knew the house fairly well because Sheila had lived in it until she had turned seventeen, when she had gotten work at a now defunct seafood restaurant. She had never asked to stay with any of her friends but first had taken a little room at the home of the restaurant owner, then gotten her own apartment on the day she turned eighteen. Kelsey could remember her folks talking about Sheila, saying that they should take her in. But there had been a hesitance in their wanting to do the good deed, and since Sheila had pointedly told Kelsey she wanted to be entirely on her own, she hadn't pushed the matter.

She wondered now if things might have been different if she had.

Even as she turned off the main road and headed southwest down the poorly kept county road that led to the few scattered houses on the street, the sun seemed to take a sharp drop toward the horizon. There were still some pinks and grays in the sky, which was good, since Latham had no outside lights on, and the front yard was dangerously overgrown with shrubbery and weeds.

So much for it being daylight.

Kelsey couldn't quite get her little Volvo into the drive, so she parked on the heavily rutted street. Getting out of the car, she wished she had changed into jeans. Twigs and high grass teased her legs as she made her way to the excuse for a front walk, and she was certain that every creepy crawly thing in the brush was making a beeline for her bare legs.

At the door, she knocked, looking at the sky. She reminded herself that she wasn't afraid of Andy Latham, he was just a scuzz.

"Yeah? What do you want?" Latham demanded, throwing open the door.

The strange thing about Andy Latham was that he wasn't a bad-looking man. He had been younger than Sheila's mother by about five years when they had married, Kelsey knew. She reckoned that made him about forty-five now. He was tall, with the lean strength of

a man who spent his life occupied in physical labor.
When he wasn't fishing, he worked odd construction
jobs and had managed to keep his lean appearance all
these years. His face was weathered, like that of many
men down here who had spent years outside in the sun.
He had keen hazel eyes and a full head of dark hair, only
lightly dusted with gray. Tonight, he was dressed de-
cently in jeans that appeared to be both clean and fairly
new. He was wearing a polo shirt that also appeared to
be clean and even pressed.

"Why, if it isn't little Kelsey, all grown up," Latham
said before she could speak.

"Hi, Mr. Latham. Yes, it's Kelsey Cunningham."

"Come in, come in," he said, stepping back. Kelsey
felt as if he were wearing the look of a spider who had
unexpectedly come across a fly already caught it its
web.

Looking past him, she could see the interior of the
living room. It hadn't changed much. The old place actually had a coral rock fireplace, and the overstuffed
chair in front of it was the same one that had been there
as long as Kelsey could remember.

And also just as she had remembered, there were
beer cans littering the floor next to it, along with wrappers and leftovers from various fast food chains. Latham
had never air-conditioned the place, preferring to leave
the back glass doors open to the patio all the time for the
breeze. Air-conditioning cost too much money; natural
air was cheaper. Many people relied on it when their
houses were set in the shade of overgrown trees, taking
advantage of the cooler air that came off the water. But
in Latham's case, the open doors didn't seem to bring
in the breeze. The smell of decaying fast food and fish

seemed to permeate the house. Flies buzzed around an empty French fry wrapper.

Kelsey didn't want to set foot inside the house.

"No, no, Mr. Latham, I didn't come by to bother you. Looks like you're ready to go out."

"I am, I am, but there's always time for an old friend. Come on in. Can I get you something? Beer, or…beer or water, I guess. Aren't you looking fine, young lady. Well, I guess big city life agrees with you."

"I have a good job that I like very much," Kelsey said. "Really, I don't need to come in, I just came by to ask you about Sheila."

If she was going to talk to Latham, she was going to have to step inside, Kelsey realized, since he was already walking into the living room.

She entered cautiously, leaving the door open behind her.

Latham had to check two beer cans before finding the one that still had something in it. His back was to her as he finished off the contents and stared into the fireplace.

"Mr. Latham, I was just wondering if, by any chance, you knew where Sheila was."

He turned to face her then, hands on his hips, staring at her.

"Why? What has the little tramp done now?"

"She hasn't done anything, Mr. Latham. She was supposed to meet me down here, but she hasn't shown up since I've arrived. We were supposed to meet yesterday at lunchtime. She hasn't been home, and it seems no one has seen her in a week."

To her amazement, he started to laugh.

"She's only been missing a week, and you're worried?"

"We had plans, Mr. Latham."

He looked her up and down for a long moment. "You can call me Andy, you know. You're an adult, all grown up."

"Yes," Kelsey said politely. "But since you'll always be Sheila's stepdad to me, it's just more comfortable to call you Mr. Latham."

Kelsey didn't know why it seemed imperative to keep as close to the door as she could, but it did.

Latham started shaking his head as if he were looking at one of the craziest people on earth. Then he laughed again, a sound with no amusement. "Well, missy, I can promise you—I'm the last person Sheila would come to and report her whereabouts. Raised her when her ma up and died on me, and what the hell did I get for it? A slap in the face and a kick in the ass. She never once thanked me for keeping her after her ma died. Never realized that I hadn't adopted her, that I didn't owe her squat, that I put myself out to keep her in clothes and put food in her mouth. From the time she was ten years old, she was a little bitch, hassling me for the way I lived, knocking me for not making enough money. She hightailed it out of here the minute she could. And she only comes back when she wants money."

Despite her unease, Kelsey felt compelled to defend her friend. "If I'm not mistaken, Mr. Latham, Sheila's mother left money to you for the express purpose of raising Sheila. And I believe there are also several joint trust accounts."

"Little wise ass, aren't you, girl? The whole lot of your generation, not a bone of gratitude in you. What do you think it costs to keep a kid in school? Go to the doctor, the dentist, buy books, paper, clothes. Hell, her mother couldn't have left enough money for what Sheila has cost me. I don't give a damn whether I ever hear from her again or not."

"But she has to keep in touch with you, because of the money," Kelsey persisted.

Latham took a step toward her.

Out on the streets, she thought, he wouldn't have scared her. If she hadn't known him, he might even have appeared to be a decent looking and friendly kind of fellow. An all-around American male, the type to watch football on a Sunday afternoon, play armchair quarterback and show up for work on Monday morning to talk over the game with the guys.

Except that he smelled a little like fish.

But she did know him. She knew he had taken a belt to Sheila several times when she had lived at home.

And he made her nervous as hell.

She took a backward step toward the door.

"Look, I'm really worried about Sheila," Kelsey said. "If you do hear anything from her, anything at all, please have her get in touch with me right away."

"And where would that be, missy?" he asked. He was walking toward her again. She had the strangest sensation that if he touched her, she would somehow be marked for life. The remaining light outside had faded. The living room was lit by one weak bulb in a lamp with no shade. The pale light fell on the carcasses of mounted fish on the wall, and the head and neck of a tiny key deer with glassy eyes.

"Just tell Sheila to get ahold of me if you hear from her. She'll know where I am."

"You're staying out at her place, eh?"

"Mr. Latham, you did raise Sheila. You must have some feelings for her."

"Yeah, I hate the little bitch."

"I'm worried, and she's missing. And the police will be around to talk to you," Kelsey said, her sense of both uneasiness and indignation rising within her.

"The cops?" Latham said, then he repeated the words, his voice seeming to rise to a roar. "The cops! You called the cops on me because that little twit of a girl has gone off with some poor Joe she intends to milk for all he's worth?"

At that point he was almost upon her. Dignity and courtesy be damned, Kelsey was getting out. She turned and headed for the door. She heard him following after her. She felt his breathing.

His hand clamped down on her shoulder. She almost screamed as he spun her around. "Don't you go causing trouble for me, you hear? You mark my words— Sheila is off with some man—a fool with money, with any luck. Getting the police involved is just going to get her into trouble. Maybe she'll even see some jail time, understand? Don't go getting the cops involved with Sheila and me. Don't you do it over that riffraff girl!"

He had powerful fingers. They were digging into her shoulder. His face was taut with tension, and his eyes had a hard yellow gleam about them.

The stench of fish wafted over her.

"Let go of my shoulder."

He smiled. The man had amazingly good teeth. Very white. It could have been a good smile, but instead it was full of menace and pleasure at the fear he was sensing in her.

"You came to my house to throw accusations in my face, little lady," he said quietly, not releasing her.

"Accusations?" Kelsey said. "I didn't accuse you of anything. I asked you if you had seen Sheila, and if you could tell her I'm looking for her if you *do* see her."

"If you didn't accuse me of anything, why are you calling the cops on me?"

His grasp had a definite biting quality. He was strong, or, at least, stronger than she was.

Cindy had been right. She shouldn't have come here. Alone. At night.

Alone at any time, she thought.

She wanted to remain calm and rational; she also wanted to scream and jerk away from him. She tried to remember all the movies she had seen, all the programs she had watched about dealing with dangerous situations. Don't show fear? Or scream like blue blazes, push away with all her strength and run like the wind?

She didn't have to make a decision. She heard the slamming of a car door and a man's voice. "Hey, what's going on there?"

Latham's hand fell from her shoulder. They both recognized the voice. Latham shook his head with disgust, his eyes moving from the newcomer back to Kelsey once again. "There he is, the big military man, ready to knock my lights out," he said. "I wasn't about to hurt you, little girl. And you want to know where Sheila is? Ask her good buddy, the half-breed coming up the walk."

She'd known from hearing him, without turning, that Dane Whitelaw had arrived. She'd been relieved.

But Latham's words gave her a chill.

She turned, Latham's words echoing in her mind.

"You want to know where Sheila is? Ask her good buddy, the half-breed coming up the walk."

Dane was coming up the path. He wasn't looking at Kelsey; he was staring at Latham.

His hair was combed back, freshly washed, a little long at the collar, but off his face now. He was in khakis and a short-sleeved blue tailored shirt. Dane wasn't exactly a half-breed. His grandfather had been a Miccosukee Indian who had married a Swedish tourist. The two had set up shop in the Keys, died together in an automobile accident and left his father with ownership of Hurricane Bay. His dad had made a career out of the military, retired, turned to fishing off his peaceful property for an extra income, and then married Mary Smith, a woman who could claim ancestors all the way back to the Mayflower. Kelsey could just barely remember Dane's mother. She had welcomed every kid in the world into their house. She had been quick to laugh, to entertain, to love children. She had wanted twenty, she had told them once. At least a dozen little sisters and brothers for Dane. But both she and Dane's father had married late in life, and complications had set in when she'd finally gotten pregnant again just before Dane's tenth birthday. She had died months before the baby was due. Dane's father had never remarried. He had always been a wonderful man when the kids were around, but he had seldom left his own little island, except to sell his catch.

Dane Whitelaw seemed to have inherited the best to be had from his background. He had dark eyes, a chiseled face with slightly broad cheekbones, dark-wheat-colored hair that was always sun-bleached to a lighter shade, and the height and stance of a Viking. She had adored him growing up. He'd been her brother's best friend. But then Joe had been killed, and their little world had changed for everyone.

Dane reached the open doorway, still staring pointedly at Andy Latham. His dark gaze had never wavered once.

"What the hell are you doing here, Whitelaw?" Latham asked.

"I was in the neighborhood," Dane said, an obvious lie. There was nothing in the immediate neighborhood that could have drawn him.

"You're trespassing on my property."

"Don't worry. I'm getting off it." He stared at Kelsey.

She was tempted to stay just because she didn't want Dane helping her, not when he was top on her list of... well, not suspects, but highly suspicious people. And not when he had been such an ass that afternoon. Maybe she had approached him badly. But he should have cared. He should at least have frowned with worry and tried to say something good about Sheila.

Then again, maybe she just disliked Dane because of what had happened after Joe had died.

"Kelsey, were you staying?" Dane asked when she didn't move.

"No, I have a dinner engagement," she said.

She turned to walk down the overgrown path, certain this time that creepy things were touching her flesh when the overgrown brush swept over her legs.

She reached her own car. Dane was right behind her, Andy Latham still standing at his door. Dane waited until she had gotten in the driver's seat, closed her door and started the engine.

Then he walked to his own car, a Jeep with oversize

tires. Necessary, she knew, for living out on Hurricane Bay. The road to the little island was private, not state or county. Dane's grandfather had built it; his father had improved it. Now Dane kept it up. It still wasn't much of a road. During a heavy rain season or after a storm, it was often underwater, sometimes so deep that the only way on or off the island was by boat.

Dane started up his car but didn't start moving until she did. She drove away with Dane just a short distance behind her.

In the rearview mirror, she could see that Latham was still standing in his doorway. Watching.

Andy Latham muttered as he watched the cars go. Then he walked back into his house, cursing his step-daughter and her friends. In the kitchen, he reached into the refrigerator for another beer. There was a big fat palmetto bug, a winged cockroach, sitting right next to his beer, waving his antennae.

He cursed the cockroach and reached for the can, then splatted it down on the roach before the filthy creature had a chance to move.

He thought about cleaning the carcass out of the refrigerator, but it seemed like too much of a project for the moment. He hadn't really wanted another beer; he'd wanted to get going. He liked nightlife. No, he loved nightlife. Nightlife took him away from his hell of an existence and made him feel like a man. He'd been ready to go when Sheila's little buddy had shown up. Kelsey.

Drinking his beer, he decided to make a pit stop. In the mirror over the sink, he surveyed his features. Good. He was still looking pretty good. He really wasn't old at all; those kids just didn't realize it, because he had made the mistake of marrying an older woman.

Well, she'd had some money. A virtue. She'd had her faults, as well. A hell of a lot of them. Who would have thought that she considered herself a match for any man?

And worse, who would have thought she'd leave the money tied up in a trust that could only be accessed little by little, and then only by him and Sheila at the same time.

He picked up the comb sitting on the sink and ran it through his hair. The face that greeted him in the mirror pleased him. He had good features and fine eyes. His skin was tanned and creased, but women seemed to like the weathered look. He was built just fine. Not muscle-bound, but tight as piano wire. Sleek, hard-toned. He was in good physical shape. The whole package was still just fine.

Funny. Once upon a time he'd had a thing for older women.

Now he liked them younger.

Yep, that Kelsey was looking darned good. Too bad he'd been saddled with Sheila. The girl had poisoned everyone against him. Hell, if it hadn't been for Sheila, he might not have known Kelsey at all as a kid. Who knows? She might have let him buy her a drink at a bar.

She might have let him do more.

He tensed, remembering the way she had looked around the house. As if he were lower than a pig.

Lower than the cockroach he had crushed in the refrigerator.

He shrugged. Imagine that. The damned thing had been in the refrigerator. Maybe that was why it had been so easy to kill. Maybe it had already been cold, shaking in its little cockroach boots, frozen right to the spot.

He looked around the bathroom.

Hell, maybe he should get a maid.

Of course, it would have to be someone who wasn't afraid of cockroaches.

He exited the bathroom, humming to himself. He started to leave the house, then paused and looked around, damning Sheila once again, thinking of the way Kelsey Cunningham had looked around his house. Fuck them both. Fuck them all. Everyone knew that Sheila took off whenever the hell she felt like it. Everyone but Kelsey, coming back here as if she were something special, raising all kinds of trouble.

Still...

He looked around his domain. Strange, once it had been clean. Sheila's mother had been good for something. She had cooked, too.

But he couldn't really remember what the place had looked like back then. There had been food in the refrigerator, and not so many beer cans. The cockroach would have died a lot happier if he had come all those years ago.

Now the place was a dump. Nothing but fast-food wrappers and beer cans. So what if the police came? They would probably leave damn quick.

He left the house, not bothering to lock his door. No one ever came out this road. There were only two other houses, and a bunch of mangrove roots and water. Angus Grier lived in the closest house, and he was ninety if he was a day. And the kids who had rented the other place...they were stoned out of their minds most the time. There wasn't much reason to lock up his place. If a thief came by…well, hell, he was welcome to steal anything in the place.

Because once he drove away from it, Andy Latham knew that he was a different man.

Chapter 3

Dane followed Kelsey back to the duplex.

She was probably going to accuse him of stalking her, but he still wanted to see that she got home safely. Besides, he could just knock on Cindy's door after he made sure Kelsey had gone on into Sheila's side.

He knew Kelsey was aware that he was following her, but she pretended not to see him as she parked, exited her cranberry Volvo and entered the house. Dane parked the Land Rover and took the steps up to Cindy's door. As he tapped on it, Cindy appeared at the door to the other half of the duplex, Sheila's half, now Kelsey's.

"Dane! Hey, we're over here."

"Hey, Cindy."

He walked across the tiled concrete front porch and greeted Cindy with a quick peck on the cheek. She never changed. Sweet and smart, Cindy always expected the best from everyone. But then, she'd never met with much personal adversity. Both her folks were still living just down the highway. She had two younger sisters and a ten-year-old brother. Her father, a transplanted Yankee, owned one of the largest charter fishing boat companies in the area.

Cindy had called to tell him that Kelsey was on her way out to talk to Andy Latham. Dane hadn't at all liked the idea of her being out there alone. Of course, he'd known that Kelsey wouldn't be particularly glad to see him out there—she would hardly think of him as a knight in shining armor—but he'd made tracks to get out there as soon as possible anyway.

"Come on in," Cindy said. "We were about to have quiche and beer." She wrinkled her nose. "Reheated quiche and beer. But it's still good. I can cook. Well, kind of, anyway."

"Sounds great, Cindy, but I already ate."

"Come in for a beer, at least. I mean, you're here, aren't you?" she demanded, blue eyes wide.

"Sure." He needed to talk to Kelsey, and it was damn certain *she* was never going to invite him in.

He followed Cindy into Sheila's side of the duplex. Kelsey was seated on a bar stool, a plate and a beer in front of her. Her shoes were off, one ankle curled around a leg of the stool. The sunglasses were gone, and he could see her eyes. Blue-green. Like a color that had been plucked right out of a shallow sea on a sunlit day.

He could see that she was surprised and definitely not pleased that Cindy had invited him in.

"Look who's here," Cindy said pleasantly.

"Surprise, surprise," Kelsey murmured.

"You're sure you don't want some quiche, Dane?" Cindy asked.

"No, thanks."

Cindy reached into the fridge and produced a bottle of beer. "But you'll have a beer with us, right?"

"Sure."

"Right. He hasn't had enough to drink today," Kelsey said.

For a moment Cindy looked as if she was going to try to ignore the obvious hostility between them, then she sighed, putting her hands on her hips. "Hey, kids, we're all grown-ups here."

"All right," Kelsey said. "Hi, Dane. Have a beer. You *are* all grown up. If you want to spend your life drinking the days away, I guess that's all right."

He stared at her and took a long swig from the bottle, ready to tell her that she hadn't seen him in years, she had no idea of what he did with his days, and she sure as hell had no right to judge him.

"That's right, Kelsey. If I want to be a drunk, it's my prerogative."

"Dane isn't a drunk, Kelsey," Cindy said.

"Sorry, then," Kelsey said. She made a point of yawning. "You know what, guys? I haven't had much sleep since I got back. Maybe you want to move your little party over to Cindy's half of the place."

"Maybe, but not yet," Dane said. He walked to the counter where she was sitting and set his beer bottle down. She tensed, and for a moment he thought she was going to jump up and try to escape.

But that would mean having to touch him because the way he was standing, at her side, hands on the counter, she would have to push past him to get by.

"So now you want to talk," she said.

"I'd have been happy to talk earlier—if you hadn't come on as such a bitch," he said.

She blinked, and he could hear her teeth clench. "You were drunk, and I was worried. And Nate had just told me that you and Sheila were…that you and Sheila had a big argument the last time he'd seen her, and that she'd told him afterward she was going out to your place. He said you weren't very nice to her."

She wasn't apologizing. She was still accusing him. And she sure as hell wasn't about to thank him for coming around when she might have been in trouble at Latham's. Of course, as far as any of them had ever known, Latham was just like a cockroach. Nasty as all hell, and germ-carrying, certainly, but not physically dangerous.

He inhaled a long breath before replying to Kelsey.

"Kelsey, I'm glad that your life is going so great that you feel you can judge everyone else. Although I'm curious as to how you got to be such a good judge of a man's level of alcohol consumption."

Her eyes narrowed. "I know you've been lying as low as pond scum, Dane, because Sheila told me."

"She did, did she? Kelsey, you need to listen to me. You haven't been around, and you don't know anything about anyone here anymore. What you've got is a bunch of hearsay and assumptions. Maybe you don't like what you think I've become, and maybe there's even some truth to it. But what you're doing here is dangerous. What do you think you are suddenly? Some kind of a crusader? Leave it alone. Quit running around accusing everyone of doing something to Sheila. You're going to get yourself into trouble."

Kelsey stared at him, eyes cool and hostile. "Dane, you didn't want to talk to me this afternoon, and now you're suddenly here telling me to keep my nose out of things. This is ridiculous. Apparently I'm the only one who's really concerned about Sheila. And since I *am* concerned, my nose is going to be everywhere until I know where she is. And I know you were seeing her."

"You're not listening to me. You're going off half-cocked and making a lot of assumptions. You know I was seeing Sheila because Nate told you so. Sheila hung around the Sea Shanty. So do I. So do Nate and Cindy—Cindy because she keeps up with old friends, Nate because he owns the place. And guess what? Lots of other people around here go there on a regular basis. It's the in place for the natives. Sheila saw dozens of people at the Sea Shanty. Big deal. But Andy Latham doesn't go there anymore, because Nate barred him. He got to be a little too obnoxious with some of the women customers. That's why Cindy called me when she knew you were going to go over and start throwing accusations at Latham."

Kelsey's eyes instantly shot toward Cindy with recrimination. Cindy flushed but shrugged, still feeling she had done the right thing.

Kelsey took a sip of her beer. "Latham is a horrible man. We all know it. He's a filthy, mean bastard—but that's all. He's scuzzy, not dangerous."

"How the hell do you know he isn't dangerous?" Dane demanded, wishing he weren't feeling his own temper soar. Kelsey knew he was right; she just wasn't about to admit it.

"He's been around for years," she said, waving a hand as if dismissing his words. "I used to go to that house when I was a kid. So did you, so did Cindy. He yelled, he was rude, and he created an environment no kid should have grown up in, but he never hurt anyone."

"Really? And here I thought you were Sheila's great friend. He sure as hell hurt *her*."

He had her on that one, and she had the grace to flush. "When he was angry, he beat her a few times with a belt. He'd be arrested for child abuse now, but back then…parents used to spank their children."

"Strange. Mine never beat me with a belt. And neither did yours. Or Cindy's."

"Okay, he's a horrible man!"

"Listen to what you're saying. He *beat* her with a *belt*."

"When our folks were in school, the deans used to walk around with big paddles."

He shook his head, growing angrier, fighting his rising temper and trying to tell himself that Kelsey wasn't his concern. If she wanted to be a stubborn idiot, there was nothing he could do.

But she was *his* concern.

He had to keep her from acting like a stubborn idiot. She would understand that—if only he could tell her the truth about Sheila.

But that was one thing he couldn't do. Kelsey would have his ass in jail so fast his head would spin. And then…

Then there would be nothing he could do.

"Don't go out there again," he said, forcing his jaw to unclench and allow him to form words. His voice came out ragged and rough.

Her eyes narrowed further still, and she replied with

cool, "who the hell are you to tell me what to do?" dignity.

"Look, Dane, no one around here is really paying any attention to me. Don't you understand yet? Someone needs to be concerned. No one else is. Therefore, in my opinion, I have to be."

"It's not that we're not concerned," Cindy murmured.

They both ignored her. Dane spoke firmly. "Don't go out to Latham's again."

"Dammit, Dane!" she said, losing her composure at last, her eyes sizzling, her fingers tightening on her beer bottle. "Don't come on to me like the gestapo. You're not my father," she said.

He caught her eyes then, held them hard. "Let's hope not," he said.

She flushed slightly. Her gaze fell from his, and she studied the quiche she'd been pushing around her plate, the grip she had on her beer bottle becoming white-knuckled.

"Kelsey, I'm not trying to come on like anything or act like a father. It simply isn't a good idea to visit a man like that alone. Okay, maybe I am sounding like the gestapo. But he's not just mean and nasty, he's damned scary. Pay attention to me. Don't go near him again. *Please.*" He would try anything. It was imperative that she understand Latham was dangerous.

She looked up at him, then looked down again quickly, silent for a moment.

"Kelsey, listen to him. He's right," Cindy suddenly pleaded.

Kelsey threw up her hands, almost knocking over her beer bottle, barely catching it. "Okay, look, both of you, I'm sorry. I was wrong. I shouldn't have gone out there, and I won't go visiting Latham alone again. Actually I wasn't planning on visiting him again anyway. It's not like it was a social call. But the trust funds mean that there's a connection between Latham and Sheila. I was just hoping that maybe she had said something to him. I want to believe with all my heart that Sheila is just being rude and careless, forgetting all about me. I'd love for someone to tell me she's on vacation in Switzerland with a wine baron. But I just don't believe it. And asking Andy Latham if he had seen her, if he knew where she was, seemed like an intelligent move to make. She may hate him, but whether she likes it or not, they're connected through her mother's will."

"He'd be the last person Sheila would go to," Cindy murmured.

"Yes, but because of the money, she might have told him if she was going to be away, or she might have made an appointment with him regarding the trust or something. Look, he's never been my favorite person, either. But I still don't think he's actually dangerous," Kelsey said, defending herself.

From somewhere a muted ringing sounded.

"Excuse me," she said, looking pointedly at Dane. He was still blocking her way. "Cell phone."

He backed away. Just a hair. She didn't want to touch him, but she was going to have to brush by him.

She did. She scraped by his taut form. She still carried the aroma of a subtle perfume.

Once past him, she dug into her purse, which she had tossed on the far end of the bar. She glanced at the caller ID and said a cheerful, "Hey!" into the phone. She listened to the voice at the other end, then spoke again. "No, she hasn't shown yet." She looked across the kitchen at Cindy and Dane, who were both staring at her. "I'm not alone," she said into her phone. "Cindy and Dane are here."

Cindy arched a brow to Dane, but her question was quickly answered.

"Larry says hello to you both," Kelsey said.

Larry Miller. The weekender who had almost been one of them. Dane had heard that Larry was around now and then, but he hadn't seen him. Larry's father had passed away, and his mother had moved somewhere up north. They had sold the condo they kept on the Keys, as well, so even Larry's little place was gone. Maybe property was what made a place home. He had Hurricane Bay, so perhaps it had been inevitable that he would come back.

Larry hadn't really been an islander, but he'd still run with their crowd. Good old Larry...

Poor Larry.

He had fallen in love with Sheila, married her, tried to give her the world. A decent guy. Studious, cautious, a talented artist.

"Tell him hello for me," Cindy said.

"Ditto."

Kelsey nodded. "Cindy and Dane say hello." She listened while Larry spoke, staring out the sliding glass door from the kitchen to the patio. "Yeah, I know, everyone is saying the same thing." She gazed at Cindy and Dane again. Her look said that phone calls should be private. But she didn't move away, and Dane wasn't about to be courteous and suggest he and Cindy go somewhere. Kelsey kept talking into her phone. "Maybe she'll show up, maybe she won't. Anyway, I'm still going to spend the week at the duplex. With Cindy. Yeah, she's right next door. Nate's in good shape—hey, he said he saw you a couple of weeks ago. You didn't mention that you'd been down here."

Whatever he said next, Kelsey didn't answer. "Listen, I'll call you as soon as I hear from Sheila or find out what she's up to, okay?"

She touched a button on her phone and returned it to her purse, then slid back up on the bar stool. "Larry is concerned," she said.

"Poor thing. He never fell out of love, did he?" Cindy said.

"Maybe not," Kelsey said. "He still cares about Sheila, but he's certainly gotten over her. He's been doing all right. He's great to look at, smart, has a good job. He was dating one of our models. Beautiful girl. But a man can move on and still think of his ex-wife as a special person. He doesn't get down here that often, but he still thinks of the old gang as his friends. Funny, though. He said he'd been down about a week ago and heard that Sheila was around, but he couldn't track her down. When I told him what I was doing with my vacation time, all he said was that he'd been down on business and hadn't had a chance to really do anything or see anyone."

"Maybe he didn't think it was worth mentioning. He must have come and gone really quickly. He didn't see me, either," Cindy said.

"He said he was down here with a client, just long enough for a drink and dinner," Kelsey said. "Apparently he saw Nate, though. But Nate didn't mention to me today that he'd seen Larry. That was strange, don't you think? Especially when he knows Larry and I work together." Kelsey had been musing aloud. She didn't seem to mind that she had spoken in front of Cindy, but when her eyes touched Dane's, she seemed to stiffen again.

Somehow he had become the enemy. Things hadn't been right between them for a long time. He hadn't expected hugs and kisses, but even so, he didn't want to be the enemy, not when it was so important that she listen to him. But she was in no mood for that now, so he might as well get going.

Dane set down his beer bottle. "Gotta go," he told Cindy, giving her a kiss on the cheek.

"You have to go? It's early," Cindy said.

"I have an appointment."

"A date?" Cindy asked hopefully.

"An appointment," he repeated.

"At night? Does it have anything to do with an exciting investigation?"

Dane laughed. "Cindy, so far I have surveillance cameras looking for disappearing bait and a few other jobs that are equally mundane." Well, that was both true and not true. He had taken a job with the principal of a local private school to tail a few of the rich teenagers who seemed to be getting their hands on a fair amount of drugs.

He was pretty sure he had the answer to that one. It had been at the top of his list of jobs to pursue...until this morning.

"Wow, Dane, you're just full of fire and energy," Kelsey said. She was speaking to him but studying her beer bottle as she peeled the label from it.

"See you, Kelsey," he said.

"Sure." She looked at him at last. "It's been great."

"Hey," Cindy said thoughtfully, as if she were totally oblivious to the last exchange, "you know, I've got a great idea, Dane. Why don't you have us over for a barbecue?"

"Cindy," Kelsey protested. "That's rude. We can't just invite ourselves over. And think about it. Dane likes his *mundane* lifestyle. I'm sure that's just what he wants to do. Get out of his lounge chair and cook for a group."

Dane had the feeling that he could turn into Emeril and Kelsey still wouldn't want to show up at his place to eat.

But Cindy was persisting. "Remember in the old days, when you and your dad had those great cookouts. Maybe Larry can come down for the weekend, and maybe Sheila will even have shown by then. Nate can get another bartender on and come, and who knows who else might be around."

"We'll see, Cindy," he said.

He was startled when Kelsey suddenly seemed to rouse herself and let go of her hostility. She slid off her bar stool, approaching him, but pausing a distance away. "Actually, Dane, you know, it would be nice if you had a barbecue and had us all over."

"You *want* to come visit ye olde town drunk?" he said, staring at her.

Cindy must have felt as if lightning were crackling around her, because she suddenly seemed anxious to get away from the two of them. "I'm going to wash the dishes," she said.

Kelsey stared at her. "We used paper," she reminded her.

Cindy gave Kelsey a little shove that almost sent her into Dane. "Look, you two, I don't know what's going on here, but good friends are hard to come by. Both of you, shape up. Kelsey, you're being a real bitch. Walk Dane to the door and tell him you don't think that he's a washed-up, inebriated has-been. Go on."

There was something going on in Kelsey's ever-calculating little mind, Dane knew, or else she would just have turned away with that air of superiority she could don like a cloak, walk herself into the bedroom, and shut the door.

"I'm being a bitch?" she said.

"Oh, yeah," Dane said. "Beyond a doubt. You're being a super bitch."

"And Dane is Mr. Nice Guy?" she said to Cindy.

"Actually I've been damned decent, considering the way you accosted me today."

"Go on, Kelsey. Walk Dane out."

"I'm sure Dane knows the way through the living room to the door, but what the heck. Come on, Dane."

He thought she was going to touch him, take his arm, but she apparently decided against it, crossing her arms over her chest as she walked to the door.

"You should have that barbecue," she said, opening the front door and leaning against the wall as she waited for him to exit.

He wasn't sure what the hell she was up to, but he was determined that she understand how dangerous any reckless course of action might be. She might have been unnerved earlier tonight, but she hadn't been nearly scared enough.

"Kelsey, *promise* me you're going to stay away from Andy Latham."

She shrugged. "I told you both, I was wrong, you were right. I only went to talk to him and find out if he knew anything about Sheila. I've talked to him. I have no reason to go back."

"All right." He hesitated. "Kelsey, seriously, get your nose out of this."

Her eyes seemed as opaque as clouds, hooded. "I'm the only one determined to find Sheila. I have to nose around."

"Look, I'm telling you, I *am* concerned. I swear to you…" He hesitated for a moment, thinking of the irony. "I swear there is no one more anxious than I am to find Sheila. I have a P.I. firm, Kelsey. Let me do this."

Her eyes narrowed. "So you *do* think there's a reason to worry about Sheila."

"Let me do the worrying—and the question asking."

She shrugged. "You're the P.I. Go for it."

He started out the door, aggravated and exasperated. He wanted to shake her. Make her understand. He also needed to get the hell out. He had to make that appointment.

"Kelsey…"

"I mean it. Go for it. I'll even hire you. Is that an inspiration for you? I assume your rates are high, but I can pay them. No slacking off, though. I want her found."

"Kelsey, I don't want your money. I told you—I want to find Sheila myself. You stay out of it."

She didn't agree that she would. Instead she persisted with her original question. "Are you going to have the barbecue?"

He froze where he was, half out the door. He turned back to her, suddenly realizing just why Kelsey was pushing so hard when he was certain she wanted to be nowhere near him.

"Kelsey, you want to come over and search my place?

You don't need a special occasion for that. Come on over anytime."

There was the slightest flood of color to her cheeks, but she didn't flinch.

"If I wanted to search your house, you wouldn't care?"

"Not in the least."

"You should still have a barbecue."

"So you could have lots of help while you searched?" he said.

"Yes."

"Bye, Kelsey."

He strode away down the walk.

"What time do you start work in the mornings?" she called after him.

"Whenever the hell I feel like it!" He stopped, turning on his heel, staring at her. "You know...once I rise from my drunken stupor. And I lock my doors when I leave, so you'll have to call if you want a personal guide while you try to find incriminating evidence against me."

Kelsey had come out the doorway behind him and was standing on the porch.

He was about to walk away, aware that he would slam his way into his car. Instead he strode back to her so quickly that she didn't have time to back away.

"What the hell is it, Kelsey? What did I do to you that makes you mistrust *me*—yet you run out alone in the dark to see a man like Andy Latham?"

He hadn't touched her—he had managed not to do that. But he stood a breath away from her. He saw the flash of fire in her eyes and the tightness that gripped her from head to toe. He thought she was about to deny that there was any reason at all. But she didn't.

"You know what you did to me," she told him. Then she gritted her teeth, turning pale, and it was painfully apparent that she was horrified that the words had come out of her mouth.

"What I did to you?" he repeated. "I didn't do a damn thing to you, Kelsey. In fact, *I* should be angry for what you did to me. So that's what this is all about?"

"This is all about the fact that I came to see Sheila, but she's nowhere to be seen, and Nate said I should ask you because you had an argument with her and then she took off to your house. And she hasn't been seen since. And because you could have done anything with your life and you're spending it drinking yourself into some kind of oblivion in a lounge chair. It's because there's something going on, and you're the only one with the knowledge and the training to deal with it, but instead you're wasting your time in self-absorbed flagellation."

"You don't know anything about me, Kelsey. Nothing at all. Not anymore. Maybe I *should* have a barbecue. Let you tear up my place while I have friends around. Maybe I shouldn't trust you alone at my house."

With that, he made his way to his car. He managed to open the door without ripping it from its hinges and even closed it without slamming it.

In fact, he made it halfway down the block before punching the dashboard.

Chapter 4

Jesse Crane was standing out by the dock when Dane returned.

Dane didn't particularly mind darkness himself, but he kept a floodlight trained on the front and rear entries to the house and the dock. The last thing he wanted was someone stumbling onto his place despite the huge Private Road notice on the turnoff to Hurricane Bay and taking an accidental dive into the water. He'd never had a fear of thieves; the value of Hurricane Bay was in the island itself. Most of what he had that might be considered of value had more of a sentimental worth, though he supposed some of the collections his folks had gathered were good ones.

Still, out on Hurricane Bay, he'd never even locked his doors—until today.

"You're late," Jesse called to him.

"Yeah, I know. Sorry."

"No big deal. I would have watched the TV, except the house is locked." Jesse was tall and gave the appearance of being lanky. He wasn't. He was honed to a *T*. His hair was nearly black, dead straight and worn short. His eyes were a light hazel, almost yellow, and he had a way of looking at a person as if he already knew everything they might be trying to hide. He'd been with the Metro-Dade force until his wife, also a cop, had been killed. At that point, he'd left the force and joined the tribal police.

He was Dane's second cousin, and he had mixed blood, as well. His just wasn't quite so complex of a cocktail, as he liked to tell Dane.

"When did you start locking the door?" Jesse asked him.

"Today. I'm setting up surveillance cameras, too."

"Your chosen line of work is getting to you?" Jesse said.

"Maybe. Come on in."

Dane opened the screen door, then unlocked the old Dade County pine door behind it. Both men stepped in.

The house was concrete block and stucco and Dade County pine, built against the storms that periodically ravaged the area. It had withstood a great deal, even being pounded by hurricanes, because the construction was so strong. The man who had owned the island before Dane's grandfather had been blown out even before they'd started naming storms. All he had wanted to do was unload the place; he'd called it Hurricane Bay, and the name had stuck. It was Dane's grandfather who'd built the house. Dade County pine was at a premium because it was almost impossible to acquire anymore.

It repelled termites and stood strong against most of the
dangers inherent in a subtropical climate. The living
room was completely paneled with it. The house boasted
two coral rock fireplaces, one in the master bedroom
and the other in the living room. A large mantel had
also been chiseled to match, and on it stood one of his
father's great treasures, a stuffed 'gator called Big Tom
in life, and—since the taxidermist had been excellent at
his craft—for posterity. His father had caught the alli-
gator, which had been terrorizing a residential canal in
Homestead. The reptile hadn't gotten hold of any children, but he had managed to consume two poodles and
a too-curious cat before being taken down.

A soft leather sofa, matching love seat and two arm-
chairs rounded out the grouping in front of the fireplace.
The walls boasted some fine Audubon prints and interesting family photos.

"Want a beer?" Dane asked as they entered.

"Sure."

Jesse followed Dane through the dining room. The
antique claw-foot dining table held Dane's computer and
stacks of papers. They passed through the dining room
to the kitchen, which fronted the house, along with the
living and dining rooms. Way back when, his grandfather had figured people would want to be outside, so
both the dining room and kitchen had large windows
that could be opened up to the porch, where there were
outside counters and rough wood tables. The back of
the house faced both the dock and the little spit of man-
made beach, so the floor plan made it easy to be outside most of the time.

Jesse leaned against the kitchen counter, looking out at
the night and the water as Dane went into the refrigerator.

"It's been a while since I've been out here," Jesse said, accepting the can Dane handed him.

"Yeah?"

"Of course, you haven't been back all that long."

"Almost six months."

Jesse didn't comment. He knew what had brought Dane back. There was no need to talk about it.

"Okay, so what's going on?" Jesse asked. "Do I have a stray tribal member harassing the tourists? Is some local all pissed off because he lost big at bingo or something?"

Dane shook his head, thinking that his second cousin's dry expectations might have amused him at a different time.

"No, actually, I need to ask you about something."

"Shoot."

"A couple of months back, you found a strangling victim out in the Glades."

Jesse frowned and nodded. "Yeah, I found the body," he said. He studied his beer can. Then he looked at Dane again, his forehead still furrowed. "I've seen a hell of a lot, between Miami-Dade and just living out where fools can go astray. But…hell. That was bad."

"Mind telling me about it?"

"I think I talked to you at the time."

"You did, but I'd like to hear about it again."

"You have a reason."

"Yes, I do."

"Are you planning on sharing it with me?"

"Soon. I just need a little time."

"You haven't found another body?"

"No."

Jesse studied him for a long moment but accepted

the fact that Dane would tell him everything when he was ready.

"I think it was just about three months ago now. The first body was found three months before that, up in Broward County."

"And the Miami-Dade boys and Broward homicide think it was the same killer?"

Jesse inclined his head. "Looks like it. It's a tough case. Both bodies were found in such a bad state of decomposition, it's been a bitch for forensics."

"That's why it was so bad when you found the girl?"

"She'd been in the water almost two weeks, in a canal in the Everglades. I don't really need to tell you what that means, but suffice it to say that nature takes its course."

"So you think she was thrown into the canal by someone who knew the Everglades?"

"Not necessarily. There are a few pretty decent roads leading off of the Tamiami Trail. And the day I discovered her was…a Tuesday. Right after those torrential rains we had when it was supposed to be dry season. A Mack truck could have driven back there and the tire prints would have been washed out. Of course, a Mack truck would have sunk in the swamp, but you know what I mean. In that area, after heavy rains… you're not going to find anything resembling a print or a track. And since the body was in the water, tangled up in some tree roots, there wasn't even a way to tell exactly where it had gone in, since it might have traveled with the current."

"From what you told me at the time, and what I read in the paper," Dane said, "they knew she'd been strangled with a necktie, because it was still around her throat."

"Right. And it was a tie manufactured by the thousands, available in any department store in any state."

"Anything else?"

"She was naked, except for the tie. That's about it."

"Did you notice anything in particular when you found her?"

"Yeah, that she was dead. I didn't need to feel for a pulse. And where I found her…it's in an area that might be considered reservation land and might be counted as county. It's not one of those places anyone really wants to fight over. I roped off the scene where I found her and called in the Miami-Dade homicide guys. Specialists. She wasn't one of ours."

"You knew that from seeing the body?"

"I couldn't even have guaranteed you that she was a she from seeing the body," Jesse said.

"Then…"

"I'd have known if we'd been missing anyone," Jesse said. "We're one damned small tribe out there, you know. Less than five hundred. They pretty well wiped out the big numbers during the Indian wars and relocation. Bingo and the casino have been our best revenge, you know."

"They did identify her, right?"

"Cherie Madsen. Twenty-three, a dancer at a Miami strip club. She'd been a missing person at the time, and she was identified by her dental records."

"And did the police have any leads?"

"Sure, they had leads, but no real suspects. They traced every name they could find for the night she disappeared, but lots of guys who go to strip clubs use cash and aren't necessarily regulars. They talked to all her old boyfriends, same as they talked to everyone about the murder in Broward County. The first girl was found in a canal off I-595. Same thing—she was in the water at least a couple of weeks before she was discovered. Strangled, tie around her neck. There had been rain that time, too. The body had probably traveled. The girl was naked, and once again the tie could have been bought anywhere. No way to get any prints. The girl hadn't scratched her attacker, so there were no skin cells beneath her nails, nothing. I have a friend in homicide at the Broward sheriff's department, if you want to talk to him further about the case. And you know the guy handling the case for Miami-Dade. It's Hector Hernandez."

"Yes, I know him. I've known him for years. Big time fisherman, down here a lot. He's a good cop."

"Yeah, he's definitely a good cop. He can help you more than I can, since you're apparently after something. I kept up with the case some, since I found one of the victims," Jesse said quietly. "But not being Miami-Dade homicide anymore, I don't have the same access to the experts. And it's not my case anymore, anyway. You know how small the Miccosukee force is. Something like this, Miami-Dade comes in."

"Did you hear anything about a psychological profile?"

Jesse nodded again, taking a long swallow from his can. "The cops in both counties got together and asked the FBI to give them a hand with the profiling, and they brought in an expert who has been pretty right on with each case he's profiled that has been solved. White male, twenty-five to forty-five, has a day job, maybe a wife and family, maybe not. Even though the second girl was found out in the Everglades, the profiler is certain the killer is a *white* male. Someone who knows the area and may even know what happens to a body in the water. He probably looks decent, maybe he's even good-looking, and he may have a certain charisma. He's an organized killer. Nothing is left to chance. He's smart enough to keep his prints off any traceable materials, use a condom and dump the bodies where nature will take care of the rest. There might be two different killers, one copycatting the other, but the homicide guys don't think so. They kept a few details about the first body secret, and those same details were also consistent with the second victim." Jesse shrugged, taking another long swallow from his beer can. "In private, of course, the homicide guys admit to having just about nothing to follow up on. Both girls were strippers. They've questioned every man they could get a lead on who was at either club the night the girl was last seen. They've questioned family and old boyfriends. They've looked for witnesses. They don't have prints, fibers, tire tracks or anything else. They haven't given up, but they've followed every lead they had, and the trail hasn't gotten them very far. It would be bull to suggest they're not hot on it because of what the girls did for a living. They're just working with nothing."

"I never suggested they weren't working every angle."

"You didn't, but some guy wrote it up in the paper that way."

"Was he questioned?"

"You bet. He was just some jerk who's down on the police. He writes up every scrap of corruption he can get his hands on. He tried to suggest years ago that the cops didn't really give a rat's ass when a psycho was killing hookers on Eighth Street. Then the cops cornered the killer and he had to eat his words. But there were witnesses on that case. At least they had the make and color of the car to go on. They don't seem to have a damned thing this time. Then there was the guy a while back who was killing working girls, cutting them up and stuffing them in suitcases. They thought they had it all solved when they were able to trace a guy to the last victim—except she hadn't been a prostitute, she'd been a lounge singer, and the guy they traced was her ex-boyfriend. Turned out he hadn't killed the prostitutes, he was just hoping to get away with murder by disposing of the body in the same manner. They caught him, but they still don't know who did in the other women."

"Think it could be the same man?"

"With a change in style? I don't know. I don't know enough about criminal psychology to answer that, but the guys I know seem to think they're looking for two different killers. Since they haven't found new bodies in suitcases in a while, they're afraid the guy they called the 'Bag-man' might have moved on. He was a slasher. This guy strangles. Apparently a different psychology brings about the difference in methods. Hey, you took a lot more classes in criminology than I ever did. You should know."

Dane shrugged. "It's not likely that a slasher would become a strangler," he said. "In this case, though... well, I just hoped you might have some insight. You saw the body in situ and all."

"I told you—I called in the specialists the minute I found her. I mean the *minute*. I knew damn well that I didn't have the manpower or equipment to investigate a crime scene like that, to protect every little hair and fiber that might turn up." He was quiet for a moment, studying Dane. "So why your renewed interest in the case?" Jesse asked.

"Sheila's missing," Dane said. He was comfortable saying that much.

One of Jesse's dark brows arched against his forehead. "What do you mean, missing? Sheila is always off somewhere, and she always turns up again. Why are you worried and connecting her to this case? She doesn't fit the victim profile. Or has she started wearing pasties and dancing?"

"No. But…she was running pretty wild."

"She may still be running wild. Sheila's taken off for long periods of time before, hasn't she? I don't think she came back to Key Largo much before you showed up down here again. And before that, if I understand it right, after her divorce from Larry, she took off for Europe for a while, came back and gambled in Vegas, then hopped around some more before settling into renting that duplex with Cindy. Why would you suspect she might be a victim just because she didn't share her plans with anyone? Cindy told me that even after they rented the duplex, Sheila often went off for a few nights. Cindy would start getting worried, and then Sheila would suddenly call her from the Bahamas or somewhere to say she was all right."

"She hasn't called anyone this time."

"Still…well, you're talking about Sheila."

"Call it a hunch," Dane said.

Jesse stared at him. "It's more than a hunch, but, hey, you'll tell me when you're ready."

"I'm still dealing with it myself," Dane said.

"Have you been to the local cops?"

"No, but Kelsey is down. She was supposed to meet Sheila here. And she said something about having gone to the cops."

"I'm sure they mollified her and filled out a report. And that's about all you're going to get. Not that you haven't got decent guys working the Keys. It's just that Sheila is a grown woman, a woman known to leave her home for long periods of time without giving notice to those around her. She's over twenty-one and doesn't really owe explanations to anyone."

"She hasn't just gone off. I have to find—" He paused, wondering if he was being an ass, if he shouldn't just bring Jesse in on it now. But he wasn't ready. It was just this morning that he had seen the photograph. "I have to find her myself."

"If there's anything I can do, let me know."

"Thanks. How are you doing out there?"

"I'm doing well," Jesse said, swallowing the rest of his beer. "And I'm going to get going on this one beer. I don't think it would make for good public relations if a Miccosukee cop was stopped for driving under the influence. Come out and see me sometime. I'll show you where I found the girl, and I'll let you see the file I have on the incident."

"Great. Thanks. I'll take you up on that."

"Let me know when you're coming, so I can be available."

"You've managed to get your hands on a cell phone that can find a signal in the Glades?"

Jesse laughed. "No, not really. But the office can rouse me on the radio if I'm not around."

"I'll be out soon."

Dane walked Jesse out through the front of the house. A broad hallway stretched from the living room to the front foyer, a formal room decorated according to his mother's era, with a library to the right and a breakfast room to the left directly behind the kitchen. A curving stairway led to the two big bedrooms that took up the entire second floor of the residence.

They all used to slide down the banisters when they'd been kids. It had driven his mother crazy.

Jesse left by the front door, and Dane went along with him as he got into his car—his own, a beige Jeep, and not the patrol car he used when he was on duty. Jesse preferred his Jeep, though he was free to use the patrol car when he chose. There had been some torrential rains lately. Maybe he'd been afraid the road to Hurricane Bay would be badly rutted.

And sometimes he liked his own car when he was off the reservation because he got tired of tourists pointing at him as if he were Tonto on a pinto.

"You know, when you feel you're ready for my help, I'm there," Jesse told him.

"Yeah, I know. Thanks."

Jesse drove away.

Dane started back to the house, but hesitated, looking at the eaves over the porch that led to the roadside, the official entry, of the house. He mentally placed a security camera in the eaves. He'd get on it tomorrow.

He walked back in, heading for his computer. He sat down, keyed in some entries and followed them. For an hour, he gave his attention to every detail he could glean from the news articles he was able to call up online.

After a while, mind churning, he logged off, stretched and walked out back. He stared at the dock

and walked around the angular corner that brought him
from the dock and the deeper water to the spit of shallows and beach.

That was where she had been.

Rain, surf, sand, time. Nothing. The area looked as
peaceful as ever.

He walked back into the house and looked around
the living room, feeling a renewed surge of fury, sorrow and anger.

In his own room, he threw open the closet door,
looked at the organized rows of clothing. The space
where an article was missing. He'd been through it all
in his head, over and over. He'd searched the house.

He went over it again.

The entire house, top to bottom. Out back, he trod
lightly over the small dock, hopped aboard the Urchin
and once again went slowly and minutely over every
detail of his boat.

At last he went back to the house, locked both doors
and made certain that his .38 special was loaded and
beneath his pillow.

Still, sleep eluded him.

Someone had been in his house. And they had done
a lot more than eat his porridge or sleep in his bed.

Only one thing had been taken.

He told himself he couldn't be sure. The house was
filled with the accumulation of years.

Still, he knew in his gut that there was definitely
one thing missing.

And that one thing could damn him.

Kelsey jerked up and nearly screamed at the sound
of loud pounding at her door.

She hadn't wanted to admit it, but going out to Andy

Latham's had spooked her. And Dane had been acting strangely, too. It was weird how life could change. She had adored him so much once; it had almost been hero worship. Then there had been the years when she kept a polite and civil distance at those few social occasions when they were at the same place at the same time. They'd gone from being best friends to stiff acquaintances. Then they hadn't seen each other at all for…two years, at least. Since the last time she had seen Sheila.

And now…

She could still hear Sheila's voice in her mind. She hadn't seen her in a long time, but she had known Sheila well. Known her when she was angry, caustic and careless of the feelings of others. Known her when she was depressed and down on herself. She knew the way Sheila sounded.

And this time, she had sounded…

Scared.

Kelsey had found herself upset when Dane left. And oddly frightened and unnerved when Cindy left—and she was only on the other side of the wall. Face it, she was actually feeling scared, though of what she didn't know, when she'd locked the door and gone to bed for the night. And she hadn't really slept. She'd dozed and awakened, dozed, and awakened again. She hadn't really been asleep when the knocking had sounded; it had just been so loud and sharp against the dark and quiet that it had startled her.

Bolting to a sitting position in the bed, she took a moment to tell herself that the noise was just someone knocking at the door—and thieves and psychos rarely knocked.

She crawled quickly out of bed. Since her night attire consisted of a long, heavy cotton, one-size-fits-most T-shirt with a frazzled duck saying something about needing coffee, she walked through the darkened house to the front door without a robe, not bothering with slippers, either.

Her mom still got mad at her for walking around without shoes all the time. Even in the Keys. Walking around barefoot and getting your feet dirty made you look like white trash, or so Jennie said.

Amazed at the thoughts that came to mind in a darkened house in the middle of the night, Kelsey reached the door and looked out the peephole. The yellow porch light beamed down on two men: Nate Curry and Larry Miller.

She opened the door, no longer at all frightened, but quizzical and irritated. "What the hell are the two of you doing out here in the middle of the night?"

Nate, a true beach boy, tanned to pure gold, blue-eyed, blond-haired, seemed taken aback. "It's not the middle of the night. It's just after two."

"It's 2:00 a.m.," Larry said, his expression somewhat rueful. Even when he was standing in cutoffs in the sand, Larry Miller looked like an executive. His dark brown hair always gave the appearance of a neat, fresh cut. Kelsey didn't think she'd ever seen him anything but clean-shaven—five-o'clock shadow didn't dare darken his door. He was dressed casually in a polo shirt and knee-length Dockers, but both were pressed and clean. His boat shoes didn't have a scuff. The overnight bag he carried, which should have looked as laid-back as a duffle, bore a designer name. He had the profile to fit the image, as well. Features chiseled like a classic Greek statue.

"I don't close the bar on weeknights until 2:00 a.m.," Nate said. He stared from Larry to Kelsey. "Okay, so maybe to some people that's the middle of the night."

"I was just going to go to a hotel," Larry said, looking at Kelsey, still apologetic. "But I went by Nate's. He reminded me that this place has two bedrooms. And if Sheila shows, I can just bunk over with Cindy."

Kelsey stepped back, letting the men enter. "Larry, you're more than welcome here—as much as I am, surely. You'll have to take the spare room. I'm in Sheila's—I know it sounds silly, but it makes me feel closer to figuring out her moves somehow. But what are you doing down here at all?"

He shrugged. "Two things. You sounded upset on the phone, and I didn't want you to go getting all worried about Sheila. She's been known to take off before. Second…I don't know. You'd been to see Nate, Cindy was here, Dane had come over…I guess I was seized by a rush of nostalgia and decided I had to come down, too. My nostalgia was tempered with reason, of course—I didn't want you to be alone and upset."

Nate made his way past both of them. Unlike Larry, he unmistakably belonged here. His tan was straight from the beach, not acquired in any artificial bed. He had a complete ease of manner in cutoffs or swim trunks, a T-shirt or his bare chest. He could dress well when he needed to and looked like a million bucks. But an hour or so with a tie on, and Nate went crazy. He'd been born in the islands, and he loved them. He'd never had the least desire to leave. He'd gone far enough north to get a degree from Florida International University in hotel and restaurant management, just so he could further improve the Sea Shanty. A vacation to Nate meant taking a boat over to the Bahamas. He had no desire to head for the snow and couldn't care less if he ever saw a country that didn't offer a good reef for diving, sun, sand and warmth.

"You got coffee, Kelsey?" he asked, heading straight for the kitchen.

"Yes, I have coffee," she said, glancing at Larry with a shrug and following Nate. "But it's 2:00 a.m. You'll wind up staying awake all night."

"Nope. I never stay awake all night," Nate assured her. He was already digging through the cabinets.

She walked behind him, caught a prying hand and said, "If you want coffee, let me make decaf, and that way Larry and I can join you."

"She's in her mid-twenties, and already her spirit of adventure has departed," Nate said to Larry, over Kelsey's head.

"My dislike of lying awake all night unable to sleep has kicked in, that's all," Kelsey said. Giving Nate a little push out of the way, she found the decaf and began preparing the coffee.

"You got anything to eat in here?" Larry asked.

"You just came from Nate's place—why didn't you order food if you were hungry?" Kelsey asked. She didn't want to say that she was actually glad to see them, as annoying as they might be. They were giving her a pleasant sense of security.

"His late-night menu doesn't offer a lot," Larry said.

"Hey!" Nate protested. "Conch fritters, conch chowder, snapper sandwich, veggie burger, hamburger. What are you expecting at this hour of the night? A sissy fruit and yogurt salad, or some alfalfa sprouts?"

"Your eating habits will give you a heart attack one

day," Larry said. "I can already hear your arteries choking."

"You're going to be one of those health freaks who does marathons and drops dead running down the block," Nate told him.

"You have cereal?" Larry asked Kelsey.

"Raisin bran. Help yourself." She was measuring coffee.

Larry had no problem helping himself to food. "Ah-ha! She has yogurt and fruit. I knew it."

"And beer," Nate said, taking one.

"You just left a bar."

"I never drink when I'm working my own bar."

"You just asked me for coffee."

"The coffee and the beer will cancel each other out."

Kelsey shook her head and let the coffee perk. She crawled up on a bar stool next to Larry. "What about work? We're both gone now."

"Tomorrow is Friday. I left a message with my secretary that I was working at home. I'll drive back in on Monday sometime," Larry said. "Don't worry, I'm a golden boy at work, you know that."

It was true.

"Um. Let's hope you're not so golden that they don't get the idea to cut my vacation short," Kelsey told him.

He laughed. "You're the golden girl. The idea lady. The creative genius. You're safe."

"Is that coffee done, Kelsey?" Nate asked.

"Looks like it. Why don't you pour me some, too?"

Larry jumped when the phone on the counter in front of the coffeepot rang.

"Who the hell would be calling at this hour?" Larry asked.

"Yeah, two o'clock in the morning," Kelsey murmured. "Answer it."

Larry did so. Even from where they were sitting, the others could hear Cindy's voice over the phone. She had recognized Larry's "Hello?" But she wanted to know what he was doing in Kelsey's place in the middle of the night.

"Time is relative," he told her. "Actually when I talked to Kelsey earlier, she sounded a little down, and I thought seeing you and Dane sounded really good, so I decided to play hooky from work and drive on down. For the weekend, at least."

Cindy said something Kelsey couldn't quite catch. Larry hung up the phone.

Kelsey and Nate both stared at Larry.

"She's on her way over," Larry said.

"Why not?" Kelsey said. "Time is relative." She got off her bar stool to walk to the front door and let Cindy in when she appeared in just a minute's time. It didn't take long to get from one side of a duplex to another.

"Hey!" Cindy said when Kelsey opened the door. She swept on in. Larry had come from the kitchen and greeted Cindy with a big hug.

"Wow!" he said as she hugged him back. "Little but powerful. I feel like I just got a hug from an anaconda."

"Sorry, too tight?" Cindy said.

Larry shook his head. "Hugs are never too tight. I just never realized before how powerful you are."

"It's a short thing. Being small, I work out a lot, so the big guys can't push me around. Kelsey, you should come to the gym with me tomorrow. I have a membership over at the new hotel. They've got all kinds of machines, a pool, a sauna… If you work out, you'll feel better about everything."

"If Sheila shows up, I'll feel better about everything," Kelsey said.

Nate had joined them in the passage between the living room and kitchen. Along with Cindy and Larry, he stared at her. They were all looking at her as if they were adults and she was a child still convinced there was a Santa Claus.

"She's gone off for more than a week before," Cindy said.

"She left me for lots more than a week," Larry said. There was no pain in his voice. He was matter-of-fact about Sheila.

"She acts on whims," Nate said softly.

They still had that look in their eyes as they watched her. Kelsey shook her head. "Come on, now, we're her friends. We've got to be concerned."

Larry cleared his throat.

"Okay, so I was barely in touch with her for a couple of years. But you know what it's like. We all grew up together. We have a bond. At first Sheila just e-mailed me, and I e-mailed back. Then we talked. Then she said that she really needed to see me, because I knew her so well, and she could trust me with her deepest, darkest secrets. Then she told me she was feeling desperate, and please would I make arrangements to spend time with her. So, you see, don't you, why I'm so worried?"

Larry groaned softly. "Kelsey, don't you remember how pissed off Sheila was when you took my side during the divorce?"

"I didn't take your side. Larry, I don't take sides in

the breakup of a marriage, which is always a very sad thing."

"Okay, you didn't take sides," Larry said. He stood staring at her for a moment, then groaned. "Well, great, I'm glad we're all best friends because it's still kind of embarrassing to admit all this. Don't you remember? She cheated. I was hurt. Really hurt. You were cool to her. I remember her standing in your office, and you telling Sheila that she had owed it to me to say the marriage wasn't working, that she shouldn't have hurt and humiliated me the way she did. She said you were her friend, so you should have understood whatever she had done. And you told her that she was a grown-up and could live the life she wanted, but she needed to start watching out for crushing other people."

Kelsey remembered the day well. Larry had just found out about what his wife had gotten up to. He'd blown an important presentation because of it, and she'd been worried about his job.

And it was true. Sheila *had* been angry with her, and she'd flounced out of the office. Next time they had made a date—at Sheila's insistence, because she had wanted to tell her side of the story—Sheila hadn't shown. The next time Sheila had tried to see her, Kelsey had still been angry herself. She'd come up with an excuse. And that had been it until just about six months ago, when Sheila started e-mailing her, and then the phone calls began.

"Sheila is our friend," Nate said quietly. "But she's kicked us all in the teeth."

They were all silent for a minute.

"So what are we supposed to do?" Kelsey said.

"You went to the police, right?" Nate said.

Kelsey nodded.

"Then we let them handle it. What else are you going to do?"

"Track her down," Kelsey said.

They all continued to stare at her. She let out a sigh of exasperation. "We follow her footsteps, talk to anyone she might have seen."

"Great," Nate said. "That would include the entire populace of the Keys. And let's not forget Miami."

"Dane has an investigations firm," Cindy said with impatience. "The smartest thing is to let him handle it."

"The problem with Dane is the same problem with you all," Kelsey said. She didn't know why she was reluctant to point out to Nate the fact that he had been the one to tell her he was pretty sure Dane and Sheila had been seeing each other as more than friends, and that then the two of them had argued at the bar, and that Sheila had implied she was heading out to Dane's place the last time he had seen her. "No one seems to be really worried," she said.

"Except you," Larry pointed out.

"All right, here's the deal," Cindy said. "Kelsey, tomorrow morning you come to the gym with me. I swear, it will make you feel better. Then we'll all go to see Dane. We'll have that barbecue at his place."

"He didn't exactly invite us for a barbecue tomorrow," Kelsey said.

Cindy waved a hand in the air as if being invited was entirely immaterial. "We'll bring all the stuff. We'll just show up at Hurricane Bay in the morning with all the fixings. He won't mind."

"Wait a minute," Nate said. "What time?"

"I don't know. Sometime in the morning," Cindy said.

"Morning is relative. It's morning now. Closing in on three," Nate said. "I wasn't planning on waking up too early."

"How about one?" Larry suggested. He yawned. "I'll sleep, Cindy and Kelsey can go get buff, buy the food, come back, then we all meet here and head over at one."

"There. We have a plan," Cindy said. "Good night. Kelsey. Will nine be too early for you?"

Kelsey had the feeling the last thing she was going to want to do in the morning was go to the gym.

"Sheila came with me sometimes," Cindy said. "You can ask around and find out if she said anything to anyone."

"Nine, then," Kelsey agreed.

"Night, guys," Cindy said. Walking past them, she let herself out.

"I should go, too," Nate said. He looked at Kelsey. "This seems strange," he told Larry.

"What's that?"

"Leaving you in a house, sleeping with my ex-wife."

"He's not sleeping with your ex-wife," Kelsey said.

"She won't sleep with me," Larry told Nate.

"No?"

"I've asked her," Larry said, winking at Kelsey. "She rebuffed me kindly, but with determination."

"She's like that."

"Hell, she married you."

"She married me because she was a friend who liked me. It was a mercy marriage, and that was all."

"She likes me, and she still won't sleep with me."

"Nate," Kelsey said firmly, "let's face it, you're just too pretty to be tied down by one woman. And, Larry, you're sleeping with one of the most beautiful women

I've ever seen, and she seems to be nice, on top of it. Nate, go home. Larry, the extra bedroom is right there. Cindy is going to get me up in a matter of hours and make me do painful things to my body, so go away, both of you."

She pushed Nate toward the door. He protested playfully, "I can do painful things to your body, if that's what you want."

"Out!"

She shoved Nate out the door.

"Lock it," he told her from the outside.

"You bet," she said.

She knew that Nate was waiting to hear the sound of the bolt sliding into place. She obliged him. "It's locked."

"Good girl. Good night."

"Good night."

She turned around. Larry laughed, putting up his hands. "I'm on my way into the spare bedroom this minute."

To prove it, he turned and walked through the doorway and across the living room.

Kelsey returned to the kitchen for a moment and unplugged the coffee machine. She decided to set it up for the next morning. She'd gotten Cindy and Nate out, and Larry off to bed. She could go back to sleep.

Except that now she was restless.

The day had been busy. She was really exhausted. She wanted to lie down, close her eyes and black it all out.

But now, in the silence that came in the wake of the others' departures, she felt wired.

So tired, but wide-awake.

She gave the kitchen a thorough cleaning. When that was done, she looked around the living room. It was already clean. Sheila wasn't the type to keep bric-a-brac lying around. Nor did she pile up magazines or bills. Of course, she would have to have some kind of paperwork lying around. Utility bills, if nothing else. Kelsey made a mental note to go through every drawer in the place the next day and really start prying into Sheila's business. With that determination made, she returned to the bedroom at last. Sheila's room.

She lay down again, got up, washed her face, brushed her teeth, turned the television on to a cable movie. An old mummy movie. Black and white, with no computer or high-tech gimmicks, it was just a darned good movie. Good acting, lots of suspense.

She warned herself that she would fall asleep and dream about bandage-wrapped creatures rising from the grave to come after her.

But she didn't.

She dreamed about the past.

And hours later, when she awoke again to the streaking pink and gold colors of a new dawn, haggard and still exhausted, she wished that she *had* dreamed of ancient monsters.

They were far less unsettling than the memories of a not so distant time.

Chapter 5

An endangered American crocodile had somehow made it into the waters just off Coconut Grove, so close to the marina that those who made a living scraping barnacles from the hulls of the many pleasure craft had been afraid to go into the water. But the wily reptile had been caught and brought back to a crocodile reserve. Two accidents had tied up US1, and a woman had been arrested for aggravated child abuse after bringing her injured baby to a local hospital. Another Hollywood star had been arrested on Miami Beach for DUI.

Waking early, Dane listened to the news on the television, then scoured the morning paper.

No bodies had been discovered in the last twenty-four hours. And it was daylight. Time to take the offensive. He owed it to himself—and to Sheila.

He left the house and started out with a visit to Gary

Hansen at the local police station. Gary had come down from Minnesota. In the sun, his blond hair had turned to a platinum that was almost white. He always wore very dark sunglasses, mainly because his eyes were nearly as light a blue as his hair was a blond. The sunlight hurt him. He was fair-skinned, as well, and despite the amount of sunblock he used, he was usually burned to a shade of brilliant pink most commonly found on tourists unaccustomed to the sun. But despite his body's seeming protest against the climate, Gary loved Key Largo. He was never leaving.

He was a decent guy of about forty, the kind who would slap a drunk driver in the can overnight without mercy, but who would deal mercifully with minor infractions of the law. He gave the appearance of moving slowly, of being a leisurely guy, but in the few cases that had brought them together since Dane had opened up shop in the area, he'd proven himself to be sharp as a tack.

"Hey, Dane, what's up? Caught any thieves on video?" Gary asked him.

"No, I just came in to ask you a few questions."

Gary groaned. "You're not going to ask me for files that aren't public domain, are you? There are laws to protect the criminals out there, you know."

Dane grinned at the joke despite his lack of humor at the moment. He took a seat on the edge of Gary's cluttered desk. "No, I think a friend of mine was in here yesterday. Seems we have another friend who hasn't been seen for a while."

Gary nodded, eyeing Dane closely as he leaned back in his swivel chair, lacing his fingers behind his head. He'd known exactly why Dane had come.

"Kelsey Cunningham. She reported that your friend Sheila hadn't been seen in a while."

"Have you done anything?"

"Filled out the papers. Asked a few questions."

"That's all?"

Gary hesitated, then shrugged. "Actually I would have come to see you today. Miss Cunningham said that Nate Curry out at the Sea Shanty told her Sheila was heading for your place the last time he'd seen her."

"She did. She came to my house. Left early the next morning. I haven't seen her since." That was God's truth. He hadn't seen her.

Not in person.

"Did she say anything to you about going away?" Gary asked him.

"No. Not to me."

"Well, there are some other locals she hangs with, who we might want to question…just for being questionable locals. Still, Miss Cunningham says that her friend's car is gone, as well. We'll treat the situation as a missing person, but from past history…this lady comes and goes as she pleases. Look, Dane, I know Sheila Warren, too. Not like you old-timers here know her, but I've met her, and I know about her. She isn't employed and lives off that trust fund left by her mother. She island hops, continent hops…seems to me she's a free spirit. Sorry, Dane, I know the woman is your friend. Maybe she's still a lot more, from what I've heard from a few people. But, hell, she's a grown woman. Apparently she…likes making new friends and traveling with them. Have you been hired by someone to look for her?"

"Yeah, myself."

"Great. We'll help each other. But…this isn't a big

city like Miami or anything, but still, we had a big
drug bust the other night, I've got to find a husband
who broke his wife's jaw at the new hotel the other
night…there's a string of burglaries, and…well, you
know the routine. It's hard to get too concerned over
a woman who regularly goes off with whomever she
pleases whenever she feels like it."

"I understand your position. But I have a suggestion.
Talk to Andy Latham, Sheila's stepfather."

"Yeah, I'd intended to do that." From his tone, Gary
Hansen obviously considered it an unpleasant proposi-
tion. He eyed Dane for a minute. "I heard around town
that Sheila was getting into drugs."

"To the best of my knowledge, she wasn't into anything heavy," Dane said. "She wasn't shooting up, if
that's what you mean."

"How do you know?"

"Okay, she wasn't shooting into her arms, at any
rate. I know because she was always bare-armed when
I saw her."

"You did have a relationship with her for years,
right?"

"Yeah. I wouldn't say high school sweethearts, because neither one of us was particularly sweet. After
high school, I went away to college, and then into the
service. Sheila went her own way."

"So it had all cooled down by now?" Gary said, still
studying him. He didn't wait for Dane to answer. "Yeah,
I guess it couldn't have been much of anything now.
Heard about what happened up in St. Augustine. I'm
sorry about that."

"Thanks. And as to Sheila, whether or not she was

buying weed or pills on the street, I don't know. She might have been. It's an angle I wouldn't rule out."

"The problem with searching for Sheila is that there are miles and miles of angles that have to be checked out," Gary said.

"Keep me posted, will you?"

"Sure."

Dane stood and started for the door.

"Hey," Gary called.

"Yeah?"

"You keep me posted, too, huh?"

Dane nodded. He felt an uncomfortable rise of tension in his throat. It might be the best thing in the world if he did keep the cops posted with the truth.

The whole truth and nothing but the truth.

No, he'd thought it all out. There was nothing he knew that could help the cops do anything.

Except charge him with murder.

Working out with Cindy made Kelsey feel like a novice climber trying to scale Everest next to the pros.

She had never considered herself to be in particularly *bad* shape—she did slide on into the gym in Miami now and then, she loved to go bike riding on a decent day, and she spent at least several late afternoons a week in her condo pool.

But watching Cindy on an exercise bike was like watching a tornado set down. She seemed to pedal close to a mile a minute.

They shared no conversation at the cycles. Kelsey was lucky to be able to breathe while trying to appear to keep up with Cindy's speed.

From the cycles, they went on to free weights.

Cindy could apparently press more weight than most of the men. Two-hundred-something pounds. Kelsey didn't need to spot Cindy while she was lifting—something that probably wouldn't have done much good anyway, since she couldn't begin to lift the weight that Cindy could—because there was a roomful of muscle-bound guys more than ready to help out.

Kelsey played with the five-pound weights she used in her own exercise routine, said hello to all the lifters to whom Cindy introduced her, and decided that her own meager workout was done. Cindy, true to her word, asked if anyone had seen Sheila in the gym lately.

No one had.

Three guys—Jim Norris, Ralph Munroe and Ricky Esteban—apparently knew Sheila. And knew her fairly well.

None of them seemed in the least concerned about her whereabouts. Ralph was short and, with his muscles, seemed as wide as he was tall. Killer pecs. Jim was the opposite, so tall that the scope of his muscles seemed smaller, though certainly as well honed. The man didn't seem to have so much as a quarter inch of body fat. Ricky Esteban came in a body shape right between the other two; standing about six feet even, he had a very attractive build. He told Kelsey that he and Sheila had spent a night on the town about two weeks earlier, and he hadn't seen her since then.

He watched Kelsey with curious amber eyes, then told her, "You know…Sheila's the kind of girl who doesn't believe in double standards."

"Meaning…?" Kelsey asked him.

Ricky shrugged, dragging damp hair back off his forehead. "What's good for the gander is good for the goose. I guess I'm trying to say that she does whatever the hell she wants to do. It aggravates her that men seem to think nothing about going to a strip club, or that they can go to a bar at night in hopes of getting lucky with a total stranger, and that women generally get labeled— not nicely—for doing the same thing. She told me once that she was a voice for her sex."

Kelsey stared at him blankly as he went on. "What I'm trying to tell you is that you shouldn't be too worried. If Sheila met a guy and liked him, and he was heading to Alaska for the week, she wouldn't think twice about going with him."

"She would have called me," Kelsey insisted.

Ricky shrugged. Then his expression changed, and he asked her what she was doing with her vacation time in the Keys.

He was flattering—and damned good-looking.

She hesitated and wondered why she did. Dinner with him would probably be nice.

She gave him a vague answer, though, escaped out to the entry area and bought a bottle of water, then sat in one of the comfortable spa chairs to wait, breathe and hope the pain she'd incurred by trying to keep up with Cindy would go away.

She damned the fact that Dane Whitelaw had returned to Hurricane Bay. She wondered if, had she not seen him, she might have gone out with Ricky.

Ricky had admitted to dating Sheila.

Then again, she wasn't sure she had met a guy yet who hadn't dated Sheila. Everything she was learning was disturbing. And yet people kept telling her these things so she wouldn't worry.

Unfortunately, all these tidbits about Sheila's wild lifestyle only made her more concerned.

The bottle of water went quickly.

She wanted coffee.

The gym was very nice—Cindy had spoken the truth. There was the gym itself, along with a complete spa in the west wing of the new hotel. The spa sold all kinds of juices and herbal teas. Healthful offerings.

She just wanted coffee. Strong, caffeinated coffee.

As she debated heading out to the hotel area, she was startled to hear her name called.

"Kelsey? Kelsey Cunningham? It *is* you, isn't it?"

She twisted in her chair to see a man coming from the free weight room. He was a good six foot two and wearing a tank top, so it was apparent that he was muscular. He had hair so dark it was almost ebony, able to defy the effects of the sun that had tanned him to such a deep shade that he was nearly brown. His eyes were just as dark as his hair. Within two seconds she recognized him and smiled. "Jorge!"

He walked over to her, about to give her a hug, then backed off, apologizing. "Sorry, I'm sweating like a pig. If pigs really sweat. Quick kiss on the cheek. How are you? I haven't seen you in ages. Actually, I should have expected you—Sheila mentioned that you were coming down for vacation."

She rose and gave him a hug, despite the sweat. Jorge Marti hadn't been one of their intimate crowd, but he had been a friend. While they had all taken various jobs throughout their high school years, Jorge had really worked. His folks had come over during the Mariel boat lift from Cuba, and for many years had barely eked out an existence. Jorge hadn't spoken a word of English when he had arrived as a nine-year-old. Now his accent was barely discernible. They'd all liked him, and on those few occasions when he hadn't been studying or working, he'd spent his free time with them.

In high school, though, he'd had a period where he'd mixed with the wrong crowd. Only the intervention of Dane's father had kept him from going to jail and acquiring the kind of record that would have stayed with him all his life.

"Jorge, it's wonderful to see you. And yes, I came to meet Sheila, but it seems that she stood me up."

"Stood you up?"

"She isn't here. Have you seen her in the last week?"

"Sure…wait…no, I haven't. The last time I saw Sheila…was at the Sea Shanty. She'd been making the rounds, then ended up sitting with Dane. I think they had an argument or something. He left…and she left right after. Hey, have you talked to Dane?"

"Yes, I have."

"Well, you know Sheila."

Did she really know Sheila anymore?

"So how have you been?" he asked her.

"Great, thank you."

"Still doing commercials?"

"Commercials and print advertising."

"Great. And you're still working with Larry Miller?"

"Yes. In fact, Larry was the one who got me the job."

"Glad to hear it. You look wonderful."

"Thanks. So do you. How is your business doing?"

"I'm happy with it. I've got two captains working for me now, so I don't have to take out every charter myself. It was a good way to create a company, but man…it made for some long hard hours and very little social life."

She smiled. "Jorge, you were always the best worker, the go-getter. One day you'll probably have a fleet of ships to rival the navy, and captains for all of them." She thought about Dane and the way he appeared to be spending his life in a lounge chair with a beer. She didn't know what had happened in St. Augustine that had made him close up shop, then close up life. But here was Jorge, who had certainly been as beaten up as any man alive when he was a little kid, and he just kept moving forward. "And you've done it all from nothing," she added.

He looked at her peculiarly, almost as if he had been watching her mind working. "Remember where you are. Here we believe in smelling the flowers along the way, you know. We're in the Keys. Sun, sand and ocean breezes."

"Alcohol and drugs," she added.

"Well," he said, his tone light, "there is a fine line between making a place in the world and forgetting that we only live in it so long. So, are you planning to take the world by storm? Eventually own every advertising agency in the state?"

She gave him a rueful grin. "No. I'm sorry, did I sound as if getting ahead was the only important thing in the world?"

Jorge shook his head. "I was just remembering how you loved to paint, and how you always had a camera, no matter what we were doing. Still painting?"

"I still have a camera most of the time. As for painting…"

She never finished the sentence. Cindy came out,

blond hair pulled back, her workout tank damp, her muscles gleaming with a sheen of perspiration. "Jorge!" she said with pleasure. "I didn't see you in there."

"I saw you, but you were lifting the equivalent of the Titanic, so I didn't interrupt," Jorge said.

Cindy gave him a kiss on the cheek, still smiling. "We're going to have a barbecue at Dane's in a couple of hours. Why don't you come?"

He looked surprised. "Dane invited everyone over for a barbecue?"

"Yes," Cindy said.

"No," Kelsey corrected.

"Yes," Cindy argued.

"We suggested he have one," Kelsey said. She looked at Cindy. "And we're surprising him with the time and date. You don't think we'll be welcome? Have you seen much of him since he's been back down here?"

"Sure, everyone from the old crowd runs into everyone else down here, what with Nate owning the Sea Shanty," Jorge said.

"Has he been…rude?" Kelsey queried.

"No, no, nothing like that. Quiet. Reclusive, maybe," Jorge said. "I've respected his privacy, that's all."

"Well, we're not going to let him be private anymore," Cindy said firmly. "Show up. We're going to make him have a good time."

"All right, maybe," Jorge said. He wrinkled his nose. "I'm off to the showers. Kelsey, great to have you home."

She wasn't really home, she thought. She was just passing through. "Thanks, Jorge."

He left them, heading into the men's locker room. Cindy sighed in his wake. "He is *so* good-looking."

"Yes, he is," Kelsey agreed. "He hasn't married? He isn't seeing anyone?"

"He works," Cindy said. "And I guess he sees lots of people. Oh, well, let's head out. We need showers, too," she said ruefully. "I must smell like a trucker who's been on the road for a week."

"You work out like a boxer aiming for the heavy-weight championship," Kelsey told her.

Cindy laughed. "Like I said, I think it has something to do with being short. Let's go, shall we? Showers, then barbecue shopping. Too bad Dane didn't really plan this. He'd have gone out and brought us back lots of fresh fish. Maybe there will be something fresh at one of the markets. Or maybe we'll just go with red meat. Or chicken. Or both." She led the way out, hesitating as they exited the building. "I hope Jorge shows up," she said.

Dane had thought that he would have to drive all the way into the city of Miami and meet Hector Hernandez in the downtown area, but Hector had suggested that they meet at the seafood restaurant at the southern end of Florida City. Being with the Metro force meant that Hector handled anything to the Miami-Dade county lines, and that meant the Trail into the Everglades out to Collier County to the west, and Monroe County at the line just before the Keys. Where they met was still Hector's territory, although his assignments were more often in the city of Miami proper and the surrounding communities.

There were enough murders there alone to keep plenty of men busy, Hector had told him once. Not that he felt his beloved county was so bad. Put that many people together and bad things happened. That was the way of life, unfortunately. Miami-Dade had a tendency to have its bad news well publicized. But Hector didn't believe that a *place* could be bad. Now, as to people, well, they could be pure evil. And it was true that South Florida had endless miles of coastline, miles and miles of Everglades and the capacity to include almost any illicit operation known to man. It was incredibly easy to get rid of a body.

Yet the bodies usually surfaced. Eventually.

Hector was already there when Dane arrived, munching down on a big plate of calamari, drinking ice tea.

He grinned when he saw Dane, rose, shook his hand, still chewing.

"Good to see you. Since you asked me to lunch, I thought I'd order everything on the menu. Got surf and turf coming after this. Filet and lobster. Maine lobster. Love this place we call home, you know, but our overgrown crawfish don't come anywhere near close to the taste of the Maine guys. You're going to get one hell of a lunch bill. Detectives are underpaid, you know. I hope your new business in the Keys is going well."

He was a big man, resembling the old Frito Bandito.

"It's going all right," Dane said. "People are into the high-tech stuff these days. Store owners want camera setups, surveillance, tapes, all the kinds of stuff they've seen catch thieves on the television shows."

"Nothing too big, yet, huh?"

"You know life down there. A bit easier."

Hector made a face. "It would be easier up here if it weren't for all the fancy attorneys. We nabbed a guy who killed his wife and kids a couple of years ago, and they got him off. You know what his defense was? He hadn't meant to kill them. He'd been threatening her because he was convinced she was cheating on him. And the gun just went off. Three times. All three shots somehow accidental. You listen to what I'm saying, and you know it's crazy. But he got the right attorney, and the jury bought it. Can you believe it?"

Hector sat down again when Dane did. "Then there was the old guy who beat the old lady to death in the nursing home. He got off, too. The defense? His medication was wrong. And the old lady wanted to die. It was a mercy killing. Oh, yeah, he beat her mercifully. What really bothers me, though, is what a bad rap the city gets. And you know what? One of those survey companies just did a study on crime in the city. Seems that a lot of crazies like to come down here to do their dirty work. They're born and get crazy somewhere in the north, then come south to be homicidal. Not that we don't have our share of domestics," he said with a shake of his head. "Or greed. Stupid greed. I've got a case right now where some asshole shot an old man just to steal his car. That was a sorry one. The wife is inside, the husband goes out for the newspaper, sees the fellow trying to take his car and decides to stop him. The perp shoots the guy, gets blood on his clothes, goes inside the guy's house to steal a new outfit, and the wife is watching television all the time."

"Did you nab him?"

"Not yet, but we will. He left his bloody clothes on the victim's floor and went out without the wife ever knowing. The perp was no brain surgeon. He left fingerprints everywhere and has a rap sheet longer than the Bill of Rights. But you see what I mean? He shouldn't have been on the streets at all. He should have been locked up. There are too many loopholes in the law. And the prisons are so overcrowded that the parole boards are pushed into letting criminals go when they shouldn't. But you know how all that goes. And you didn't come here to ask me about any of the no-brainers."

Dane started to speak, but Hector lifted a hand. "Order first. Have the squid. They know their calamari here. Lightly dusted with breading, tender as a baby's bottom."

Dane ordered the yellowtail, instead, guaranteed fresh by their waitress. He opted for ice tea, as well, and when the waitress had gone, he plowed right in. "I'm interested in one of your open cases."

"The tie-strangling?" Hector said, wiping his mouth and reaching for his tea.

"Yeah. How did you know?"

"One in Dade, one in Broward. They're what we've got going right now with the biggest media attention and the least to go on. Both girls were strippers. If you were friends with one of them, your name has never come up in the investigation. What's your interest?"

"A friend of mine, a girl named Sheila Warren, hasn't been seen around in about a week," Dane said. He was going to stick with honesty while talking to Hector. The truth—just not the whole truth.

"Sheila…" Hector mused over the name for a moment. "Yeah, I know your friend Sheila. I've gone out on charters with your buddy Jorge Marti a few times when he had her aboard, cooking, running around, fishing… just being charming. Beautiful woman. Okay, before I keep going, is she a friend or more than a friend?"

"We were hot and heavy way back in the old days," Dane told him. "But we've both changed a lot. She'd gotten used to living a bit on the wild side, and she's been known to take off with new friends, so the local police aren't very concerned."

"But you are."

"Yeah."

Hector was quiet for a moment, mulling Dane's words as he chewed. Then he said, "I'm not sure where you're making the connection. Both girls strangled by the Necktie Strangler were strippers. And customers have gotten more than lap dances at both clubs by paying extra to have private 'shows.' Your friend wasn't a working girl, was she?"

"No. But she was definitely walking the wild side."

"So what makes you think the strangler might have gotten hold of her?"

"If I'm remembering correctly, both girls were missing persons before their bodies were discovered."

"True. Look, we haven't had much to go on. The bodies were badly decomposed. We haven't found so much as a fiber to give to forensics. We've questioned the families, the friends and the other employees at the clubs. We've tracked down customers through interviewing the proprietors about their regulars and through credit card receipts. Have we found all the customers? Hell, no. A lot of guys won't use a charge card at a strip club—their wives might want to know what they were doing there. We've had plain clothes guys sit around both clubs, watching for weirdos. And do you know what we've gotten?"

"What?"

"A hell of a lot of weirdos. But not a single lead has panned out."

Their waitress came to the table, delivering their food and refilling their glasses.

"I hope you're making the big bucks down there," Hector said, looking at his plate with relish. "Look at that baby! A two-pounder. I was so hungry, I almost ordered the five-pound guy. But then I thought about the old arteries."

Dane looked at Hector's plate. "I can see you're really concerned," he said dryly.

Hector shook his head. "It's all right. I start out the day with oatmeal." He waved a hand for the waitress. "I think I'm going to need a little more of that melted butter," he told her.

Dane took a bite of his fish. It was fresh, and broiled to perfection. "I hear there are details about the murders that are being held back from the media."

Hector had been smiling in delight at the succulent taste of his lobster. Now, he scowled. "Where'd you hear that? Oh, yeah, I forgot—you're related to Jesse Crane."

"Second cousins or something like that," Dane agreed.

"He tell you that?"

"No."

"Good, because it's not supposed to get out."

"So you're not going to tell me?"

"No," Hector said, but he pulled a pen from his breast pocket and started writing on the paper place mat beneath his plate. "But I will give you this. The names of both clubs—I'm pretty sure that both of these girls were targeted when they were working—and a few of the names of the girls we interviewed at each. Who knows? Maybe you'll get something we haven't been able to come up with. Sometimes these girls can spot a cop a mile away, and they're not always so willing to talk to the cops, even when their own lives might be in danger. And if you get anything, anything at all, you come to me with it, you hear?"

"If I get anything from a lead you've given me, you know damn well I'll come right to you."

Hector nodded.

Dane asked him about his family then. Hector told him about his teenaged boys with pride, while still managing to consume his entire meal and ask for dessert, and then coffee.

Dane had coffee, too. When it was served, he asked the waitress if they were in the smoking section, then pulled out a pack of cigarettes.

"Thought you gave that up," Hector said with a frown.

"Yeah, I did. I picked it up again just before I left St. Augustine."

Hector shook his head. "And you're giving me a hard time about the food I eat?"

"You've got a point," Dane said.

Hector downed his coffee, glanced at his watch and said, "I've got to get back to work. Thanks for the lunch. Good luck."

"You don't mind me in your territory, asking a few questions?"

"Hell no." Hector was standing, but he hesitated. "First body was found just about six months ago, second body was found just about three months ago. These guys...the profilers say they work in cycles. That could mean we're due for another body. They say that kind of killer doesn't stop. He keeps going. If anything... Never mind. You took classes in criminology."

"Yeah, but, if anything…what?"

"You know. The killings will just get worse. This guy probably started out squashing lizards as a kid. Maybe he went on to drown kittens, or take a BB gun and use it on puppies. It's likely he progressed to battery or rape, and then…well, now we have our bodies in the canals. That's the psyche of such a man. So believe me, I don't mind you asking questions at all. I don't feel the least possessive about finding a monster like this one. Just don't hold out on me, huh?"

Dane looked at Hector, an honestly good man, and was tempted to tell him all he really knew.

He couldn't.

Hector was too decent a guy. A by-the-book cop.

And Dane needed time. His palms felt itchy. He was determined now, but every once in a while, he felt a cold sweat break out as he wondered what the killer might do next.

"Hector, the minute I've got anything that might help you catch this guy—if and when I ever do—you know that I'll be in your office with the speed of light."

Hector nodded. "Thanks for the fish. And good luck. Who the hell knows? This guy could have moved on. They may be pulling strippers out of a bayou in Louisiana next. I wish I could say that we always get our man. Take care of yourself, Dane. Sorry about the situation in St. Augustine. I'm real sorry. Heard the fancy-pants lawyers got *him* off, too."

Dane folded the place mat Hector had written on. He thanked the waitress, paid the bill and decided he might as well start that night with the club in Miami.

He left the restaurant, mentally berating himself as he did so.

He *had* concentrated on psychology, human behavior and criminology during his years at VMI. While Joe had dived headfirst into his love of flying, Dane had been studying with the men from the FBI offices at Quantico. His expertise in the service had been in enemy psychology, the study of religious and behavioral influences on the movements and actions of different peoples. He had worked in both diplomatic negotiations and in "observation tactics," out-of-uniform exercises among the populace in various zones of action in order to determine the mood and reactionary tendencies of the people.

But he'd been back a hell of a long time now. And though he'd opened his investigations agency in St. Augustine with energy and determination, even that seemed a long time ago. For all that he had learned in the classroom, he had discovered some basics—it was easy for people to become fanatical, and it wasn't always possible to discover just why people became brutally homicidal. Years of study, training and research came down to one dogma—there were simply some bad-ass people out there. Some wore their penchant for cruelty in a manner that was almost as easy to read as an open book. Some were well dressed, charming and could talk such a damned good line that in the very midst of destroying other lives, they could come off looking like victims themselves.

He realized that he'd come home to Key Largo knowing that he'd had to get the hell out of the St. Augustine area. And that he'd also come with the fatalistic belief that none of it had meant a fucking thing. He'd opened an agency again not because he'd been interested in the cases he might acquire but because he'd needed an income if he didn't want to go through his savings and his inheritance like toilet paper while literally leading the life of a lounge lizard, as Kelsey had accused him.

He could set a camera, a wire, any manner of surveillance, easily. He could keep an eye on hours of tape in the event of robbery or an employee pilfering from the till, of drug deals taking place in a parking lot. Easy. Like breathing. Waking up, showering, dressing.

No thought involved.

Maybe he *had* turned into a lounge lizard. Because his first thought, after the whack in the face of the photograph the other day, had been to lie low. To act normally, to watch, to wait.

Hell.

Maybe the old days were kicking back in. And maybe it was just an instinct for survival. He was suddenly as determined as all hell that he was going to crack what was going on.

Yeah, well, he had to be. He'd been bitter because he felt the system had failed him. So he'd walked away. It hadn't been the system. He had failed himself.

And then he had failed Sheila.

He owed it to her to find the truth.

Not to mention what the alternative could mean to him. Hell, this was Florida. He could get the death penalty.

He drove mechanically, traveling US1 southward as he had throughout his entire life. He gave the problem at hand the majority of his concentration until he pulled onto the private road to Hurricane Bay.

Then he groaned.

He had company.

Several cars were drawn up by the walkway. He recognized Cindy's minivan and Nate's full-size Wagoneer, with the name Sea Shanty and the mile marker of the establishment written in script along the side.

As he pulled up the gravel driveway in front of the house, Cindy came running around from the dockside of the property to meet him.

She was smiling as if it was Christmas.

"Dane, surprise! We've brought the barbecue to you."

Chapter 6

Dane was definitely not delighted to be having a barbecue, Kelsey thought, seeing the tension in his features as he walked with Cindy around to the dock side of the house.

Cindy was smiling. She didn't seem to notice that Dane was less than pleased. "And look who made it down here," she was saying excitely. "Larry Miller."

"Larry, hey, how are you?" Dane said. Larry had left the patio chair where he'd been sitting to walk over and shake Dane's hand. He was wearing a T-shirt, cutoffs and sandals, apparel similar to Nate's, but he still had a haircut that looked pure office. Nate was blond and shaggy, and looked like the native he was.

Some things didn't change.

Dane had been somewhere off the island, she thought. He was wearing chinos, dock shoes and a short-sleeved

tailored shirt. Blue. A good color for him. It emphasized the dark quality of his eyes and the bronzed tex-
ture of his features. He was far from formally dressed,
but in the heat and breezes and casual lifestyle here,
ankle-length pants and a nonknit shirt were akin to
being dressed up.

"I'm good, thanks, Larry. Nice to see you. What are
you doing down here?"

Larry shrugged, grinning a little sheepishly. "Well,
Kelsey was down here, and she was upset because
Sheila didn't show. Then you were at the duplex, Cindy
was there…and Nate. I admit it, I felt like a kid left out
of a party. So I drove on down."

"Nice to see you here. It's been a while."

"Actually I've been down a few times here and there.
But they've been business dinners, quick trips to a restaurant and back, and with a client. Every time I drove
down, I'd think, man, I'm an hour away, and I love this
place, and I never get here. So here I am."

"So we had to have a barbecue," Cindy said.

"Like old times," Nate put in. "Except, of course,
that we meant to surprise you. Instead the tables were
turned—we were the ones surprised when you weren't
here. But I made these guys hang in for a while. I had
faith that you'd show up eventually."

"But we meant to surprise you with no trouble to you
at all, of course. You name it, we brought it," Cindy said
with pleasure. "Hog dogs, hamburgers, steaks, chicken
and fish. We brought the charcoal, corn on the cob—
wrapped and ready for the grill, mind you—baking
potatoes, salad, chips, beer and wine. Oh, and paper
plates, napkins, paper cups, plastic utensils."

"Great," Dane said. The word was right, but Kelsey

thought his inflection was off. He had the look of a man running down a street with a destination in mind, only to find a brick wall in his path.

At least he wasn't going to throw them off the property.

He'd had plans, she realized. But he was going to forgo those plans, rather than share them or make explanations.

Nate rose from the railing where he'd been sitting. "Hey, Dane, when did you start locking the house?"

Dane walked to the door, replying with a shrug. "I'm in the business of investigations," he said. "I supply people with security. I guess in telling people they need to lock up and take precautions I realized that I left my own place open all the time." He twisted his key in the lock and opened the door. He looked straight at Kelsey then. "Come in. The house is always open to you."

Nate walked in, carrying a cooler of groceries. Cindy followed, plucking a grocery bag from the floor of the porch. Larry did likewise, and Kelsey came last, aware that Dane was still staring at her, his hand on the door as he held it open. Her cheeks felt hot as she walked by him. Well, she had basically accused him of…something. At the very least, of keeping information regarding Sheila from them. And she had more or less told him that she was interested in coming here to search his house.

And here he was, opening the door.

She slid by.

"Didn't you want to get one of the bags?" he inquired politely.

She turned back, her flush seeping down to her throat. She picked up a bag, and he turned for the last two.

Cindy was already in the kitchen, emptying the bags.

Nate was searching through the supplies for the char-coal. "I'll go right out and get the grill going, Dane, if that's all right?"

"Sounds like a good way to start, since it will take a while for the coals to heat up," Dane said. He walked over to the cooler Nate had brought in, helping himself to a beer.

"I hope they heat quickly. I'm starving," Cindy said.

"Everyone is starving," Larry said. "How about you, Dane?"

"Actually I just had lunch, so I'm fine. I'll get some bowls so we can break out the chips and dips for you guys while we wait to cook all that meat."

"I'll get the meat ready," Kelsey said, needing something to do. She delved through the bags until she found the hamburger meat, hot dogs, chicken, sirloins and seasonings. She found a place on the kitchen counter and started to form hamburger patties.

It felt strange, coming to Dane's place. Like the Sea Shanty, it seemed a bastion of all that had been good about her childhood. She had come here so often as a little kid. There was a lot of dockage, but not so much beach area in Key Largo as people tended to think. Hurricane Bay had both dockage and a spit of beach. Man-made, like a lot of the island itself, but it was beachfront, and over the years so much sand had been brought in that it was surprisingly clean and nice. The dock looked straight out on the Atlantic, ocean as far as the eye could see, while the beachfront area was protected by a curve in the property. Mangroves still surrounded the area. In fact, on the beach side of the house, lying on the sand, it was possible to feel as if you were marooned on a private subtropical isle in the middle of nowhere, with total privacy and a distance from the entire world. Many years ago, they had played pirates here. Dane's folks had never minded having kids around, whether they were actually with Dane or not.

Things had changed a little bit when his mother had died, but though his father had become something of a recluse, he had still welcomed the kids. Maybe he had done it in her memory, and maybe he had just liked kids himself. But there had always been something special here. Lemonade or ice tea and home-baked cookies when Dane's Mom was here, and canned soda and bags of Oreos once she was gone. The welcome always remained.

And the house was wonderful. A veritable museum.

"Watch the chicken," Cindy said.

"What?" Kelsey said, startled from her memories.

"The chicken. Wash it well, and don't let it get near anything else. Germs, bacteria…you know."

"I'll watch it like a hawk," Kelsey assured her dryly. Cindy gave her a grave nod. "Are these pieces ready? I'll take them on out."

They were alone in the kitchen. Kelsey could hear the guys talking out back around the barbecue.

"Cindy, actually, I know you'll do a much better job with the chicken than I will," Kelsey said. "You get to work here. I'll take this stuff out and let them get it going on the grill."

Kelsey didn't give Cindy a chance to protest. She picked up the plate of raw meat and headed out of the kitchen.

In the dining room, she paused. There, on the table, was Dane's work station. His computer. Mail. Stacks of paper. Sheets of information he had apparently downloaded and printed out. She held still for a minute, listening to Cindy talk to herself about the dangers of salmonella. She moved forward a few feet and looked out the window to the deck, assuring herself that the men were still talking around the grill.

She balanced the plate of meat in her left hand and moved to the printer, where she saw that he had been downloading newspaper articles. She sifted through the sheets and saw that the columns all referred to the murders of two women. She placed the plate of meat on the table and picked up the top sheet. "Second Stripper Found in Canal." She scanned the article, but it wasn't really necessary. She remembered reading it when it had come out about three months ago. Cherie Madsen, twenty-three. A business major at a local university by day, a stripper by night. Her friends had said that she'd found it the best way to make the money for her tuition. She didn't intend to get old dancing and taking her clothes off, but she had always said that she was good at what she did and that it beat the hell out of selling clothing at a department store or working in a coffee bar. Cherie was her real name. She'd been reported missing about a week before her body had been discovered.

"Excuse me. We need the meat."

Kelsey was so startled that she dropped the paper. It wafted from the table to the floor, landing at Dane's feet.

She just looked at him wide-eyed. He betrayed nothing with his expression.

"Do me a favor. Don't get grease all over my papers."

"I—I wasn't. I just saw this headline. I remember when the murder was the top story in the news. Sad, huh? I didn't mean to get anything on your papers. The headline is kind of gripping, you know."

"It jumped right out and bit you, right? From the far end of the table."

She stood still, staring at him. He shrugged. "You told me you wanted to search the place. I don't know why I should be surprised. But I do have business that's confidential and that has nothing to do with Sheila. So... do you mind? And we *do* need the meat."

She shook her head. She moved forward to pick up the errant paper just as Dane reached down to get it himself. Their heads butted, and they both backed away. "Kelsey, take the meat out. I'll get my papers," he told her.

She nodded, picked up the plate and fled from the house. When she returned, having given the food to Larry to throw on the grill, she found Dane putting his piles of papers into the filing cabinets against the walls. She was about to go into the kitchen for more meat, but she hesitated, staring at his back. She knew he was aware that she was watching him.

"Why are you following the cases of the murdered strippers?" she asked him.

"None of your business, Kelsey."

"Do you think those stories have something to do with Sheila?"

He turned to her. "Do you think Sheila was stripping?"

"No."

"Then why do you think my interest has something to do with her?"

"Because you're supposed to be trying to find Sheila."

"I am."

"Then why—"

"You guys showed up over here for a barbecue," he reminded her.

"Kelsey?" Nate popped his head through the door. "You're supposed to be getting the rest of the meat."

"It's coming," she said.

Nate went back out. Kelsey stared at Dane. "I think you know something about Sheila that you're not telling me."

"Kelsey!" Nate said again, popping his head back in from the porch. "The meat. We need the meat."

"Okay," Kelsey said.

Again Nate's head retreated.

"Kelsey, I'll just get the meat," Dane said. He shoved his file drawer shut and walked past her to the kitchen. She followed him, picking up packages of buns and rolls.

"Make sure the chicken is cooked, really cooked," Cindy said, scrubbing her hands at the sink.

"Will do," Dane assured her.

Once they were outside, Kelsey started setting up the tables. The guys were talking about their favorite spots for fishing. Cindy came out carrying one of the coolers. Dane went to help her. Nate snorted. "She may be little, but she can bench press her own weight," he told Dane.

"That doesn't mean I don't like it when you all pitch in to help," Cindy told him.

"Dane can probably bench press his own weight, too," Larry told Nate.

"I think P.I.s are supposed to be in shape, aren't they?" Nate said.

"Either that or they're fat as houses and take up all the space behind their desks," Larry said.

"I think they come in all sizes," Dane said. He set the

cooler down and stared out at the corner of the house. "Who else is coming?" he asked.

"Maybe it's Jorge Marti," Cindy said. "We asked him."

Kelsey set down a napkin and stared around the corner as well. She was suddenly aware of a horrible and overpowering odor.

"It sure as hell isn't Jorge," Dane said, starting down the porch steps and around the house. Kelsey found herself hurrying after him. She was right behind him when he came face-to-face with Andy Latham.

Latham was shirtless, in cutoff denims. He seemed to gleam with oil and sweat, and he was bearing a big bucket. The odor was coming from the bucket.

"You take your fish back! You take your rotten fish, and from now on, you keep the hell off my property, do you understand?"

Latham was shaking as he spoke. Whether it was with fear or fury, or a combination of both, Kelsey couldn't be certain.

"What are you talking about?" Dane demanded.

Latham turned the bucket over. Bloated, rotting fish spewed forth. They'd been dead a long time, and they'd been left in the sun. Some had exploded from the heat.

Dane stared from the fish on the ground to Latham, who took a step backward. "Oh, yeah, that's right, you're such a big man now. They taught you how to kill in the military, so what the hell, I just ought to be afraid and sit here and take everything you're dishing out on me," Latham said. He was still shaking, and still keeping a distance from Dane. "But you remember this, Mr. Tough Guy. A bullet goes through any man. You come on my property again and I'll put a bullet through your head." Latham backed up again.

"You ass!" Dane said. "I don't know what the hell you're talking about."

"The fish. The fucking fish! You came and dumped these right in front of the doorway."

"The hell I did!" Dane said.

"Who else?" Latham charged back. By then Larry had come to stand on one side of Dane and Nate on the other.

"I don't know who else. God knows, Latham, you'd never win a popularity contest around here," Dane told him.

Latham pointed a finger. At first Kelsey thought he was pointing at Dane, then realized he was pointing past Dane, at her.

"You! You little trouble-maker. You probably did this. Or you put the half-breed up to it. You...you'll get yours!" He was so angry, he was foaming at the mouth like a dog. Spitting as he spoke.

But just the same, he kept his distance.

Dane seemed to snap, taking a step forward. "You're as crazy as a loon, Latham. None of us dumped fish at your door. And if you threaten me or Kelsey again—"

Dane didn't finish speaking, because Latham broke in, shouting, "You heard him! You heard him. He's the one threatening *me*. You stay away from me. Stay away from me, and stay off my property, all of you!"

With that, he turned and ran.

"Whew!" Larry said.

"We're never going to be able to eat our barbecue with this stench in the yard," Cindy moaned. "What in God's name was all that about?"

"We'll eat in the house," Dane said. "Why don't you guys go get the food and bring it in? I'll get the fish picked up."

"Man, this is disgusting," Larry said.

"Get in the house. I'll get some bags and get it out of here before it permeates my whole place."

"I think he's gone crazy," Cindy said as they followed Dane. "Andy Latham never seemed really sane. Now I think he really has gone crazy."

As Dane went into the house, Kelsey started collecting the plates, plastic ware and cups she had been setting out on the porch tables.

"Cindy, hold that plate so that I can heap this food on it," Larry said. "Hey, who do you think really dumped these dead fish in his yard?"

Dane had already been in and out of the kitchen. He had two black plastic garbage bags in his hands and a roll of paper towels. "Who the hell knows?" he muttered. "Anyone could have done it." He walked away, followed by Nate. Cindy coughed and gagged. "I can't stand this. I've got to get into the house."

"We can't use the dining room," Larry said. "Dane's got it set up as an office."

"Head to the kitchen," Cindy said, leading the way.

A few minutes later Dane came in, followed by Nate and Jorge Marti.

"Jorge," Larry said, lifting his beer to greet the newcomer.

"Good to see you, Larry," Jorge said, walking over to shake Larry's hand.

"You made it," Cindy said with pleasure, walking over to kiss him on the cheek.

"Yeah, I got here just in time to be cleanup crew." He

wrinkled his nose and lifted his hands. "I hear old man Latham paid a visit and brought food. Maybe he thought he was invited and that it was supposed to be a potluck occasion. Hey, gorgeous," he said, stopping by Kelsey. He kissed her cheek, as well. She kissed his back.

"That was one bad smell out there. How weird. Latham just came by and dumped a pile of rotting fish?"

"He thinks Dane dumped them on his property," Kelsey told him.

"Why would he think that?"

"Because I went out there last night to ask if he'd seen Sheila, and Dane followed me out at Cindy's insistence," Kelsey explained.

"Apparently he's crazy as a loon," Jorge said, shrugging. "I've heard the guy isn't making the catches he used to get anymore."

"Did you wash your hands?" Cindy demanded.

"With antibacterial soap," Dane said, walking into the kitchen. "We're safe, Cindy." He smiled at her, amused. "I swear it."

"He made us all scrub," Nate assured her, coming in behind Dane.

"Well, God knows what might be on those disgusting little fish corpses," Cindy said, making a face.

Nate went for a beer. "It was a real waste of good fresh fish," he said.

"The man is crazy, and that's all there is to it," Cindy said. "So, Jorge, how's the charter business going? The snowbirds are mostly gone now, with summer coming in full blast."

"Business is good," Jorge said, sitting on a bar stool and accepting a beer from Cindy and a plate of food from Larry. He lifted his drink to Larry. "Thanks to you Miami businessmen trying to shake the ties and white collars during the weekends. Lobster season is coming, too. I guess Latham hadn't heard from Sheila and none of you has, either?"

"No sign of Sheila," Larry agreed.

Jorge looked at Kelsey and smiled. "She'll show up."

"Sure," Kelsey said. She realized Dane was watching her. "She will show up, right, Dane?"

"Oh, yeah. I'm positive she will. Eventually," he said quietly.

Kelsey didn't like the way he said it. Not flippantly. And not with reassurance. He spoke with somber certainty. He knew something.

And it had to do with the murders of the two strippers, Kelsey thought. Putting it all together scared her to death, but she knew he wasn't going to share whatever it was that he knew with her. Whatever he was onto…

She had a computer, too.

Dane thanked God for the placement of his property and house. The stench had been enough to choke a dung beetle, but with the breezes going through, it didn't last long. In fact, with the fish double-tied in trash bags and set back for disposal, the afternoon and evening became so nice that they were able to head outside after they had eaten. He set up the volleyball net, and they played a few games. They switched teammates and sides, but somehow, Kelsey always wound up on the other side of the net from him.

The exertion of playing sent them all into the water, but again, though there was a lot of dunking and fooling around, Kelsey kept her distance. Later, they all rinsed the saltwater off with the hose he had rigged up as a shower by the porch, then dried off and ate dessert—packaged brownies—outside. The brownies were so-so. The coffee Kelsey ground and brewed was great. He hadn't figured out yet if she was simply keeping her distance from him because she was never going to forgive him for the night that followed Joe's funeral, or if she was actually afraid of him. He damned himself for not filing away his down-loads before leaving the house that morning, but then, he hadn't expected company.

Now she knew he was interested in the murders. All the better, once the reason for his interest was known.

Dane finished his coffee and lit a cigarette. Cindy and Jorge were sitting on the porch swing, talking about gym equipment. Larry had begun passionately explaining the value of top-notch advertising to Nate.

Kelsey had headed out on the dock and was sitting there with her cup of coffee, watching the sun begin to set.

He rose, determined to join her. He knew that she heard him coming over the wooden decking, but she didn't look up. At first he thought that she was staring at his boats, both of which she had seen before, the snappy little Donzi for zipping around on quick trips, and his larger boat, the thirty-eight-foot Chris-Craft. The Chris-Craft was probably the one material object that meant a lot to him. He and his father had chosen the boat, refurbished it together, and spent countless hours on her out at sea. She could sleep six but still offered an enormous captain's cabin along with private guest quarters, a huge galley and salon, and large deck spaces. She was an old girl now, built in the early eighties, but he had tended her lovingly over the years.

But Kelsey wasn't staring at his boats. She was simply looking down at the wood of the deck. She wasn't seeing anything at all.

Dane sat next to her on the dock, where she dangled her legs over the edge. The wary look in her eyes as he joined her was disturbing.

"Hey, it *is* my dock."

She nodded. "You're right. It *is* your dock." She hesitated for a moment, staring at the water. "Your dock. I was actually just wishing that there was still something here, in the Keys, that was mine. It's strange, not having a place here. You know, the house doesn't even exist anymore."

"I know. So…how are your folks?" he asked.

"Good, thanks. Doing really well. You knew that they moved to Orlando?"

He nodded. "Yeah, I knew."

"I guess you weren't very far from them when you were up in St. Augustine."

"Probably not. Just a few hours."

"You never saw them?"

He shook his head. "I was always afraid that I would just be…well, a reminder of Joe."

"They'd probably really like to see you."

"I don't know. It was hard on them."

"It was hard on everyone."

"Joe was their son. And your brother."

"Your best friend."

She was actually looking at him again, and the mistrust seemed to have faded from her eyes for a moment. He found himself looking ahead at the dazzle of the sun on the water, rather than at her.

"Actually I thought that it was harder on you than

anyone else." He paused for just a moment. "Do you remember feeling that—"

"I don't want to remember," she said. There was an edge to her voice. He knew what she didn't want to remember.

"Don't go getting your hackles up," he said. "I'm talking about the break you had with your parents. Joe worried about it."

"Oh," she said, her cheeks growing bright. "You mean…the way I thought they preferred their son?"

"Yeah," he said softly. He was treading on personal ground. She would either get furious and walk away, or else they would have a chance to bridge the gap that lay between them.

She kicked her feet in the water like a kid, watching the waves she made. "I felt, after Joe died, that I didn't quite come up to what he had been in their eyes. And that my folks really had loved him more, and that I wasn't anywhere near as important." There was a curious, wistful expression on her face. Kelsey was beautiful. Her hair had dried in the breeze and was wafting around the perfectly molded contours of her face. Her eyes reflected the water. She was still in shorts and a bathing suit top. Her throat was long and smooth, and her breasts rose high and tight against the bikini bra. He had taken a seat close enough that their skin nearly touched. Something was stirring within him.

So much time yawned between them. She'd been his best friend's kid sister, so the instinct to protect and defend had always been there. The instinct to touch her, to have her, had only pushed to the surface once. Now both waged war within him. She brought out something protective in him. He realized, as he had on that long-ago night, that she also brought out a hell of a lot more.

Odd that something so brief could be remembered so long. So clearly.

He tamped a lid on the urge to reach out and touch her.

He lifted a hand. "Your dad was gung-ho military. Joe followed in his footsteps. Naturally he was interested in every move Joe made."

She laughed. "You're being kind. To my father, the sun rose and set on Joe. And I still remember feeling totally inadequate because I didn't seem to be able to do anything to make my brother's loss any easier for my parents. For so many reasons, I was in such sorry shape then, and I did such sorry things—"

She broke off. He could feel the warmth emanating from her.

He was sure that he had been one of those "sorry things."

He decided to ignore that for the moment.

"They always loved you equally, you know. Like I said, Joe just had a lot in common with your dad."

She smiled, and the curve of her lips was both rueful and nostalgic. "Hey, it's okay, time has gone by, and I don't need any assurance. Actually the past is one of the reasons things are so good between us now. Dad called me a couple of years ago and asked me to come up and spend some time with them. I did. We sat together one night, and he apologized to me, told me that he probably had set more store in Joe, and that it had been shameful of him not to realize that he had shown so much favoritism. We both cried, drank too much, talked about Joe all night, and fixed everything that might have been wrong. I see my folks often now. It's only a four, four and half hour drive up to their new place. They're not on the water. They have a couple of acres in an area zoned for horses. Dad and Mom have started riding together, and they're thinking about buying a couple of horses of their own."

"I'm glad to hear they're doing so well."

"Thanks."

The silence stretched out between them. Not a comfortable silence. She drew her knees in, rested her chin on them and looked at him. "So what happened in St. Augustine?" she asked him.

He felt himself stiffen. "Someone died."

A frown tensed her brow. "And it was your fault?"

"Yes. No. Look, it's not something I like to talk about."

"Hey, you came out and sat down next to me."

"Yeah, I did. So how is your life? No marriages after Nate over there?"

He heard the sound of her teeth grating. "No. No marriages. How about you? Is it true? Have you and Sheila been getting close again?"

He shook his head, aggravated, trying not to lose patience. He stared at Kelsey, and she stiffened where she sat, not turning from him, but definitely tense. "What is it that you still haven't figured out? Sheila was looking for something, and it wasn't me. Yes, we hung out together at the bar. Yes, she came out here. But I wasn't in the best shape to try to solve her psychological problems, and she certainly wasn't any kind of a balm for me."

"But you were the last person to see her."

"No, I'm certain that someone else saw her."

"Who?"

"Dammit, Kelsey, that's what I don't know."

"You think she's dead," Kelsey said, watching him.

"Kelsey, I'll find Sheila."

"Hey, out there!"

They were interrupted by the call from the yard. Looking back, they saw Cindy, Larry, Nate and Jorge standing and waving.

Dane got to his feet and instinctively reached down to give Kelsey a hand. To his surprise, she accepted the lift and didn't wrench away immediately.

"We're going to take off," Nate called. "I've got to go by the bar."

"I need a real shower," Larry said.

"I may have a hot date," Cindy contributed.

"I *am* someone's hot date," Jorge said.

Dane walked back along the dock and reached the yard. Cindy took a step toward him before he could reach the group, rising on tiptoe to kiss his cheek. "Thanks for letting us invite ourselves over."

"Thanks for everything you brought."

"Just call us dial-a-party," Nate said. "Hey, come by the bar later, if you can. I've got a new band starting tonight. They do everything. Pop-rock, jazz, reggae, calypso... you'll like them."

"I'll try to make it."

"I'm off," Jorge said, lifting a hand with his keys in it. "Thanks, all of you. It's good to get together."

"Yeah. We'll have to do it again," Larry said. "We're heading back to the duplex," he said to Kelsey. "Are you coming?"

"I've got my own car. I'll be along."

"You sure?" Larry said.

"I'm sure that's my car," Kelsey said, smiling.

"No, I meant—"

"Kelsey will be right along," Dane assured him. "I have plans tonight."

He thought that maybe her cheeks reddened, but she replied smoothly to Larry, "I'm just going to make sure we picked up any messes we made in Dane's place." She turned and started for his house. The others took off for their cars, waving their last goodbyes.

Dane looked at the dying sunset. Strip clubs didn't get going until later anyway. He followed Kelsey into the house.

She was in the kitchen, rinsing out the last chip bowl.

He leaned in the doorway, watching her. "Are you sure you don't want to go through the rest of my papers?"

She turned and looked at him innocently. His gaze slipped to her breasts. He forced it back to her eyes.

"I have my own computer, you know."

"What?"

"I don't need to go through your papers. I can download old newspaper articles just the same as you can."

He clenched his teeth with aggravation. "Kelsey, leave it, please."

"I just want to know what you're going to do to find Sheila."

"I will do everything in my power. Kelsey, please, trust me on this. Let me do the investigating."

"There's a little coffee left. Do you want more, or should I just pour it down the drain?"

"No, I'll drink it."

He walked over to the coffeepot.

"I'll get it for you," she said.

He paused. Kelsey was suddenly being far too nice.

"You know...I think I left my lighter outside. Why

don't you join me for coffee? I'll meet you in the living room."

He walked out of the kitchen and through the house. Outside, he leaned against the support wall and looked in through the dining-room window. He watched as Kelsey came out of the kitchen, set the cups down on the coffee table and looked around the room. She was headed back toward the dining room when something caught her eye. He frowned, seeing Kelsey get down on the floor on her hands and knees.

He walked back in. She jumped up as he did so, her cheeks bright red. "What the hell are you doing?" he demanded.

She stared at him in silence for a moment. "Just friends," she said. "There was nothing hot and heavy going on? There was nothing serious?"

"What are you talking about now?" he asked, aggravated.

She dangled something in front of him. An earring. Sheila's earring.

He crossed his arms over his chest, staring at her. "So?"

"This is Sheila's earring."

"You know that?"

"Of course I know that."

"How?"

"I gave her these earrings. The stones are emeralds. They were my gift to her when she was the maid of honor at my wedding."

"So Sheila lost her earring. What does that mean? She's been in this house many times."

"Right. But her earring was here, on your living-room floor. If you look at the way the loop closes, these aren't the kind of earrings that just fall out."

"Kelsey, what the hell are you saying?"

"You two were...you were having an affair again."

He walked over to where she stood, staring into her eyes as he plucked the earring from her fingers. "All right. One more time, Sheila was here. I never said to anyone that she wasn't. Were we having an affair? No. We honestly were not having an affair. Nothing so grand. Did we have sex one night? Yes. One night. We both knew that even what we'd had as kids was long over. Did I do something horrible and evil to Sheila? No. Pay attention here. *No.* There it is, the truth. And I really don't give a damn whether you believe me or not. Take it or leave it."

Kelsey's teal eyes lit hard on his for a long moment. Then she brushed past him. He didn't move and didn't turn.

He heard the sound of the door closing as she left his house.

Chapter 7

Kelsey was surprised to arrive at the duplex and find that neither Larry nor Cindy had gotten back before her. They had probably gone with Nate to the Sea Shanty. Or else the hot date Cindy had mentioned was with Jorge. She had no desire to follow them and have a more social night, and was relieved at first to be back alone. She wanted to shower, huddle into bed and sleep. It was unlikely that she would sleep easily, but at least she could shower, get into bed and mull over her thoughts of the night.

Strange, though, the minute she turned off her car's engine, she felt her solitude. The night wasn't still; there was a soft breeze blowing. But the trees and shrubbery seemed to hang heavily around the driveway and create a host of shadows. The short distance from the driveway to the house became very long. Darkness almost seemed to whirl in pockets of ebony, constantly changing the shapes that were nothing but illusion but appeared to be sinister creatures lurking in the night.

They had forgotten to turn on a porch light. It was only the street lamps, standing high and at a distance, that gave any glow to the night and turned the lengths of branches into bony fingers, stretching out over the yard.

Kelsey realized she was just sitting in her car, staring at the house.

She told herself she was ridiculous, opened the car door and started for the duplex. None of the shadows jumped after her, though breezes rustled the branches, seeming to create a whisper on the night air. To her annoyance, she fumbled with the key while getting it into the lock. Once she had gotten the door open, she burst in, then turned and closed the door as if there were a tiger on her tail. She locked it quickly, then stood in the entry feeling like a fool. Shadows. She didn't tend to be afraid of them, or of darkness, or of the night.

Yet as she walked through the living room to the kitchen and dining area, tossing her purse on a chair, she felt uneasiness creep over her.

The strange sense that she wasn't alone.

She found herself retracing her footsteps to the front door, as anxious to get out again as she had been to get in. But before she reached the door, she managed to tell herself she was being absurd. The duplex had been locked. There was nothing out of order that she could see. There was no reason to think she was anything but alone.

Still, with the uncanny sense of something being off persisting, she decided that her first course of action had to be an inspection of the apartment. Living room.

Definitely no one there, unless it was an ant-size person. She opened the door to the second bedroom where Larry was sleeping, going to the bath and looking behind the shower curtain, then checking out the closet.

She was feeling silly again when she thought she heard a sound…like a thumping, coming from the back. Standing in a closet that held nothing but a few of Larry's shirts, she felt a chill sweep through her. Great. She was inspecting the house like a sane person, but if there did happen to be an intruder, she had nothing with which to defend herself other than a tailored shirt and a hanger.

Great.

She looked around the bedroom. Nothing. She stepped back into the living room and decided her best bet for protection was one of the heavy pewter candlesticks on the coffee table. She grabbed one and walked toward the back.

Great. The porch light wasn't on but the lights inside were. If there was someone lurking in the shadows in the back, they would be hidden in darkness. She might as well be on wide-screen television.

Kelsey hit the switch on the wall, pitching the main room into darkness. She inched into the dining area and quickly hit the lights there, as well.

Now the world seemed a pool of darkness.

She stood still, listening. Night sounds came to her, almost imperceptibly. The breeze against the house, the rustle of branches. The longer she stared out through the plate glass, the more her eyes adjusted to the darkness. Seconds stretched into minutes. Minutes seemed an eternity. She realized she wasn't breathing and exhaled a long stream of air, then inhaled. She neither saw nor heard anything out of the ordinary. After a while she once again felt like a fool. She left her silent vigil at the back window and walked into her bedroom.

Sheila's bedroom.

The drapes were open in there, as well. She could see out to the back. A long palm frond dipped low over the pool, as if it were a bony hand with pointing fingers, indicating some horror within the water. She chastised herself for her ridiculous imagination and total cowardice. She still had a death grip on the candlestick.

The moonlight showed little more than shapes in the room. She was almost frozen with the fear that one of them would move. Again she stood still and waited. She almost screamed aloud when she heard another thumping sound from the back, not by the pool, but by the fence to her right.

Nine-one-one, nine-one-one, nine-one-one, just call the police! her mind raged. But call the police and tell them what? That she had heard a thumping noise from her backyard?

So much for being alone, for being grateful for solitude. Where the hell was Larry?

Cindy?

Anyone?

Dane had been looking up information on murdered strippers. He had gone to bed with Sheila. He had caught her snooping through his work. Maybe she was getting too close to the truth. Maybe he had followed her home, and now he was out there, thinking she should share Sheila's fate.

She formed the thoughts in her mind, but she didn't believe them. Dane couldn't have followed her so quickly. He certainly couldn't have been here before her.

Besides, she didn't want to believe evil of Dane. How insane.

She kept staring out into the darkness, watching, fighting the sense of panic. The shadow-shapes in the room seemed to loom larger. The bed, she knew. The chair. The wing shape was merely the jacket she had tossed over the back of it.

Nothing was changed, she was certain.

And yet…

She had the oddest sensation that someone other than herself had been in here.

Sheila…

She almost said the name aloud. Was she fine, perhaps in hiding for some reason, slipping in and out of her own home without telling a soul, simply because she was afraid?

But with no valid reason, no logic, no sense, she was just as certain that Sheila hadn't returned as she was that someone had been in the room.

Staring out the back, straining to see, to hear, she almost missed the sound that came from the front of the house.

But she didn't.

Subtle, soft, barely perceptible. But a sound. A clicking. A soft clicking. Like a door opening. With stealth and menace.

The front door. She had locked it.

Hadn't she?

Had she imagined the sound? Worked herself into such a silly panic that she was imagining noises everywhere?

But no…once again, some form of sixth sense or instinct was kicking in.

She was not alone in the house.

The thumping had come from the back. The clicking had come from the front. If she had really heard either.

She realized that she was standing like a deer in the road, blinded by the lights of an oncoming car, standing still and simply awaiting the deadly impact.

In a single instant, she decided that she would rather take her chances outside than be trapped inside the house with a...

Killer.

In a whir of motion, she reached for the latch on the sliding door leading out to the porch, pool and yard. The door didn't give. She pulled at it, then realized there was another latch closer to the floor. She bent down to unlock it.

And then she knew.

There really was someone in the house.

She could hear the swift quiet footsteps against the carpet. She could feel the displacement of the air, as someone was rushing toward her, out of the shadows, out of the darkness.

She gripped her candlestick tightly in her left hand and pulled at the sliding glass door once again with her left. She pulled hard, with an adrenaline-charged strength that sent the glass sliding with a vengeance across the runner.

But before Kelsey could catch her balance and go flying out, the phantom that had been only sound became real as a figure burst through the bedroom door and came barreling toward her.

With no choice, she turned rather than flee, ready to attack in self-defense.

In a split second, she lifted the candlestick.

And screamed.

There were no prints on the Polaroid.

Dane knew it. He hadn't brought the photo into any lab; he just knew that he was dealing with someone who had carefully plotted every aspect of his crime.

He had once heard an FBI profiler give a lecture on the perfect crime. He'd claimed there was no such thing.

But sometimes, by accident, a killer could commit a perfect crime. When a woman was murdered, the husband, ex-husband, boyfriend or lover, immediately fell under suspicion. Except in the case of serial crime. Most of the time, serial killers committed their crimes against strangers. And when there was no one with whom to compare physical and trace evidence, the evidence, no matter how carefully collected, was of little use. Husbands, lovers and boyfriends were easy to track down; strangers were not so easy to find.

There were always clues.

But what had gone on here had been, at the least, orchestrated with extreme detail and careful planning. Accidents could create a perfect crime. This killer had planned on accidents of nature. There were so many tiny fragments with which forensic experts could now work. Prints and blood were huge by comparison; in a lab, a case could be made with a tuft of carpet, a broken strand of hair, a remnant of ash.

Could.

Nature could preserve. Insects could give time lines and tell a million tales.

But nature could also take away. And the whipping fury of a storm could wipe away any trace evidence.

So much for his own powers of observation, his training, his years in the military.

The killer had known when he was away. Had known when he would return. The killer had performed his savage act when Dane had been gone. He had delivered the photo when Dane had been gone.

But not before any evidence had been destroyed. He had planned his act to coincide with the storm. A violent storm, with whipping winds, a massive surge. Normally it would have made sense to go through the motions. To follow procedure. But Dane knew that he had been targeted, watched and used. He was intended to take the rap, to go to prison and possibly to meet his fate through lethal injection. The crime had almost been a challenge.

None of it made sense when brought beneath the scrutiny of everything he had ever learned. The Necktie Strangler was considered, by all the law enforcement agencies that were involved, to be a serial *signature* killer. Often a serial killer's MO might change. He might target strippers who practiced prostitution on the side, then change to picking up women who were merely promiscuous. But the man's *signature* had been in his acts against the bodies of his victims, the fact that he had left them stripped, with the weapon of their strangulation still around their necks. He didn't leave the bodies in the open; he hid them in the water, knowing that time and the elements would take their toll on the corpses. Though this implied organization and planning, it didn't fit with a body being left on his property—and a Polaroid picture of the body being taken, then shoved beneath his door.

There were, of course, killers who wanted to be

caught. Killers who knew they couldn't stop but still had enough conscience left to want to be.

Tonight, as he stared at the picture, stomach still churning at the sight, nerves raw, emotions burned and cold, he felt again the sorrow. And the tumult. If he brought this piece of evidence in, he would go to jail. He had owned the old Polaroid camera that had taken the shot.

He had owned the tie that was knotted around her neck.

Any evidence pointing to the real killer had been washed away in the fury of the elements.

Sheila had been with him. There might still be DNA evidence on the body that could prove it.

And yet...

Hiding the picture was withholding evidence. He loathed what he was doing. If his actions brought about another woman's death...

He closed his eyes. If he was arrested, another woman might still be murdered. Because they would be holding the wrong man.

Kelsey was already convinced he was involved. She would be passionately determined on justice for Sheila.

He rose, ready to leave the house, a man with things to do, people to see, and a desperation to do them all before time closed in on him.

He returned the photo to the place beneath the floorboard in his bedroom and headed out. But before he was out the door, his phone rang. He let the machine pick up. He was surprised to hear Jesse Crane's voice.

"Dane, call me. They've found another body in a canal."

* * *

"Kelsey!" Larry yelled.

He said her name with barely enough time to prevent her from bringing the heavy pewter candlestick down on his head.

"Larry!"

The room was suddenly flooded with light. She and Larry were caught in a bizarre embrace. Nate and Cindy were standing in the doorway.

"I could have killed you!" Kelsey said furiously. "What were you doing, sneaking around in here?"

"Me? We came home and heard someone creeping around the house, and there were no lights and no sign of you," Larry protested.

Shaking, Kelsey dropped the candlestick. Larry jumped away, watching it fall.

"We really thought someone had broken in," Cindy said. "Kelsey, you didn't have any lights on. I whispered your name, but I guess you didn't hear me."

"Why didn't you just call my name loudly?" Kelsey asked.

"We couldn't call your name loudly if there was a thief or a...or a thief," Nate said lamely.

Kelsey exhaled a long breath. "I thought I heard someone sneaking around. And I heard a thumping sound out back."

"There's a mango tree out there. The fruit was probably falling," Cindy said impatiently.

"Let's take a walk out back and look around anyway," Larry said.

He walked past Kelsey. They all followed. The whole thing had been silly, she thought, with her sneaking around in the darkness and thinking someone was about to attack her, and the three of them certain that *she* was the intruder. And still, when they walked out back, they were all unnerved.

Larry laughed suddenly. "Nothing out here but a pool."

"Grass and trees," Cindy said, sounding almost giddy with relief.

Kelsey turned around, wanting to feel more relieved than she did. "Well, I have to admit, I'm glad you're all back."

"It's getting late," Nate murmured. He looked at Kelsey. "Maybe I'll bunk out on the sofa."

She was about to tell him that wasn't necessary, since Larry was staying in the guest room, but then Cindy chimed in again. "You don't need to sleep on the sofa here when there's an extra bedroom in my half of the place. If any of us gets the heebie-jeebies in the middle of the night, we can just bang on the walls."

"Doesn't sound like such a bad idea," Larry said.

"Okay, then, I'm off to bed," Cindy said. She gave Kelsey a hug and started back into the house. They all turned and followed her.

"Wait," Larry said, checking the glass doors to the back and assuring himself that the rear of the house was completely secured. He gave a satisfied nod to Kelsey. "I'll lock the front once the crew is out."

"Great. See everyone in the morning," Kelsey said.

She closed the door to her room once they were all out but found herself standing still, listening intently until she had heard Larry lock and bolt the front.

The light was on in her room. Larry was out front, the house was full. She still felt that sensation of uneasiness.

She turned and leaned against the door, surveying

the room, and she knew what was still bothering her. There wasn't anything that was an exact giveaway, but she still felt as if someone had been there. Someone who hadn't come to rob them, who hadn't taken anything. Someone who had come to do something worse. To invade…

To invade what?

She didn't know. But the pillow didn't seem to be on the bed at quite the angle that she had left it. The spread seemed to be a bit off. The items on the dresser seemed to have been moved just a fraction of an inch.

Kelsey checked the door again, searched the closet and the bath. She was definitely alone now.

She hesitated, then looked under the pillow.

Sheila's diary remained right where Sheila had left it.

Yet it, too, seemed to have been moved. Just a fraction of an inch…

Maybe she was simply losing her mind, so convinced that something terrible had befallen Sheila that she was making up evil ghosts in her mind.

Telling herself that she was crazy didn't seem to help any. Kelsey took a long shower, a couple of Tylenol and went to bed.

And stared into the murky darkness of the room, eyes wide-open, listening…

Listening…

Andy Latham, who was as crazy as a loon, was convinced they had thrown dead fish in his yard. And then there was Dane, who was behaving so suspiciously. He'd slept with Sheila, then she had disappeared. He'd been the last one to see her, and now he was reading about the Necktie Strangler. But Dane couldn't be guilty…

Why not?

Because she didn't want him to be.

A branch tapped on her window. She almost screamed aloud, then realized it was just a branch and she was being ridiculous. She had been so frightened tonight over nothing; they had all been stalking one another, when there had been no one here, no one outside...

Logic didn't matter.

In the night, in the dark, she was suddenly very afraid.

"Jesse," Dane said, grabbing the phone.

"Dane, good, you're there."

"Is it...could it be...?"

"No, definitely not Sheila. Some fishermen pulled up a body today. Just bones. They've been taken to the morgue, but the medical examiner said the victim has definitely been dead nine months to a year. They'll try to ID her as soon as possible, of course."

"But it was the Necktie Strangler?"

"They aren't even sure of the cause of death. But the preliminary investigation suggests it's a young woman. And if they do connect her to the other murders, it means our guy started off long before any of us suspected. I don't have much real information to give you yet, but I wanted to let you know. The bones were found just west of Shark Valley. And I wanted you to know that it wasn't Sheila, so you wouldn't worry when you saw it in the papers."

"Thanks, Jesse."

"Ready to tell me what's going on yet?"

"Soon. I want to do a little more investigating first."

"I'm here if you need me."

"Thanks."

Dane hung up, then left the house as he had intended. It was late, but there were some places in South Florida where the night was just beginning.

Morning was hell.

Sunlight made its way through the drapes, and, though muted, it seemed to pierce Kelsey's eyes with a vengeance. She had barely slept.

Rising, she drew the drapes anyway, recoiling and blinking in pain as the light increased. Still, it was the best way to wake up.

She jumped in and out of the shower, dressed, then made coffee. With her first cup, she felt more awake. And then foolish. Larry was still asleep in the spare room, and the shadows of the previous night became benign trees, gently waving in the breeze. Fear faded. Determination returned.

She thought about turning on her computer and tracking down the stories Dane had been reading, but decided instead that if she was looking for Sheila, first she needed to delve more deeply into her friend's life. She returned to her room, second cup of coffee in hand, and reached beneath the pillow for Sheila's diary.

It still surprised Kelsey that Sheila had kept any kind of a diary. She had always seemed far too busy living life to take the time to put anything down on paper.

The diary began shortly after Sheila had moved back to the Keys. The first page was a simple entry.

Home again, home again, home again. Things change, and yet they don't change at all.

Two days later, there was another entry.

The tourists are flocking. Busy little bees. Almost had to drag a lady out of a chair at the bar at Nate's. I told him he needed reserved stools for the locals. Naturally, being Nate, he took me seriously and tried to explain that he couldn't do that. And he had the nerve to say I wasn't really a local anymore. Ah, men, how quickly they forget. But that's okay.

Most of them are far too forgettable themselves.

The next few entries were basically just as mundane, yet typically Sheila.

How strange Dane has become. Somber. Not like him. Cool, though, that he's come back now, too. Told him I might wind up needing his services. He gave me a really strange look. God knows what he's heard about my past. I told him I wasn't thinking about stud service, that I might want to use him as a private eye. He said I should hire someone better. Poor guy. Wonder what happened. He won't talk about it. Thought he was just lying around drunk in a lounge chair, but he wasn't drunk, since he was drinking soda water, or so Nate said. He was just lying around. Strange to see Dane so beat, yet when he looks at you, when you see his eyes... well, there's life in there yet. Just have to reach him. Ah, well, I'm living in a piece of Paradise. Lots of pretty boys on the water. Better yet, lots of pretty rich boys on the water. Still, sometimes the old boys are the best boys. Time will tell. Meanwhile...

Saw Izzy.

Now there's quite a high.

Good old Izzy. His stuff just gets better and better.

And old Izzy isn't bad himself. He likes to bargain. Which is okay by me. Izzy has Latin rhythm down pat. Running his stuff keeps him in good shape. Another laugh. Officially he's in the fishing trade. Some fish. He takes tourists out and makes them so happy they couldn't care less if they get any fish. Cindy says she sees him at the gym now and then, but he must be work- ing hard at his craft—running! What do I care? I'm hardly the FBI or DEA. Not likely. No, I'm the down and dirty kind, but hell, what would you expect? Still, the way he flirts and bargains is pretty cool. Makes me feel...okay, not exactly Madonna-Like-A-Virgin-ish, but damn cool close.

Combine Izzy and the stuff...

Not a bad deal. And I really do have one hell of a good time. If I were a guy, no one would think a thing about it. The shrink said I'm looking for some- thing I can't have. He's full of shit. I was married. I had the good-looking guy with money, and I was bored to death. Maybe he was just the wrong guy. But if so, I threw away being what the other guy was looking for years ago. Just reread this, and I'm not making sense, even to myself. But maybe I don't want to make sense. Maybe I don't want to see the truth, even if it's just for my eyes only.

A knock on the bedroom door startled Kelsey so badly she might as well have been a guilty teenager. She jumped up and shoved the diary beneath the pillow.

"Hey, Kels? You awake in there, kid?"

"Yeah, yeah, Larry, I'm awake."

She walked across the room, glancing at her watch. It was already one in the afternoon. She opened her door. Larry, somehow still looking like a *GQ* adver- tisement in shorts and a crew neck shirt, was smiling at her. "What do you think this is, vacation?" he teased. "Want to get some lunch?"

"Lunch?"

"Yeah, you know, the meal that's typically eaten sometime around noon."

"Lunch? No," Kelsey said, making a sudden decision. "I've got a few errands to run. But I'd love to have dinner. Let's meet at the new fish place just past Nate's at seven. How's that?"

She didn't really care how it was. She brushed past him, already on her way out for her purse and keys.

"Wait a minute, Kelsey. First of all, we'll probably hurt Nate's feelings if we eat somewhere else. And second, where on earth are you going? Cindy is going to wake up and want to know where you are. We were all spooked last night. She'll be worried, then she'll be pissed at me for letting you go."

She paused at the door. "You're right, we don't want to hurt anyone's feelings. We'll meet at Nate's place at seven sharp." Then she left before he could ask any more questions or give her any further argument.

Jesse Crane leaned against his desk and handed Dane the top dispatch from the stack. As Dane read, Jesse talked. "Looks like our killer has been busy a lot longer than any of us suspected. Forensics found remnants of threads around the neck. Down here, in the Everglades and the heat, a body can decompose quickly, but the ME's office still estimates the girl had been dead close to a year. There's no damage to the bones, though there's also no proof that she didn't drown. There were remnants of fabric found in the muck near the bones, and forensics may be able to discover what they came from. No actual clothing, no purses or shoes or other personal effects of the victims have been found, so it's quite possible that the remnants came from a tie. They managed to identify her quickly. Her name was Alsie Greer, aka Janice Thorson, aka Lydia Farning. She had a nice long rap sheet for drugs and prostitution, and worked in a really low-down joint up in Palm Beach County. Alsie cared for her teeth, though. She'd been reported missing eleven months ago, and the computer matched up the dental records right away. That was a lucky break. You know how long it can take just to identify a victim, much less—"

"Find a killer," Dane ended.

Jesse shrugged. "The statistics say there are probably a couple hundred serial killers at work in the country at any given time. And most of them are never caught."

"This one has to be caught. You know that or there will be more victims. And it looks as if he's picking up his pace."

Jesse shook his head. "Dane, we really don't have a clue as to what his pace is. South Florida holds endless miles of waterways. You know that as well as I do. Last year they finally found four teenagers who'd been missing for almost twenty years. They'd driven into a canal and disappeared without a trace. And the businessman from Philadelphia who disappeared after a night on the town? He was found in a Fort Lauderdale canal after more than a decade. The list of people found in the water after they've been missing for years is staggering."

Jesse nodded. It wasn't that South Florida law enforcement didn't have excellent dive teams, because they did. Some of the best in the world. It was that the waterways were endless and often mucky, murky and dense with vegetation. Thanks to the divers, many people survived after driving into canals, and most of the time the missing were found. But then there were times when finding someone in the endless waterways was like finding the proverbial needle in a haystack.

"Come on," Jesse said, taking the paper from Dane and setting it on the desk. "I'll take you out to the site where the remains were found."

They took Dane's Jeep, though. The road they followed wasn't nearly as bad as many of the seldom used paths into the Everglades. It was treacherous country for the unwary, though. Summertime heat was on, and though the area had gone through a drought, it had turned to storm season. Technically the Everglades was not a swamp. The whole area was really an incredibly slow-moving river, heavily subject to the whims of nature. After the recent storm, the gator holes and canals were deep. One twist of the steering wheel could land a car in the water and muck, and then the car and its inhabitants could disappear from view, maybe forever.

Today, as they drove, the sky was a beautiful blue, with light tufting clouds. There was a breeze, bending the saw grass low, like shimmering sheaves of green wheat. They passed canals where unwary egrets, herons and other water birds played perilously close to the watchful gaze of alligators, their bodies cooled from the brutal heat beneath the water's surface, their eerie, reptilian eyes sharp and ever on the alert just above the water's edge.

"There's another storm moving across the Atlantic," Jesse said.

"Yeah, I saw the paper," Dane said.

"They think it's going to turn up and head for the Carolinas," Jesse commented.

"They tend to do that."

"I think this guy likes to dispose of his victims just before a storm," Jesse said. "I think he even plans his murders by the weather."

Dane felt a strange chill despite the near hundred degree heat of the day.

Jesse was right. The killer would strike again soon.

"Whether that storm turns north or not, we're probably in for some weather…in three, four days' time," Dane murmured.

"Better stop ahead. We'll move down to the waterfront on foot."

The term "waterfront" didn't actually apply. Once they stepped out of the car, they were in several inches of muddy water. The muck oozed around their feet and created sucking sounds with each step they took.

A few minutes' walk took them to the actual canal, swollen against its banks. A Metro-Dade uniformed officer stood an unhappy guard beside the yellow crime tape that surrounded the area where the body had been found. The man miserably swatted at a mosquito and greeted Jesse with a hello, then nodded at his introduction to Dane.

There wasn't much to see at the actual site. Dane knew that forensics experts and crime scene investigators had spent the morning looking for any minute scrap of evidence—a hair, a fiber, anything at all that might one day link the victim to a suspect, should a suspect ever be apprehended. The tiniest carpet fiber from a vehicle could link a killer to his victim. Forensics had made convictions possible in many cases where it had seemed there was no hope. A perpetrator always left some tiny piece of physical evidence behind, just as he took some piece of evidence with him, a victim's blood, a fiber from their clothing, a strand of hair.

But after nearly a year in a swamp...

"See what I mean, though? The road isn't your average tourist track," Jesse said. "But it's more than possible to get your average vehicle near enough to dispose of a body. Of course, it's also possible that the body traveled."

Dane nodded, looking around. The heat was intense. The buzzing of the flies and mosquitoes was like a monotonous song. This was one instance when the detectives were going to have to rely on the age-old methods of hunches and a lot of footwork.

"I went up to the Broward club last night," Dane told Jesse.

"Yeah?"

"The girls are leery about talking," Dane said. He shrugged. "They're convinced they're safe because one of them has already been killed, and the killer seems smart enough not to strike in the same place twice. They don't trust the police, and I spent a lot of time trying to convince the girls I wasn't a cop."

"Did you learn anything?"

"Not yet, but I believe I will. I want to get into the Miami club, as well. Jesse, I didn't have time to read everything on that report. When this girl disappeared, someone evidently filled out a missing persons report, right? So I'm assuming her friends and co-workers were questioned."

"I've pulled up what information is in the records. It's the same story. She was at work one night. She wasn't there the next. She lived alone. Neighbors don't remember anything. She might have come home, she might not have. She left the club sometime between four and five in the morning, and that's the last time anyone can remember seeing her. In this case, she didn't drive, so there wasn't a question of looking for her car. There was no record of her calling a cab from work, and though her cell phone disappeared with her, the company records were requested, and there were no calls to a cab company. The last place she contacted was a language school—she had asked about taking French lessons. She never went to the school, though, so that was a dead end. She'd had a boyfriend, but he checked out. There were witnesses to prove he'd been at a party in West Palm the night—or early morning— she disappeared. He passed out in the living room at the party, and there were four people to attest to the fact that he didn't wake up until after the girl's shift started the next night. The police in three counties are follow- ing every lead, not that there are many. Warnings are going out on the news daily. And other than that…well, the population down here is in the millions, once you take in the three counties. Every possible lead dries up. You know that can happen. A killer is usually caught when he slips up. This guy hasn't slipped up yet. And the police can't interrogate every man who steps into a strip club in South Florida."

"I think I can narrow it down," Dane said.

Jesse studied him gravely.

"The Necktie Strangler has to be someone I know," Dane said.

"Someone you know?" A deep, concerned furrow creased Jesse's forehead.

"Or someone who knows me," Dane said.

He wasn't ready to elaborate further. Jesse, being Jesse, would accept that.

Dane decided to end the conversation there.

"I've got to get back. There's a lot I have to do. And I don't think I have a lot of time."

Chapter 8

The sign read simply Izzy's Charters.

Izzy Garcia's fishing boat, the *Lady Havana*, was docked next to a dozen others. Kelsey was glad for the other people around. From what she understood, Izzy was ostensibly living the perfect Keys life, working when he chose, then taking off for the pure pleasure of it when he chose, as well. But if the rumor was true—which she was certain it was—Izzy *didn't* actually take off for the pure pleasure of it. He ran drugs.

She wasn't sure why some government agency hadn't cornered him by now. Except that he was probably good at what he did. He knew every tiny island and inlet, Gulf-side and Atlantic-side, of the Keys, knew when to hold and when to fold, and how to rid himself of a cargo quickly.

He had apparently taken out a morning charter. What

seemed to be a family of tourists hovered on the dock, two kids watching with fascination as Izzy gutted and filleted their catch. His knife was sharp, his expertise with it swift and fascinating. Kelsey had spent many an hour with a fresh catch herself, and she was nowhere near as good as Izzy. Few people probably were.

She hadn't seen him in years, but she recognized him right away. He was tall and bronzed, more wiry than massive, but Kelsey had to admit that he was very good-looking in what she might term a "smarmy" way. His hair would have been long if it weren't so curly, oily and dark. His face was lean, with a sharp chin and narrow cheekbones. His eyes were deep-set and very dark. He moved with a strange, natural grace, and knowing Sheila, Kelsey knew what Sheila saw in the man. His tan was so dark that he was beyond bronze and more the color of nutshell brown. His skin was shiny in the sun and heat. Like many a boat man, he was in nothing but cutoffs. His feet were bare.

As if he sensed her standing on the dock, he looked up. Since she'd had no trouble recognizing him, it shouldn't have been strange that he recognized her immediately.

"Kelsey Cunningham," he breathed, pausing for a moment as he stared her up and down. Again Kelsey understood Sheila's attraction. There was nothing hidden in the way he looked at her. His assessment was slow and complete. He didn't just undress a woman with his eyes, he went all the way.

"Is that the last of them?" the mother of the two children asked. Her nose was white with sunscreen. Her cheeks, missing the protection, were lobster-red.

"The last," Izzy said, still staring at Kelsey, a curious smile twisting his full lips. He wrapped the fish in brown paper kept at the dockside station for just that purpose. "Don't overcook the fish. Just a little olive oil in the pan, a touch of butter…" He brought his fingers to his lips and made a kissing sound, still looking at Kelsey. "Voilà! Your fillets will be like butter themselves!"

"Thank you," the husband said. He had the kind of belly that protruded over the waistband of his shorts. The slice of stomach that was revealed was as red as his wife's cheeks.

The group started to move off. Izzy finally looked away from Kelsey. "A tip is customary," he said flatly.

"Oh, yeah, sure," the man said, digging in his damp pockets.

"Tip him good, Daddy!" the little girl said. "He helped me catch my fish."

"Oh, yeah, sure, we had a great time," the man said, giving Izzy a wad of bills.

Izzy grinned. "Of course. Little girls, just like little boys, should learn to catch fish. To go for it all in life, right…Susie?"

"My name is Shelly," the little girl said, frowning.

"Ah, yes, Shelly." Izzy tousled her hair, grinning. "Of course. And now you know how to catch fish with the best of them."

"My fish was bigger," the little boy said.

"You both did well," Izzy said complimentarily.

The kids seemed happy, as did the parents. They waved as they walked away from the dock, studying Kelsey curiously and nodding as they passed her.

"Think she's his girlfriend?" the little girl asked the little boy in a whisper as they passed.

"I'll bet he has a dozen girlfriends!" the boy said confidently. "At least a dozen."

Izzy laughed, watching them go. "So...Kelsey Cunningham. What an honor—and a surprise. So, have you come to be one of my girlfriends? City life getting to you? Did you come down to slum it with a real man?"

She walked to the table where the flies buzzed around the fish remains. "I came down to see Sheila," she said.

His smile didn't alter a hair. He shrugged. "Sheila. Now there's an unusual woman. A real woman. Maybe more of a real woman than I am a real man."

"So you've seen her?"

"Of course I've seen her. She knows where to come when she needs me."

"Lately? Have you seen her lately?"

He set his hands on his hips and cocked his head, thinking. "I saw her...eight days ago? I think. Before the storm."

"Not since?"

"No, I don't think so. You know Sheila. She comes, she goes."

"Were you seeing her...regularly?"

Izzy let out a long laugh. "Was I *fucking* Sheila? Is that what you want to know?"

Kelsey suddenly felt both a surge of anger and a sense of her own stupidity. What the hell did she think—that Izzy was going to confess he'd taken Sheila off and dumped her in the ocean?

She started to turn away. She was startled when his hand fell on her shoulder and he quickly apologized. "Kelsey, don't go so fast. I'm sorry. You were never mean to me, you were never interested in me, either, but I'm just surprised to see you, that's all. But if I can help you, I'd be happy to. So are you concerned about what Sheila has been doing—or what Sheila has been getting? Did you come to me for...something?"

Despite herself, she felt her cheeks flood with color. He thought she had come to an old acquaintance to make a drug purchase.

"I was supposed to meet Sheila here on Thursday. She hasn't shown up yet."

He made a face that clearly showed her that she was talking about no time at all, the way Sheila would see it.

"Sheila sees me one day...then disappears for a week or more. She has other things to do." His long lashes swept over his eyes for a moment. "So many people to meet. Me, I fulfill some of her needs. But she has... many needs, and I can't satisfy them all." As if sensing her discomfort, he changed the subject. "Would you like to come aboard? I've got cold drinks in the refrigerator."

He picked up on her hesitation immediately.

"I don't bite—unless I'm asked to."

It might be the stupidest thing in the world to walk onto his boat. But the dock was filled with people. A lot of the charter fishing captains took out a morning group and an afternoon group. They were all between right now. At least a dozen people would see her when she stepped aboard. And she wanted to see for herself where Sheila had been spending time.

"Sure. I'd like to see the boat. And I'd love a cold soda."

He arched a brow in surprise that she had agreed so readily. Then he smiled broadly. "Miss Cunningham, do come into my parlor. I promise to be on my best behavior."

Kelsey followed him from the dock, taking his hand as he helped her jump down to the deck of the *Lady Havana*.

"You haven't joined the DEA or anything have you, Kelsey?" he queried. "Because I know damn well you don't trust me."

He was still holding her hand. She didn't allow herself to pull it away, though she wanted to, and finally he released her.

"I'm just worried about Sheila."

"I'll tell you what I can."

They didn't stay on deck. He led the way to the few short steps that descended into the cabin.

Dane's concentration had been on focusing the lens of his camera on Izzy Garcia. Bringing his face into full view as best as possible from this distance. He clicked a picture, then another, then a third. A decent full frontal shot as Izzy stepped off his boat. A good profile shot as he turned to the woman passenger, assisting her from the boat. Then, on the dock, cleaning his fish.

He was patient in his quest, waiting for a good, clear shot. He stared at the dock area, where the object of his attention was working. He refocused, noting the mother, father and two children. Then, through his lens, he saw Kelsey.

Hair pulled back into a cool ponytail, she was in a tank top, shorts and deck shoes.

From the midst of a tangle of sea grape trees, Dane watched in amazement as Kelsey disappeared from view, entering the cabin of Izzy's boat.

He hadn't expected to find her here. And he sure as

hell hadn't intended to confront Izzy himself. If he were even halfway rational, he wouldn't confront Izzy now.

But he couldn't see Kelsey. And that suddenly meant that he wasn't rational at all.

He pocketed the small camera in the cargo shorts he was wearing and headed toward the dock.

Kelsey was an idiot.

At this moment Dane didn't just dislike Izzy Garcia, he hated the man.

Though he could travel the distance from the off road hummock to the sandy path, the dock and then the boat in a matter of moments, he thought even that was too long a time for Kelsey to be alone with Izzy Garcia.

His heart rate and sense of unease escalated when he saw Izzy on deck again, releasing his mooring lines.

"Shit!" Dane swore, suddenly at a sprinter's pace as his feet hit the dock.

The *Lady Havana* was already pulling away from her berth.

"We'll just take a little spin out on the water," he'd said, again offering his smile of amusement at her obvious mistrust. "Twenty people just saw you get onboard," he'd reminded her. "And I have another charter in less than an hour. But that way no one will be able to interrupt us. I can talk to you."

Then he'd left her in the cabin and gone up top. She was still nervous, but he was right—she had gotten on his boat in broad daylight, in front of plenty of witnesses. And Izzy had never done anything to her or to anyone she knew.

Unless, of course, Sheila…

She could swim, she reasoned with herself. If she

didn't like what was going on, she could just jump overboard and swim to safety.

Besides, she wanted a few moments alone in the cabin. Time to snoop. Not a lot of time, but she was willing to use anything she could get.

Of course, not only was she looking for a needle in a haystack, she didn't even know what needle she was looking for. But she'd found Sheila's earring at Dane's, and though he'd had a reason for it, she'd learned something.

Actually, more than she'd wanted to know. But it was important to know everything.

And here, in Izzy's boat...

Charts by the radio. And Izzy's cell phone. She glanced up the steps to see him busy on deck and hit the phone book key on Izzy's phone to get his stored numbers. She was carrying a small knit bag, so it was easy to find a pen and paper. She started writing, keeping her eyes on the steps. He was going to have to steer out of the marina area. That would take at least a few minutes.

She found the number to the duplex and the number to Sheila's cell phone. And others that startled her. Cindy's number, Nate's...Dane's. Dane's number at the house and at the office he had rented on US1. More numbers. Even the number to *her* house. She was so surprised that she froze for a minute, then started writing again. She didn't recognize half the area codes.

She heard his footsteps overhead. He was still maneuvering the boat out of the channel.

In a frenzy, she wrote down every number she could. She wondered if she would be able to decipher her own chicken scrawl later. She heard the motor idling down and quickly set down the phone and looked around the cabin. A simple place, loaded with fishing gear. A refrigerator, a small cooktop, a door reading Head. A small archway to an aft bunk. Cushioned seats lined both sides. She lifted the seats, knowing there was storage beneath. More fishing gear. A couple of metal boxes holding…what? A woman's bikini, neatly folded. Sandals on top. Sheila's? A purse…

Kelsey glanced back toward the steps. Listened. The motor was still running. She opened the purse. Lipstick, pen, small plastic bag holding a greenish-brown tobacco-like substance. She sniffed it. Grass. A compact initialed with the letters *SEW*. Sheila Elizabeth Warren.

The motor went still.

Kelsey dropped the purse back in the seat, closed the cushion lid. Sat. She was breathing as if she had just run a marathon. She willed her heart to stop pounding.

Izzy came down the steps. "Soda or beer?"

"Just a soda, please."

She was amazed to hear her own voice. It was low, calm, polite. It should have been a squeak.

"Cola or lemon-lime? Store brand, I'm afraid. Fishing charters don't pay enough for me to supply the tourists with anything better. Besides, out in the heat, on the ocean, what do they care? If they catch fish, they're happy. Half of them don't even eat fish. They just like to catch them, watch them struggle and say they caught the biggest one. What do you think that says about people?"

"I think it says most people realize that the big fish are born to hunt the little fish. That they rip apart their own kind at the first sign of weakness," Kelsey said.

"Not like people, eh?"

"Is it your opinion that people rip other people apart when they sense weakness?" Kelsey asked him.

"Me? I've seen it happen, if that's what you're asking. I saw the revolution in Cuba, the good and the bad. Little children helping old people, old people sacrificing themselves for the children. I saw a man jump into the sea and drown so that the overloaded raft he was on would make it across the sea. And I saw another man knock his wife from a raft so he could survive himself. All this I saw as a child. Yes, I would say it formed opinions in my mind."

"So whatever you do to anyone is all right, so long as it helps you survive?"

Izzy laughed, bringing Kelsey a soda and sitting at her side. Close. Brown legs against hers. "No. I think what I do is all right when I fulfill other people's needs. I told you, I fulfilled many of Sheila's needs. But look at you, Kelsey. Such a pretty girl. And a sweet girl, mostly. But you're so stiff. This is right, and this is wrong. I bet you've never even jaywalked. And now you work for an uppity advertising agency. You go to long lunches with clients at the best restaurants, silly places where they take ten words to describe a piece of lettuce. I bet you live in a gated complex, up high, looking down at the world."

"Are you going to tell me about Sheila?"

"You know Sheila."

"Not like you know Sheila."

"Right. And I like Sheila. There's no pretense about her. She knows how to have fun. And while she's having fun, she takes what she wants. If a man appeals to her, she goes after him and enjoys him. If he has money and gives her beautiful jewelry, all the better.

If he's jealous, she laughs. She'll order filet mignon or a hamburger, drink champagne or a beer, have sex on the sand, in the mud...wherever."

"How deep into drugs was she?" Kelsey demanded.

Izzy smiled, white teeth flashing against his bronze skin. "Did she shoot heroine? No. Did she enjoy some good pot or hash? *Sí*. And ecstasy? Oh, yes, Sheila is a woman of the senses. You see, I didn't have the diamonds to give her, but I had something else. A world of fantasy—and, of course, myself. What I offer is good. Safe drugs."

"Safe drugs?" she inquired.

"See, there you are, Miss Moralist, Miss Purist, perfect little nose in the air. You've got to learn to have fun. Let your hair down." He set a hand on her knee.

She moved it, staring at him.

He was amused. "You married Nate. He runs a bar. You think drunks are safer than people who've smoked a few joints?"

"Izzy, it doesn't matter what anyone's moral opinion is, it's legal to drink and it's illegal to do drugs."

"I still think you need a joint. You should chill out a little."

"Izzy, I don't want to chill out. I want to find Sheila."

He frowned suddenly. "I told you. Sheila comes, and Sheila goes. Except that..."

"Except that *what*, Izzy? Please, help me."

He shrugged. "Sheila did tell me that she had been a fool. She said that when a man was part of the past, he should be kept in the past." He hesitated, then looked at her squarely. "You know, Sheila saw a lot as a child, too. Maybe that's why we understand each other so well."

"What are you talking about?"

"She never talked to you about her mother?"

"Her mother? Her mother died."

"She did. But she was a busy lady before that. She and old Andy Latham, they were two of a kind. She had the money, but she was willing to do a lot of things for old Andy. And that included looking away."

"Looking away from what?"

Izzy suddenly stood, shaking his head. "Talk to Sheila. I've said too much. It's not my business to share."

"Izzy, please, that's why I'm here. What exactly are you saying? That Sheila's mother ran around after she married Latham?"

"She ran around *with* Latham is what I'm telling you. He needed more than…more than just one woman. Maybe two women. Maybe just watching. And Sheila… she saw a lot."

"Izzy, please, stop talking in riddles."

He walked back to her suddenly, arms braced on the wall to either side of her, his face just inches from hers. "Sheila has done too much, but you…you haven't done enough. Kelsey Cunningham. I always liked the sound of your name. Good Kelsey, beautiful Kelsey, prim and proper Kelsey. Take a chance, Kelsey. Life is to be lived. I can show you why Sheila couldn't stay away from me."

"Don't you have a charter this afternoon?" she asked him.

"Screw them."

He moved closer, but Kelsey wasn't afraid, just impatient. She wanted to get back to talking about Sheila and what Izzy knew about her. She wanted to know what Sheila had meant when she told him that the men in her past should remain there.

"Izzy—"

"Sí?" His dark-lashed eyes were half closed; his face was barely an inch from hers.

She was about to respond when an explosive slam suddenly sounded in the cabin and Izzy was jerked away from her as if by the hand of God. A too-familiar voice rang out in fury.

"Get the hell away from her, you drug-dealing asshole!"

Izzy had gone flying and crashed against the door to the Head. In the middle of the cabin, dripping sea water, stood Dane Whitelaw. Dark hair was plastered against his head. His feet and chest were bare, but his cargo shorts dripped like a leaky hull.

"Dane, what the hell are you doing here?" she asked angrily.

Izzy had recovered from his impact with the door. He shook off the blow, stood and pulled a switchblade from the pocket of his cutoffs.

"Izzy! Drop it. Dane, what the hell is the matter with you?"

Both men ignored her. Dane's face was set, harsh. Izzy looked ready to kill. He came forward in a rush.

She had never seen what Dane was capable of before, and he scared her. Izzy was a well-built man, muscled and lithe. But Dane sidestepped him in a second, smashing the arm with the blade and capturing him in a headlock.

"Stop it!" Kelsey screamed, leaping to her feet, grabbing Dane's right arm.

"Get the knife, Kelsey."

She picked up the switchblade, shaking, and realizing she didn't even know how to close the weapon.

Izzy swore in Spanish, a spew of venom, frightening. But Dane's headlock kept him from moving.

"Topside, Izzy," Dane said. "And get this rust bucket back into her berth."

Izzy kept swearing, but Dane was dragging him toward the steps. Dane determinedly forced Izzy up, then out to the open deck. Kelsey followed behind, shouting at Dane. "What the hell are you doing here? He was just talking to me about Sheila!"

"What the hell are *you* doing here? Trying to meet the same fate?" Dane countered. He shoved Izzy toward the helm. The two of them stood like a pair of game cocks, tension knotting them so tightly that they seemed like a display of bulging neck veins and wet muscle, like a pair of fighters about to be photographed for an anatomy class.

"You have no right to be here, Whitelaw," Izzy said. "Kelsey chose to come aboard. I can have you arrested for breaking and entering, and assault and battery."

"Izzy, I can have you arrested for so many felonies, your head would spin."

"You can't have me arrested for what you think, Whitelaw, and you have no proof of anything."

"You might be surprised at what kind of proof I have, Garcia."

Kelsey didn't have the slightest idea what was going on, but Dane's words gave Izzy pause. He turned around, cursing Dane in Spanish. She and Dane were both well enough acquainted with the language to know what he was saying, but the words had no effect on Dane, who didn't move, just stood stolidly watching as Izzy raised anchor and gunned the motor. The sound of it suddenly filled the air, and he walked to the helm, guiding the *Lady Havana* back toward the marina.

As the boat moved, the breeze picked up. Other boats filled the horizon, sailboats, fishing boats, dive boats. The sky remained blue, lightly touched by clouds. Oddly beautiful.

As the *Lady Havana* slowed into the "No Wake" zone, they all remained stiffly silent. When they reached the berth, Dane leaped from the boat, ready to tie her to the moorings. As the two men secured the boat as naturally as men who had been working together all their lives, it seemed impossible to believe that they had just been at each other's throats. The moment the boat was tied, Dane reached down to help Kelsey onto the dock. She ignored his hand, hopping out. She had been around boats just as long as the two of them had.

Izzy's afternoon group, five men of varying ages, all pale, two with the paunchy bellies of the weekday-business-warrior-weekend-couch-potato, were waiting on the dock, confused because there had been no boat waiting for them.

Dane spoke softly. "Don't even think about taking Kelsey out again, Izzy."

"Why? You afraid of what I'll say to her?"

"I'm afraid of what you'll do to her. You want to discuss this more now, or do you want to carry on your business and take your tourists out?"

Izzy turned his back on Dane. His easy smile back in place, he approached one of the waiting party with his hand extended. "Señor Huntsville. Good. You're on time."

As Izzy kept talking to his group. Dane started walking down the dock, toward the path out to the parking lot.

Kelsey ran after him, tapping him angrily on the back and forcing him to turn around.

"Look, I don't need a bodyguard. I could have taken care of myself with Izzy."

"You think so?"

"We were talking."

"Kelsey, you can't even close a switchblade."

"So? Izzy wasn't going to rape and kill me."

He looked at her with disgust and turned, ready to walk away again.

"Dane!"

"What?" He turned back with aggravation.

"What the hell just went on back there? How did you get on the boat? Why were you so convinced I was in danger, and what is it that you think Izzy has done?"

"Izzy is scum. I can just about prove that he's the supplier behind the drugs being sold at the local high school. He's dangerous, Kelsey, whether you want to believe it or not. As to how I got there, I hitched a ride on a dive boat, dove in and swam across. I destroyed a shirt and lost a good pair of boat shoes in the process, too. And what the hell kind of thanks do I get from you? None. You're too busy telling me that you didn't need a bodyguard."

"I've known Izzy most of my life."

"So? Did you know he has a rap sheet for assault? Or that he was also accused of date rape? The girl refused to prosecute, probably because she was paid off. I just didn't want to see you in her position. You don't want to believe me? Talk to Hans at the sheriff's office."

Kelsey could feel her cheeks going red as he spoke.

Maybe she *had* been crazy. *Really* crazy. She had found a purse that definitely belonged to Sheila, but then again, he hadn't denied that he saw Sheila frequently.

Sheila's earring had been at Dane's. Her purse had been on Izzy's boat.

Then there were all the numbers she'd found on Izzy's cell phone.

It was true that for a few minutes she had been afraid. But now she found herself inclined to believe that Izzy wouldn't have hurt her, nor would he have forced her into anything. He had pushed, but pushing was his way.

"Lots of people saw me get on that boat. Only an idiot would have harmed me."

"Or a guy so aggressive and confident he believes himself immune to the law. But hey, Kelsey, what the hell? I'm the last person you want help from, right?"

"It's not that, Dane, but you really don't have to follow me around."

"I wasn't following you around, Kelsey. I simply happened to be there at the same time you were. But what the hell, you're right. You're free and over twenty-one. I can't stop you. Just keep on seeing every psychotic scumbag in town. I'll do my best to quit trying to keep you from putting yourself in harm's way."

"Excuse me, but how the hell am I supposed to know *you're* not a psychotic scumbag?"

He turned and started walking again. She found herself following him, regretting her words already.

"Okay, I don't *think* you're a psychotic scumbag." He was still moving. He either didn't notice or didn't appreciate the light touch she had tried to give her words. "Dane, I'll buy you a new pair of shoes," she told him.

He kept walking.

"And I'll replace your shirt."

He was still walking. She could have kicked herself for following him, but she couldn't stop herself. "He told me things I didn't know, Dane. And he might have told me more."

He stopped at last and turned back to face her. "You've known Sheila forever. What could he have told you that you didn't already know?"

"That…well, I always knew Andy Latham was a creep, but according to Izzy, Sheila's mother was just as bad."

Dane studied her for a long moment. "That's a surprise to you? And you think it will help you find Sheila now?"

"Everything I learn is a help, Dane. And—" She broke off. Dane wasn't telling her everything, so she wasn't going to tell him everything.

"And what?"

She shook her head. "I just feel that if I could have talked to him long enough, he might have said something that would have helped. I think Sheila was spending a lot of time with him, off and on."

He looked down at the ground for a minute, then met her eyes again. "Kelsey, if you were going to spend time with everyone Sheila had been seeing, you'd need way more than a week's vacation." He waved a hand in the air. "Sheila was…it was almost as if she was on a quest to prove that she could have whoever she wanted whenever she wanted him."

"But why? If we knew, it might lead us to her. Or to whatever…happened to her. We have to find out why."

"I *will* find out why. I told you that."

She was silent for a minute. "But I could find out things you don't know."

"Not a chance."

"Oh?"

"Why do you say that?" His eyes narrowed.

She shrugged. "Because people who might not be willing to talk to you might be willing to talk to me."

She walked past him.

"Where are you going?"

She hesitated. "Back to the duplex. Are you going to follow me?"

"You're really going back there? You're not going to go into the computer and see if you can find another violent career criminal to visit?"

"I'm really going back to the duplex."

He nodded, then headed for his Jeep.

"Are you coming over?" she asked him.

He shook his head. "I have things to do."

She hesitated, watching him climb into the Jeep. He turned on the motor and took a pair of sunglasses from the dashboard, but he didn't move the car. He just watched her through the dark lenses.

"We're meeting for dinner at Nate's at seven," she told him. "Care to join us?"

She could read no emotion on his features, and she couldn't see his eyes.

"Yeah, I'll be there," he said.

She turned and got into her car. A block down the street, she realized that, despite what he'd said, he was following her. He wasn't even pretending not to. When she parked at the duplex, though, he remained in his car. She walked over to him. "Are you coming in?"

"No, I just thought I'd see you safely in."

"I thought you didn't care if I put myself into dangerous situations anymore."

"I lied." He adjusted his glasses. "Go inside, Kelsey."

She turned impatiently and walked to the door, fitting her key into the lock. She stepped inside, calling Larry's name. He didn't respond, but she hadn't expected him to, since his car wasn't in the driveway. She hesitated before closing the door, remembering her uneasiness the night before. She ran through the duplex, checking out closets and bathrooms, then back to the front. Dane was still there, still staring impassively out from behind his sunglasses. She waved to him and closed the door, listening to him drive away.

She hesitated. Her half of the duplex was empty, and she knew it. So why did she still have the feeling that someone had been there who shouldn't have been? That someone had searched the rooms? That the space had somehow been violated?

She glanced at her watch. It wasn't quite three. She had plenty of time to run over the list of numbers she had taken from Izzy's cell phone. She walked to the kitchen, set her purse down and dug out the paper. She marked off the numbers she knew, amazed that he seemed to have so many that should have meant nothing to him at this stage of all their lives. He had Larry's home phone keyed in, as well as her own, and that of the company where they both worked. Nate's home, Nate's business. Cindy. Dane. There was one listed only as "JM." She was willing to bet that number was Jorge Marti's. Just to double-check, she went to the phone and punched in the numbers. The phone rang, and then an answering machine picked up. "Hi, this is Jorge. Please leave a message. I'll get back to you as soon as possible."

She hesitated, then said quickly, "Hi, Jorge, it's Kelsey Cunningham. A group of us are meeting at seven at Nate's for supper. We'd love it if you could join us."

She hung up, then picked up the phone again, ready to try another number. After a moment she hung up without dialing, not wanting to call from the duplex.

Everyone had caller ID these days.

She drummed her fingers on the counter, wondering why she hadn't told Dane about Sheila's purse being on Izzy's boat, or that she had taken the numbers from his phone.

She really didn't know what the hell to do with the numbers. She knew it was somehow important that Izzy not only had all their numbers, but that he kept them on his cell phone. But as to finding out anything about the other numbers...she really didn't know how to go about it.

Dane would. He was a private investigator.

Maybe she would tell him. Soon. She was still disturbed by the fact that Sheila's earring had been at his house. That he had admitted to sleeping with her just before she disappeared.

What did it all mean?

Dane arrived at the Sea Shanty late. Before joining the group, he observed them from the doorway. Cindy was looking small but perfect in a backless sheath that showed off the definition of her shoulders, pecs and back. Larry was as perfectly pressed and tailored as ever in tan slacks and a black short-sleeved knit.

Nate was wearing a surf shirt and knee-length Dockers, and he was enthusiastically discussing something with Larry. Kelsey was leaning back in her chair, her hair shimmering in the Tiki lights, curling over her bare shoulders. Her dress was a flowered strapless concoction that clung to every curve of her body. She was listening to the man in the chair at her left, Jorge Marti.

Jorge looked good. Dark, handsome, he was the only one in a jacket. His navy shirt was open at the throat underneath the beige blazer. Like Kelsey, he had the knack of looking both well-dressed and casual. Whatever he was saying to her was making her laugh.

Before joining the group, Dane discreetly took a few photos. Then he slid the small waterproof camera into the pocket of his black windbreaker and strode over to join them at their table.

Kelsey heard him coming and looked up. He couldn't tell if she was pleased by his arrival or not. Cindy, as always, jumped up with the effusive pleasure she showed to all her friends. "Dane, we were afraid you weren't coming."

"Sorry I'm late," he said, sitting and picking up a menu, though he knew it by heart. "Jorge, how are you doing?"

"Great, thanks. You?"

"Moving right along," he said. "I hope I didn't keep you all from ordering?"

"We're in the Keys," Larry said. "We're not supposed to be in any hurry. We planned on giving you half an hour, at least. Then we figured we'd spend another fifteen minutes being disappointed that you hadn't joined us."

"I knew you'd show," Nate said. "By the way, those

hidden cameras worked great. Fired a kid today. Caught him right on tape with his hand in the till. Thanks, man. You saved me a bundle."

"What can I say? Security works," Dane said.

"I guess it's good," Larry volunteered. He smiled at Kelsey across the table. "I don't know. At work, I feel like Big Brother is watching. The frigging cameras move. They follow you around."

Dane gave him a rueful smile. "Good cameras. They're probably expensive. They must think highly of the work you do."

Larry sniffed. "Either that, or they think we're going to make off with all their art supplies. Ah, well, such is corporate life."

"Since Dane is here, let's order," Cindy said. She looked at the suddenly silent group. "Okay, it's the Keys, but I live here all the time, and I'm starving."

Laughter followed her words. Nate summoned the waiter, and they ordered. "I hope you're not disappointed," he said. "This place isn't exactly gourmet."

"We'll go gourmet another night," Kelsey assured him. "Tonight we'll go with friendship and down-home good food."

"Thanks, sweetie." He lifted his glass toward her. She lifted hers in return. "To the best ex-wife I've ever had."

"Thanks. Of course, I'm the *only* ex-wife you've ever had."

"Scary to think I could have gotten married over and over again." Nate shuddered. "I think you've made me a single man for the rest of my life."

"Great, there's a real testimonial," Kelsey groaned.

"No, no, I didn't mean it that way," Nate protested.

"None of us really seem cut out for marriage. Take Cindy, for instance. She may end up an old maid."

"Thanks for the compliment," Cindy murmured.

"We're all in the same boat. I'm a reformed man, Dane doesn't show the least inclination toward marriage, God knows what goes on in Kelsey's mind, Jorge, you're still on the loose. And Larry...Larry and Sheila were a total disaster."

"We weren't a total disaster. I still love her," Larry said.

"Sheila wasn't meant for marriage," Jorge said, without meeting Larry's eyes.

Larry shrugged. "You guys don't all have to stare at your drinks. Let's face it, my ex-wife has hopped into bed with every guy here." He lifted a hand before any of them could protest. "Not while we were married— not with you guys, anyway—and if I'm wrong, I don't want to know. But it's true, I still love her."

Dane noticed that Kelsey was staring at her ex-husband. He wondered if she knew about her ex's relationship with Sheila, or that he had been just as big a lech as any other man alive.

"Okay, here's to you for being such a decent guy," Cindy said. "But you know what? Guys will sleep with anyone."

"Oh, yeah. I'm just a walking pile of testosterone," Larry said.

Cindy had to laugh. Even Dane felt the twitch of a smile at the other man's mournful tone. "Kelsey says you're dating a model."

"She *is* pretty gorgeous," Larry admitted.

Cindy continued. "That's the problem. There just

aren't that many decent guys out there anymore. And all the ones I know are my old friends."

"That doesn't mean we aren't willing to oblige you in any way you might desire," Larry told her, grinning.

"See what I mean? You're dating a gorgeous model, but you're ready to oblige me."

"Hey, I was kidding. Besides, who knows what the future holds? It's awfully easy to find yourself available. I learned that the hard way."

Cindy smiled. "Poor Larry. I'll keep the offer in mind—for the future, of course. I just hate to lose a really good friend by dating him."

"Hey, Kels didn't just date me. She married me and divorced me, and we're still friends," Nate said. "But then, I took the divorce awfully well."

Kelsey stared at him, shaking her head. "Nate…"

"Hey, it's your loss. Isn't that what they say?"

"My loss. You're a good guy, Nate," Kelsey assured him.

"Hey, at least she divorced you before sleeping with half the town," Larry said.

"You know, Larry, you have Kelsey in the office with you all the time," Cindy pointed out.

Kelsey groaned. "I never date co-workers."

"And she means it, dammit," Larry said.

Kelsey shrugged. "I hate to lose friends, too, and I also hate the idea of being uncomfortable at work if it didn't work out."

"Good policy," Jorge said. "You should never date clients, either." He spoke casually, but when he met Dane's eyes, he blushed, despite his dark complexion, and looked uncomfortable. Dane wondered just how much his friends knew about what had happened in St. Augustine. Enough, apparently.

"This whole conversation is depressing me," Cindy said.

"In that case, we'll talk about something else," Larry told her.

"Oh!" Cindy said. "Did you hear that they dug up another skeleton in the Everglades?"

A dead silence followed her words. Dane studied the faces around him, wondering whether they were afraid to ask if the remains might belong to Sheila.

Kelsey sounded as if she was strangling as she asked, "Bones? Just…bones?"

"Uh-huh," Cindy said. "They've been out there almost a year. That's what they reported on the evening news, anyway. Apparently the police suspect that the woman might have been a victim of the Necktie Strangler. They've already managed to ID her. Another stripper, thank God. Lord, that sounds awful, doesn't it? It's not that I have anything against strippers. Everybody has to make a living. Except that it seems the victims were all prostitutes on the side. And that's why I'm grateful. This guy is targeting a certain kind of woman. If there was a killer on the loose who chose his victims randomly…well, I know I'm not desperate enough to start hooking, so I don't have to be afraid of my own shadow."

"You should always be careful," Dane told her.

"I wish we knew where Sheila was," Nate said.

"Sheila doesn't work in a strip club," Jorge said.

"But the way she behaves…" Larry murmured.

"Right. Taking off without letting anyone know," Cindy said firmly, refusing to acknowledge any similarities with the dead women. "Sheila is fine, and she'll show up soon. I know it."

There was silence again.

"Wow, what a fun time we're having," Nate groaned. "Anybody here have anything cheerful to talk about?" Nate said. "So far we've gone through failed marriage, the lack of romance in our lives, our worry about Sheila, and, just to make us all a little more anxious, we've thrown in a serial killer."

Jorge turned to Kelsey, who was still looking worried. "Sheila is going to be all right."

No, she's not, Dane wanted to shout.

Which would be an insane move.

"We can talk about politics," Cindy suggested.

Nate groaned more loudly this time. "Hell, let's throw in abortion, gun control and religion. We won't have to worry about being old friends by the end of the night."

"Hey, Kelsey," Jorge said. "Are you planning on doing any painting while you're down here?"

"Maybe. I haven't done any in a long time," she said.

Jorge began talking about some of the areas she might want to sketch. Then Cindy asked Dane about his work, while Nate and Larry turned to a discussion about a new rock group from the Keys that was starting to gain national prominence. The food came and went; coffee and dessert were served. Dane glanced at his watch.

He looked across the table to find that Kelsey was studying him. He leaned as close to her as he could. "You're not visiting anyone tonight, are you?"

She arched a brow. "I'm here with friends."

"Stay with them," he told her. Then he rose. "I've

got to get going. This was great, seeing everyone. And just to assure you all of the success of my career, let me get the check, Nate."

Nate grinned. "Hell, no. I'm getting it here. You can get it on…say Monday. We'll try that nouvelle cuisine place right down the road. It will be much cheaper for me that way."

"Nate!" Kelsey protested.

Dane was unperturbed. "That's fine with me. Monday night. Seven again?"

"Seven," Cindy agreed. "Ugh. Monday is a workday."

"That from Miss Workaholic," Jorge teased.

"True—usually. But with us all together now…I'd love to just play for a few days. Head out to the beach. Go boating, diving, exploring. Like when we were kids."

"Actually I wasn't part of most of your excursions back in those days," Jorge said. "I feel a bit like an intruder here. Sure you want me along?"

"Oh, definitely," Kelsey said, looking at Jorge.

"Of course we want you to join us," Cindy said.

"You've got to be there," Dane said, nodding his agreement with the others. "Nate, thanks for dinner. The Sea Shanty rules, as always. Good night, all."

He waved and headed out, taking the path for the parking lot.

He hesitated, hearing a rustle in the bushes. He looked back.

He could see a touch of color through the foliage. Someone's shirt?

He walked again.

Listened.

Yup. He was being followed.

Chapter 9

Earlier Kelsey had planned to leave the Sea Shanty and head straight back to the duplex for a tub of hot water, a cup of tea, a Tylenol P.M. and a night's sound sleep.

Instead she forced herself to sit tight for a moment when Dane left, then feigned a yawn and begged off. She left quickly and followed Dane's footsteps. When he stopped to light a cigarette, she froze. As soon as he was in his Jeep and heading out of the lot, she ran for her own car, gunned the engine and sent pebbles flying as she hurried to catch him. He had entered the flow of traffic, heading north.

Her hands were shaking on the wheel. Dane knew something he wasn't telling. She was sure of it.

Of course, she wasn't giving him all the information *she* had, either. Meanwhile, she was determined to follow him tonight.

Dane's relationship with Sheila still disturbed her.

Why? She shouldn't have been surprised that he had slept with Sheila. It hadn't been anything new. They had been a duo all through high school, after all. And she hadn't needed to find the earring or hear from Dane himself that he had been with Sheila. When she had first reached Key Largo and Sheila hadn't been there, she had heard right away from Cindy that Sheila had been seeing Dane.

Before that, on the phone, Sheila had told her that she was seeing him, though there had been a strange wistful tone to her voice that hadn't seemed to fit the words.

Kelsey realized how badly she wanted to believe in Dane. She didn't know why. Maybe it was impossible to be with him without feeling an attraction. After all, he had been Joe's best friend. There for most of her life. Older, handsome, assured, determined on his future, confident in his ability to get where he wanted to go.

Or maybe it was just because of *that* night.

As she drove, trying to focus on following the Jeep, she found that a certain honesty was bubbling to the surface.

She shouldn't have come to Key Largo. She had been married to Nate—a disaster from start to finish—but she didn't feel a thing when she was near him except for an old affection. She'd spent one night with Dane and all she had to do was see his face to feel a rush of sexual longing so strong it was humiliating. She could tell herself whatever she wanted, she could lie or hide it from others, but it was hard to keep the truth from herself. She didn't want to mistrust Dane, she didn't want to think that he had come home to waste his life, and she hadn't wanted to believe he had been back with Sheila.

But he had been.

She was able to keep a safe distance behind him while the highway was divided into four lines. But then they hit US1 on the way back to the mainland and Florida City. The road narrowed to two lanes and there were several cars between them at that point, so she could no longer see his Jeep.

But there was nowhere for him to go except north. She stuck to the tail of the car ahead of her as she drove. She didn't know why, but she hadn't expected Dane to leave Key Largo. She hadn't expected such a long drive, but, checking her gas tank, she knew she was fine. As long as she didn't lose him once they reached Florida City.

Coming up to Florida City, she strained to catch sight of his Jeep. She found him and followed, taking the ramp onto the turnpike.

At the toll booth, she had to scramble for change to get through. He had shot on ahead of her. She hit the gas hard, trying to keep up. Eventually he took the turnoff for South Miami. Amazingly she didn't lose him when he exited, back onto US1. He didn't drive far from the exit. She saw the Jeep pull into the parking lot of a strip club.

She drove by once, then returned and entered the parking lot. She surveyed the area. The club was called Legs. It sat in the middle of the parking lot; a strip mall stretched behind the freestanding building. Ironically the mall included a day care center, a health food store, a coffee shop, an insurance agency and a gym.

The parking spaces nearest the club were filled. The lot was large, stretching back to where a border of trees separated the property from the gas station next door.

Floodlights illuminated the area, so though the area by the trees seemed a bit dark and foreboding, the rest of the parking lot seemed to be fine.

Kelsey found a space in the far back row, next to the trees. She parked the car but remained in it, staring at the club. She wasn't sure what to do. She'd never been inside a place like that before and had no idea if single women ever just wandered into such a place. She'd been invited once to go on a girls' night out to a male strip club, but something had come up at the office, and she'd been too tired to join the others.

She sat in the car for another couple of minutes, then got angry with herself. She was an adult. Surely she could walk into such an establishment without feeling like a guilty child.

Of course, she wanted to walk in without Dane seeing her, and without attracting attention.

Only one thing to do.

She exited the car and strode across the parking lot. Odd, she already felt as if she were walking peculiarly.

The door opened as she approached it. She was afraid she would find herself immediately accosted by a bunch of drunks.

There were no drunks, just the doorman. Or bouncer. He wasn't more than six feet even, but his shoulders appeared to be about three feet wide. He was wearing a casual suit and had a pleasant smile. "Welcome to Legs," he told her.

"Thanks," she murmured. She started to walk by, blinking to adjust to the dark and smoky club where, strangely enough, a country tune was playing.

"Excuse me," the man called to her.

"Yes?"

"I'm sorry, there's a cover. Pay right over there."

"Oh, of course."

So much for not attracting attention. She saw the booth where a woman was sitting. She wasn't exactly topless, but strategic lace-rimmed holes in her shirt meant she might as well be.

Kelsey tried not to stare as she paid the admission, then slipped into the club. She was grateful that she could slink around the back of the room, far from the stage, and take a seat in a dark corner.

She wasn't sure what she had expected. A pack of dirty old men with scraggly cheeks and beer bellies, all leaning around the stage, tongues hanging out.

Maybe she'd been watching too much television.

The club was actually rather nice. She had expected something seedy, with dirty floors, dank walls and rough, litter-strewn tables. But though the place was dark and smoky, the tables surrounding the stage were clean, polished wood, sporting candles and even fresh flowers. She liked the darkness; it allowed her to feel invisible.

She looked around. The customers were not what she'd expected.

For the most part, they were clean-shaven. Or, if they had facial hair, it seemed to be trimmed and in good order. Some were dressed casually in denims and polo shirts, and some were in suits.

Some were with women. *Normal*-looking women.

Okay, Kelsey, she asked herself, just what is normal?

It wasn't time to get into a philosophical debate with herself. She had come to find out what Dane was doing.

At the moment, country music was playing because the performance was…country. The girl on stage was a tall, beautiful blonde. As Kelsey took her chair, the girl was removing her hat and swirling her hair. She wore a white-tasseled skirt and matching jacket and moved with a sensuality that defied the wholesome lyrics of the song.

The cocktail waitress who came to her table was wearing a short black skirt and low-cut silver bustier. She was pleasant and professional, and didn't seem either surprised or annoyed when Kelsey asked for soda water with lime.

There were catcalls rising around the room. The girl on stage shed the short skirt to reveal a G-string, a pretty piece of nothing so studded with rhinestones that they might as well have been glued to her skin.

"Hi there."

Kelsey looked up. A nicely dressed, older man with steel gray hair was standing by her table.

"Hi."

"Are you alone?" he asked. "Want company?"

"No...I'm waiting for my fiancé. But thank you."

She breathed a sigh of relief when he moved away. The waitress returned with her drink, and this time she seemed to eye Kelsey curiously.

"Thanks," Kelsey told her.

The woman smiled. "You look nervous. Don't worry. They don't let guys come on too hard to the women here—customers or dancers—unless it's obvious that's what they want. Did you come here looking for some action?" she asked.

"No, I...I'm waiting for my fiancé."

"Sure."

The woman wasn't going to press it, but Kelsey knew she wasn't buying that for a minute. "Actually,

I've never been in a place like this. I just wanted to see what it was like."

The waitress smiled again. "You mean you followed your old man here to find out if he was just out with the guys or ordering a private lap dance?"

Kelsey was surprised to hear herself laugh. "No, honestly, I just came to see what the club was all about."

The woman suddenly frowned. "You're not from the press, are you? This really is a decent establishment, and after Cherie was found, the cops and the news people were all over us. If you're here to start writing more moralistic trash—"

"I'm not! I swear, I'm not a reporter," Kelsey said.

"All right, then," the woman said, nodding. "If you need any help—if any of these guys come on too strong—you let me know."

"Thanks. Thanks very much."

The woman shook her head. "You look like a babe in the woods," she said as she walked away.

Kelsey was a little irritated by the remark. The cocktail waitress didn't look as if she could be over twenty-two by any stretch of the imagination. She knew she was definitely older, and surely more mature, than her newfound champion.

A babe in the woods…

Her eyes scanned the tables, and at last she saw Dane. He was in the front row. He had a drink in front of him, something clear with lime. Just like hers. Dane was drinking soda water, too. His attention was on the cowgirl, who had shed the white-fringed top.

The woman on stage was beautiful. Perfectly built. Kelsey wondered why she had always thought that only desperate women would take to dancing like this for an income. This woman could clearly do whatever she wanted, and yet she was here.

The woman moved along the stage, dancing, achieving positions that surely were matched only by the world's best contortionists. Her eyes were on Dane, and he seemed to be returning the stare.

"Hey there, cutie."

This time the man who approached Kelsey slid right into the chair across from her. He was younger, and one of the scruffier-looking patrons in the place. She met his eyes across the table. "I'm not alone."

"Sure looks that way."

From her purse, her cell phone started ringing. She dived for her bag, wondering who was calling her at this hour, yet glad of the chance to pick up the phone and end this conversation before it began. She stared at the man as she hit the talk button. "Do you mind?"

He didn't move.

"Kelsey? Kelsey, is that you?" It was Larry on the other end.

"Yes, sweetheart, it's me," she said.

"Sweetheart?" Larry echoed dubiously.

"What's up?" she asked cheerfully.

"I was worried. You didn't come back. I was afraid you'd decided to take off and throttle old man Latham or something like that."

"No, I'm fine."

"What the hell is that music in the background?"

"I'm having a drink."

"Kelsey, you don't sound like yourself. And you called *me* sweetheart. If you're in any kind of trouble, I'll come and get you, wherever you are."

"That's wonderful. But I'm fine." She lowered her

voice, made it soft and husky. "We'll discuss all that… later."

"Kelsey, now I'm really worried."

"Oh, don't be worried." She stared at the man at her table. "No one's bothering me here. I know you're built like Conan the Barbarian, honey, but you really don't need to rush to my rescue. Honestly, I can handle myself."

To her surprise, either she sounded good or she must have looked as if she meant it. The man threw up his hands, rose irritably and walked away.

"Kelsey, since when have I been built like Conan the Barbarian? You aren't making the least bit of sense. Where the hell are you?"

"Just at a club, having a soda. Larry, I know I'm sounding ridiculous, but, please, it's okay. I'll explain later. Don't worry about me. I swear I'm fine, and I promise I'll call you if I have any problem whatsoever. Bye now. Get some sleep."

She clicked off before he could keep talking.

She did so just in time to keep Larry from really worrying, since it seemed that the entire place was now kicking into a chorus of "Home on the Range" to go along with the antics of the cowgirl on stage. The girl had lost all semblance of a top, and her bottom half was the next closest thing to completely bare.

The men in the place had all made an almost comical shift, leaning closer to the stage, even those men who were with their wives or girlfriends.

The cowgirl lay down and started gyrating sensuously on her back again. Then she got up and, with the sinuous movements of a prowling cat, she made her way to the tables closest to the stage. She was there to accept money from the appreciative audience, and there was only one place for them to put the bills they were eagerly pulling from their wallets.

As Kelsey watched, Dane leaned forward, tucking one in. He smiled at the cowgirl, who seemed to watch him a second longer than the other men who added to her collection.

Kelsey realized that she was grinding her teeth and staring down at her soda as if she had been watching something not just sexual, but intimate. It made her furious with Dane, despite the logic flooding through her and telling her that she had no reason to be offended— he was an adult male without a commitment to any woman, so he certainly had the right to attend a strip club and slide bills into a dancer's G-string if he chose.

She wanted to slosh a drink over his head.

"You seem to be doing all right, honey."

She was startled to find the waitress standing at her side, giving her a broad grin.

"I'm fine, thanks." She noticed that Dane's waitress had gone back to his table. He was talking with the girl, and he had taken something from the pocket of his jacket and was showing it to her.

"Want another soda water?"

"Pardon?"

"Another soda water?"

"Sure, thank you."

"That's Katia," the waitress said. "She's the best. I wish I could move like that."

"So do I," Kelsey murmured, and realized she meant it. Katia the cowgirl had evidently had years of dance lessons before beginning her career with the pole.

"She's a nice woman."

Kelsey looked up at the waitress. For some reason the woman seemed bent on proving to Kelsey that the people who worked there weren't as shady as most people supposed.

"I'm sure she is."

The waitress was staring at the stage. "She and Cherie were really good friends."

Kelsey instantly remembered the news articles she had scanned at Dane's. "Cherie…she was the girl who worked here who…was murdered."

The waitress, still looking at the stage, nodded. "She was a really sweet kid. Some guy had broken her heart, but she was determined to make it through school and get ahead in life. She always quoted that old adage about success being the best revenge. I knew…I knew she was giving some guys more than lap dances, and…I guess she went off with the wrong one."

"Aren't you afraid now when you leave here?" Kelsey asked her.

"Hey, Sophie! We need another round over here," a heavyset man in a business suit called. He was at a table with a number of well-dressed Japanese men.

"Coming," the waitress called. She told Kelsey quickly, "Since I'm Sophie—Sophie Smithfield—I guess I'd better get moving. I'll be back."

The waitress moved on. The cowgirl had left the stage, and "Sheherazade" was being announced next. The music changed to something Arabic and exotic. The new dancer was definitely exotic herself; she was almond skinned, with dark slanting eyes and a head of rich dark hair that cascaded down her back.

Kelsey watched Dane again. He was leaning back in his chair, arms crossed over his chest as he watched the stage. The waitress approached him again, slipping him a note.

A few minutes later, he rose and walked toward the back of the club, disappearing through a door at the left. Kelsey gave thanks for the darkness, which had kept him from seeing her.

Frustrated, she stared after him. She felt the rise of illogical anger once again.

"Another soda," Sophie said, arriving at her side and placing the drink in front of her.

"Thanks. I'll take the check, too, I guess."

"Sure thing. Oh, you asked if I was afraid to work here now. Not really. There's a super nice homicide guy on the case. He seems to really care that Cherie was killed. And he told us that this guy is no idiot. He'll move on and choose his next victim somewhere else—if they can't catch him first, of course."

"That's good to hear. But you've still got to be really careful, you know."

"Of course."

Sophie gave her the check, and Kelsey produced a large bill and told Sophie to keep the change.

"That's really nice of you."

"Thanks. *You* were really nice. I might have felt like a real idiot, sitting here by myself, but talking to you helped."

"Come back sometime."

"I might. I swear I'm not a reporter or a cop, but I might ask you more about Cherie sometime, if you don't mind."

"Why?"

"I have a friend who is missing."

"A dancer?"

"No, but…well, it's complicated. I'll explain some-time."

"Sure, and thanks again."

Sophie started to walk away. Kelsey rose and stopped her quickly. "Sophie, that door back there…where does it lead?"

"Back there? That's where the guys go to get private lap dances."

Sophie smiled and moved on. Patrons were calling her again.

Kelsey made her way out of the club, then hesitated just outside the door. One of the floodlights that had illuminated the parking lot had evidently burned out. The lot suddenly seemed very dark, and she was parked across the way, under the trees.

As she stood there, the door opened behind her. She almost jumped. It was just a couple, leaving for the night. They gave Kelsey a friendly smile and moved past her.

She sprang into action herself, moving quickly across the parking lot.

Shadows seemed to lurk everywhere.

The couple's car was close to the door. Kelsey's was not. They got into their car. She kept walking.

A shadow loomed, looking high and tall. She thought it was a man, then realized it was just one of the trees separating the parking lot from the gas station beyond.

She exhaled a sigh of relief and purposely slowed her footsteps, since she could hear the thumping of her heart. She didn't know why she was suddenly so scared. There was no real reason, except that it was night.

And a girl had left here one night, never to return.

Her decomposed body had been found floating in a canal.

She heard laughter and spun around.

Just another couple leaving.

She kept walking, her pace quickening once again. Then, like Lot's wife, she found herself turning back.

The entry to the club was in deep shadow, the bouncer nowhere in sight. There was definitely the shadow of a man this time.

And he was watching her. As he moved from the doorway to the parking lot, she was certain he was looking directly at her. Without the floodlight, she couldn't see his face, couldn't tell anything about him. Except that he was tall, his build formidable.

Even at a distance, she heard his footsteps in the otherwise silent parking lot. Sharp, fast, coming her way.

Her keys were out. She clicked the button to unlock her car and moved briskly toward it. The footsteps kept coming. She quickened her pace. Behind her, the footsteps quickened, as well.

Kelsey began to run.

She reached her car door and threw it open, sliding into the driver's seat. She reached for the door handle to slam the car shut.

But a hand fell on the frame of the door, stopping her.

"Not so fast!"

Kelsey opened her mouth to let out an earsplitting scream.

Nate Curry looked down the length of the bar, saw that everyone seemed to have a full glass and gave a little nod of satisfaction. He'd brought on a new kid, a college junior from the University of Miami, so he wouldn't have to feel so wed to the place himself. Since he'd been joining his friends tonight, he hadn't planned on working at all, but hell, being here, he had to kick in. Especially since he was down one employee, after uncovering the thefts. But the new kid, Bill Edgeham, seemed to have everything under control. The Saturday night band was playing as usual, conch fritters and chowder were being served right and left, the tables were filled, and the bar was busy. A good Saturday night—even if the gang had all departed long before he had thought they would. Kelsey and Cindy usually loved to dance. And it was fun to party with the old crowd. Fun…and, of course, intriguing as all hell.

He still felt uneasy. He wished Kelsey hadn't left so quickly. And he wished that she'd gone straight home, which he knew she hadn't. Larry had called earlier to say she hadn't returned to the duplex, wondering if Nate knew where she was. He was worried about her; she was so determined to delve where she shouldn't in her attempt to find Sheila.

At the end of the bar, he picked up the phone and called the duplex.

Larry picked up. "Have you heard from Kelsey yet?" Nate asked, trying not to sound too anxious.

"Yeah, I talked to her."

"Well, where the hell is she?"

"At some club. I don't know what she's doing. She sounded strange, kept calling me sweetheart, and said something about me being built like Conan the Barbarian."

Nate frowned. "You?"

"Hey, I resent that. I'm in good shape."

"Yeah, but hardly Mr. Universe."

"Don't go sounding jealous on me. She didn't mean anything by it. She said she was at a club. She was probably just talking like that to keep the sharks away, though what the hell she was doing in a club to begin with if she was avoiding sharks, I don't know."

"But she was all right?"

"She said she was fine, and that she'd call me if she had any problem."

Nate couldn't help feeling a little rise of resentment, even though he'd barely been married to Kelsey for a month, and that many years ago now. She'd cried rivers when she'd broken it off with him, sorry that she had used him as solace the way she had, begging him to forgive her. She'd sworn that she would always love him—as a friend.

He wound the phone cord around his fingers. Kelsey and Sheila. As different as night and day. Kelsey, who felt she'd sinned the minute she was with him, because she had to admit both to herself and to him that she didn't love him.

Sheila, who was generous to a fault. Heedless of anything she did with a guy, whether she loved him or not.

And here he was, feeling a rush of heat to his face and a burn of anger in his soul because Kelsey had said that she would call Larry if she needed anything. Well, what the hell. He and Kelsey had hardly been married. Kelsey and Larry worked together.

But I'm closer to you, Kelsey. Closer in your heart. And I know you. Even if you've forgotten the time when we were close. I remember. I'm the one you should depend on.

"Nate, you there?" Larry asked.

"Yeah, sorry. Well, I was just worried. But since you've talked to her and know that she's okay, then I'll quit worrying."

"I never said she was okay. She's got me worried. She's obsessed with finding Sheila." Larry's sigh came through loud and clear. "She just hasn't gotten it yet, that Sheila will show up when she's ready."

Nate felt a prickling at his nape. "Yeah, sure."

"If Kelsey doesn't get back soon, I'll call you."

"You're going to stay up?"

"Sure. I've got work here with me. I can always stay up."

"All right. See ya. And tell Kelsey to give me a call in the morning. Unless you don't hear from her. Then call me, because I'll be worried."

"Of course."

Nate hung up and turned just in time to see Andy Latham, his eyes wild, standing on the other side of the bar.

"Latham, I told you, you can't come here anymore. The women complain."

Latham shot out a fist, catching Nate hard in the jaw before he could duck.

"Damn!"

Dane swore as he clamped his hand over Kelsey's mouth. He looked around the parking lot. No one was anywhere near them, and the music blaring from the club would drown out pretty much anything, anyway.

Cars were going by on US1, but not one of them had even slowed.

"What the hell are you trying to do, get me arrested?" he asked Kelsey angrily.

She caught his fingers, drawing his hand from her mouth. Her blue-green eyes met his with a narrowed anger. "What the hell are *you* trying to do, give me a heart attack?"

"I followed you out to your car. Hell, you saw me. You turned around and looked right at me."

"I saw *someone*. I didn't know it was you. Why the hell were you following me like that?" she demanded.

"That's not the question of the hour," he told her, voice harsher than he had intended. It was disturbing, though, to realize how easily he had been able to accost her.

And the way that she had screamed…without anyone noticing at all.

"Why were *you* following *me*?" he demanded, his words sharp.

She stared at him where he leaned against the open car door.

"What makes you think I was following you?" she asked.

"How about the fact that you jumped up the minute I left dinner, and then you followed me."

"Maybe not. Maybe I just decided to check this place out on the same night you did." She didn't intend to admit a thing.

"Kelsey, you suck as a liar."

"Say that I actually *did* follow you. Maybe my reasons were entirely innocent."

Dane felt himself growing impatient. "Entirely innocent? Right. You followed a man to a strip club. What were your innocent reasons? You decided to get your jollies by watching me get a lap dance?"

Kelsey looked away from him, hating the flush that filled her cheeks. "Don't be ridiculous."

"Then what do you think you were doing?"

"Trying to figure out what *you* were doing."

"Stuffing money into G-strings. That was obvious, I'm certain. But then I know I don't have to tell you anything, because you were watching me from the minute you walked into the club."

She looked startled. "You didn't see me. I was in the—"

"Kelsey, I knew you were following me all the way north, and I saw you the minute you tried to walk in without paying."

"I didn't know you had to pay!"

"Kelsey, I don't know what the hell to do with you. I've told you often enough that you have to trust me. All you do is get yourself into trouble. So far, you've had a confrontation with Latham, and you've gotten me into a fight with Izzy Garcia. One would think you would have gone home tonight. Will you please listen to me now? I want to find Sheila just as much as you do. More. Dammit, Kelsey, let me handle it."

She looked straight ahead again. "I can see how you were handling it."

"Did it bother you?" he inquired, amazed that he could feel amused.

"Your sex life is your own concern."

"I don't know, Kelsey. You're looking like a disapproving schoolmarm at the moment."

"I don't give a damn if you fu—" She cut herself off, fell silent, then said, "I'm just not real sure that your current…techniques will do anything to help in your investigation."

"Kelsey, this *is* a strip club."

"A strip club where a murder victim worked," Kelsey said.

Dane exhaled a long breath, shaking his head. "Isn't that the point? I'm here, therefore you don't have to be."

"I do have to be," she said stubbornly. "You're following the tracks of a murderer known as the Necktie Strangler." She looked at him then with a certain naked anguish in her eyes. "You think that Sheila is dead, don't you?"

He was silent for a long time. Then he told her, "Move over."

"Move over? You don't need to ride with me. Your Jeep is here."

"Yeah, and we'll just leave it here for now. I don't particularly like the idea of you riding back down to Key Largo alone."

"Dane, I drive alone all the time. I'm a career woman, living alone in Miami, a fairly street smart kid."

"It's almost an hour's drive back. Move over."

"You know, I don't have to go back to Key Largo tonight. My condo is fifteen minutes away, just down US1, on Brickell. I'll be fine."

He straightened and quickly walked around to the passenger side, then opened the door and sat before she could think to lock him out.

"Go. I'm just dying to see your condo."

"You're not going to stay at my condo. Certainly not tonight," she told him.

There she was, he thought. The imperious Kelsey.

"I touched a stripper? Does that make me diseased?"

"You didn't need to touch a stripper to be an unwanted houseguest, Dane," she said flatly.

"You want to talk, Kelsey? Get to the bottom of some things? Then drive."

She stared stubbornly at the windshield, jaw clenched. He was sure she was mulling over the possibility of dragging him out of her car.

Evidently she thought better of it.

She twisted her key in the ignition. The car roared to life.

"I hope they tow your Jeep," she said.

"Oh, I doubt it. The club stays open until 5:00 a.m., and by then the coffee shop is open, so there's no reason why there shouldn't be a car parked in the lot."

"Sounds like you know the place well," she said, eyes on the road as she pulled out on to the highway.

"Well enough."

"I see."

"Just drive, Kelsey."

Chapter 10

It felt strange, having Dane come into her condominium with her, Kelsey thought. He always seemed to be observing everything, dark eyes watching as she flashed her pass to the guard on duty at the gate, looking over the parking beneath the building, noting the security cameras in the lobby as they walked to the elevators.

He didn't speak, and neither did she, as they rode to the fifteenth floor. He gave his attention to the hallway again as they left the elevator and walked to her unit.

"How many apartments on each floor?" he asked.

"Four. There are actually four towers," she told him, opening her front door. "Four apartments on each of sixteen floors per tower. In the center of the building, there's a rec room, and out back, a pool."

He followed her into the condo. She turned on the lights, wondering why it felt so odd to have Dane here.

Because, she decided, this was *her* life now. Her

life in which she had moved forward. It wasn't part of the past.

The past was what should bother her. But it had been comfortable, being back at Hurricane Bay, though maybe it had been comfortable in a bad way. She had experienced a proprietary feeling at Hurricane Bay that she never should have felt. The place was his. Just because she had been welcome all the time as a child, that didn't give her any right to feel as if she were home when she was there.

She stood in the hallway, waiting as he surveyed the entry, living room and kitchen. He walked to the large plate-glass window and looked out on the bay.

"Nice view."

"Yes."

"Small rooms."

She shrugged. "It's an expensive area. This is what I could afford. I took it because I do like the view."

He stared out the window for a moment, then turned to her. "Aren't you going to offer me something?"

"You want a drink?"

He laughed. "You sound as if you've joined the Temperance League. No, I don't mean a drink. Coffee or tea would be nice."

She walked into the kitchen and opened the refrigerator. "Regular, flavored or decaf?"

"Regular."

He remained by the window, just staring out, as she measured coffee and poured water. While the coffee brewed, she came around the counter, leaned against the wall and watched him.

"Well?"

"Well what?"

"We're here so you can tell me why you're trying to track Sheila down at a strip club," she reminded him.

He turned and looked at her, studying her in silence for a minute. "Kelsey, I keep telling you to stay out of this. And I mean it. You're dangerous to yourself and everyone else. But I have the feeling there's something you're not telling me. That you have an insight into the whole thing that I'm missing. From just about the minute you showed up, you were on *my* tail over Sheila's disappearance. *Mine.*"

"That's not fair. You're the one who followed me over to Latham's, and you were the one who went ballistic when I went to Izzy's boat to question him about Sheila."

"That was *after* you stormed after me. I was first. Why?"

She shrugged. "Come on, Dane. You know the reason. I got in, there was no Sheila. Cindy hadn't seen her since she'd been at Nate's place. Cindy suggested that I talk to you. She said you and Sheila had been talking at Nate's. She was convinced you two were doing a lot more than talking. And she was right." He didn't argue with her; just kept standing by the plate-glass window, watching her. "Cindy told me that you'd been different since you got back. Bitter in a way she'd never seen you before. And prone to, well, like the song says, wasting away in Margaritaville."

"There's more to it than that," he told her. "Unless you've really been carrying a grudge all these years. Andy Latham is downright slimy and scary, but you immediately decided to come after me, forgetting all about him until later that day. And Izzy is a pure sleaze, but you only decided that you just had to go talk to him today."

She was startled by his words, which were spoken dispassionately, as if he wasn't judging her, wasn't feeling offended.

"Don't be ridiculous," she said. "You were the last one seen with Sheila, that's all."

"That can't be all," he said, shaking his head, dark eyes on her intently, giving her the impression that she was a book being read. "When you were making plans to meet Sheila, she must have said something to you, implied something. And anything she said could be important now."

"She never said she was going to strip clubs, if that's what you mean."

Her comment didn't perturb him in the least. "So what did she say?"

"You mean...after she e-mailed me the first time?"

"Of course." His eyes narrowed suspiciously. "Did she write something else?"

"No," she lied.

He didn't know about the diary. But the diary hadn't really given her anything yet.

"Dammit, Kelsey, give me something to go on here."

"Why were you in that strip club?"

He stared at her for a long time. "Because I *am* trying to track down the Necktie Strangler. I didn't go in the back for a lap dance, Kelsey. I was showing the girls pictures of people."

"People? Who?"

"Andy Latham, Izzy Garcia..."

"And?"

"The cowgirl was good friends with the murdered

girl. She's going to study the photos I gave her and see if she can remember anyone."

"She couldn't tell you now?"

"She wasn't sure. She wanted to take time to look at all the faces. And I couldn't stay."

"Why?"

"You were leaving."

"I was only going to drive home."

"Yeah, sure."

"Where did you think I was going?"

"God knows. After your visit to Izzy, nothing would surprise me. Kelsey, will you please tell me about Sheila? What she said on the phone or in her e-mail. Anything that might help."

Kelsey hesitated, then shrugged. "I heard from her for the first time in ages when she e-mailed me after renting the other half of the duplex where Cindy was living. She said that being back as a permanent resident was strange. You were different and distant. One time she'd write that you needed help, the next time she'd write that *she* needed help. She was chatty about Nate and Cindy, and she wrote about Jorge and Izzy, as well. She admitted to drinking quite a bit, and I think—well, now I know—she was doing drugs, as well." Kelsey paused for a minute. "She wrote that she was having some strange problems, but that she didn't want to go into them. That her past was catching up with her. She said she really needed to see me. And that was why I decided to come down and spend a week with her."

"And that's it? That's why you were all over *me* first thing?"

Kelsey stared at him for a long moment. His dark eyes never wavered in their intense perusal of her.

"No."

"Then what?"

"She said that she needed to talk to you. Really talk to you. Because she was nervous."

"If she was nervous about something, and the some-thing was me, why would it be me she wanted to talk to?" he demanded.

Kelsey threw up her hands. "I don't know. But every-thing led to you. Her e-mails led to you, Cindy and Nate both told me about Sheila being with you at the bar, then going off after you. And that's the last time anyone saw her. And you admit to having a relationship with her."

"It wasn't a *relationship*," he murmured, looking away from her for a moment and staring out at the lights of the city again.

"Okay, so you slept with her."

"Once. And she couldn't have written to you about that, because that was the last time I saw her. And I told you how it happened."

She threw up her hands. "It's just that Sheila always implied something about you. And your name came up first with everyone. That's it. Really," she said.

Dane never seemed to give anything away in his voice, or with his eyes, his face. Yet she thought he looked relieved.

"So you aren't still bearing a grudge?"

She lowered her eyes. "We were one night, ages ago, in another lifetime."

"Yeah, well, we're feeling the same thing now."

"Oh? What?"

"That we both failed Sheila. But I'm begging you, Kelsey—please be careful. Don't follow me to strip clubs. Don't go to Latham's. Or to Izzy Garcia's. Give me a chance. Believe in me."

She watched him for a long moment. "Dammit it, Dane, I want to. But I want to know…things."

"Such as?"

"To start with, I want to know what happened in St. Augustine."

For a moment Kelsey thought he was going to remain silent, rejecting the question as totally irrelevant, but then he shrugged. "You really want to know? Right now?"

"You want me to trust you. To believe you really want to find Sheila. So let's start with what happened in St. Augustine." She was silent for a moment, then added, "Please. I'd really like to know."

"I'm not sure what you've heard," he said.

"Nothing, really. I suppose I was so determined to find Sheila that I didn't ask many questions. I know that something went wrong." She hesitated. "And that one of your clients was killed."

"Yes, a woman was killed. And she was more than a client," he said.

Kelsey thought he was going to end it there, he paused for so long.

"You'd been in St. Augustine for a while, right?" she asked, prodding despite the fact that he might turn around and inform her curtly that it really wasn't any of her business. He was silent again for a minute, then seemed to decide it didn't make any difference. He was still wary of her, and probably with good reason. It was true—she had gone after him, when she had first seen him at Nate's, as if he were the most detestable being alive, something she hadn't quite understood herself.

Or maybe she did. Better to go in attacking than be dismissed as an annoyance from the past. No, that wasn't quite it. Better to go in attacking than wonder how you could still want someone after so many years, still care so deeply when there had been so much so wrong.

"Right," he said, eyes on her as if he could see the soul beneath the flesh. "You really want the whole story?"

"I do."

"All right. I had been working up there for a couple of years. Nice life. I liked it. The ocean was still at my fingertips, but it wasn't Key Largo. And…I just didn't want to go back to Key Largo."

Kelsey understood what he meant.

"I'd heard you were up there," she murmured. She suddenly felt warm and uncomfortable, remembering the morning when he'd left. Three days after her brother's funeral. She hadn't seen him off at the small airport. She'd fled his house as if all the demons of hell had been after her. She could remember hearing his voice, calling her name. And she could remember seeing him standing at the top of his driveway, a towel around his hips, watching as she gunned her car and drove away.

He'd flown back to his base, and a week later, he'd been back overseas. His father had been dead by then, and Joe was gone, as well. He'd never called or written. The way he was watching her now, she knew they were both remembering that time.

"I knew the minute I went back after my leave that I wasn't going to become career military like my father. And St. Augustine seemed pleasantly tame after I'd gotten out of the service. Not that I hadn't opted for the kind of work I was doing in the Middle East and Eastern Europe. Joe loved to fly, and he was good, really good. I loved to filter into a different society and find out about the way people thought, and why, how they were likely to react to a situation. I liked the prospect that I could save lives by finding out about terrorist activities or ethnic purges before they could take place. My knowledge of a number of languages was useful, and with my strange coloring—both so dark and so light—it wasn't easy for anyone to figure out my ethnic background. I was young, and despite some of the horrors I had seen, I still believed in my own immortality. After Joe died, though, things just changed. I wasn't so sure that I was anything more than a grain of sand on an endless beach. I wasn't as sharp as I had been, and twice, I almost got myself killed. I had some money, so I found an agency in Key Largo to see to the maintenance of Hurricane Bay so I could wander around a while. Finally I knew I still wanted to live in Florida. Not too far south. Not too close to home. St. Augustine had history and a certain charm. The city was small, but not too small. It was on the water, but far from Hurricane Bay. Joe was gone, my father was gone, God knew what steps Sheila was taking to get where she wanted to go…and you had run."

"I hadn't really run. Not at that point. I went away to college," she said.

Dane shook his head. "No. You had already run. You were running the morning I last saw you. So there was no point in going home. Oh, Larry was coming and going, Cindy was around, and Nate was entrenched at the Sea Shanty, but I knew there was something of the past that we could never recapture, and I didn't want

to look back. I toyed with the idea of hiring on at a police department in the north of the state, but after my
years in the military, I wasn't ready to start taking orders again. So I got my license and opened an investigation firm. Which was tedious at times."

"From what I understand, very tedious," Kelsey said.
"Hours and hours of just sitting around, watching people."

"Sometimes, yes. But I was my own boss, so I could
take on the cases that interested me. Still, a lot of the
work I took on was small stuff. I wasn't going to save
the world with what I did, but I had to find a niche in
the civilian world, which isn't always easy when your
training has equipped you to infiltrate and—" He hesitated, looking at her again. "And kill people. Anyway,
I was good at what I did, so I started gaining a certain
respect in the area. I took a lot of cases in Jacksonville.
Bigger cases, more interesting cases. A few with some
really high profile companies. Sabotage, fraud. I had
a small but decent place on the water, a dock for the
Donzi…a good enough lifestyle in the off-hours, and
plenty of work to make me feel useful, and worthy of
the fairly exorbitant fees I charge. Then I met Kathy
Nottingham."

"The woman who died," Kelsey murmured.

"The first time she came into the office, she was very
nervous. She walked in, a beautiful young woman in
dark glasses. She didn't have a deep mystery about her,
though—she just wanted a standard service, information about her husband. I told her that I wasn't working domestic cases anymore. But then, when she finally
took off the glasses, I saw the shiner she'd been given.
She said she was clumsy, tripped, some excuse. The
usual. She wanted to have her husband followed. She

knew that he was seeing other women and she didn't care, she just wanted out, but he didn't intend to let her go. She had to find a way to force his hand. I tried to tell her again that I wasn't taking that kind of case, but there was something about her...I told her I knew she was lying, that she didn't need a P.I., she needed the police. But she was afraid that if she called the police, her husband would kill her. She said she had heard that I was discreet. She thought that if she had enough against her husband, she could get a divorce and custody of her children. I agreed to help her, if she'd get help herself. Anyway, to make a long story short, I couldn't budge her that day. She said that as long as he thought she'd be his good little wife at home, he'd shove her around a little but keep up with the life he was living. She had to operate in secret until she had enough to really get away.

"I started feeling really sorry for her. She'd been a poor kid who'd gotten married right out of high school to an older guy with an income. She'd gotten pregnant right away. And right away, he'd gotten angry when the dishes weren't set out on the table properly, when a piece of dirty clothing was left for a minute in the bathroom, when she wasn't perfect. At first he only yelled. Then he started pushing her around. Dragging her over to point out where a vase was off center or a glass had been left. She was so frightened that day that I finally swore I wouldn't give her away to anyone, and that I would help her. So I started to follow her husband. I got pictures and video of him in compromising situations. And when I'd see Kathy again, she'd be wearing more bruises.

"Finally I got really angry. I was afraid I was just going to go up to the guy and belt him in the jaw—

which wouldn't have helped her. I told her I couldn't help her anymore if she didn't get out, and I convinced her that no one should live with such abuse. She took her two little girls and left him, and headed straight into a shelter. Her husband realized how badly it could go against him when the first thing we did was get a restraining order against him. He sent his lawyer to give her anything she wanted. She was kinder and fairer than he deserved. She said it wasn't for him but for their children—she didn't want the girls to lose their father. Every kid had a right to love their parents—both of them. She was still afraid, but she went through with the divorce. I was with her in court, and afterward, I told him that if he ever touched her again, I'd kill him. He seemed to believe the threat. He acted as if he was ashamed, and just grateful that she was still going to let him see the kids. She got the house, custody, and he got a weekend with his daughters once a month. He wasn't allowed to go inside the house. He was to pick up the girls outside and return them outside. On the street, in full view of neighbors and passersby. Time went by, months, and she seemed to blossom like a rose. She got a job as a hostess at a restaurant. She was happy."

"And you two started seeing each other," Kelsey said.

"Right. She loved the water, boats…a day in the sun. Just existing, without being afraid. I enjoyed her company. She was so alive, intrigued by every little thing she hadn't experienced before."

"And then…?"

"Then one day he went to pick up the kids. And he ran her right into the garage door. She was pronounced dead on the way to the hospital."

"My God, I'm so sorry," Kelsey said. Silence

stretched between them. "He was arrested, right? He went to trial?"

"Oh yeah. He went to trial. The police had him before I could get my hands on him. I was so livid, I could have gone up for murder myself." He stopped and looked at Kelsey, a certain mistrust in his dark eyes again, along with a flat honesty. "He got out on bail, and I ran into him at a club and wound up in jail for a night. I might have killed him if I hadn't been stopped. When he went to trial, he got off with manslaughter. He convinced a jury that it had been a terrible accident, that he had thought he had his car in Reverse…anyway, he'll be out in a few years."

"Dane, that's horrible, and I'm so sorry, but how was it your fault?"

He sat, still staring out at the water. "I should have seen that the danger was still there, that he was homicidal, and that he wasn't really going to let her get away. There I was, a guy with his own P.I. agency, ex-military, and in the end, I couldn't do a damn thing to protect her. And the bastard got away with it."

Kelsey shook her head. "It's not your fault. No one can guard another human being every minute of the day. She decided he had the right to see his children. Because of that, he managed to kill her. What could you have done?"

"I could have—should have—seen just how deadly he could be. Most of the time, men who beat their wives are cowards who fold as soon as someone strikes back. He played the part. He was remorseful. He was ashamed. He said he knew he needed help. He was polite and followed the rules set up by the court. Kathy even believed that in time he might marry again and be decent to another woman. But all the while, he was just being devious and cunning, waiting for his opportunity. And when it came, he seized it, but because he'd been clever and played his part well, he got away with a vicious, premeditated murder."

"No one can really read another human being," Kelsey said.

"Yeah? Well, I should have been able to. So you were right. Bottom line, I fucked up big time in St. Augustine and came back to waste away in self-remorse. I just really didn't give a damn. I would have been happy to drink the hours away. It wasn't a sense of decency that made me open up an agency down here—sheer tedium did it. I couldn't drink enough to make the day any shorter. Then, after a while, I guess I became alcoholed out. And I didn't want to piss away everything my father had done. Cindy is a good kid, Nate's place is pleasant... I started thinking living down here again wasn't so bad. Then Sheila came around again. Seeing the way she was living should have scared the hell out of me. I found myself being disgusted and angry instead. I lectured her. But not enough. I slept with her. I shouldn't have. She'd asked me for a 'mercy fuck.' It was so wrong in so many ways. At the time I was still wallowing, but living and breathing. And now, according to all accounts, I was the last person around here to have seen her...to have seen her."

Kelsey wondered at his strange hesitation. It was as if he had been about to say *I was the last person around here to have seen her alive.*

"Except that I wasn't," he said flatly. Then he stared at her, impatient and angry. "The point is, I've screwed things up with Sheila, too, so you don't have to hound

me every step of the way and put yourself in jeopardy.
I intend to find out what happened to her, and I don't
need your money or your pressure to do it. In the mean-
time, though, I want you to stay the hell out of it. Do
you understand?"

His sudden about-face took her off guard. "You seem
convinced she ran into the Necktie Strangler," Kelsey
said, her voice rigid. "A guy who kills strippers and
prostitutes. I'm neither."

"Sheila didn't actually fit the description, either."

"She was running around, living the wild life,"
Kelsey said.

"And you're running in her footsteps."

"So let me run with you."

"No. Not on your life. You should go back to work.
Hell, if Sheila *is* in a canal somewhere, she might not
be found for years. Jesus Christ, they're always dragging out someone who's been under water for years...
decades, even. Kelsey, have you gone daft? The cops
might not be able to solve this thing. Sometimes serial
killers are caught, and sometimes they're not. Do me a
big goddamned favor and don't make me feel responsible for your death, too."

So much for any closeness that might have sprung
up between them. Kelsey rose abruptly. "Let's go. I'll
drive you back to your car."

"No."

"Who's daft now? This is my place, and I don't want
you here. I'll drive you back to your car, or you can
take a taxi."

He looked up at her, dark eyes hostile, face set.
"What are you going to do, Kelsey? Throw me out?"

"That's exactly what I'm doing."

"I'm not going. You'll have to call the cops."

The challenge in his eyes was so great that she was tempted to do it, just to drag him down a peg. But she wasn't going to, and she knew it.

She walked away from him, going to the hall closet. She dragged out a pillow and sheets and went back to throw them at him where he remained stubbornly seated.

She didn't say a word to him, just turned again and retreated to her bedroom. She slammed the door and locked it. Childish. And pathetic. He wasn't coming after her.

She was both wired and tired as hell. Determined that she was going to salvage a few hours' sleep, she decided that she was going to pretend he wasn't on her couch. Mechanically she went through the steps to prepare for bed, brushing her teeth with such determination she was lucky she didn't rub her gums raw, then standing beneath what must have been the hottest shower endurable by man. She dressed in her most comfortable, threadbare cotton nightshirt, turned off the lights and crawled beneath the covers.

Her eyes remained open and fixed on the darkness.

The events since Sheila had failed to appear at the duplex ran like a broken tape through her mind. *Dane had opened up to her tonight. A lot. Not enough. He had not been pleased to find them at his house yesterday. He thought Sheila had been a victim of the Necktie Strangler. Why? Why think that, just because she had disappeared? Yes, Sheila had been running wild. Yes, she had been seeing Izzy Garcia. A lot. But Dane was the one she'd been with last. Izzy had had Sheila's purse* on his boat, but she hadn't told Dane. Why not? Dane was still holding something back from her.

He'd gone to the strip club. She'd followed him. Home had held nothing for him, no reason to come back to Key Largo. She had run...run from the very beginning. Sheila had gone to him. Necktie Strangler. He had failed someone he had loved. Wasn't going to fail again. Didn't need her or her money. He wanted her out of it. Sheila had been seeing so many people. They all admitted it. Larry had said that every man at the table had slept with his ex-wife. No denials.

Nate had never told her about being with Sheila. Maybe he had been too embarrassed, too polite, or maybe just too macho at heart to say he hadn't had what every other man there had had.

She'd been with Dane last. There had been something there. Sheila had gone to him...because after all these years, the good, the bad, the friendship, there had always been that thing *about Dane that made him seem strong and compelling and sexual. A thing that compelled and drew...*

Kelsey had run. He had run. They had all run. Just like a first-grade reader. Run...run...run. Because Joe had died. Because she shouldn't have needed to be held so badly. She shouldn't have found something so strong that it had swept the pain away. She shouldn't have been with a man who had once been Sheila's. Sheila was gone... Necktie Strangler, strip clubs, bars, drugs, she could have been into anything. He had been the last one to see her...

Kelsey kept staring into the darkness.

When she finally rose, it wasn't with a real plan. But

she got out of bed and opened the door. Tea, a drink, something to make her sleep.

She walked back out to the living room.

It was dark, only the dim lights of the city drifting softly in. The sheets were on the couch. He was stretched out, one below him, one on top of him. His chest was bare. His clothing lay on the coffee table.

Sleeping? She couldn't see his eyes without approaching him.

She veered from her path to the kitchen. She stood over him. His fingers were laced behind his head, and he was watching her.

"What?" he asked curtly.

"I just...wanted to see if you were sleeping."

"You've seen."

She nodded.

She was startled, but she didn't jump back when he suddenly swung into a sitting position with a silent speed like lightning. He reached up and caught her wrist.

"What do you want, Kelsey?"

She could feel the pulse beating in the vein in her throat. Breath coming too fast. Blood on fire, racing through her veins.

She hadn't come out for tea.

She felt the heat in his fingers where they wrapped around her wrist. She didn't need light to visualize his hands. Large. Callused. Bronzed. Fingers long, nails clipped short. Blunt, no-nonsense hands. Time had never changed the way they felt against flesh.

She had never been able to read people, but she felt something hot and hostile flowing from his touch. She ignored the hostile. And felt the hot. Ignored whatever might be in the midnight darkness of his gaze, both brooding and sharp upon her, despite the shadows in which she stood.

"What, Kelsey?"

"Well, hell," she drawled out. "I couldn't sleep. I thought I'd see about a mercy fuck myself."

"That isn't you, Kelsey. The words don't even fit your mouth."

Burning with humiliation, she tried to wrench her hand free. She didn't succeed, but found herself drawn down on his sheet-covered lap, feeling the warm heat of his breath against her cheek, aware that he was naked beneath the sheet.

"I didn't say I wouldn't oblige," he told her.

Chapter 11

To say that Kelsey—stone-cold sober and asking for sex—was far more than he'd ever imagined would have been a serious understatement. To say that the simple fact of Kelsey being on his lap was pure and instant arousal would be an even greater one. Everything in him went rigid, and he knew he sounded like a Doberman when he added, "On one condition."

One condition. Christ, he was giving her conditions.

"Condition?" she said. A whisper. Soft as the air, smooth as silk, one word sending the blood coursing roughly through him. Kelsey's magnificent backside on his thigh, her breath teasing his lips, warmth enough to jump-start a generator. Man, was he a liar.

"You're not going to run out at dawn."

"Where would I run? It's my apartment."

"You'd find a place. But you won't. I like to wake up next to a woman."

She blinked. "Did you wake up next to Sheila?"

"No. And did I hurt her in any way? No. But you know that, or you wouldn't be here. And I don't want to hear her name again. Not now." He threaded his fingers into her hair, drawing her face down to his before either of them could ruin it with any more words. Her lips parted instantly under his, her mouth sweet and deep with the seduction of liquid honey. He had a million intentions. A seduction so damned good she would never forget it. But when she shifted in his arms, her fingers running into his hair, cradling his head, the sheet fell away.

The soft cotton of her nightshirt rode up.

She wasn't wearing anything beneath.

He shoved his hands beneath the fabric while his mouth remained locked onto hers, tongue creating ravishment, deep, wet, molten. His fingers ran over her torso, settled beneath the firm fullness of her breasts, ran over the circumference, caressing, exploring. Her nipples were as taut and hard as marbles, and a breath seemed to escape from her mouth into his as he touched her. She shimmied convulsively against him, and he brought his hands down the length of her back to her buttocks, marveling at the feel of her flesh and the round tension of muscle beneath. He shifted her until she was straddling him right where he sat, lifting her just enough to bring her back down on the instant erection she had so effortlessly created. Their kiss broke and she gasped, head tossed back as her body gloved his sex, wet and giving as he brought her slowly down until he was fully inside her. She shuddered against him, head falling against his shoulder for a moment as he let her adapt to the invasion. Then his hands were on her hips and he was moving her, she was moving herself, and they were desperately bucking together like a pair of kids stealing time in the old man's Chevy. There wasn't a lot of time to think, to really rue the fact that he'd been far less than a slow and sensual lover. The eroticism of her flesh against his and the near rabid pulse of their movement were like a spiral to a carnal heaven. The sound of their breathing, the staccato beating of their hearts, seemed like a driving thunder. Her fingers dug into his shoulders, nails pressing his flesh. He managed to wrench the nightshirt over her head and toss it into a corner of the room without missing a beat. Her breasts fell against his face. His tongue moved over them as she rose and fell. His lips latched around one pebbled nipple and aureola, suckling, evoking a soft gasping cry on the wind they'd created. He felt himself bottling up desperately. Prayed for an iota of control. Moved her harder, faster. Listened to the sweet beat of their bodies, damp and writhing, sliding against each other. He couldn't take it. His arms wound around her. He ground her down against him, teeth gritting as he prayed. He heard the expulsion of her breath, felt the tension drain out of her, her body suddenly seeming to collapse against his. He thanked God. In a split second, he let himself go. His body constricted and erupted in climax, held and released, and he pulled her even more tightly against him, wet and pliant as he pulsed and withered within.

Her head rested against him. They were both sheened with sweat, wet and hot and cooling. She didn't move at all but remained on top of him, hair damp and streaming over his chest, tickling his nose.

"You're not running," he said softly after a moment,

smoothing her hair but otherwise remaining still, glad to have her remain so intimately against him.

"I don't think I can move," she murmured against his chest.

They lay content for several seconds. Dane was dimly aware of a muted sound.

And then, contrary to her words, she suddenly leaped to her feet and went running across the room to the dining area, dragging his sheet with her.

"What the hell…?"

"Cell phone," she said.

"Cell phone? Great," he muttered.

She had already reached the table where she had left her purse and was digging through it with one hand while draping the sheet around herself with the other.

"I have to answer it," she told him. "I forgot. Larry will be worried."

"Larry will be worried?" He didn't know why he was so irritated. He had no great claim to Kelsey's time or attention, and he had been less than the world's greatest lover in the last few minutes, though it had seemed like great sex nonetheless, so Larry's call was definitely unwelcome.

"Hello?" she said into the phone. "Yes, I'm fine."

He rose himself, grasping for the bottom sheet, and walked over to where she stood. "Is there a reason Larry gets to know where you are at night? Something going on there?"

She covered the little phone.

"Don't be ridiculous." Even in shadow, the look she gave him was scathing. "He was in love with Sheila forever, until this new girl finally came around."

She moved her hand. He could hear the crackle of words from the other end.

"No, no, it's all right. I'm in my condo in the city. We were at a club in Miami. We…Dane and I. It was really late, so we're going to drive back in the morning."

There was a pause as Larry spoke on the other end.

"I know it's really morning now. Larry, I'm sorry. I should have remembered to call you back. We're going to catch a few hours' sleep and be back." She listened again. "No! Is he all right?"

"What's going on?" Dane asked.

The phone crackled.

"Yes, it's Dane. He's awake, of course." She hesitated for a split second. "He was sleeping on the couch. He heard the phone, too."

Larry said something else.

"What's going on?" Dane repeated.

Kelsey told him. "Andy Latham went into the Sea Shanty and belted Nate in the jaw."

"What? Why?"

She waved a hand at him to indicate that she couldn't hear what Larry was saying. "Something about more fish," she said.

"More fish?" He reached for the phone. She surrendered it.

"Larry, what about the fish?"

"Dane?" Larry said from the other end. "Jeez, you two had me worried. I didn't really think too much about Sheila being gone, but when Kels said that she was at a club earlier, then never came back…I was sitting here like a worried parent. Then Nate calls, nursing his jaw, because old man Latham walked into the Sea Shanty, straight up to him, and belted him in the jaw.

I wasn't there, but it caused quite an uproar. Latham is sobering up in jail, but he claimed it was because 'one of us snot-nosed kids' kept throwing dead fish on his property. Bizarre, huh?"

"Definitely."

"He's crazy as a coot," Larry said. "But they've got him cooling his heels right now, though they'll have to let him go in the morning."

"Tell him we're heading back right now," Kelsey urged at his side.

Dane looked at her in the shadows, then glanced to the plate-glass window, where darkness was beginning to ease into the softer, pastel tinted shades of day.

He wondered when he would next get the chance to see Kelsey standing next to him in a sheet.

"You know, there's really no reason."

"I'd feel better if we were back."

"I'd feel better if we just moved this into the bedroom."

The blood seemed to drain from her face, but she said, "I'm not running anywhere, Dane. I'd just feel better if we drove back now."

He still wondered when he would see her in a sheet again. And he wished he'd given her a hell of a lot more to remember.

"What?" Larry said from the cell.

"Nothing." Dane stared at Kelsey. "I was just saying she should get some sleep, but Kelsey wants to get back, so we'll be there in a couple of hours."

"Hey, tell her as long as we all know she's all right..."

Kelsey was already heading for her bedroom. The sheet wasn't really wrapped around her all that well.

"I'm going to take a shower," she said.

She had her front covered just fine, but she undoubtedly didn't know that the long sleek line of her back was bare, and one buttock was exposed.

"Yeah, we'll see you soon," Dane said.

He didn't hear Larry's reply. He pushed the end button on the cell, tossed it back in Kelsey's purse and followed her.

He'd already proven he could be quick.

The water was already running; she stood beneath the spray. He joined her. The water sluiced down over the two of them as she gave him a reproachful look. "We've really got to get back."

"We will."

"Then…"

"Right after I lick you all over."

"We said we'd be right there."

"I'll lick quickly." He pulled her against him. Soaking wet, smooth as velvet. Kelsey was tall, but still several inches shorter than he was. Each part of her seemed to fit in a perfect place against him. He pressed his lips to her throat. Found the pulse. His hands slipped over the wetness of her breasts, down around her hips, between her legs.

"Dane…"

"Quickly…but thoroughly."

He picked her up, lifted her from the shower stall. He didn't bother with the water. It dripped from them as he carried her into her bedroom. They were still soaked when he brought her down on the designer sheets of her bed.

"We're wrecking the bed," she murmured.

"It will dry by the time you get back."

Wet, tasting faintly of soap, she was delicious. He'd

promised "all over," so he went for it. Throat, belly, lips, long and lingeringly, inner thighs, dead between them, long and lingeringly again. So much for quickly. Kelsey forgot time. The pastels of morning were beating back the grays. She was bathed in soft golden yellows. He made a mental note of just how she looked, tanned against the softness of pale sheets, belly flat, legs wickedly long, breasts full, body writhing...words incoherent as they escaped her lips. He felt himself drown in her taste, musky on his tongue. When he sank completely into her at last, he'd aroused himself to a frenzy and time no longer mattered. She moved as only Kelsey could move. The world came down to the driving desire for release. Damp bed, Kelsey, wet flesh, sliding, rocking, friction, Kelsey, words, whispers, cries. Explosion...

But once again, he had barely eased his weight off her before she was shooting up.

"I'm going into the shower. Alone. For two seconds," she said. Pleading.

"Sure." He lay there as she left.

A moment later, she was out. He strolled into the shower himself.

Within ten minutes, they were on the road.

Two hours out, two hours in.

Aboard his main boat, *Free as the Sea*, Jorge Marti could see the night lights of the marina. He was almost back. The night was cool, touched by the ocean breeze, which had been heightened by the storms out on the Atlantic. Hurricane season. There was always a weather system sliding off the African coast. And if that wasn't enough, killer winds would form in the Gulf, slip off the Yucatán Peninsula, the islands or South America, and whip into something lethal right before they struck.

Then the winds would churn, making a beeline for the Florida coast, or maybe turning in a matter of seconds and heading straight toward the Carolinas.

Fishermen and charter captains always paid attention to the weather forecasts. They listened carefully and learned to make sane judgments. Of course, there were times—more often in the Keys than on the mainland—when evacuations were mandatory.

Tonight...

Tonight the forces of nature, far out over endless miles of water, simply made the ocean a thing of pure beauty. A gentle, deceptive softness kissed the air.

It was beautiful coming in. The very first edges of dawn were beginning to break. He had planned on beating the light. Maybe he would. His mantra kept running through his head.

Run slow...run slow...

The soft sound of his motor, just above an idle, still seemed as loud as a chorus of growls. Yet looking ahead, he could see that there was a stir of life on the dock. Fishermen began their day with the coming of light. But the activity seemed natural. People arriving... not so many, only the real fishermen. The lights were shining an iridescent yellow. Joe Palumbo, who kept his boats two berths down, was loading groceries onto the deck. Izzy Garcia's *Lady Havana*, farther down the way, was showing lights. Old man O'Connell, who was so wizened and brown no one could really estimate his age, was at work on the aft of his boat. Nothing unusual.

Two hours out...

Two hours in.

Dawn was still just a promise.

Jorge guided the boat carefully past all the buoys, keeping his wake down to nothing more than a ripple. He ran with his lights and speed conforming to all laws and regulations.

He came in close enough to see old man O'Connell's face. He looked up, waved. Jorge forced a smile, waved back.

He cut his motor.

He brought in the *Free as the Sea*, running from the helm to the rigging, securing her first with one tie, then leaping to the dock to bring her closer in before hopping back down to secure her completely.

He was standing on the dock, securing the last tie, when he felt a tap on his shoulder.

His blood ran cold, and he felt a sheen of sweat break out on his skin.

He turned. Izzy Garcia was standing there, staring at him.

"Izzy. Hey."

"Estúpido," Izzy said softly, reverting to Spanish. "I will be blamed for what you are doing."

Jorge stiffened, staring at Izzy. The light was becoming more pronounced.

"I don't know what you're talking about."

"Yes you do."

"Izzy, you'll never be accused of my...crimes."

Izzy threw up his hands. "If I go aboard your boat now, I will find nothing there?"

"With what you do, you should get off my ass," Jorge said quietly.

"I say again, if I go aboard your boat, I will find nothing there?"

Jorge was in good shape. He worked hard, when he wasn't working, he went to the gym. Nor was he a coward.

But Izzy was honed like a razor blade.

Jorge was still tempted to smash him in the face, though it would accomplish nothing. He would wind up lying on the dock, bleeding like a freshly killed fish. An ambulance and the police would come for him.

Or the coroner's wagon.

And there was more to lose than his life.

"I have sometimes kept silent when I shouldn't have," Jorge reminded Izzy. "You owe me the same."

"You've kept silent?" Izzy sounded amused. "I have seen things I shouldn't have seen. I have seen parcels go into the water…from your boat."

"I've seen what you discard into the water as well… from *your* boat."

"So we have both seen things go into the water. And how do we prove that now? But I play a game I know how to play. And you…well, you are all emotion and passion, and you will get caught. So you do what you must. But I tell you this. You get me in trouble with the law on anything, *amigo*, and I will kill you," Izzy told him. "Do you understand? I will not blink. I will kill you, and they will never find your body."

Over Izzy's shoulder, Jorge could see that the activity on the dock was growing. It was time for him to deliver his package. And Izzy was still threatening him, though naturally it appeared that they were doing nothing but having a friendly conversation.

"I will never get you in trouble."

"You remember that. Every second."

"I just said, I will never get you in trouble."

Izzy nodded. "All right. Just so long as you know. You do so, you are a dead man." He folded his hands together. Very powerful hands. He tightened them, as if showing Jorge just what he could do with them.

Jorge wished he had a gun. Bang, bang, you're dead. Then it wouldn't matter how tough and powerful Izzy thought he was.

Bang, bang...

Jorge allowed himself the luxury of watching Izzy fall limply to the dock in his mind's eye.

No guns. That would just destroy them both.

"I hear you, Izzy," Jorge said.

Izzy smiled again. A scary smile, and yet Jorge could see why women thought it had a certain dangerous appeal.

Loathing him, Jorge watched as his countryman walked away down the dock.

Pink light emerged in the sky, but the air remained touched by a distant storm.

The day was serene.

Jorge turned quickly back to his boat to complete his night run without further incident.

The ride was both too long and too short.

Intimacy could be very strange.

In the condo, it had been as if time had rushed away. Kelsey *knew* Dane, as she had known him years ago. Dressed, sitting next to him as he drove her car, she studied his face and realized anew how much time had passed. She didn't know him at all anymore. And yet, maybe it was time to speak out loud about her reasons for being so quick to think him capable of harming Sheila.

"Dane?"

"Yeah?" He was deep in thought.

"I think I came right after you because of what had happened…years ago."

He glanced her way. "You *think*?"

She instantly grew defensive. "Hey, excuse me, by your own admission you were the last one to see Sheila."

He shook his head. "You want to go way back? There was nothing wrong with what we did. Joe was your brother and my best friend. We were always close as kids, even when I was tight with Sheila, which I wasn't at the time. You came to me for comfort. We wound up in bed. I was fine with it, you weren't. Sheila and I weren't together, and you still felt as if you'd intruded on something private that was hers. Well, I *wasn't* hers. Hadn't been for some time. She was already moving in the direction she intended to go. She wanted a hell of a lot more than love from a man, though I don't think she even knew herself just what that was. The sad thing is, Sheila wouldn't have blinked before sleeping with someone you loved."

"It wasn't just Sheila," Kelsey told him. She shook her head. "My brother was dead. And there I was… enjoying life."

"Kelsey, as long as we are alive, we have to live. And that's all you were doing. Joe would have understood."

"It's all easy now, isn't it?" she murmured.

He shook his head firmly. "Nothing is easy now."

She was silent for a minute. "All right, you can tell me now that I was a fool when I ran away before, but look at what you just did. You came back to Hurricane Bay to waste your life. You said it yourself. You were only pretending to go through the motions of making a living."

He stared at her. "Maybe. Or maybe, whether I knew it or not, I came back to pick up the pieces of my life."

"You looked like a drunk that day."

"I have been a drunk."

"So...?"

"Kelsey, that night, with you, after Joe died, I found out that I want to survive. There's something about life...we want to live it. And while we have it, that's what we do—we live. I intend to make it past...all this."

She didn't have a chance to reply. They had pulled into the parking lot where he'd left his Jeep.

The coffee shop was already doing business, though it was slow and laid-back, on a Sunday morning.

"Sit tight," Dane told her, after he had left the driver's seat and she had taken it. "Please. Okay?"

She nodded.

He left her in the car, walked into the coffee shop, and returned within minutes with two cups of coffee and the morning paper.

"Kelsey, I'm begging you, please go straight back to the duplex. I'll be right behind you."

"Dane, it's daylight. And I'm not a stripper or a hooker. I live a dull and boring life, with all my fantasies going into ad campaigns."

"Maybe so. But we've already established the fact that you're bent on visiting men who may be psychotic killers. Please, promise me you'll go straight back to the duplex."

She nodded, waited until he was in his Jeep, then started out along the road for home.

As he had promised, he followed right behind her.

Stupid-ass thing to do.

Stone-cold sober, by the light of day, Andy Latham

knew that what he had done had been one really big stupid-ass thing to do.

He sat in his jail cell. Day had come. They brought him coffee and breakfast. Breakfast wasn't too bad—for jail. The coffee was good.

He rubbed his chin and felt the stubble on it. He must look like hell. Clothes slept in, hair unkempt. It was the alcohol. Usually, he was smart enough not to drink too much. But last night...

It was the fish. The dead fish in his yard. Again and again. And he couldn't help but believe it was those uppity rich kids throwing the bloated corpses in his yard. The smell...

He had smelled fish all his life. His sense of smell was both inured and heightened. Fresh fish smelled good. Dead and decomposing fish smelled like such awful rot that it could make a strong man vomit. It was as if someone knew how he hated the smell once the creatures started going bad.

He'd had too much to drink, and he'd lost his temper. It had felt good when he'd bashed Nate in the face. Now he knew that it had just been stupid. All the things he'd done in his life, and he'd avoided a cell—until now.

But here he was, all because he'd popped a rich kid in the nose.

A cold sweat suddenly broke out over his flesh.

He had to get out of here. Had to get out and had to get out fast.

He heard a jangle of keys. Someone coming toward his cell. Sheriff Gary Hansen. Pink-faced as always. The fool should move back to the north. Some people belonged here, some people didn't. Hansen didn't belong, yet he seemed to think he owned the island.

The door to his cell opened. Andy stood up, wavering just a little. Not because he was still drunk, because he'd been sitting too long. And because he was wary of Hanson.

"What's going on?" he demanded.

"Your attorney is here. Looks like you get to go home," Hansen said. "If it were up to me, they'd lock you up for a hell of a lot longer. Unfortunately there's still such a thing as due process."

"They ought to fire your ass for saying that," Latham told him, his mouth twitching uncomfortably as he spoke. His eye was twitching, too. Hell, maybe he could sue the sheriff's department.

"You're going before the judge, you'll post bail and walk away," Hansen said, staring at him with disgust. "But don't get too cocky there, *Mr.* Latham. You'll still be charged with assault and battery. And you may yet do some real jail time."

Andy Latham paused right by Hansen. "And you, you porker. You might still trip one day and dry up in the sun, just like a slug. Or fall off your boat and drown. The fish would be delighted."

"Get out, Latham, before I think of a way to hold you longer."

Latham left. His attorney, a fastidious man in a suit, despite the heat, was waiting. He looked good. Andy found himself suddenly burning with an inner fury. He could look good, too. He could be a handsome man, appealing. He had his charms. He had proven it many times.

It was all right to smell like fresh fish.

Just not decayed fish. He needed a bath. A beer to

chase away the trembling from the night before. He needed to grab a nap, change his clothes…

And get away.

He thanked God for the due process of law.

When Kelsey pulled into the driveway of the duplex, she was startled to see the front door to her side open and Larry, Nate and Cindy come running out to greet her, like a welcoming committee for a long lost child.

She barely got the door open and a foot on the ground before Nate was pulling her out, hugging her. Then Larry, then Cindy, all chastising her at the same time.

"You scared us to death!" That came from Nate.

"You just took off after dinner without saying a word." Larry was reproachful.

"Thank God you're back," Cindy said.

Dane's Jeep pulled in behind her car. Both Larry and Nate looked at him as if he had done something totally morally reprehensible.

"We were worried," Nate said indignantly.

It was then that Kelsey got a good look at his face. The left side was swollen and red, his eye area bluish and swollen.

Kelsey gently touched the other side of his face. "Are you all right?"

"Oh, yeah, sure, I'm all right. I'm more embarrassed than anything. Humiliated that I let a slug like Latham get past my guard."

"What could you have done?" Kelsey said. "He walked up to you and slugged you, right?"

"He's in jail, isn't he?" Dane asked quietly.

"I'm fine, and yes, Latham is in jail. But you know

they won't hold him long. He'll be out on bail. And slugging someone isn't like a capital offense or anything."

"But you're going to press charges," Dane persisted.

"Part of me feels badly," Nate said. "He's such a loser, I'll just be adding to the degradation that is his life. But then again, he's a scary piece of scum, so, yeah, I'll press charges. Though I guess the state is already doing that. I don't know that much about the law."

"I believe you'll have to press charges," Dane said.

"It's hot as hell out here. Let's go in," Cindy said.

Dane shook his head. "I'm going over to the jail. I want to see if Gary Hansen will let me talk to Latham," he said. "You're all going to hang out together today, right?" He stared meaningfully at Kelsey.

Nate and Larry each slipped an arm around her. "We won't let her out of our sight," Nate said possessively.

Kelsey frowned, looking at Dane. She had thought that he would stick around. That she would have time to talk to him.

She wanted to kick herself. They'd had so much time together and she hadn't said anything. And now she suddenly wanted to spill everything. She wanted to tell him what she'd seen on Izzy Garcia's boat. She wanted to give him the phone numbers she'd stolen and let him try to figure out why Izzy had them.

She wanted to tell him that Sheila had kept a diary, and that she was ready to quit running around, questioning people, until she had read the entire thing.

"We'll take good care of our Kels," Larry said.

She was between them, finding their joint embrace kind of sweet, but when Dane started toward the Jeep, she pulled away.

"Wait just one second," she said, running after him.

Seated in the Jeep, he looked up at her with weary exasperation. "Kelsey—"

"Shut up and listen. I…yesterday, on Izzy's boat…I prowled around a little before you, er…arrived. I found Sheila's purse in the storage compartment beneath the seat, port side. And I took these…" She dug quickly in her own bag, producing the list of phone numbers. "These numbers were programmed into his cell."

He stared at her incredulously. "You're giving these to me…*now*?" he said.

She stared back at him. "Better late than never—isn't that what they say?"

She heard his teeth grate. "Yeah, I guess it is. You've got my cell number, Kelsey. Anything, anything at all… get hold of me right away."

"All right."

"*Anything*, Kelsey."

"I'm not an idiot, Dane."

His expression told her that she had done little to prove it, but he didn't say anything else, just gunned the motor of the Jeep and pulled out onto the road.

"You know what we should do?"

Cindy was behind her, her voice as cheerful as ever.

"What should we do?"

"Just take off. Get in a boat, take off for a few hours. We can dive, snorkel, fish. Get away. Just us. The old guard."

"Cindy, there are things…"

"We're all worried sick about Sheila, Kelsey."

She nodded. Of course. "I'm really tired, too."

"So are we because last night we were up late worrying about you."

"I told Larry I was okay, that I was with Dane."

"You know us…we stayed up anyway. C'mon, let's take off. It *is* Sunday, you know."

"You want to go to church?"

"The next best thing. Let's head out to the reef and the Christ statue. Say a little prayer under water. Kelsey, we have to quit driving ourselves crazy."

Larry had come up to them. "There's an idea. Come on, Kels. Let's do something."

"Whose boat?"

"Nate has his down at the same marina where Izzy and Jorge keep their charter boats. He has plenty of gear on board for all of us. We'll just do a day trip."

Kelsey thought quickly. She wanted to read the diary, but she could take it with her. If she stayed at the duplex, she would just read and pace, read and pace.

Maybe they were right.

"All right. If that's what you all want to do. I need a few minutes to grab a few things."

"Me, too," Cindy said.

"What? What's up?" Nate asked.

"You're taking us out for a spin," Larry told him.

"A spin?" Nate said.

"On your boat," Cindy told him.

He threw up his hands. "What the hell."

Kelsey walked past him into the house. She went to her bedroom, digging into the suitcase she hadn't really unpacked for a bathing suit, shorts, T-shirt and cover-up. She had started for the bed to grab the diary from beneath her pillow when a strange sensation told her that she wasn't alone. She held still, looking around the room. Again she realized that things were just slightly out of order.

She turned to the door of her bedroom. Nate was standing there, good eye soulful.

"Sorry, Kels. I didn't mean to disturb your privacy. It was a long night. You know, after Latham slugged me and the cops came and I spent hours with ice on my face, worrying about the fact that you hadn't come home and that you were calling from some club...and that...well, that you were with Dane."

"You shouldn't have been worried if you knew I was with Dane."

He shrugged. "Okay, maybe I was jealous."

"Jealous? Nate, after all this time? I thought we were friends, good friends."

"We are, Kelsey. It's just that I still get one of those macho, possessive things going on now and then. Oh, nothing serious. I'm over it. Really. Hell, I like Dane. And I guess we all saw something there all those years ago when you...well, when you didn't know it."

She just stared at him, brows raised.

He lowered his head. "Anyway, I started looking around. I wasn't digging into your things, honestly. But Sheila had mentioned something to me once about keeping a diary. I thought I'd look around for it."

"Did you find it?" Kelsey asked cautiously.

He shook his head. "But I didn't want you to think you were crazy, and I didn't want to lie to a friend. I was looking around in here last night. Or this morning. Whenever the hell it was."

She nodded, still watching him speculatively. He appeared so sheepish that she decided not to yell or lecture.

Larry suddenly appeared behind Nate. "Are you two ready?"

"Just a second," Kelsey said. "Would the two of you get out of here? For just a minute?"

"Oh, sorry." Larry turned and walked away. Nate followed and closed the door softly in his wake.

She walked quickly to the bed and found the diary, then stuffed it into the canvas bag she was bringing for their day at sea.

"He's gone. Out? Free?"

Dane was incredulous as he stared at Gary Hansen.

Hansen, seated at his desk, stared back at Dane, shaking his head. "What the hell did you think I could do? A drunk punched a guy in the face. The drunk had an attorney. I don't make the laws, I uphold them. And besides, Dane, Andy Latham may not be a popular man around here, but hell, what can you do? He got drunk and punched Nate. You can't execute the guy for that."

Dane exhaled a long breath.

Hansen's eyes narrowed. "What's with you?"

"What's with me? Gary, his stepdaughter is missing and we've had dead women popping up in the water."

"Dane, there's still nothing to say that Sheila Warren won't come back anytime. She could come sashaying in any day now, be incredulous that we had the gall to want to know where she was and with who."

"And there's nothing to say that she will," Dane said flatly.

Gary leaned forward. "Dane, you find a reason for me to keep Andy Latham in here and I'll be happy to oblige. Like I said, I don't make the laws, I uphold them. And I can promise you, I'm not the only lawman in the country sick to my stomach at the ability of fancy lawyers to let criminals walk. But as it goes right now, Andy Latham is walking free. Legally."

"How about you keep an eye on him, then?"

"We're trying to do just that. But you know what? We have to cover a hell of a lot of people and a hell of a lot of area. You keep an eye on him, too, if you're so damned convinced he's dangerous."

"He's proven he's dangerous."

"By punching a guy in a bar?" Gary shook his head in weary disgust. "Dane, do you know how many men we'd have to keep under permanent lock and key if that were a crime punishable by years of incarceration?"

"Sorry, Gary. Sorry."

"Get me something. I'd love to see him put away."

Dane left the sheriff's office and drove out to Latham's place. The guy wasn't there. His truck wasn't parked in the driveway.

He tried a few of the local hangouts but could find no sight of his quarry.

Dane stopped at a local donut shop for more coffee, gazing over the list of numbers Kelsey had given him. Why the hell had she taken so long to tell him about Sheila's purse being on Izzy's boat—and about the numbers? He felt a chill along his spine, knowing that Izzy had been keeping tabs on all his old acquaintances.

Coffee in hand, he headed out for the docks and Izzy Garcia.

His cell phone rang. He picked it up quickly.

"Dane, it's Kelsey. What happened with Latham?"

"Nothing. They'd already let him out."

"They let him out?"

"Yeah, yeah, he's out. Where are you? What are you doing? Your voice is fading in and out."

"Oh, we decided to spend the day out on the water. Cindy thinks it will be good for all of us."

"Out on the water?" He wasn't sure why that disturbed him.

"Yeah. Don't worry. We've taken Nate's boat. It's just Larry, Nate, Cindy—and oh! We ran into Jorge at the docks, and his captains are taking out all his charters, so he decided to tag along, too. We're going to do the tourist thing, go to the Christ statue, see the tropical fish. You know, all that stuff. We'll come back in around—"

The phone went dead in his hands. He clenched his teeth, telling himself that she had just gotten out of satellite range somehow. He dialed her back. A taped voice told him that Kelsey Cunningham wasn't available and to please leave a message. With an oath, he tossed his phone down.

He was already heading to the marina.

But when he arrived, Izzy's boat was gone. Naturally. Charter time.

He stared at the dock impotently, thought of all the things he could do to make wise use of his time, then turned and walked to his car.

Screw it.

Something was bothering him. Something he couldn't fathom.

When he got back to Hurricane Bay, he didn't even go in the house. He headed straight for his boat.

Chapter 12

Kelsey lay on the deck. The sun was brilliant, a fantastic orb in an unbelievably blue sky. Larry had mentioned that the National Weather Service was still talking about a storm, but according to the forecast, the tropical depression now being called Hannah was heading toward the Carolinas. Kelsey still thought the sky was beautiful in the way it often was just days before the wind really ripped and the rain came in a deluge.

Lack of sleep had meant they were all fairly exhausted when they started out, but Cindy had been right. Being out on the sea was great. They had chosen to visit a few of the popular reefs around John Pennecamp Coral Reef State Park. The underwater park was protected, so there was an abundance of fish for them to look at. They started off north of French Reef, diving down to the wreck of the *Benwood*. The *Benwood* had been hit by a torpedo during World War II, then, while trying to get home, hit hard by another ship. Now she hosted a wealth of undersea wildlife. Beneath the surface, Nate pointed out a big grouper and mouthed a name. Old Henry. She hadn't seen him before. Sometime during the last few years he must have realized with his little fish brain that Pennecamp was a good place to live.

They stopped at Key Largo Dry Rocks, as Cindy had suggested, and went down to the Christ of the Deep Statue, a copy of the Christ of the Abyss Statue in the Mediterranean Sea just off Genoa. It had been a gift from an Italian industrialist. It was a beautiful statue, about twenty feet beneath the surface, arms upraised, face sculpted with peace and serenity.

After waiting for the tourists from the hired dive boats to leave, they all paused around it. Cindy folded her hands in prayer and they all followed suit. A while later they rose, and Nate suggested that they leave the park behind and do some fishing in legal waters. They hadn't made any plans for a restaurant for dinner that night, so a good catch of fresh snapper, dolphin fish or grouper would be good.

After just having met Old Henry, Kelsey was more in the mood for dolphin than grouper. Lying on the deck, feeling the air and the sun, she gave half her attention to the discussion going on between Larry, Nate and Jorge.

Jorge said that since they didn't seem to be catching anything from the boat, they should think about doing a little spearfishing.

Kelsey glanced at Cindy, who was lying on a towel near her. She appeared to be sleeping.

Kelsey had almost dozed a few times herself, but

she had brought Sheila's diary topside with her to read
as she lay in the sun. So far, she wasn't getting anywhere. Sheila had written about the men she met, but
there were too many of them to keep track of. Plus she
often used initials that meant nothing to Kelsey. So far,
especially since she had sheathed the diary in a plastic
book saver, no one had asked her what she was reading.
She often had a book or a sketch pad with her, and she
loved reading, just as Cindy loathed it, so apparently no
one thought it worth bothering to ask about.

Just as she had very nearly dozed off again, she came
to a section that alerted her.

*Saw the asshole my mother married again yesterday.
Had to see him to go to the bank. He was all dressed up.
Told me he was enjoying a new nightlife and meeting
lots of women, real women. They found him appealing.*

*I don't care what he says. He can take a bath and
pour on a liter of cologne, but he'll still smell like rotten fish. He always did. I told him so, too. Maybe that's
why I left the Keys before. I can't stand the smell of
rotten fish. Always reminds me of him. Reminds me of
being a kid. Reminds me of the things he made me do.*

I don't want to remember.

Despite the heat of the sun, Kelsey felt cold. She
closed the diary, biting her lip as she stared up at the
sky. She should have known. She had been naive all her
life. Sheila hadn't really spelled it out, and neither had
Izzy, but suddenly she knew the truth.

Andy Latham had molested Sheila when she had
been a child. And if the things Izzy had said were true,
he had done it with—if not her mother's consent—at
least her mother's knowledge.

Poor Sheila! What a rotten life. And now...

Out of the blue, tears stung her eyes. Maybe just because she was so tired.

And maybe because she knew, just knew, that Sheila was dead. They could pray at the Christ Statue all day, and all they could hope to achieve for Sheila was peace.

She closed her eyes. For a moment she almost felt sick to her stomach. Then she was outraged. When Sheila had become an adult, she should have brought charges against her stepfather.

She pushed herself up on her arms, suddenly needing to get into the water again. Rinse off, cool down—except that she had chills. Rinse off and warm up, then. The water was warm today, especially here in the shallows.

She started, realizing that Nate was sitting next to her. Cindy was gone and Nate was there.

"Hey."

"Hey. You okay?" he asked her.

She nodded.

"Really, really worried, though, huh?"

"Yeah."

"So am I."

She watched him. He hugged his knees to his chest. "Sheila was really going off in a bad way. I tried to talk to her, but..." He hesitated, then stared at Kelsey. "I really did care about her. You know..." Again he hesitated. "Well, you heard Larry last night. I had my fling with Sheila, too."

"Yeah, I heard Larry."

"I always loved you best, though."

"Nate, you know how much I care about you. I always will. But you don't have to apologize to me for sleeping with Sheila. We've been divorced for a very long time. And it was wrong to begin with, our getting married."

He looked away for a moment, then back at her. "Why do you think we barely lasted a month? Was there...something the matter with me?"

"No!" Kelsey protested quickly. "Nate...it was me. I hurt you, and I had no right to. I didn't really want to be married. I was just so hurt when Joe died, and I felt that...that I needed to belong to someone who was... mine, I guess. There wasn't a thing wrong with you then or now. You're handsome, charming and dependable."

He looked at the sky again, then lowered his head and his voice, as if someone might hear him. "Was I..."

"Were you what?"

"Okay in bed?" He sounded anxious.

"You were just fine," she assured him.

He still looked uncertain. Then he made a funny face, wincing. "I don't think that's what Sheila would say. She made some comment that I think was out of a movie. That you needed a microscope and a tweezer to find anything if you wanted to have sex."

Kelsey quickly lowered her head, determined to hide her smile. Leave it to Sheila.

"She was just being mean, Nate. You must know that. I mean...well, you made it through school, you were on the football team...you've been in locker rooms, and surely you've been with other women. You know what she said wasn't true."

"Didn't do much for my ego, though."

"I can imagine. But you know Sheila. She has a habit of striking below the belt. But..." She hesitated. "Nate, you know she was writing to me, calling me...and I've had a chance to read a few of the things she wrote in her diary. All these years, Sheila has been a bitch. She could be mean as a kid, but we all tolerated her. You know why?"

"We're a pack of fools? There weren't that many kids to hang around with?"

She shook her head. "I think Latham abused Sheila from the time she was a little kid. I'm pretty sure that's why she had no respect for sex whatsoever. And I think that, even when she cared about people, she hurt them. She was probably afraid to care too much about anyone. And if you use people, then they usually don't get a chance to use you in return."

"You think it was that bad?"

"Nate, I don't really know anything. Sheila kept things hidden from all of us. But I think that growing up must have been horrible for her."

"And then her mother died."

"Yeah. And she loved her mother, but I think maybe she wasn't much better than Latham."

"You mean her mother allowed whatever went on?"

"Maybe. Like I said, I don't really know anything. But I don't think you should let anything Sheila said upset you, or even give your ego the slightest scratch. Sometimes she just liked to strike out at people. I think she hurt you just because…it's better to hurt someone than to be hurt by them."

He squinted, looking up at the sun again.

"I could see it if we'd been headed for a monogamous situation or something like that. She just wound up being with me." He hesitated, then shrugged. "I think…I think she wanted Dane. But Dane had come back not wanting anybody. Of course, though they came back at nearly the same time, I think Sheila had been through half the lower Keys before he even came on the scene. And she knew about him…knew that his life hadn't been going real well. Do you think everybody has one great love in life, and even when it doesn't work, it's always there?"

"I don't know. But the world is full of people. And a lot of them are very nice." She paused, frowning at him. "Nate…are you saying that Sheila was the great love in your life and she crushed you?"

He started to laugh. "Hell no. You were the great love in my life. And *you* crushed me."

Kelsey felt the color flood her face. "Oh God, Nate, I am so sorry."

"Hey, that was years ago. Don't go apologizing. You just gave me back my manhood. I'm grateful to hear from you that I didn't suck as a lover. And I hope you're not lying to make me feel better."

"You didn't suck as a lover. I did."

He brushed her cheek with his knuckles. "All you had to do was be and you were great. But…"

"But?"

"You weren't really there. You were never really there. I thought…I thought there was someone else. Then you became a workaholic after we split up. You were never dating when I talked to you. Are you…"

"Am I what?"

"Nothing."

"Am I *what*?"

"Gay?"

She felt her cheeks darken again. "No."

"Hey, there's nothing wrong with it if you are."

"I agree. But I'm not. And I do date. Just not often. You're right. I have been something of a workaholic."

He leaned closer to her suddenly. "You know, girls, more than men, experiment."

"What are you talking about?"

"When Larry made that comment that Sheila had slept with everyone at the table, he meant everyone— and he wasn't off by much. That is, if you're being honest."

"I still don't get you."

"I think Cindy and Sheila had a thing."

"You think?"

"I do think so."

"I don't think you should say things unless you know they're absolutely true," Kelsey said. "And maybe not even then. If they did…experiment, as you say, it isn't our business."

"Sure. Sorry."

"Dammit, Nate, don't be sorry. I just think you should watch what you say."

"Yeah, maybe. And I do believe Cindy is looking for the right guy, though the years are going by."

"We're not living in the Civil War era. We don't become old maids at the age of seventeen or eighteen anymore," she told him dryly.

"Right." He shook his head. "Man, I'm sorry about Sheila. And I'm sorry as hell I let that asshole stepfather of hers get a fist on me! Wish I could have belted him back."

"I'm glad you didn't. The fact that you restrained yourself probably makes it a clearer case of assault."

Nate laughed. "Hell, it had nothing to do with restraint. He caught me by surprise and I fell flat. And by then…the cops seemed to be right behind him. I will prosecute, though. For Sheila. Because she was a friend…even if she did set out to humiliate me. At least…well, now I understand."

He rose suddenly. "They're still talking about spearfishing. Are you coming?"

"Maybe I'll come in later." She grimaced. "I never really liked spearfishing."

"Oh, yeah. Big difference. Catch a fish on a hook and let it flop around and asphyxiate, or shoot it cleanly with a spear."

"We can, you know, just order in a pizza," Kelsey said.

"Where's your spirit of adventure, woman?" Nate asked. "We need to eat fish!"

"We can order anchovies on the pizza."

He gave her a look of disgust. "We're going to have fresh fish. And if you don't catch any, you're going to get to clean them."

"Maybe I'll join you guys. Give me a few minutes. And if all else fails, I will call for that pizza."

He let out a sigh, still staring at her. "Good book?"

"Um." She nodded and smiled at him, feeling a bit of a guilty twinge. Then she gave her attention back to the diary, aware that he walked off with a snort of impatience.

Men. Men, men, men. Can't live with 'em, can't get them when they're nice and then shoot them when they become obnoxious.

The best ones out there—the cutest, the funniest, the most courteous—are all gay. They're even the best built, half the time. They make the best friends, that's for sure.

Maybe I should go that way myself. Try it, anyway. I can make anyone think I love them. It's fun.

But I need more. Want more. Just what do I want? I

should probably be in therapy. Good old Larry. He always told me I needed help. He's too involved. He thinks he can fix me, and we'll fall in love all over again, even get married again. Poor boy. I know I'm self-destructive. I'm trying to get even with someone. Or prove something. I really should get therapy. There's something in me. Every time I get near someone, I have to prove I can seduce him. And I get something from everyone, like a little trophy. I think even the fact that women are supposed to be so much more selective and discreet makes me want to prove everyone wrong. I hope Kelsey comes. I want to spill all this to her. I need to tell her how I'm suddenly afraid, even though I'm not sure why.

Once upon a time I might have been in love. But even then, the evil seed was blooming in me. I know some people would say it wasn't my fault. But if it wasn't my fault, why do I always feel so guilty?

Dane is at Nate's all the time. Oops, there I go again.

Hafta have, hafta have. Hafta prove I can take what I want. I think it's the chase. I need so much. But maybe not in this instance.

Okay, I will look into a therapist.

Kelsey set the diary down, feeling a strange chill sweep through her. *Had* Sheila made a play for Cindy just to experiment with her own prowess?

She stood, feeling acutely uncomfortable. She didn't really want to know all the private thoughts, emotions and deeds, of her friends.

But she felt she had to finish the diary if she was ever to have a chance of finding Sheila.

Or of finding out what had happened to her.

Because, like Dane, she was beginning to sense that Sheila was dead.

She realized that, despite the chill that had swept through her, she was baking. At least she'd had the sense to apply sunblock. She looked around. The others were all in the water and the dive flag was up on the boat.

She walked aft. She saw Cindy's head bob to the surface, then Larry's. They were laughing about something.

Their voices carried over the water. "What the hell were you aiming at, Cindy? We can't eat a cute little yellow tang for dinner."

"You didn't see the snapper?"

"We're not down here to massacre fish, children," Larry called back.

"I'll get a bigger fish," Cindy assured him.

Her head disappeared beneath the water.

Kelsey looked around. Since they had anchored, several boats had joined them at the sandy-bottomed fishing spot. The sun was glinting so brightly, she couldn't make out much about them. The charter captains often came here. On the outskirts of Pennecamp, where fishing was allowed, there could be a good catch. Fish naively left the safety of Pennecamp and wandered into the area where they were fair game.

Kelsey went over to the equipment and found her mask and snorkel. She leaned over the port side of the boat to spit in her mask and rinse it, then jumped into the water.

Dane had tried many of the usual haunts before trying the fishing spot. He didn't know why, but his sense of anxiety had been growing ever since he had learned that Andy Latham was back on the streets.

Latham had a tendency to fish the Gulf side, but when the fishing was poor there he went over to the Atlantic.

The shallow bank near Pennecamp was a favored spot. Some of the best reefs were close by, and not far away was a small, barren island, almost a sand spit, with a few tenacious grasses and trees. It was a popular picnic spot for boaters. Beneath the water's surface there were long spits of sand, as well, making it a safe place to anchor without harming the coral, while still being close enough to several small outcroppings of reef where the fish tarried before—hopefully—falling prey to rod and reel. There was also the wreck of a fishing boat that had gone down before they had been born. It provided a place for barnacles to form and sea life to find a home. It made the spot a special place, good for fishing, diving and, especially, for snorkeling, since the water ranged from twenty to forty feet deep.

As he motored in slowly, Dane surveyed the boats already anchored there.

"Bingo," he said softly.

He could see the *Lady Havana*, *Free as the Sea*, Nate's *Madonna*, and two of the other charter boats that went out from the same marina. Jorge Marti wouldn't be captaining the *Free as the Sea*, since he was with Kelsey and the others.

Izzy Garcia might well be aboard the *Lady Havana*, though.

He set his anchor and picked up his binoculars. He could see the groups aboard the *Lady Havana*, the *Free as the Sea* and the other two charters, the *Key Kiwi* and the *Sea She*. He studied the *Lady Havana* closely, but he didn't see Izzy among the men with their rods.

He turned to study the *Madonna*. There was no one topside, and the dive flag was up.

He set the binoculars down. The view before him

was almost picture-perfect, entirely serene. The day
was spectacular, without even the customary puffs of
white clouds above him. The sky was a crystal blue,
the sea shimmering in shades of blue and green. The
waves were light, without a hint of chop, and the boats
at anchor rocked gently where they lay.

And yet…

He should have been on the phone with the women he
had met at the strip clubs, pushing and prodding to find
out if they recognized any of the people in his pictures.
He should have been tracking down Andy Latham, calling every number from the list Kelsey had taken from
Izzy's cell phone, or bribing or conniving a friend at
the phone company to give him names and addresses
for those numbers he didn't know.

Instead he was here.

There was no reason to suspect that Kelsey should
be in any kind of danger. She wasn't a stripper, and she
didn't lead Sheila's lifestyle.

But she never shut up. She was determined to find
Sheila. She was always asking questions, and her questions were an awful lot like accusations.

The temptation to get in the water and find her was
overwhelming. He felt like an Alfred Hitchcock trailer.
"Have you ever had a premonition…?"

Dane put up his own dive flag, went for his snorkel
equipment and dived in. Surfacing, he headed straight
for the area where the *Madonna* lay at anchor.

Kelsey took a deep breath and dived. She could see
Cindy ahead of her. Cindy could be a pure predator. She
had apparently shaken Larry, having decided he would

scare her fish away and ruin her catch. Now she was headed toward the scattered coral.

Something brushed Kelsey. She instinctively moved, then realized it was only a piece of seaweed. There was a lot of it today. Whatever was happening with the storm out in the Atlantic might be driving it in.

She surfaced and took another gulp of air.

Her lung capacity was good. Probably because she had grown up an islander and spent almost as much time in the water as she had on land the whole time she was growing up. They were all good, of course, though Larry wasn't quite up to par with the rest of them. But then, he had been a weekender. And no one was quite as good as Dane, but then...well, he was Dane.

Joe had been as good, though.

Kelsey swam toward the coral and found a tiny flatfish digging into the sand. She teased it with a finger and watched as it dug deeper. She surfaced and found herself pulling away from a big patch of seaweed again. For a moment she floated, staring up at the sky. She found herself thinking that she was going to make a point of calling her parents that night. She remembered her feeling, after the initial anguish of Joe's death, of failure that she wasn't all that Joe had been, the perfect son.

It all seemed so petty now.

She was grateful to them; she loved them so much. They were so normal and they did love her. They had given her a good home, a good education and so many of the silly things she had wanted over the years.

She had not led Sheila's life.

She turned in the water, took a deep breath and made another dive.

She was very close to what could be classified as a reel reef. And, she realized, she was by the old wreck. How far had she come from the boat? As experienced as she was, she never went diving alone, and even when snorkeling, she was careful to stay close to the others. The best swimmers in the world could drown because they were too confident in their own abilities.

She would surface, get her bearings and head back.

Now, she saw, she was right over the wreck. The scattered coral near it was intriguing. As she headed up, she was surprised to catch a glimpse of green curling around one of the larger pieces near the rusting hull of the boat, and she found herself taking a breath and slipping beneath the surface again. She dived down low to the ground, wondering if a moray eel was making a home here. She swam deep. Tangs, parrot fish and medium-size grouper swam past her, the grouper eyeing her warily. She kept her distance, circling, watching.

She was startled at a whooshing sound in the water, close by.

She spun around and saw nothing, but the fish that had been near her were all darting to and fro in sudden confusion and fear.

She turned around in a full circle but still saw nothing.

The old boat sat decaying in the sand and rock, silent and still.

The fish around her slowed again, their movements easy through the water.

As she turned back to the little spit of coral rock, she was pleased to spot an eel. It poked its head out from a hole in the formation of living rock, then ducked its head back in.

Treading water, she waited at a safe distance, anxious to see the moray again. She'd missed being in the water like this. She loved the serenity in the water, the beauty of the creatures that lived there.

The moray tentatively peered out.

She was careful not to move.

How long had she been down? At one time she could make almost five minutes. She probably wasn't that good anymore.

The eel seemed to accept her.

Then...

It jerked back so suddenly it was almost like a disappearance into thin air—or water, as the case might be.

She heard the whooshing sound again...

And saw...

A streak of silver.

A spear...

Some idiot was spearfishing right here, with her in the water. Surely, despite the coral and the seaweed, she could be seen.

She couldn't see anyone attached to the spear that had just shot by her, dangerously close.

She looked around...and again...the whoosh.

Damn tourists!

Was someone in the hulk of the old boat, thinking they could do better if they were hidden in the rotting wood and rusting metal of the wreck?

She got ready to kick her way to the surface, out of the fishing grounds. Before she could do so, she nearly screamed as a hand landed on her shoulder.

She turned in alarm. Dane. He grasped her hand, pulling her upward.

They broke the surface together.

"Dane, what the hell are you doing here? You scared me half to death!"

"*I* nearly scared *you* to death? Jesus, someone down there is using you for target practice! Get back to the boat, Kelsey."

"Back to the boat? Where are you going?"

"Back to find out who is down there."

He pulled free, about to dive. She grabbed his hair, jerking him back up. His dripping head and blazing eyes reappeared.

"Dane, you idiot, there are tourists down there who don't know what they're doing! You've got to come with me. We'll call the Coast Guard."

"Kelsey, dammit, get back to the boat. I don't think that's some dumb tourist taking potshots. Let me go."

"You're not going after someone with a speargun. You're unarmed!"

"Kelsey..." He was impatient.

"Dane!" She was adamant.

"Kelsey, go back to the boat. Now."

"But—"

He dived. She didn't stop him, but she couldn't turn and leave him, either. She surveyed the ocean floor beneath her.

She could see the coral, but the fish had all disappeared.

The old wreck sat like a silent sentinel, as it had for years. No activity was evident in or around it.

She couldn't see Dane.

Seconds ticked by with agonizing slowness, but she still couldn't see Dane.

Or any sign of life.

Minutes.

Minutes went by.

He was good. He could hold his breath for a long time.

She still couldn't see him. How far had he gone? Where had he gone?

She gasped, inhaling water along with air as she felt a hand on her back. She turned, coughing, treading water as she wheezed and struggled for breath. Dane. He had come from the other direction.

"I told you to get the hell out of the water!"

"Don't yell at me!"

"Kelsey, you idiot, I think someone was trying to kill you."

"Here? With at least half a dozen boats around? Dane, it was some idiot tourist who should be arrested. You were in as much danger as I was."

"We may still be in danger, Kelsey, and while I'm wearing a dive knife sheathed at my ankle, you haven't any protection but a blue bikini. So swim, Kelsey. Let's both get back to the damn boat."

She turned and started for the boat, but she couldn't help thinking he was crazy. No one would want to kill her.

And yet...

Why would someone search for concealment in order to spearfish?

Unless they were fishing for a human prey.

Chapter 13

When they reached the boat, Larry was just climbing up the ladder. He was jubilant.

"Will you look at this? I got a dolphin fish—a big one. Cindy, Nate and Jorge got *nada*. Call me a weekender, will ya? Look at this baby. Hey, Dane, where the hell did you come from?"

"Where the hell did you catch that?" Dane demanded. Larry's smile faded, and he pointed north, away from the wreck. "Over there somewhere," he said, scowling. "What the hell's the matter with you?"

When they reached the ladder, Dane urged Kelsey to go first, then followed her up.

Kelsey, sorry that Dane had been so curt when Larry was so excited, explained quickly. "Larry, someone was over by the wreck with a speargun, and they missed me by a matter of inches."

"Damn!" He stared at Dane, who was dripping onto the deck. "Stupid tourists. Did you tell them to stop?"

"We couldn't find them," Dane said. "But I'm calling the Coast Guard and reporting the incident. Where are the others?"

"Coming in."

Dane, his hands on his hips, was staring toward the other boats still anchored nearby.

"It's gone," he said.

"What's gone?" Larry asked, perplexed. The spear he had held so proudly, bearing his captured fish, was now lowered by his side.

"Izzy's boat. The *Lady Havana*."

"It was out there?" Larry said.

Dane nodded, studying the fishermen still at anchor. "Jorge's boat is gone, too."

"Jorge is with us."

"I know. But his boat was here when I anchored."

"So?"

"So we need to know exactly who was out here."

"Those charters usually just do rod and reel fishing," Larry said.

"I know."

Jorge came climbing up the ladder, his spear empty. "Hey, Dane," he said in greeting.

"Where were you?" Dane asked him.

Jorge frowned and looked down at his torso, glistening from the sea. He looked back at Dane. "In the water."

"Where were you spearfishing?" Dane clarified.

"Toward the boats in the crescent there. Why?"

"Someone nearly speared Kelsey," Larry explained.

"What?"

Cindy was on the ladder then, with Nate right behind her. "Maybe we should explain this to everyone all at once," Kelsey murmured.

"I'm calling the Coast Guard," Dane said, and headed below deck to use Nate's radio.

Kelsey wound up explaining. They were all indignant, and certain that anyone so careless with a speargun had to be a tourist.

"I mean, come on, Kels," Larry said. "Why would anyone be aiming at you?"

She shook her head. "I don't know."

Dane had come back topside.

"You really called the Coast Guard?" Nate said slowly, as if they might wind up getting someone in trouble for a piece of stupidity.

"What happened was serious," Dane said.

Cindy was frowning. "Dane...how did you get here?"

He sighed and pointed. "My boat."

"Oh. You were just coming out to join us?" Nate said.

"Something like that."

"Cool," Nate murmured. "Hey...they're all leaving."

"Did any of the rest of you notice what other boats were out here?" Dane asked.

They looked at each other. "I didn't even notice that Jorge's *Free as the Sea* was out here," Larry admitted ruefully.

"And I hadn't seen Izzy's boat," Kelsey said. She hadn't paid the least attention to the other boats. She had been involved in the diary, and then she had gone in the water.

Dane looked at them all one by one. Kelsey could feel a certain tension rising. "You were all within sight of each other, right?"

A silence followed his words.

"Kelsey was right—we should have decided to order pizza," Nate said, staring hard at Dane.

They heard the loud blast of a horn from a Coast Guard cutter, and a moment later the vessel was lining up with theirs and an officer hopped aboard the *Madonna*. He was young, and very serious and attentive as Dane told him that he had gone looking for Kelsey, only to see a spear go streaking through the water, nearly missing her.

"Well, who shot it?"

"I don't know," Dane said impatiently, ruffling the feathers of the young officer. "She was nearly killed. There were at least two spears, maybe more. And whoever shot them was hidden somewhere. In the wreck, I imagine."

Then the officer stared at them all curiously, since they had obviously been spearfishing.

"Every one of us knows how dangerous a speargun can be," Nate said firmly.

"And we weren't anywhere near the wreck," Cindy said.

The officer took information from each of them, then asked what other boats they'd seen in the area. Dane rattled off the names of at least five of other boats anchored.

"We'll do what we can," the young officer said, then shook his head. "If you'd only seen someone..."

"Yeah, I know that," Dane said impatiently, "but when you're being shot at, you try not to swim right back into danger."

"And you're sure," the officer said, narrowing his

eyes at the group once again, "that none of you was...
careless in any way?"

"We're positive," Jorge said with disdain.

"Right," Larry murmured. He nodded toward Kelsey
and Dane, and said, "Humans there." He picked up his
catch. "Fish here. We know the difference."

Once again the officer stiffened. "You don't need to
be sarcastic. We're on the water to save lives."

"Of course. And you do an excellent job," Cindy
soothed.

"We deal with drug peddlers, modern-day pirates
who would just as soon shoot you as look at you, refugees and—"

"Assholes," Nate supplied.

The officer lifted a brow and at last cracked a small
smile. "Yeah. So if I offended you with my questions,
at least you'll understand why."

"No one is offended. We appreciate your work,"
Dane said carefully. "But you will check out everyone
on those other boats, won't you?"

"Yes, we will. I know most of these boats. And you
think there were a few more with names you didn't
catch?"

Dane nodded. "Yeah." He sounded angry with himself.

"You didn't mention that boat over there." He
pointed.

"She's mine," Dane said.

"Oh? So you came out in two different boats?"

"I knew my friends were out here," Dane said.

"And you just happened to dive in the water and found
your friend in danger from an unseen spear fisherman?"

"Yes," Dane said. Kelsey realized then that everyone was staring at Dane.

"Good timing," the officer said.

"Yes, it was."

The officer kept staring at him.

"I don't even own a speargun. I was never into spearfishing," Dane said impatiently.

"All right. We'll do our best." He handed Dane a card. "I've got your name and numbers. And you can contact me if you think of anything else," he said.

Dane accepted the card. "Thanks."

The officer returned to his boat, leaving them with a cross between a wave and a salute.

They were left alone, silent for a few minutes, staring at one another.

"I guess it's a pizza kind of night after all," Cindy said, trying to break the spell of silence with a light tone.

"I think we should head back in," Nate said stiffly, his eyes on Dane. "I'll bring you back to your boat."

"What about my fish?" Larry asked sorrowfully.

"We'll clean him and freeze him at the duplex," Cindy said.

"But it's fresh now."

"It won't feed us all," Cindy said.

"Well I can't exactly throw him back. He's as dead as dead can be."

"All right, we can have dolphin tidbits with our pizza."

Nate pulled in the anchor as they spoke and started the motor. As it roared to life, Dane leaned close to Kelsey.

"Come with me."

"I can't."

"Why not?"

"My things are all on board this boat. It'll take me ten minutes to get them all together."

"Leave them, then."

"I have things I can't leave."

"Nothing is more important than your life, is it?"

She stared at him incredulously. "You know, I can see where you think I was an idiot for running over to Andy Latham's. And it might have been even stupider to go on board Izzy Garcia's boat alone with him. But this is a group of our oldest friends."

"Yeah, great. We've barely seen each other in years."

"I've barely seen *you* in years."

"Kelsey, someone was shooting at you."

"None of these guys."

"Wouldn't it be nice if your belief in the goodness of man was a guarantee?" he murmured, then returned to the original topic. "What the hell can you have on board that's so damned important?"

She looked at him and hesitated for a moment, then said, "Sheila's diary."

For once she took Dane completely by surprise. But he was able to mask his emotions almost instantly.

"Who knows?" he asked in a whisper so low she barely heard it above the hum of the motor and whipping of the wind.

"No one."

Apparently Nate didn't plan on tying up with Dane's boat. He cut the motor about twenty yards away. Normally it would have been no big deal. The day was still beautiful, the sun hot. There was no reason why Dane shouldn't swim back. The problem was the reason why they'd stopped where they had.

Nate was wearing a resentful and stony expression.

"Dane, we're going to make it a pizza party tonight," Cindy said cheerfully, speaking loudly, since Nate was revving the motor in a ridiculously impatient manner.

Dane smiled at Cindy. "Pizza party," he muttered beneath his breath.

"Oh, yeah, it's going to be just great. A really happy, friendly occasion," Kelsey said. She stared at Dane. The moments of fear she had felt beneath the water were quickly fading. This episode in her life definitely had a logical explanation. One they used often, to explain any aggravation.

Tourists.

They could be annoying as hell, but the Keys could hardly exist without them.

Dane walked aft to dive off the end of the boat. "Dane, you're coming over, right?" Cindy called hopefully.

Bless Cindy, Kelsey thought. Ever the peacekeeper. Just what *had* her relationship with Sheila been? Kelsey couldn't help but wonder.

She felt queasy. She wasn't going to go through life wondering about Sheila and everyone she knew.

Yes she was. Until they found Sheila.

"I wouldn't miss it for the world," Dane assured Cindy.

He leaped over the hull and into the water. Kelsey could see him swim with clean, swift strokes to his own boat.

Nate didn't wait for him to board.

He gunned the motor, and they headed back for the marina.

* * *

As he headed in, Dane tried to keep a vein of rationality running through his head.

Kelsey was right. Their entire group of friends could hardly be conspirators in the Necktie Strangler cases. And Kelsey wouldn't be alone with anyone for the next few hours, not since they were all heading for the duplex to order pizza.

He'd never felt like quite such a madman in his life, not knowing what to do first. He needed to talk to the strippers again and find out if the girls could pick out anyone from the pictures he had brought to them. He needed to accost Izzy Garcia before he could get rid of Sheila's purse, and he also needed to be with Kelsey. The whole thing was getting crazier by the minute. Kelsey wasn't a stripper or a prostitute, so she shouldn't be in any danger. Except that she had been asking questions.

So why would anyone want to kill Kelsey, even if she had gone around asking questions of everyone?

Perhaps because she'd gotten too close to the truth.

He made his decision as he headed back toward the Key. Veer to the left, he brought his boat straight in to Hurricane Bay and made it as fast as he could to the duplex.

Or, veer to the right and head for the marina.

As they brought the *Madonna* into her berth, Kelsey was surprised to see that the young Coast Guard officer had decided not to waste any time. The majority of the charter boats were back in, and it appeared that a number of officers were walking the docks, talking with each captain and his passengers.

She paused, seeing that a tall, well-built black officer was on Izzy's deck.

"Want to hang around?" Larry asked her.

She shook her head. "No, I'd rather let those guys do their work and get back to the duplex." She looked at him. "What can I do? Run around and stare at everyone they're questioning?"

Cindy was behind her. "You know, that might not be such a bad idea. Give them the eye, see if anyone breaks down and confesses."

"No one is going to break down and confess. Let's get out of here. I want to take a shower, chill out and order pizza."

They kept walking toward the parking lot. Kelsey hadn't been lying. She needed a shower. The sun seemed to be baking the sea salt permanently into her flesh. Though it was dropping now, the heat was still so intense that it shimmered over the pavement. She wanted a long shower, soft, clean clothing and the company of no one but friends.

"Think Dane will show up?" Jorge asked.

"We can hope not," Nate said, casting a sideways glare at Kelsey. "*She'll* just let him in if he does."

"Oh, come on, Nate!" Larry said. "Kelsey could have been killed. Naturally he's afraid. Especially after he fucked up in St. Augustine."

"How do we know *he* wasn't down there with a speargun?" Nate said.

"He didn't come out of the water with a speargun," Jorge reminded them. He had stopped walking. "I wonder if I shouldn't stay behind for a bit. Check on my captain, see what's happening on my own boat. I'll be there later, though, so don't count me out."

"Of course not," Kelsey told him. "We all need show-ers, downtime. Let's do the pizza thing about seven or eight, how's that?"

"Good by me," Jorge said. He lifted a hand to them and started back for the dock and the berth where the *Free as the Sea* was docked.

"Nate, chill," Cindy commanded.

"How many years have I known that guy?" Nate said. "And he suggests that *we* might have been care-less with spearguns. Hell, was he suggesting one of us might really have been down there on purpose, trying to hit Kelsey?"

"Nate, he reacted to a situation, that's all. He's got a thing for Kelsey, always has had, and we all know it," Larry said with a deep sigh of impatience. "I'm not going to throw out a friendship over this. Do you re-ally want to? Hell, the guy has helped you. He set up the cameras that caught your thief, and he spends half his life at the Sea Shanty."

Nate shrugged, dug around in the pocket of the short-sleeved tailored shirt he'd thrown on, found a pack of cigarettes and lit one. His fingers were shaking.

"I thought you quit," Cindy said with reproach.

"Yeah, I did."

Cindy shook her head and started walking toward the parking lot again.

"Hey, guys, come on, this is my vacation time," Larry said.

Nate nodded. "Okay, okay. Let's go get ready for our cozy little pizza party." He hesitated suddenly, looking back toward the dock.

"What is it?" Kelsey asked him.

"I was just thinking...do you think old Andy Latham might have gotten in his boat and gone out there? Even Dane said that he didn't notice the names of all the boats out there. Do you think Latham could be smart enough to go after you like that? Would he even be capable of such planning and subterfuge? I mean, whoever was down there was either one lucky asshole or one very clever would-be killer."

Kelsey looked at Nate. "I don't know. I really don't know," she said. "But if Latham's boat had been there, don't you think one of us would have noticed it?"

"Hell, I didn't even notice that Jorge's boat was there, and Jorge was with us," Nate said.

"I didn't notice what other boats were out there because I wasn't paying any attention. But if Latham's boat had been out there, Dane would have seen it."

Cindy turned back. "Are you guys coming? If Latham was out there, who the hell says he was even on his *own* boat? Please, can we go? I feel like a salt lick for an entire herd of cattle. Whatever happened out there doesn't matter right now, because we're all together. Let's hit it."

Kelsey and Nate started walking, but Kelsey found herself stopping and looking back again.

Izzy Garcia was standing barefoot on his dock, hands on his hips.

Staring after her.

She couldn't see his eyes or read his features. But even at a distance, it was easy to read his body language.

The man was furious.

Sunday afternoons tended to be crazy, which Dane knew. He returned to his house, docked his boat, opted for a two-second shower and clean clothes, then drove down to the marina.

Sunday evenings could be quiet. Dead quiet.

In the time it took him to get back, the activity at the marina had died away. But it was Izzy Garcia he wanted to see first, and the *Lady Havana* was at her berth.

He left his car and hurried down the walkway until he reached Izzy's charter boat.

He glanced at his watch and then at the sky. It was nearly nightfall. On a Sunday night that meant a lot of people were heading north to Miami-Dade and beyond to prepare for Monday morning and the workweek. The tourists and daytime fishermen had taken their catches and headed on home or to their hotels. Cocktail time was drifting into the dinner hour at the local restaurants. But the hectic pace at the marina had slowed to the lazy crawl that came at the end of such a day.

Dane headed straight for the *Lady Havana*. There was no sign of Izzy or anyone else on the boat. He jumped lightly from the dock to the deck. The *Lady Havana* rocked ever so slightly at her mooring.

Before he could reach the cabin, Izzy emerged. His features were so tense it looked as if he barely had enough skin to stretch across the bone structure of his face.

"Took you longer than I thought," he told Dane, and headed back down into the cabin. He opened the refrigerator as Dane followed. *"Tú quieres una cerveza?"*

"No, I don't want a beer. I want answers."

Izzy took out a beer for himself, popped the top and swallowed for a long time before lowering the can with a sigh and staring at Dane again, as if he were watching a rabid dog.

"Maybe the pressure is making you *loco, amigo*," he said. "Now you think that I take out a charter, leave the clients on board, grab a speargun and go after a woman everyone has always liked?"

"So the Coast Guard came."

"Oh, yeah, the Coast Guard came." He waved an arm vaguely to indicate the cabin. "To the others, they ask a few questions. Me? Me they grill for twenty minutes."

"You *are* a dope-peddler. Occupational hazzard," Dane said. "You know, cops and such wanting to talk to you."

Izzy gave him an icy smile. "You think I'm selling at the high school?"

"Yeah, I do."

Izzy shook his head. "I sell recreation to adults. Maybe some people with whom I've worked have gotten careless and greedy. I will make it stop."

"What do you think, Izzy? That you can make me stop wanting to nail your ass?"

"You're not here about the drugs today. You're here about Kelsey. No, it's more than that. You're here about Sheila."

"Someone tried to nail Kelsey in the water today. And Sheila…"

"You think Sheila is dead."

Dane didn't respond.

Izzy walked through the cabin, lifting the seat cover on the port side of the boat and pulling out Sheila's purse. "You have come for this, I believe. Kelsey found it. I knew that, of course. But I don't know where Sheila is. Maybe she is dead. Sheila played in many scary places. Maybe she knew things she shouldn't have known. And maybe she did things she shouldn't have done. But I didn't kill her. Here, you take this. Go ahead and waste your time hounding me. I didn't kill Sheila. I could swear to that, but it wouldn't mean shit to you if I did so. I didn't go in the water with a spear gun, and I didn't kill Sheila. Now get the fuck off my boat."

Dane didn't move.

"You keep an interesting set of numbers in your phone, Izzy," he said.

Izzy swallowed the rest of the beer. "Yes, I watch everyone. I know where everyone is and what they are doing. It's good to know things about people. Maybe I'll become a private investigator, too, one day. And maybe I'll be better than you. I make it my business to know what goes on with the people who think they know me too well."

"Izzy, I would never claim to know you too well. I just know *about* you."

"That thing. In St. Augustine. What happened wasn't your fault."

Dane felt his jaw twist, but he didn't allow his emotion to show.

"Trying to suck up to me?"

"Why? I don't need to suck up to you. You can't prove anything against me."

"I must be awfully close."

"I don't think so. You see, that is why I make it my business to know about the people around me."

"If you make it your business to know about people, why can't you tell me more about Sheila?"

Izzy arched a brow, then gave Dane a sardonic grimace. "No one really knew about Sheila. She couldn't anticipate her own movements. But you—you should be careful. Here you are on my boat. The big military man who learned all about killing." He mimed aiming a gun with his fingers. "Don't you know? Even tough guys can be killed by the crazy people out here. And even some who are not crazy, just businessmen. You could wind up dead, you know."

"Now, now, Izzy. First you suck up to me, then you threaten me."

"Hey, I'm just talking. Pointing out some of the facts of life."

"Tell me, Izzy, would you happen to be the Necktie Strangler?"

Izzy could be a good actor, Dane knew, but the look he gave him then registered genuine surprise. Then he tightened his features into a snarl of real disgust. For a moment Dane thought he was going to spit on the floor of his own cabin.

But he didn't. "The Necktie Strangler? Do you think I'm some psycho? Look around you. I do well with women, my friend. Very well. Perhaps not with women like Kelsey, who think they know me too well, same as you. But you should see some of the corporate wives who come aboard this boat with their paunchy husbands. They long for a man who doesn't have a fat white tire for a middle. The Necktie Strangler…he is some sick reject, desperate, seeking revenge, perhaps. Or maybe he was just born bad. Evil. He is probably what they call a bad seed. And I am not. I've chosen my way in life. I like to take a few chances. I disagree with some laws, but I am not evil inside."

"You're quite the upstanding citizen, Izzy."

"Yes, I am. And you should know this—*if* I wanted someone dead, it would not be like that. Perhaps you should look at some of your friends. Why don't you find out what Jorge Marti does out on the ocean in the middle of the night?"

"Why don't you just tell me?"

"I don't actually know for certain," Izzy said. "That's the truth. But I know that he is out there. And I know that whatever he does, he does in darkness. There, I've told you what I know and what I've seen," Izzy told him. "Now get off my boat. I've given you what was Sheila's. Yes, she left it here when I saw her last, but that was before *you* saw her last. If what you really want is the truth about Sheila, you're wasting your time with me. I didn't kill her. It did not even occur to me that she might be dead or a victim of the Necktie Strangler—which apparently you do, or why accuse me of being such a man? I didn't hurt Sheila. Ever. I gave her a great deal of pleasure, actually. So, lay off. Get off my ass and leave me alone."

Dane folded his arms over his chest. "If you know anything, Izzy, it would be good for you to tell me."

"I've told you all I know. Now will you leave? Or were you planning on beating me to a pulp. Maybe break my arm?"

"Your face, actually," Dane said. "But I can't afford to spend a night in jail." He started out of the cabin and up topside, to the deck. Izzy followed him.

On deck, he stopped. "What about those rape charges that were filed against you, Izzy?"

"Filed and dropped," Izzy said.

"Maybe the lady was afraid she might wake up dead one morning."

He smiled. "And maybe the little *puta* realized she wasn't going to get anything. She filed charges because she wanted a one-woman man. And that's not me. She got pissed off because she wasn't so special. That's it. You're going now? You'll leave me alone?"

"I'm going, Izzy. But I'll be damned if I'll leave you alone."

"Remember, everyone says Sheila was with you the last time anyone saw her." He smiled. "Alive, that is."

Dane was tempted to risk a night in jail for one good wallop. Just one punch, enough to flatten Izzy's nose. Instead Dane took a long stride that brought him from the deck of the *Lady Havana* to the dock. Then he turned back. "Be seeing you, Izzy."

Izzy just glared.

Dane strode along the dock. With or without Izzy's approval, he intended to talk to Jorge Marti. But the *Free as the Sea* was not in her berth.

Well, maybe that wouldn't matter. Jorge would be coming for pizza at the duplex. He knew that he himself would be hardly wanted there, not after today. Nate was the most put out.

Too damn bad.

Nate and the others had been in the water with spearguns.

He stood on the dock for a moment, watching the ripple of water in the place where Jorge's boat should have been berthed.

Then he turned and headed back for the parking lot.

Izzy was still topside on the *Lady Havana*, watching him every step of the way as he departed.

He hated Izzy because of what Izzy did.

He'd learned a hell of a lot about the man when he'd been hired by the private school to find out who was supplying the kids. Discreetly placed cameras had caught a number of the pushers in the act.

Thus far, though, even when threatened with prison, no one had been willing to identify Izzy as their supplier.

The guy was the epitome of bad news. Sleaze. Slime. A pusher.

But was he a cold-blooded, organized psychopath who killed with his bare hands?

Dane stopped, lit a cigarette and looked back over the flame of his match.

The man was still watching. And he knew that Dane was watching him.

Izzy lifted a hand, formed his fingers into the shape of a pointed gun, pretended to aim and fire, and then smiled.

Dane ignored him and started walking again. He could still feel the heat of Izzy's gaze as the man watched him while he reached his Jeep, stepped into it, gunned the engine and left the parking lot behind.

"What?" Kelsey cried, startled.

She had jumped at the sound of the knock against her bedroom door.

She hadn't really been scared, just startled, because she had become so engrossed in what she was doing.

She was seated on the floor in front of Sheila's dresser, still wrapped in a towel after her shower. She wasn't sure what had made her suddenly decide to lift the lining beneath Sheila's elegant undergarments before getting dressed, but her curiosity had been rewarded. A folder had yielded all kinds of interesting papers, even if they weren't particularly relevant to her disappearance. An award Sheila had earned for being top speller at the local competition when she was in third grade. A picture of her and Dane together at his

high school prom. A half-written letter to Larry, trying to explain why she couldn't stay married to him. A
page, apparently written when she had been very young,
on which she practiced her penmanship with the line *I
hate my stepfather* written over and over again.

"Kels, can I come in?"

Larry. She jumped up, wrapping her towel more se-
curely around her and cracking the door open.

"Hey," she murmured. "Sorry, have I been a long
time? Are the others here?"

"No, no, it's all right. Cindy is still next door, and
Nate went by the bar just to check on things. He called
and said he'll be along. The pizza place doesn't deliver, so I'm going to go pick up our order. I wrote you
a note—it's there on the table—but then I thought I'd
just see if you were out of the shower before I left."

"I'm out. I'll get dressed right away, just in case anyone shows up while you're out."

"Can you think of anything else? I ordered one pizza
with just cheese, one pepperoni, one vegetarian, and an
order of anchovies on the side."

"Anchovies on the side sounds great. Anyone who
likes little hairs on their pizza is welcome to them."

"Do we need beer, soda, wine?"

"I went shopping when I got here. We're fine."

"Maybe I'll pick up an extra six-pack."

"Whatever you think."

"All right, then, see you soon."

She closed her bedroom door when Larry left and
returned to the dresser. She dropped the towel and
she suddenly found herself looking toward the rear
window. The drapes were open. There was faint light

out in the patio and pool area, but bright light in the bedroom.

She cursed herself, grabbing the towel, suddenly afraid that she was being watched. She grabbed her underwear and bra and raced into the bathroom, then discovered that she was shaking as she slipped into them. Of course. What she had done was idiotic. Every woman knew not to dress with her shades open.

And great. Now she was wearing a bra and underwear, but her jeans were still in the dresser. She was really getting stupider with every passing moment. She should have simply closed the drapes.

And now...here she was.

She was suddenly afraid to stay in the bathroom. Afraid that she might find herself trapped there if the someone watching her made it into the house.

No one could get into the house.

Larry would have locked the door.

What if he hadn't?

She could lock the bathroom door and hole up until Larry returned, Cindy came over, or one of the others showed up.

She reached for the knob, all the while assuring herself that she was being ridiculous. But then she thought she heard another knob turning. Someone coming into her bedroom...

She waited in absolute stillness...and listened.

Seconds...minutes...

She exhaled, unaware that she had been holding her breath. It sounded to her like a jet engine. She was afraid that she might have missed some subtle noise beneath it. She held her breath again. Nothing. Nothing...

She was becoming ridiculously paranoid.
Kelsey opened the bathroom door.
And screamed.

Chapter 14

Dane tried in vain to find Andy Latham. His truck wasn't at his house, and his fishing boat wasn't tied to the pier.

He tried the usual hangouts, the bars Latham frequented, and found no sign of him.

As he pulled out of the parking lot of one hole-in-the-wall, his cell phone rang.

A soft female voice spoke tentatively on the other end. "Dane?"

"Yes?"

"It's Katia. From Legs."

He stopped the car, pulling back into a parking space to listen attentively. "Katia, hey. Thanks for getting back to me. Did the pictures jar anything in your memory?"

"Yes."

"Which one?" he asked, hearing the tight sound of his own voice.

She let out a long sigh. "The scary thing is, I see so many people. They all look familiar. Every face in the shots you gave me seemed familiar. You could probably give me a picture of some old geezer who was European royalty a hundred years ago and he would look familiar."

Dane lowered his head, listening, rubbing his temples.

"So…you might have seen these guys…and you might not have seen them."

"Well, yes."

"Thanks, Katia. I appreciate you trying."

He was ready to hit the end button on his phone when she spoke softly again. "I said they all looked somewhat familiar. But one of them…I know one of them has been coming for months."

Dane's heart quickened again. "Who?" he asked.

His hands tightened around the wheel as she answered him.

"Kelsey?"

Cindy burst into the bedroom just as Kelsey cut off her own scream.

"What is it?" Cindy demanded.

A face in the window. Or had it been? There was now a large lizard where she was certain she had seen, at the least, the shadow of a head. A very large lizard.

"Anole," she said, exhaling.

"What?" Cindy asked.

"There's an anole, a big lizard, on the window."

"You screamed because of an anole?" Cindy said

incredulously. "You've seen them all your life, Kelsey. Kelsey?"

She could feel that she was still white and shaky. She didn't know if paranoia was setting in, or if she really had seen a face in the shadows.

She stared at Cindy suddenly. "Is Larry still gone? How did you get in?"

"Larry should be back any minute. I let myself in with my key when you didn't answer my knock. Kelsey, maybe you should go on home. Maybe this whole thing with Sheila isn't good for you. You're taking it all so much to heart, and…"

"And what?" Kelsey stared at her.

Cindy shook her head. "I don't know. Have you done something to someone? It's possible someone was taking potshots at you in the water. And now you're seeing faces in the window. Kelsey, I'm going to be more worried about you than Sheila if this keeps up."

Kelsey stared at Cindy. "Maybe there *was* someone in the backyard."

Cindy answered slowly and carefully. "Right. Maybe."

"Well, I intend to look back there. For footprints or something."

"You think we have a Peeping Tom?"

"Maybe. Maybe it's something worse."

"We can check it out," Cindy said. "Of course, we can wait for the guys, too. On second thought, I may be buffer than either Nate or Larry."

"No, you're right, we should wait. There's safety in numbers."

"And there may be safety in clothing, too," Cindy said dryly, pointing out Kelsey's state of semiundress.

"Were you planning on an underwear pizza party? The guys would appreciate it, I'm sure."

Kelsey reached for a pair of jeans and a knit shirt, sliding them on quickly. She strode quickly across the room then, drawing the drapes. The anole darted away when it sensed her approach.

She closed her eyes, wishing she weren't still feeling so shaky. There couldn't have been anyone out there. Her slightest movement had caused the anole to scamper away in panic. It never would have stayed on the window if someone else had been out there.

"Hello? Kelsey? Cindy?"

"It's Jorge," Cindy said, pleased. "He can go out with us." She raised her voice. "Hey, Jorge, we're here, in the bedroom."

"How did Jorge get into the house?" Kelsey said.

"I must have left the door open," Cindy said. Kelsey stared at her. "Well, I heard you scream, I opened the door as quickly as possible…and I must have left it open." Kelsey was still staring at her. "You were screaming," Cindy said. "I thought you were in trouble."

"Well, thanks, it's good to know you're ready to run to my rescue."

"You can count on me in any lizard situation," Cindy said dryly.

"Hey…?"

Kelsey looked across the room. Jorge had come to the door. In dark jeans, a navy cotton shirt, with fresh washed, combed back hair and the slight scent of a pleasant aftershave, Jorge was both attractive and reassuring, built to take on the creatures of the night.

"You two all right?"

"Kelsey thinks she might have seen a Peeping Tom," Cindy explained.

"Or a big lizard," Kelsey admitted ruefully.

"You have to watch out for the lizards around here," Jorge said gravely. "They seem to be watching all the time. Just like Big Brother."

"Maybe we'll find out that the lizards are aliens, and they've been waiting all these years to take over the earth," Cindy murmured.

"Want me to check the yard?" Jorge asked.

"Let's all check the yard," Kelsey said. She started to open the sliding glass doors that led out to the back.

"Wait, I'll head out that way," Jorge said. "You go out the front, and that way, if there's a Peeping Tom, we'll know it because you'll see him trying to get away."

Jorge went out the back. Cindy and Kelsey went out to the front porch and ran right into Nate and Larry.

"Hey, guys, I found Nate out here, which is good, because even I—weekly-businessman-perfect-athlete that I am—cannot handle the pizza boxes and drinks all in one," Larry said. Then he frowned, staring at them. "You didn't come out to help with the pizza, did you?"

"We're checking out the yard," Cindy said.

"For lethal lizards," Kelsey explained.

"Lethal lizards? You think there's a gator back there or something?" Larry asked.

"No, just a big anole," Kelsey responded. She took the pizza boxes from Larry and nearly ran with them into the kitchen. Cindy was behind her with the sodas and beer. Then they hurried to rejoin the men, following them through the tall wooden gate of the privacy fence on the side of the house and around the back. They got to the window in question, but there was nothing there, and nothing seemed disturbed at all.

"Any footprints?" Cindy asked.

"Lizard prints?" Larry said.

"People prints," Cindy said with exasperation.

"I sure don't see any," Nate said.

Jorge was standing about five feet from the window, looking at them in dismay. "Well, actually, now there are lots of them."

"Just what are we looking for?" Larry asked. "A lizard or a person?"

"Signs that someone was here," Cindy murmured.

"I thought someone might have been back here in the yard," Kelsey said. "I—I thought I saw someone. Maybe it was just a shadow or something," she added lamely.

"She definitely did see a lizard," Cindy said. "I saw it, too."

"Let's check under all the trees," Larry said. They all split up to look around the yard.

"The pool looks nice tonight," Jorge said.

"We can always dive right in," Larry said.

"We've left all our suits behind," Nate reminded him.

"There's skinny dipping," Larry suggested.

"Or just underwear," Cindy said. "Kelsey will be all set. She's wearing her good stuff tonight."

Kelsey smiled vaguely at Cindy. If someone had been in the yard, he had left by the gate. Or else he had been in really good physical condition and scaled the wooden privacy fence around the rear of the duplex.

"There's another car out front," Cindy said.

"Let's go back in," Kelsey said suddenly. "It must be Dane."

"So he did come," Nate murmured.

"Maybe we shouldn't mention all this," Cindy said. "Dane really seems to be on edge lately."

"Good idea. Don't say anything," Kelsey said. Jorge was staring at her, frowning. "He'd rip apart the entire backyard because I saw a lizard," she explained.

"And accuse us all of being Peeping Toms," Nate said.

"Shh," Cindy said.

Dane was out of the Jeep. He saw the open gate and joined them.

"What are you all doing?" he asked.

"We just decided to come outside and see the night," Cindy said. "It's a beautiful night."

"Yeah. But wouldn't it be more beautiful from the patio?" Dane asked.

"Um, well, we were just trying to find an anole. There was a really big one on Kelsey's window a while ago."

"Hey, the pizza is getting cold," Kelsey said. Dane didn't seem inclined to press the point. He was watching Jorge, and she was curious at the way he was staring at the other man.

"We can eat out on the patio," Cindy suggested.

"That sounds great," Kelsey said. She automatically started for the sliding doors to the bedroom, while the others began to go around the front. "We can get in right here," she called.

"Yes, but then we'd have to tromp through your bedroom," Jorge said.

"It doesn't matter."

"We'll go around the front." Dane snapped out the words. The others froze, staring at him.

He looked at the group. "Oh, what the hell. Jorge, I have to talk to you."

Jorge's face, though darkly tanned, turned ashen. "Oh?"

"Let's go for a ride," Dane said quietly.

"All right," Jorge said.

"Wait a minute. You haven't even had any pizza," Cindy protested.

"It's all right," Jorge said.

Kelsey and the others stared in amazement as Dane turned and started for his Jeep, Jorge following behind him.

"Well, hell, leave it to Dane to spoil the damn party," Nate said.

"You don't think that...that Dane thinks...Jorge might have had something to do with Sheila's disappearance, do you?" Cindy asked.

"Of course not!" Larry protested. His words sounded hollow.

They stood in the yard in silence for long seconds.

"Well..." Nate said.

Kelsey threw up her hands. "Let's go get the pizza."

They walked through the house and into the kitchen. They were quiet, politely passing paper plates and plastic cups.

"It is beautiful outside," Kelsey said. "Why don't we sit around the pool?"

"Sounds good."

A few minutes later, the four of them were gathered around the pool.

"Hey, that depression is stalled over the Bahamas," Larry said.

"Hannah, right?" Cindy said.

"Yeah, they're calling it Hannah. Right now, it's still supposed to be heading for the Carolinas. I hope it doesn't turn. Since Andrew, every time it looks like the wind might blow hard they want to evacuate the Keys."

"That's natural. It's dangerous down here when a really big storm hits."

"Well, yes, but evacuating…man, I hate it. We don't get tourists for weeks afterward."

"I don't mind the lack of tourists," Cindy said. "I just hate it because all the fast-food restaurants close, and we have no electricity, which means no air-conditioning.

"The duplex is high. I think it would take a major storm for us to have to leave here."

"Nothing is high here," Larry argued.

"But we're not right on the beach. And when they evacuate…the traffic, oh, Lord!"

"If the storm is over the Bahamas, it will probably go north," Kelsey said. The pizza was good, she was hungry, but this was strange. She still hadn't shaken the feeling that someone had been in the yard. And when Dane had told Jorge that they needed to talk, Jorge had looked like a man who had been caught at something bad.

And yet the four of them were sitting here talking about the weather.

"A penny for your thoughts," Larry said to Kelsey.

"They're probably not worth it," she replied lightly.

"She's thinking, wow, let's all strip naked and jump in the pool," Nate suggested.

She smiled at him slowly, shaking her head.

"Okay, I tried. She's wondering why our friend the gestapo came in and hauled off Jorge," Nate said. "Am I right?"

"Of course."

"But none of us could possibly believe…" Cindy murmured.

"We should call him," Larry said. "Tell him we're a group and demand to be let in on this."

Kelsey stared at him.

"Well?"

"I think you're right," she said. "Let me grab my phone from inside." She crumpled her pizza plate, stood and went inside for her cell phone. She dialed Dane's cell number.

It rang and rang and rang. At last his voice came on.

"Dane, dammit it, you can't just run in, drag Jorge out and not give us anything resembling an explanation," she said. Then she frowned and clicked off.

"What did he say?" Nate demanded.

Kelsey let out a sigh. "Nothing."

"What?" Cindy protested.

"Nothing. I just got aggressive with his answering machine."

"He's not answering the phone?" Cindy said.

"No." Frustrated, Kelsey sat back down on a lounge chair.

They were all silent again for a minute.

"Well…" Larry said.

"Yes?" Cindy spoke, but they all looked at him.

"There's the whole skinny-dipping thing," he suggested.

Cindy moaned. Silence fell again.

"Damn." Nate yawned. "Well, this just sucks. We're all exhausted. No one has had any sleep in forever, and now—"

He broke off suddenly, his body tense.

"What now?" Kelsey said.

"I think I heard something."

They all jumped up and raced back around the side of the house.

"Dammit! I could swear..." Larry said. "Did you see a flash of...color, fabric, a person...?"

"Going out the gate?" Nate said. "Hell, why are we waiting? Let's find out."

He was already running.

Larry was at his heels.

Kelsey stared at Cindy. In tacit agreement, they burst into a run themselves.

Dane didn't speak at all until they were on the highway. He knew exactly where he was going, and apparently Jorge knew, as well.

"We're going to the marina?" he said. He seemed calm now that they were away from the others.

"It's as good as any place to talk."

"This is about my activities at night in the boat?" Jorge said.

"And more."

"I did not think..." Jorge began, but he didn't finish.

"You didn't think what? That you'd get caught?"

"I didn't think that you...I didn't think that you'd involve yourself."

"Not involve myself? When who knows how many women have been murdered and Sheila is missing?" Dane was so astounded by Jorge's attitude that he nearly missed the turnoff. The Jeep jerked its way into the parking lot and ground to a halt.

Jorge was staring at him incredulously. "I haven't murdered anyone. What are you talking about?"

"The strippers. The victims of the Necktie Strangler."

Jorge shook his head, frowning. "I am guilty, but not of murder."

Dane sat silently for a minute. "Someone witnessed you dumping something into the ocean, Jorge. And I'd like to know what it was."

Jorge said nothing at first, then insisted, "I have never killed anyone."

Dane stared ahead through the windshield. "A stripper at the club where Cherie Mardsen worked saw you there. Many times. She's pretty certain you were there the night Cherie disappeared. Sure enough to testify to it in court."

Jorge laughed, then buried his face in his hands. "You talked to a stripper. Which stripper?"

"Her name doesn't matter right now."

"Yes, it does," Jorge said. He looked around, then turned to Dane. "So you think I may be a killer, but you're talking to me alone."

"Right."

"Why?"

"Because you're an old friend."

"You're not afraid of me?"

"No. However, I am armed."

"Of course. You would be," Jorge said. "Maybe you don't really have anything on me."

"Maybe I don't, though I do have witnesses to your activities. But I intend to let you explain them first—if you can. Want to talk?"

Jorge let out a long sigh. "Sure." Then he hesitated and looked away before turning back to Dane. "Okay, like I said, I am guilty of illegal activity. But not murder."

"Go on."

"You said you talked to a stripper. But not a girl named Marisa Martinez."

Dane frowned and shook his head, studying Jorge. "No, I didn't speak with a girl named Marisa. Why?"

"I had business with her."

"What business?"

Jorge hesitated again. "I can show you. But…I have to trust you. If I can't trust you, then you'll have to drive me to the police."

Dane shook his head. "Jorge, if you're doing something illegal—"

"Illegal, but not…bad," Jorge said.

"All right, Jorge. If you can convince me that what you're doing isn't bad…then we'll leave it alone. But if you're pushing drugs…"

"That's Izzy's business. I think I can convince you that you need to look beyond what you have seen," Jorge said.

"I'll give you a chance."

"And I'm taking that chance," Jorge said.

"Well?"

"Drive. I'll tell you where to go."

Dane stared at him warily for a moment.

"You're armed, and I'm not," Jorge said. "You can search me if you want. Please, drive."

Dane stared at Jorge, then revved the engine. A minute later they were back out on the highway.

Running didn't get them anywhere. When they reached the sidewalk, Nate and Larry were already there, staring down the little byway that led to US1.

"What? What did you see?" Kelsey asked breathlessly.

"I think someone did run through here," Larry said.

"Not just someone," Nate added.

"Who, then? What the hell is going on?" Cindy demanded.

"I...I don't know," Larry said. "I can't guarantee it, but it might have been..."

"What?" Kelsey exploded.

"A truck. A beatup old tank of a truck," Larry said.

"Old man Latham's truck," Nate explained.

"You think Andy Latham might have been here? In the yard, staring in Kelsey's window, then hiding until he could get away?" Cindy asked.

"Maybe," Larry said. "I wouldn't put it past him."

"It's Nate he's pissed at, though," Larry said.

"I think he hates all of us," Cindy murmured. She stared at Kelsey. "Maybe you did see more than a lizard. I think we should call the police."

"Definitely. That asshole slugged me last night, and who knows what he's doing now? Stalking all of us," Nate said. "Yeah. I'm going in. I'm calling Gary Hansen's office."

"We can't prove anything. We didn't really see anything," Kelsey said.

"We should report the incident, anyway," Nate insisted.

Kelsey nodded. He was right.

They all traipsed back inside, where Nate went to the phone and called the sheriff's office.

Dane was wary as they drove down a side street, but it was true—he was armed, and Jorge wasn't. He was also pretty certain that in a fight, he wouldn't have any trouble taking Jorge down. But the street was a quiet one. And if Jorge was running drugs, it was hardly likely he would have admitted it while they were sitting in the parking lot at the marina.

But it was important to pursue this. Now.

"Just down the street," Jorge said.

Dane pulled into a yard. It was neatly kept. Someone had planted perennials in the little boxed garden area surrounding the house.

The car in the yard was an old Chevy. Like the yard, it showed signs of careful upkeep. The house itself was small but whitewashed.

It didn't look like a crack house.

Jorge got out of the car. Dane followed him as he started up the path to the house and knocked at the door.

A woman's voice answered, sounding wary. The door didn't open.

Jorge spoke to her quickly in Spanish, identifying himself. Dane's understanding of the language was good, but Jorge was speaking so quickly that he couldn't catch everything. But Jorge wasn't warning her that he was out there with someone dangerous, that much Dane could comprehend. He was assuring her that everything was all right.

The door opened slowly.

They stepped into a small living room. The furniture was sparse but polished. A handmade quilt covered an old battered couch. The tile beneath the throw rug was scrubbed and shiny.

The woman who had let them enter was young, in her mid-twenties. She was exotically beautiful, with huge brown eyes, deep bronze skin, long, dark hair, and a willowy, hourglass figure. She looked at Jorge, then at Dane.

"Marisa, *este hombre es un amigo mio*," Jorge said. "Dane Whitelaw."

"Hola," Marisa said gravely, shaking his hand.

"Dane, Marisa works at the club."

"Nice to meet you."

"She is applying for her citizenship," Jorge went on to explain.

"Good for you," Dane said.

She apparently understood some English, because she smiled and said, "Thank you."

"Call Jose," Jorge said softly.

Her eyes widened with alarm.

"It will be all right," Jorge said. "Please, call Jose."

Marisa looked at Jorge. She was clearly afraid, but she trusted Jorge.

"Jose!" She walked toward a small hallway that must have led to the bedrooms. "Please, Jose, come out."

A moment later a boy of about six came running out of the bedroom, straight to the woman. She settled her arms protectively around his shoulders as he stood before her, staring up at Jorge and Dane with the same large dark eyes as Marisa. He smiled at Jorge but looked suspiciously at Dane.

Jorge turned to Dane.

"Marisa is my reason for being at the strip club. Jose is my cargo. Marisa came here several years ago from Cuba. On a raft. Marisa and her husband were parted when they left, and Jose was with his father. Their raft began to leak, and they had to go back. She has been trying for years through legal channels to get her son here. Last year his father died. He was left alone with a very old grandmother who wanted him to come here

to his mother. She tried other means. Then she came
to me."

"So...you earn your living smuggling refugees out
of Cuba?" Dane said.

Jorge stiffened and stared at him with the coldest
gaze Dane had ever known.

"Not me. There are others who take every cent desperate people have ever made. Not me. I do this because
I love my countrymen, because I came here myself, because I love my new country. I do it for all that I have
been given."

Dane was silent. The little boy was looking up at
him. Dane ruffled his hair. "So what were you dumping in the ocean?" he asked Jorge.

"I lost a passenger once. A very old man. He wanted
to touch the shores of a free country before he died.
He didn't make it. I...had to cast the body to the sea.
I couldn't explain how I had come by it if I had not."

Dane smiled at Marisa. "Thanks," he said softly. He
grinned at the boy, mussed his hair once again.

Then he turned and started from the house.

Jorge followed him. "You can't turn me in. You can't
tell anyone about Jose."

Dane stopped. "Dammit, Jorge, I'm not going to turn
in the kid."

"I have not lied to you about anything. I am scared
every time I make a run. Scared to death. But it's something I must do, something I owe to myself, to God. I
would never hurt a woman, I swear that to you."

"Okay, Jorge, I believe you."

"So now...?"

"So now let's go back and have pizza."

Jorge studied his face. Then nodded. "Pizza. It will be cold, but it won't matter. You don't know what a world is like without fast food and pizza."

"Actually, I've seen many worlds without fast food and pizza," Dane told him dryly. "But in this world if our pizza's cold, we can order another one. So let's go."

They returned to the car. Back on the highway, Dane asked Jorge, "You're absolutely sure you were nowhere near that wreck today?"

Jorge looked over at him. "Dane, if I had seen anything, I'd be the first to say so."

"Okay, so were you, Larry, Nate and Cindy near each other all the time?"

"Sure."

"You saw them?"

"Of course. Well, not always…but there were only moments when we weren't together." Jorge spun on him suddenly, angry. "Izzy was so quick to tell you about my activities. Have you talked to him?"

"Obviously."

Jorge stared ahead. "Maybe you should talk to him some more."

"Is there something you know that I don't?" Dane asked.

Jorge shook his head in frustration. "I wish there was. Hey! Look—a sheriff's car. There are Gary Hansen and one of his deputies in front of the duplex."

Dane drove quickly onto the embankment near the front of the duplex. The motor was barely off before he was out of the car and racing toward the front door, his heart thundering with panic.

* * *

"Dane, hey!" Gary Hansen called out.

Dane looked like a thundercloud, all dark-haired menace as he walked toward the porch. Kelsey looked up as he came toward them.

"What the hell happened?" Dane demanded.

"The folks here think they might have had a visitor," Hansen said.

"A visitor?" Dane's eyes were fixed on Kelsey.

"I thought there might have been someone in the yard. Then, when we were eating our pizza out on the patio, Nate thought he saw something, so we all ran out front, where he and Larry thought they saw a truck that might have been Andy Latham's."

Dane stared at Gary. He didn't say a word; he didn't have to. Gary quickly answered his unspoken question.

"Dane, dammit, I told you, I uphold the laws, I don't make them. And so far all he's done is punch Nate and maybe trespass."

"He has to be picked up," Dane said.

"I've got an APB out on him," Gary assured him. "We can bring him in on suspicion of trespassing, something like that. But if you want me to hold him, dammit, you've got to come up with something for me to hold him *on*."

"Bring him in," Dane said, running his fingers through his dark hair. "Bring him in, and I'll come up with cause to hold him."

"You'd better. Because I haven't got squat."

Gary started down the walk toward his car. Dane stared at Kelsey, and she stared back.

"Pack up a few things."

"What? Why?"

"You're coming to my house."

Kelsey frowned. "Dane, Larry is here, and Cindy is right next door."

"Please," he managed to say quietly, gritting his teeth. "Come to my house."

Kelsey stared at him. Scary. She had slept with him last night, and now she didn't know if she trusted him or not.

No...

She did trust him. As much as she trusted anyone.

And still...

"Kelsey, please."

She didn't want to be afraid the way she had been earlier. Seeing a face in a window, wondering if it was real or just a product of her overexcited imagination.

"Come in for a few minutes." She looked past him, frowning, and saw that Jorge was right behind him. She stared at the two of them. "Is everything all right with you two?"

"Just fine," Dane said curtly.

"Are you going to explain?" she asked them.

"No," they said in unison.

"Great. And I'm supposed to go sleep at your house," she said to Dane.

Jorge set a hand on her arm. "It's all right."

"I have your blessing?" she inquired, a half smile curving her lips.

Jorge grinned and nodded.

"Great. Well, then, you two go on in and explain yourselves to the others, have some pizza. Beer and sodas are in the refrigerator." She stared at Dane, whose dark eyes never gave away a damn thing. She exhaled.

She was uneasy. No, flat-out scared. But, right or wrong, she wanted to be with him.

"I guess I'll go pack a few things."

Chapter 15

As Kelsey walked back through the apartment, she heard Nate, Larry and Cindy discussing Andy Latham and wondering why he was so convinced that one of them was throwing dead fish on his property. They were clustered together in the living room, and had moved on from pizza and beer to coffee and Oreos.

"Is Gary Hansen going to do anything?" Larry asked her, stretching to get a kink out of his neck.

"Yes, he's going to try to pick him up, and he can probably hold him for about twenty-four hours, but he can't really keep him unless we can come up with something on him. By the way, Jorge and Dane are back."

The announcement was unnecessary, because by that time the group could clearly see Jorge and Dane walking in behind her.

"Did you eat all the pizza?" Jorge asked.

"No, the leftovers are in the refrigerator," Cindy said. "Want me to heat it up for you?"

"I can manage," Dane said.

"Did you two duke it out or something?" Nate asked.

Kelsey went to the bedroom and closed the door behind her. They could figure it out between themselves, she decided. Whatever was going on, Dane and Jorge had decided not to tell her.

She sat down again in front of the drawer where she had been digging through Sheila's things. She separated out the papers she had already gone over and started leafing through some of the others. She came to a picture that looked as if it had been drawn by a small child. It had been, of course. Sheila's name was scrawled at the bottom right.

The drawing was done with the simple strokes of a grade school art class. Arms and legs were little more than sticks.

What was disturbing was that the picture, despite its simplistic form, was very real. It depicted a man and a child, his arm around the little girl. Not around her shoulders or her waist. Lower. His smile was little more than a slash of color, and yet it captured a strange sense of evil. The girl was clearly afraid of the man. Studying the crude crayon drawing, Kelsey bit her lip. She wondered if anything she was seeing could prove that Andy Latham had been a child molester.

She doubted that either Sheila's diary or her old drawing would be enough in a court of law, not without Sheila here to do something about it. Gary Hansen knew just as well as they did that Andy Latham should be locked up, but like he had said, he didn't make the laws, he just upheld them.

She stashed the picture, the rest of the papers and Sheila's diary in an overnight bag and grabbed a few more things. She walked back out to the living room with the bag packed.

"What's that?" Larry asked in surprise, an Oreo halfway to his lips.

Dane was seated in the armchair next to the sofa. He had a large coffee cup in his hands. He looked at Kelsey over the rim of it and replied to Larry. "Kelsey is going to stay with me at Hurricane Bay tonight."

"Oh," Larry said.

They all stared at Kelsey.

"That didn't take very long," Larry murmured.

"Well, I guess we've all known all along that there was...something between them," Cindy said.

"Still, three days," Larry said, looking at Kelsey with a shake of his head.

"Three days," Nate echoed.

"Three days—and how many years?" Jorge said.

"I guess I just never realized before that Kelsey and Dane knew each other so quite well," Larry said.

Larry looked at Kelsey, still confused. "Did Sheila know?"

"Did Sheila know what? That I'm going to stay at Hurricane Bay tonight because I'm spooked by what happened here?" Kelsey asked, unable to repress a certain irritation that she seemed to have three extra parents judging her actions.

"About you and Dane," Larry said with a sigh.

"There wasn't—isn't—any 'me and Dane,'" Kelsey said. "I'm just sleeping at Hurricane Bay tonight."

"It's because he thinks one of us tried to kill you

with a spear-gun," Nate said suddenly, angrily. "And I guess you think so, too."

"No!" Kelsey protested. "Nate, that's not it at all. I'm just a little uneasy about Andy Latham or someone sneaking into the yard and watching me."

"I'm here, too, you know," Larry said.

"And I live in the other half of the house," Cindy added.

"You could have come to my house," Nate said, eyeing her levelly.

"I'm glad I'm not in the middle of this one," Jorge murmured.

Nate kept staring at Kelsey as he said, "She's always been in love with him." He offered her a rueful smile.

Kelsey groaned, dropping the bag and staring at the lot of them. "I'm here, right here, you don't need to talk around me. Dane made me the first offer, so I'm just going over to Hurricane Bay for the night. I'll figure it all out from there tomorrow. Is that all right?"

Larry looked at Nate. "He was in the armed forces. And he's a private investigator."

"Carries a big gun," Nate agreed.

"Larry, if you're feeling protective, I may just stay on this side tonight, in Kelsey's bed," Cindy said.

"Sheila's bed," Kelsey corrected.

None of them said anything, their silence seeming to indicate that they shared her fear that something bad had happened to Sheila. No one even tried to suggest that Sheila might show up that night.

"There's a plan. Cindy, who can bench-press twice her own weight, is going to let me feel protective," Larry said.

Jorge crumpled his pizza plate in his hand. "Well,

I know where I'm sleeping—in my own bed. I'll wish you all good night."

He nodded around the group, then looked at Dane, who was just walking in from the kitchen. Kelsey was both baffled and curious. Dane nodded back at Jorge, as if the two of them had come to some new understanding that went beyond anything she could begin to comprehend.

It was nice, of course, since they had been friends for a very long time. But it was also annoying as all hell. She felt very much on the outside.

"I guess I'm going, too," Nate said, rising.

"And we'll be on our way. I'm about to drop," Kelsey said.

Nate was standing behind her. "Oh, yeah. I'll bet you're going right to sleep," he said softly.

She stared at him, frowning. "Do you remember that we didn't sleep at all last night? We came rushing back here because Latham decked you."

"Thanks for the concern," he said. He started out the door, then turned back. "Hey, Larry, if Latham really is getting freaky, you two do need to watch it, being here. Make sure you lock up tight."

"We'll do a thorough inspection of all windows and doors before going to sleep," Cindy assured him.

"Of course," Larry said, "we could all go to Hurricane Bay and be safe."

"Except that we're not all invited," Jorge said. "Good night." He headed out for his car.

"Good night, and, Cindy, Larry, really do lock up," Kelsey said.

"I'm on it," Cindy assured her.

Nate didn't say goodbye; he just watched Kelsey as

she climbed into the Jeep beside Dane. As they left, Cindy and Larry waved from the door. Nate at last lifted a hand.

When the others had left, Cindy looked at the two men. "It's not actually a surprise."

"You mean Kelsey going off with Dane?" Larry said.

"Of course. Nate, you're the one who used to tell me all the time that you thought something went on between them years ago."

"Yeah," Nate said.

"So why didn't they stay together?" Larry asked.

"Who knows? Maybe Kelsey felt she had betrayed Sheila or something like that."

Larry made a snorting sound. "How could anyone betray Sheila?" he asked.

"Poor Larry." Cindy put her hand on his arm. "I know she hurt you, but...but I think sometimes that she just must have been...is...so messed up inside that she couldn't help it." She watched him, hesitating for a minute. She was about to make a confession. "I... could tell you..."

"What?" Larry asked her.

"Never mind. Let's take a walk through my place, check it out, lock it up and come back here."

"You think someone might have broken into your place?" Nate asked.

"I don't know, but I'll feel better if we look around. I'm like Kelsey, just feeling a little spooked."

"Whatever makes you happy," Larry said.

"Can't hurt," Nate told Cindy. "Maybe I'll hang around on the couch tonight. We'll all be here then. Would that make you feel better?"

Larry groaned. "Just because I'm usually in a suit doesn't mean I haven't got balls, you know."

Cindy laughed. "Larry, we're not questioning your manly credentials."

"Right," Nate said. "Actually I might stay just because I'm spooked myself, and I'm not sure I want to drive home alone. I had Dane set up cameras and stuff for security at work, but hell...we haven't locked our doors around here for years. Larry, you can protect me, too."

"Cool," Larry said. "Let's start with Cindy's place, then."

They locked the door to Sheila's place, and Cindy unlocked the door to the other side of the house.

"Want us to hang out in the living room?" Larry asked.

"No, I want you to follow me every step of the way."

They did. They went through every room, checked out every closet, then made sure every door was locked. Just as an extra precaution, they shoved a mop handle against the sliding door in the back bedroom that corresponded with the one where Kelsey had been sleeping. Larry found a broken broom to use for the same purpose off the dining and living area.

"Happy?" Larry asked.

"I am," Cindy said.

"Okay, now we go through the other side," Nate said.

They walked through the house together, then secured the doors, taking extra care with the back where Kelsey had slept and where Cindy would sleep that night.

"Am I crazy?" Nate murmured, looking out the window before closing the drapes. "Are we all crazy?

Kelsey might have seen a head—or she might have seen
a lizard. I might have seen a flash of someone—or it
might have been my imagination. We might have seen
Latham's car—and we might not have seen it."

"We're all overtired," Cindy said. "We've hardly had
any sleep at all."

"All right, well…there's my bunk," Nate said, indicating the couch. "I guess you two are beat."

"Exhausted," Cindy agreed. "But…not quite ready
to sleep. I shouldn't have had that coffee. I'm wired."

"I know how to cure that," Nate said.

"How?" Cindy asked.

"Let's have another beer."

"Great. Then we can sit around and talk about old
times," Larry said dryly.

"If we have two beers, who knows what I may wind
up telling you," Cindy said.

"Something scandalous?" Larry asked.

"Low down and dirty," Cindy said.

"I'm on my way for the beers," Nate told her.

"I wish you would tell me what went on with Jorge,"
Kelsey said. "You came in the first time as if you wanted
to throttle him. You came back in later as if you were
his best buddy."

"I wouldn't say that," Dane told her, pulling onto
the road to Hurricane Bay. "Jorge just explained a few
things, that's all. No one is off the hook yet."

"Off the hook? Dane, I know that I've been the one
pressing to find out what happened to Sheila, but I think
you're becoming paranoid."

"Kelsey, have you forgotten that someone shot at you
with a speargun today?"

She turned in the seat, staring at him. "There were lots of boats out there today. You didn't even catch the names of all of them. And let's face it, most of the problems down here are caused by tourists who don't know what they're doing. And if someone around here is guilty of any of this, it has to be Andy Latham."

"I'm sure he *is* guilty of something. But that doesn't explain a lot of the things that have been going on. I didn't really look at all the boats out there today—I was too anxious to hook up with all of you—but I think I would have noticed Latham's boat. It's a floating cesspool." Dane shook his head. "Besides, I can't see Andy Latham having the intelligence to track you down, take a speargun and manage to hide himself so well."

"If he is the Necktie Strangler, he's certainly demonstrated his intelligence," Kelsey said. "He's managed to dispose of his victims so that they don't surface until it's almost impossible for the police to get evidence from the bodies."

Dane brought the car to a halt and turned off the engine. "All right, I'll grant you that."

"And if anyone was running around the yard tonight, it must have been Latham. Nate was almost certain it was Latham's truck he saw."

Dane looked at her. "Okay, Latham is the prime suspect. Now we just need some proof. Or at least something that connects him to the victims."

"If we find Sheila and she's been..." Kelsey's voice faltered.

"Yes, *if* we find Sheila," he said simply. "Here, give me your bag."

He took the small canvas bag she had brought and

exited the car. Kelsey followed him to the back door and noted that he now locked both the bolts.

"You're worried about something out here?" she said.

"I'm just worried in general," he told her.

As soon as they were inside, he was careful to lock the door again.

She had paused just in the entry. "Make yourself at home," he told her, walking past her.

"Strange, isn't it? I do feel at home here."

"Because it hasn't changed a hell of a lot, probably."

"Yes, but *we've* all changed, haven't we?"

"Maybe. And maybe not. Want something to drink? Are you hungry? Hell, I guess you're exhausted. I am."

"Yeah, I'm beat. And I know where the kitchen is," Kelsey said. She hesitated. "Where do you want me?"

"In my room," he said ruefully. "I get the impression you're still not really sure you trust me."

She took the bag from him. "Miss a chance to inspect your bedroom? Not on your life." She started for the stairway in the front, then paused. "You're going to let me go up there without supervision?"

"I have a few calls to make," he told her.

"All right. Who are you calling?"

"I promise I'll tell you if anything pans out, how's that?"

"I don't think I can beat an answer out of you, so I guess it will have to do." She hesitated, watching him.

"Yes?"

"If you take too long, you know I'll be asleep."

A slow, rueful grin cut across his face. "I'll keep that in mind."

Kelsey went up the stairs.

* * *

The threesome at the duplex were actually on their third beers when Nate urged Cindy to make good on her earlier remark.

"C'mon," he pressed. "I've confessed my horrendous dating experiences. The time I got that really hot model into bed and passed out from too much booze. Then the obvious, of course—that I couldn't keep my wife a full month. And Larry has told us all how he caught his pecker in his zipper on his first date with that art assistant. Come on, Cindy—you got us going on guy talk. You're going to have to join in. And this should be different—I mean, you're not likely to tell us you couldn't get it up."

"No..." Cindy said slowly.

"Jeez, come on," Larry prodded. "Nate and I only spilled the far-from-macho beans to get you talking."

"All right." Cindy stared at them. "I had a thing with...another woman."

"Whoa!" Nate said.

"I wound up really humiliated."

"What happened?" Larry demanded.

"Who with? It wasn't Kelsey, was it? Or wasn't she telling the truth when she said she's not gay?"

Cindy shook her head. "Not Kelsey. And, Nate, dammit, quit worrying that you weren't a good lover and that's why your marriage didn't last. I think it's obvious now what made Kelsey tick all the time."

"A better man," Nate said.

Cindy shook her head determinedly. "A different man. That's all, Nate. A different man."

"Hey, hey, hey. Enough of the rah-rah for Nate. Come on, Cindy. Do we know this broad you slept with?"

"Oh yeah."

"Who?" Nate demanded.

"I know," Larry said, eyeing Cindy over his can of beer. "Sheila."

"Sheila?" Nate exploded. "How did she fit you into her schedule between men?"

Cindy smiled. "Oh…we were doing this same thing one night. Sitting here, drinking wine. We just started talking, kind of like this, about men. I was telling her about all my bad dates, lousy relationships. I had just been out with this guy who sold T-shirts wholesale. The entire time we were doing business, he was as nice as could be. We go out for dinner, and right off he wants to head for his hotel room."

"Let's get back on topic here. What happened with you and Sheila?"

"She gave me the speech about her own life—saying I might as well get what I could out of a guy, because they were all like that at heart."

"I wasn't. I loved her," Larry said.

"She said you loved her too much," Cindy told Larry. "Maybe."

"Come on, Cindy, get to the good part," Nate urged.

"I'm not even sure where it started," she said. "I guess we decided that, on the whole, the male of the species was a total louse. Except for gay guys. They're great but unavailable. She said that was why women often preferred other women. They were nicer, sensitive…decent. The next thing I knew, she was rubbing my shoulders. She said I needed a hot bath. We wound up in the bath together with a ton of bubbles and more wine, and when we got out, she started drying me off. And she…well, she just touched the right places, and I was really drunk, and then…the things she could do…"

"Yeah, we know," Nate said huskily.

"Well, anyway, we slept together. I woke up with a terrible hangover, feeling ridiculous and uneasy. Sheila started laughing and telling me not to worry about it, she wasn't getting into anything permanent with me—I had actually been an experiment. She just wanted to prove to herself that she could seduce anyone, male or female. I was pretty pissed off—and big time embarrassed. I don't think we spoke to each other for days after that. But she was always so blasé about everything. In a week it was as if it had never happened."

"That was probably a record," Nate said. "I doubt if she ever remembered any guy she slept with for more than a week."

"Except for Dane," Larry said.

"Her thing with Dane was weird," Cindy said, shaking her head. "She wanted him, but she would push him away when he tried to get too close."

"She knew she couldn't be what Dane was looking for," Nate said. "Partly because she was Sheila…and maybe she even knew he'd had a thing for Kelsey all those years. And this time around, she knew he had been in love with that woman in St. Augustine." He was quiet for a minute, then said, "Okay, Sheila drank with you and sympathized about bad dates. I'm doing the same thing. And I'd sure love to get into a tub with you and a bunch of bubbles. What do you think?"

Cindy just laughed.

Cindy curled into Sheila's bed at long last. She was beyond exhaustion, and though she had had a great time staying up and talking with Nate and Larry, she knew she was going to regret it in the morning. She loved what she did, really enjoyed the stores, the people she met and, especially, buying the things they would sell, but it was still work. Nate could cruise into work when he felt like it, and Larry was on vacation, though he'd said he planned to do some work on the computer. She was the only one who was going to have to get up in a few hours' time.

Still, it was fun. She liked having the old crowd back. Not that she hadn't had Nate around forever, or that she hadn't seen Dane a fair amount since he'd been back. But she'd missed Kelsey. And Jorge. Spending time with Jorge was great.

She snuggled beneath the blankets, glad the air-conditioning worked so well. She lived in Key Largo because she had no desire to live anywhere else. One day she would probably be as wrinkled as a prune from her hours in the sun—despite the sunblock she had learned at a young age to apply on a continual basis—but she had no desire to live anywhere else in the world. The sun was wonderful, the water was wonderful. Snorkeling, diving, all of it. The reefs, the people, the food, the drinks…and now, the return of old friends.

Heat was great by day. At night, though, it was great to cuddle beneath the blankets in the chill blast of the air-conditioning.

The best of both worlds.

She turned and plumped her pillow, knowing she really needed to sleep.

She had almost drifted off when she was suddenly wide-awake again.

At first she didn't know what had disturbed her. She just lay there in the darkness, her eyes wide-open, her body tense from head to toe.

Then…

A rustling. Outside.

She turned and stared at the window, but of course she had made certain the drapes were closed before she went to bed, so she couldn't see a thing. She wondered if she was really hearing something, or if she was suffering from belated nerves.

She told herself that she was safe. Larry was in the other bedroom; Nate was on the sofa.

At last the tension in her muscles began to ease. She closed her eyes.

Then her lids flew open again.

There was someone out there. Someone trying to jimmy the lock on the sliding glass door.

"Hello? *Hola?*"

"Jorge, it's Dane."

"Dane?" Jorge sounded puzzled.

"Sorry, were you sleeping?"

"Yeah, but no big deal. What's up?"

"I'd like to talk to your friend again."

"Why?" Jorge asked suspiciously. "You said you wouldn't—"

"Jorge, I don't want to send the boy back to Cuba. I just need to talk to your friend. I showed Katia some pictures. That's how I knew that you'd been at the club. But she wasn't sure about the others. She thinks everyone I showed her might have been there at one time or another. Which is logical, I guess. She sees so many men. But maybe Marisa could help. I want to be sure she's seen all the pictures, too."

"She's probably sleeping now."

"I know. But I'd like to see her first thing in the morning."

"All right."

"Were you planning on working?"

"I have captains who can work my boats," Jorge reminded him, a low touch of pride in his voice. And then he added quietly, "Except when I must go to sea myself."

"Meet me at the gas station up on the highway by my place. Nine o'clock too early?"

"No. Not for you."

Jorge hung up.

Dane looked at the clock. There wasn't much else he could do until morning. Not on the phone.

He stood quickly, and headed for the stairs.

Cindy let out a scream that could have roused the dead. She jumped up and tore out of the room. In the broad hallway outside the bedroom, she collided with Nate.

"What is it?" he demanded. His blond hair was tousled, almost standing on end. He was clad only in a pair of blue silk boxers.

"The back!"

Larry, nothing but a sheet tied around his waist, came rushing out of his room.

"What the hell…?"

"There's someone at the sliding glass door," Cindy said, trying to be calm.

"You're certain?" Nate said. "You're not just having leftover jitters?"

"I heard someone!"

Larry started into the bedroom, heading for the drapes.

"I'm going out the front. Hope we can catch him this time," Nate said. Heedless of his shiny blue boxers, he headed right for the front door, unlocked it and went out.

Cindy watched Nate go, then ran after Larry. She reached the room just as he wrenched the drapes away from the window.

There was no one on the patio.

"I'm going around to find Nate," Cindy said.

"I'm right behind you."

Larry followed after her. She had just reached the door when she heard him curse.

"Shit!"

She turned back. Larry had tripped on his sheet. He was on the floor, in the buff. Despite herself, she felt the urge to laugh. She didn't want to stare at him. He looked like a kid on a bear rug, ready for one of those embarrassing photos parents liked to show their kids.

"I'm going to catch up with Nate. Come on," she said.

Cindy ran out the front door. She tore around to the side gate, which gaped open.

"Nate?" she realized that she had whispered his name.

He didn't reply.

"Nate?" she persisted, raising her voice slightly.

Still no reply. He had to be out there.

She hurried along the side of the house, walking quickly, then running, anxious to reach the patio, where Nate had to be.

Suddenly she staggered, a shooting pain going

through her head. She blinked, wondering what she had done, and tried to take a step.

She careened to the ground instead.

Kelsey really should have gone to sleep.

But she was waiting for Dane, and she knew it. When he didn't come right away, she knew she would fall asleep if she didn't do something, so she turned on the television, sitting up in bed and using the remote. Nice bed, she thought. Big. Comfortable. Four pillows at the headboard. The room wasn't overly neat—Dane had fishing magazines strewn about and some kind of trade journal describing new security products. Across from the bed was a bookshelf with an interesting assortment of titles: copies of the classics, military manuals, books on the local flora and fauna, a lot on the Everglades, and the paperback thrillers he liked to read for pleasure.

The room was done in a combination of hardwood and rattan. It was a masculine room that still welcomed a feminine presence. She felt ridiculously comfortable and at home.

Dane even had a good mattress. Clean, cool sheets. Comfy pillows.

Don't get too comfortable, girl, she warned herself. She led a different life. A fast-paced life in the advertising world. She'd only been home a matter of days, and already it seemed as if the years since her last visit meant nothing, were hardly even real. She had ended up exactly where she wanted to be. But it was a bad move. She didn't know Dane anymore. She doubted that he wanted any more than a few days with her. He'd been hurt in St. Augustine, so here he was. She'd actually gone to him and asked him to sleep with her. She was sure that was no hardship for him. But he'd slept with Sheila, as well. Before she had disappeared. She needed to think about this situation, keep her emotions in reserve.

And yet all that seemed to matter was that she was here with him now. Granted, he was downstairs. And she had warned him that she might fall asleep. Hmm. But she had also insisted that he find Sheila. And whatever he was doing, she was certain, had to do with that goal.

With that in mind, she jumped out of bed and dug into the bag she had brought along. She drew out the picture Sheila had drawn in grade school. Sheila was no artist, yet the picture was more disturbing than if it had been a perfect likeness.

She kept going through the papers, then picked up Sheila's diary, wishing that it gave more away. A diary was supposed to allow for total freedom of thought, but Sheila had only rambled. Kelsey flipped pages, wishing she could find something. Sheila did refer to people. Nate was a "silly dear." And Larry loved her so much, she wished she had been able to settle down with him. He still called her, just to make sure she didn't need anything. Izzy remained at the top of her list for fun. She enjoyed Jorge's company, but he lacked that true edge of dangerous excitement—and the ability to see her as a real equal—that Izzy had. If only Izzy didn't mind that she loved to go to bars and pick up strangers.

The only time she ever mentioned fear was in reference to Dane. In needing to talk to Dane.

But Dane had been right. If she was afraid of him, why would he be the one she turned to when she needed to talk?

She cast the diary down in exasperation. "Sheila, why the hell didn't you just come right out and say something? It was *your* diary," she said aloud.

She picked up the papers again. Riffling through them, she was startled to find another drawing she had missed earlier.

The drawing was more like doodling. But once again it depicted a man and a girl. Or a woman. The man had the woman by the throat.

"What did you find?"

Dane's voice startled her and she nearly threw the drawing into the air. He was standing in the bedroom doorway, watching her.

"A sketch Sheila did," she told him.

He walked over to the bed, taking the sketch, staring at it. Dane so seldom gave anything away. But his look as he stared at the picture was disturbed and sorrowful.

"You think she was drawing Andy Latham?" he asked.

Kelsey shrugged. "Who can tell? She wasn't much of an artist."

He looked at the journal on the bed, still encased in the book cover.

"Sheila's diary?"

"Yes," she admitted.

"And...?"

"Nothing. She talks about everyone, but...nothing."

"I should read it."

Kelsey shrugged. "Sure. Maybe you can find something I can't."

"Not tonight. I don't think I could make sense of anything tonight."

She met his eyes. "I guess you're really tired."

"Well, there's tired and then there's tired."

"Oh?"

"I'm too tired to read." He set the journal on the nightstand and collected the papers Kelsey had scattered on the bed, piling them on top of the journal. He sat on the side of the bed, looking at her. "You've got great shoulders, Kelsey."

"Thanks."

"Can I assume the fact that they're naked shoulders means that the rest of you is also naked underneath that sheet?"

"You can assume anything you want. But you are a private investigator. I'm sure you can think of some way to find out."

"Yes, I'm sure I can."

He didn't touch her then, but rose, turning off the light. He picked up the remote control and flicked off the television.

The room wasn't completely dark. They were on the second floor, and Hurricane Bay was a private island. The drapes were pulled back. Pools of soft moonlight spilled into the room.

He undressed in haste, shoes kicked off at the foot of the bed, pants and briefs discarded there. He pulled his knit shirt over his head and it, too, fell on the pile.

He pulled the sheets from Kelsey.

"Looks like my assumption was right."

"Wow, you're really good at what you do."

"Thanks, ma'am."

"I meant investigating."

"I didn't."

Kelsey laughed as he crawled in beside her.

"Humble," she murmured, as she felt the length of his body slide next to hers, hard, hot and vibrant.

"Do you want humble...or good?"

"Well you'd better be damn good now," she told him.

She saw him grin in the moonlight. "All right."

Kelsey curled her arms around him. She'd been exhausted, but suddenly she was wide-awake.

His lips found hers. He could kiss in a way that created a carnal and intimate illusion of everything he was about to do with his body. Her legs were parted by the length of his. Their mouths were locked in an open, wet fusion when he thrust deeply into her, bringing her to the brink in a matter of seconds. She wanted to hold on, to savor the moment of deepening penetration, but then he moved...and moved.

She thought she was going to die. But just when she reached that point, he withdrew. His lips started moving then. Over her shoulders, which he complimented in whispers once again. Teasing against her collarbone. Doing incredible things to her breasts.

She couldn't bear it. She pressed against him, turning the tide. There was so much of Dane she wanted to explore. Taste, treasure. She nuzzled against the hair on his chest, ran her lips and tongue in delicate kisses over his throat, down to his hips.

Great legs...

Six-pack belly. He kept himself in shape.

She teased him everywhere...then slid her mouth down the length of his sex. She heard his single expulsion of breath as he savored her every move.

He flipped her down in a sudden movement with a sound almost like a growl. Then he returned the caresses. Belly, thighs...

Between.

She tugged at his hair. He came to her.

She thanked God they were on an island, she shrieked so loudly.

And then they lay there, locked together. She was aware of the dim moonlight. And of Dane. The feel of him, sheened with sweat, beside her. So alive.

"Well?" he murmured, lips against her ear.

She smiled, turning into him, running her fingers through his hair. "You'll do."

"Thanks." He rose above her suddenly. "I'm not always so good, you know."

"Oh?"

"It's you," he said. "You're incredibly inspiring."

"I try," she said, then added. "With you."

She couldn't see his features as he lay by her side again. She curled against him, exhausted. In moments she was asleep.

She awoke to find that he was up, dressed and ready to go out. She was startled to see that there was a gun on the bed next to her.

"It's a .38 special," he told her. "You know how to use it?"

"I...yes. I haven't touched a gun in years, but...I used to go to the shooting range with Joe fairly frequently."

"Good. I'll be about an hour. I'll lock up behind me, but keep that with you—even in the shower."

He kissed her forehead.

"Where are you going?"

"To see a stripper."

"Really."

"Yes, really. But I'll be right back."

She didn't press him, because he wasn't there to press. She heard his footsteps as he hurried down the stairs.

She lay in bed, wanting to get up, eyeing the gun. It had been a while. But she did know how to use it.

She closed her eyes, and was startled when the phone rang.

She picked it up, wondering if she should have. "Hello?"

"Kelsey?"

"Yes." It was Nate. His tone was strange.

"What is it? What's the matter?"

"Are you up? I'm coming out."

"Nate, dammit, what the hell is the matter?"

"Two things, Kels. Cindy is in the hospital."

"Why? My God, Nate, what happened?"

He went on as if he hadn't heard her.

"Cindy is in the hospital…and they've found another body." He hesitated for a fraction of a second.

"And they think this one is Sheila."

Chapter 16

Cold seeped into Kelsey. A chill deeper than anything she had ever felt before.

It wasn't like the day when the military had arrived to say that Joe had been killed in action. That had been agony, anguish deeper than any physical trauma could ever inflict.

But even when Joe had died, she hadn't felt this chill. Joe had died doing what he considered his duty as an American.

Sheila had been murdered. And the anguish now lay in knowing that Sheila must have been terrified, that she must have suffered not just pain, but fear.

And the chill came from the fact that her murderer was still out there.

"Kelsey?"

"Who called?"

"A policeman called this morning and asked us to come down and identity her remains. They couldn't get hold of Andy Latham, so they tried to find Larry. Where's Dane?"

"Gone. I'm not sure where."

"All right. I'm on my way out to get you. Dane's got an in with both Gary Hansen and the Metro-Dade cops. I'm sure they'll get hold of him. Get dressed. I can be there in five minutes."

"Yes, all right." She was so distraught about Sheila that she'd almost forgotten the first news he had given her. "Wait! What happened to Cindy? You said she's in the hospital. Is she going to be all right?"

"God, yes, sorry. She thought she heard someone at the sliding glass door to the bedroom last night. I went out the back, she and Larry went out the front, and she was running, and we think she ran into the hurricane awning. Anyway, she knocked herself out. The E.R. doctor said she needed to stay in the hospital, just for observation." He hesitated. "We're supposed to pick her up this afternoon. I haven't told her that they think... that they think they've found Sheila. We thought we'd let her get out of the hospital first. Be ready, okay?"

"I will."

Kelsey hung up the phone and jumped out of bed. If she thought about dressing, she wouldn't think about Sheila.

Wrong.

All she could think about was Sheila.

Her dread had proven to be far too real.

Tears stung her eyes as she hopped in and out of the shower, then threw on clothing. She didn't think to brush her hair. She didn't even glance at the gun Dane

had left on the other side of the bed, just ran downstairs, wondering if Nate had arrived and she hadn't
heard him. She looked out the peephole in the front,
but no one was there.

She looked out back.

Nate had arrived.

He was standing on the little spit of beach to the far
left of the dock.

She hit the lock and exited the house, hurrying over
to him. She hesitated. He was standing there, hands in
his pockets, shoulders slumped, just staring at the sand.

"Nate?"

He turned to her, the sun casting a strange glow over
his features.

"There you are," he said softly.

He walked to her, placing his hands on her shoulders. His eyes were curiously dry. "Kelsey," he said.

He drew her to him.

His grip was hard.

And painful.

They had found her.

Dane had barely reached the gas station before Gary
Hansen gave him the call. She had been found on the
Gulf side by a couple of kids out fishing around the
numerous little islets that were little more than a few
mangroves grouped together.

Due to the condition of the body—and the tie around
her neck—she had been brought to the Miami-Dade
County morgue for autopsy. Since she'd been fished
out of the water where she'd been caught among the
roots of the trees, there wasn't much the crime scene
investigators could do, but they were out there working.

Hector Hernandez had told Dane that he was welcome to meet him at the morgue; they were going to need a positive identification, and they weren't sure Larry was going to be up to it.

Dane met Jorge long enough to tell him what had happened, then drove north as quickly as he could. He had given Jorge a picture of Andy Latham and asked him to go show it to Marisa and ask her if she recognized the man.

Hector was well acquainted with the morgue. At the desk, he was directed to what they called cell five. It was where she had been taken, awaiting autopsy.

When Dane entered, Hector had his notebook out as he spoke with Dr. Alfred Gray. Hector waved a hand to indicate to the medical examiner that it was all right to keep speaking with Dane in the room. Sheila had been in the water approximately seven to twelve days, but since she had last been seen a week ago Friday, he thought it likely that she had been killed soon after.

"You were the last one to see her, right?" Hector asked Dane.

"The last one to admit it," Dane replied.

He had seen the dead before. Those who had died peacefully, and those who had died after the ravages of a long illness. He had seen people who had been shot, bombed and stabbed, the casualties of war.

He had never seen anything like Sheila.

What the water and its inhabitants had done to her once beautiful face and figure went beyond terrible. The crabs had chewed on her. Fish had nibbled fingers and flesh. And then, of course, there had been the death itself. Strangulation was not a pretty way to go.

And the tie. His tie. The pattern still visible, despite the ravages of water, fish and muck.

"It is Sheila Warren, though, right?" Hector asked him.

Dane nodded.

Hector was studying him gravely. He wanted to turn away. He felt Hector's eyes, but kept studying Sheila's face.

"We tried to contact her stepfather, but his boat isn't docked and his car is nowhere to be found."

Dane stared at Hector. "I've been looking for him myself, ever since Gary Hansen had to release him after he made bail. His boat and car were both gone yesterday, as well."

The medical examiner covered Sheila's face.

"Is there a place where Dane and I can talk for a minute?" Hector asked Dr. Gray.

"My office. Down the hall."

Dane followed Hector out of cell five and down the hall. Gray's door was closed but not locked.

The office was strange, though perhaps the eclectic decor within was to be expected. A skeleton hung from a metal stand. Dane knew it was human, not a copy. The skull on the desk, however, was an excellently crafted medical tool made of plastic. There was a stack of eight by ten photos on the desk. Morgue photos.

Hector sat in the doctor's chair, indicating that Dane should take the chair in front of him. Dane sat, folded his hands in his lap and looked at Hector.

"You came to me about the Necktie Strangler when Sheila was just among the missing. I need to know why you thought we were going to find Sheila like this," he told Dane.

"That's not a great mystery," Dane said, despite the fact that it seemed every one of his muscles was tightening like piano wire. "She was missing—missing women have been showing up in the canals lately."

"And you've been looking for Andy Latham, who has disappeared, at least for the moment. Want to tell me why?"

"Because he's a scumbag, and Sheila hated him," Dane said. Staring at Hector, he still saw Sheila's face. Sheila's beautiful face...

Never to be beautiful again.

Sheila, who had said, "Dane, help me."

He felt sick. He didn't usually get queasy at the sight of death.

He didn't usually see a woman he had known all his life, slept with, grown up with, dead, and not just dead... dead the way Sheila was...lying on a slab at the morgue. Sheila was beyond suffering now. And beyond help.

There was a tap at the door, and it opened. Dr. Gray didn't enter, he just spoke briefly.

"Hector," Dr. Gray said, "if you're done...we're going to get started on her right away. You'll have my report the minute we're finished."

"Thank you," Hector said gravely.

The door closed. Hector looked at Dane again. Dane realized his palms were sweating.

"Come on, Dane," Hector said. "Talk to me."

"Hey! Let's go!"

It was Larry. He was on the dock.

Nate released Kelsey, staring down into her eyes. He shook his head in misery. "I didn't mean to...I just started thinking…oh, God, Kels, I had a death grip on you there…I'm sorry, I just…I just…"

She nodded. "Let's go."

She walked over to Larry, who looked like hell. His eyes were swollen, the rims nearly crimson.

"It—it may not be her," Kelsey said.

Neither of them answered her as they walked to the car. She knew that, in their hearts, all three of them knew that the woman in the morgue was going to be Sheila Warren.

Nate had trouble opening his car door.

"Are you all right to drive?" she asked him.

He stared at her. "I'm fine. Honestly. Come up, we've got to get up to Miami."

Larry got into the back seat. Kelsey took the front. They drove in silence.

"Kelsey Cunningham, an old friend, showed up here a few days ago because she was supposed to meet Sheila."

"I know who she is," Hector acknowledged.

"Kelsey was extremely concerned right away. She didn't believe Sheila would have gone off without telling her, not when they had arranged to get together. She came to me—and then she went out to Andy Latham's. Another friend called to tell me that she was out there, so I went after her and got her. Not because I knew anything, but because, like I said, Latham is a sleazebag. Always has been. We—Sheila's friends—believe she was probably molested by him as a child. Then Latham showed up at my house when we were having a barbecue. He dumped off a pile of rotting fish. Accused us—or me—of having dropped them on his property."

"Did you?"

"Come on, Hector, what do you think? Of course I didn't."

"Go on."

"Last night Kelsey thought someone was out in the yard at the duplex. She's staying at Sheila's place. They called Gary Hansen, so the cops came out."

"Are you sure it was Latham?"

"Sheila's ex-husband, Larry, and Nate Curry were both there, and they thought they saw Latham's truck drive away."

"They thought."

Dane lifted his hands. "Hector, I wasn't there at the time. I'm telling you what they told me. But they called Gary Hansen."

"And?"

"By the time Gary came out, they'd all tramped all over the yard."

"Did anyone dust for prints?"

"No. But..."

"But what?"

"I think he wears gloves. Some kind of gloves, most of the time. Diving gloves, fishing gloves. You know yourself, the Necktie Strangler is no fool."

"Is there anything else?"

"Yes."

"What?"

"Yesterday they all went fishing. When I heard that Latham had been released, I set out to find them. And I did. They were spearfishing. I found Kelsey, and while we were down there, a couple of spears came shooting by—far too close."

"Who was shooting? Did you find Latham down there?"

"No. I didn't find anyone."

"And did you do anything?"

"Hell, yes, we called the Coast Guard."

Hector eased back in his chair. "You're a private investigator, and you didn't find out who was shooting at her?"

"I went down...but Kelsey wouldn't go back to the damn boat without me. I didn't get to search long, because I was too afraid someone was going to find his mark."

"But you think Latham might have been out there?"

Dane shrugged.

Hector leaned forward. "All right. If Latham is the Necktie Strangler and he was determined to kill his own stepdaughter, he'd have known, once the deed was done, that she was dead. Why would he be staking out the duplex?"

Dane exhaled a sharp breath. "To kill Kelsey," he said. And he straightened. "She's out at my place now. Alone. And no one knows where the hell Latham is."

Hector shook his head. "She's not alone," he said.

"But—"

The door to the office opened, and a man, apparently a plainclothes officer, stepped in.

"The ex-husband and his friends have made it?" Hector asked.

The man nodded. "The M.E. took the morgue photo out to the ex and his friends just a minute ago," he told Hector. "They gave us another positive ID. They're out there now."

The ex-husband and his friends...

"Fine, I'll go speak with them right now," Hector said. "Come with me," he told Dane.

They left the office and headed out to the reception area. "I dislike sounding clichéd, Dane, but you're not planning any vacations or anything, are you?" Hector asked.

"Am I planning on leaving town? Definitely not. But I sure as hell hope you're looking for Andy Latham, not wasting time suspecting me."

"We are. And I assume you'll be doing the same. In town, of course."

"Yes."

"I'm going to need a lot more against Andy Latham to hold him, much less to get the D.A.'s office to put together a sound case. So far...well, I hope you can give me more than the fact that you don't like him and his stepdaughter hated him. And that he dumped dead fish on your property, and people *think* they saw him sneaking around."

"He may have been hanging around the strip club where one of the other girls who was killed worked. Where she was working the night before she disappeared."

Hector stopped in the hallway, staring at him again. "And you have found this out...how?"

"One of the girls thinks she may have seen him."

Hector was still staring at him. "I spent days at that strip club."

"You had nothing to give the girls. I brought in pictures. And you know as well as I do that girls practicing prostitution on the side aren't going to talk to the police."

As they were standing there in the hallway, Dane's

cell phone began to ring. He ignored it for a moment, staring at Hector.

"Answer it."

He did. It was Jorge, and he was excited.

"Marisa says she has definitely seen Andy Latham at the club."

Hector was still watching him, and Dane was pretty sure he had been able to hear Jorge's words.

"Thanks, Jorge."

"What now?" Jorge asked.

He winced. "Marisa may be asked to testify."

"She will have to go to court?" Jorge sounded alarmed.

"She's legal, right?"

"Yes."

"Then there's no problem, Jorge."

"I pray that you are right."

Jorge hung up. His last words sounded as if he felt he had somehow been betrayed. Unfortunately there was no way for Dane to call him back and reassure him.

"You heard?" Dane asked Hector.

Hector nodded.

"Gary Hansen put out an APB on Latham last night."

Hector arched a brow. "That's good. But now the APB will have to be amended. He'll be wanted on suspicion of murder."

They walked out to the reception room. Larry, Nate and Kelsey were there. Kelsey's red, tearstained eyes widened at the sight of him. Larry was ashen. His eyes were red-rimmed as well.

"It's Sheila," Larry said. "Oh, God. It's really Sheila. I had hoped…knowing Sheila…I just kept believing that she'd walk back in, irritated that we were so worried. That she would say she had just gone off to Paris or Rome…or, hell, Tampa. But it's Sheila…"

He was going to break down again. Kelsey put an arm around him.

Larry covered his face with his hands.

Hector stood by him, his features both sympathetic and resolute. He was a homicide detective, a man who had been the bearer of such news before.

"Thank you very much for coming down. You were called in as the closest to kin we could find. I'm sorry, very sorry. And I assure you, we are doing everything we can to catch the killer."

Larry nodded, getting a grip on himself.

"We're free to go?" Nate asked.

"Of course. I'll know where to find you when I need to ask more questions."

"We all have cell phones," Nate said.

Hector stared at Dane. "We'll catch him."

"You need to find Latham."

"Oh, we will." Hector was still staring at him. He turned and walked back toward the autopsy rooms.

"Let's get back," Nate told him.

"I need a drink," Larry murmured.

"We'll get Cindy…break it to her and go to the Sea Shanty. We'll be together."

The three of them rose.

"Kelsey," Dane said, "drive with me."

She looked at the other two, worried.

"Drive with me," Dane repeated.

"Go with him," Nate told her. "Larry and I are all right. We'll pick up Cindy and meet you at the Sea Shanty."

"All right," Kelsey murmured.

As they stepped out to the parking lot, the sky was overcast. "Looks like we're in for some weather," Nate said.

But none of them cared about the weather anymore, even when it started to spit and sprinkle as they parted, walking to their cars.

"We'll be right there," Kelsey called as the two men walked off. "They look like a pair of lost puppies," she said to Dane.

"And you...you're all right?"

She gazed at him ruefully. "No. But I'm not going to fall apart. I'm too busy being angry at myself right now."

"Trust me," he said. "Everyone has regrets."

Help me, Dane.

As they drove, silent tears trickled down Kelsey's cheeks. She wiped them away angrily. "There are people who will say she was asking for it. They'll never know what a horrible childhood she had, that she was always running. She was always trying to escape, always trying to get somewhere."

"Yes," Dane said softly.

She stared at him suddenly. "My God! You don't know."

He almost veered off the road. "Know what?"

"About Cindy."

"What about Cindy?"

"They're picking her up from the hospital. They thought they heard someone in the yard again last night, and all started running around. From what Nate told me, she ran right into one of the storm shutters and knocked herself out."

"They thought they heard someone and started running around outside again?" he said with distress.

"I guess Nate went out one way, and Larry and Cindy went out the other, trying to catch whoever it was."

"They should have kept still and called Gary Hansen," Dane said, dismayed. "They might have caught him."

"So you think someone really was out there—even though the police had been by already?"

"I don't just think it was someone, I think it was Andy Latham," he told her.

"But if it's Andy…Sheila is dead."

"Hector just made the same point."

"So…?"

"Dammit, Kelsey, don't you see? You're in danger."

"Why me?"

"Who the hell knows?" he asked her. "Because you went after him. Because you were her friend. Because he's psychotic. Perhaps because he thinks she might have said something to you. I don't know." He paused and looked at her. "I don't know, but you're staying with me and close to me. All right?"

She didn't look his way. She was staring out the window. She had to be afraid.

She had seen Sheila's morgue photo.

"Kelsey?"

"Yes, of course, I'll stay with you."

"We have a bit of a detour to make. It will only take a few minutes."

She glanced at him at last.

He reached in his pocket and handed her his cell phone. "Call Jorge. Tell him we're on our way to the gas station to meet him. I need to see Marisa."

She frowned but did as he asked.

* * *

They arrived at the Sea Shanty later than the others because of the "detour" they had taken. They had met Jorge, who was upset about Sheila but understood Dane's need to see Marisa.

They had driven to the neat little house on the outskirts of town, and she had met the young Latina stripper, who was strangely shy, incredibly sweet, and stalwart despite her fear of the authorities when Dane explained that it was imperative for her to contact Hector Hernandez and explain to him that she had seen Andy Latham at the club.

Jorge listened quietly the whole time. When Dane had finished, the girl rose and told Jorge that she wanted to go right away. She had a friend at the house, so she could leave. She wasn't due at work until later.

Kelsey still didn't entirely understand what had been happening.

"Why is she afraid to go to the police?"

"Her son was just smuggled in from Cuba."

"But…he's her son. Won't the immigration laws protect him? Does he have a father back in Cuba, or family that will fight for him?"

Dane shook his head. "No."

"Then I'm sure he'll be all right."

Dane looked at her, and she knew that he didn't want to betray a confidence, even to her. And then she understood.

Jorge Marti had smuggled the boy in.

"Oh," she said softly. She didn't intend to make Dane say more. But she felt a strange warmth inside. She was proud of Jorge. The world could be awful. What had happened to Sheila was beyond awful.

But there were wonderful people in the world, as well.

"They'll have reached the Sea Shanty before us," Dane said. "Let's just say we stopped for gas."

"Sure."

The others were indeed there. Cindy hopped up and hugged Kelsey tightly, then did the same to Dane. They didn't speak about Sheila right away, and Kelsey quickly asked her how she was.

Cindy was dismissive of her own injury and as distraught as the others about Sheila. Kelsey saw, when they took their seats at the table, that she had finished her first beer and was pouring her second.

Kelsey, at the end of the table, frowned with concern as she watched her. "You just had a major crack on the head. Should you be drinking like that?"

"I don't know any other way to drink," Cindy said, trying to speak lightly.

"Cindy..."

"I didn't take any of the pain medication they sent home with me. I'd rather douse myself with beer."

"But if you have a concussion..."

"I'm fine," Cindy insisted. "I was fine last night, but they wanted me to stay for observation. They observed me. I'm fine. I don't even have a knot on my head anymore."

"You're sure you hit the hurricane shutter?" Kelsey asked.

"What else? I was running around barefoot like an idiot." She paused and actually smiled. "Kelsey, it was just a comedy of errors. Nate went out the back. In beautiful blue boxers, I'll have you know. Larry was following me—in the buff, except for a sheet. It all happened so fast. We wanted to catch the bastard. Larry tripped on his sheet, on the way out. He was cute as could be," she said, trying to make Larry smile. She glanced at him affectionately where he was seated at the rough wood table beside her. "Naked as a jay, tummy down on the sheet. Great butt, Larry. Just thought you should know. Anyway, stupid me, I kept going, I was running, and…pow, I went down."

"You didn't see the hurricane shutter?" Kelsey asked.

"If I'd seen it, I wouldn't have slammed into it."

Dane, next to Kelsey, leaned forward. "I think she's trying to find out if you're certain that you were hit by the hurricane shutter."

"Well, what else could it have been?" Cindy asked.

Dane looked at Nate and Larry.

Nate shrugged. "I found her under the shutter."

Larry seemed to emerge from his fog enough to join the conversation. "Nate had just reached her when I managed to wrap the sheet around me again and get out there, but yes, the hurricane shutter was right there."

"And had anyone tried to jimmy the lock?" Dane asked.

Nate and Larry looked at each other.

"I don't know," Nate admitted.

"You didn't call Gary Hansen's office?" Dane said.

"Shit, we called an ambulance. We were worried about Cindy. We went into the hospital with her."

"And later…?"

"Later we were half dead, and we fell asleep…and then we got the call about Sheila," Nate said.

"But…you still haven't called the cops to check the yard?"

"Jesus Christ, Dane!" Larry exploded. "We just found out that Sheila is dead."

"Murdered," Nate said, staring at his beer.

Dane leaned forward. "And I intend to see that her murderer is caught," he said angrily.

"All of you, stop it," Kelsey protested.

"Dane, call the cops now—they'll go out and look around. Maybe Gary can even post a man at the duplex."

"Yeah, he will. The police are on the lookout for Latham," Dane said. "Excuse me while I make that call."

"Wait. Wait just a minute. We need to make a toast. To Sheila. To tell her we loved her," Cindy said. "No matter what her sins may have been."

"Right. We're the ones who cared," Larry said. "I mean, that matters, doesn't it? We all loved her. In the end, what matters is that you had people who cared."

Nate poured from the pitcher on the table into two more glasses for Dane and Kelsey. Then they all solemnly raised their glasses.

"To Sheila," Kelsey said.

"May she rest in peace," Nate added.

"Let's pray that she's found it at last," Cindy murmured.

"Amen," Dane said.

Then he rose and left the table. Cindy watched him go.

"At least…"

"What?" Nate said.

"At least Dane has…something to do. He can help catch Sheila's killer…Latham, if it really is Andy Latham. While we…well, we're just sitting here, and we can't do anything but think about her. I'm glad about Dane, though. When he first came back to the Keys…"

She looked at Kelsey and shrugged. "It looked like he was going to become a lounge rat."

Dane was standing about twenty feet away. As she watched him, Kelsey thought that it was a fitting day.

Rain had followed them.

It had stopped now. But the sky, usually so bright and blue, was gray.

Dead gray.

As if he read her mind, Nate said, "The day is right for mourning, isn't it?" He lifted his glass, as if to heaven.

"See, Sheila? Even the elements know you're gone. The day is weeping." He set down his glass and studied his beer. "We'll get that sick bastard," he murmured. "Count on it, Sheila. We're going to get him."

Dane came back and sat down. He sipped his beer, set it down and looked around.

"What's the matter?" Cindy asked him.

He smiled ruefully and shook his head. "I don't know." Then he said, "Excuse me." He stood again, and walked through the restaurant, then went out toward the parking lot.

"What are you doing?" Kelsey asked him when he returned a few minutes later.

"Nothing, I guess. Being really paranoid. I thought I saw someone."

"I'm sure you did," Nate said, indicating the tables near them, where tourists sat, having stopped in for the lazy, rainy afternoon. "Customers. It's a public establishment, Dane."

"Yeah, I know. I just had a strange feeling."

"Did you see anything?" Cindy asked, perplexed.

"No. Just a feeling."

"We're all having them," Larry murmured. He shrugged. "After all, we know there's a murderer somewhere out there."

Chapter 17

By seven that night, they had eaten and commiserated, and they were silent with one another. Dane had kept in touch with Gary Hansen, but there had been no sign of Andy Latham. They also learned from Hector Hernandez that the police were sorry to intrude, but they would all be needed for questioning, as Sheila was now a murder victim and not just a missing person.

Kelsey watched Dane's face as he spoke with Hector on the phone. His features were almost as dark as the day. She was certain that he, as the last one to see Sheila, was going to bear the greatest scrutiny, even if the police were looking for Andy Latham and might be able to tie him to all the murders.

Cindy and Larry drank heavily, but Nate was as slow in imbibing his beer as Dane and Kelsey. He had made himself the designated driver.

They stayed at the Sea Shanty until tacitly agreeing that it was time to go.

Nate, Larry and Cindy were determined to spend the night in the duplex, and they were actually hoping that the backyard prowler was going to show up, since Gary Hansen had a man from the sheriff's department stationed at the house.

They left after a round of hugs and with the knowledge that they all needed some sleep.

Dane was silent as he and Kelsey headed out to Hurricane Bay. The weather still seemed fitting. The sky had gone from dull pewter to the deep gray of a battleship. As he parked the Jeep, the wind was whipping around them, but at the moment it wasn't raining. He got out and headed for the house, then turned. Kelsey thought he was heading for the docks, but he wasn't.

She frowned as she watched him walk to the same spit of the beach where Nate had stood earlier that day.

She walked up behind him. He knew that she was there.

"I failed her," he said after a moment.

Kelsey felt the same way herself. "We didn't fail her," she said. "We were all her friends—despite her sins. Then again, it's not as if we're all without our quirks and problems. She was friends with all of us, too, no matter what. But you didn't fail her, Dane, any more than any of the rest of us did. Sheila was going to do things her own way, no matter what."

He nodded after a moment and turned for the house.

Kelsey followed him in.

Once they were inside, Dane double-locked the doors. He walked toward the kitchen. "I need an aspirin. You want one?"

She shook her head. "I'm all right." She hesitated. "I think I'm going to take a long bath and lie down. Is that all right?"

He nodded. "I'm going to call and make sure they've got a man stationed at the duplex. I want to talk to Jorge again, too, see if Marisa did go to the police."

Kelsey nodded and went up the stairs, feeling drained. She ran hot water into the tub, then found herself digging through his toiletries, wondering if she would find bath beads and glad when she didn't. She didn't want to think that Dane had downplayed his recent relationship with Sheila.

He did have shampoo. She poured some into the tub to make bubbles. Then she leaned back in the water, letting the heat warm her. But when she closed her eyes, she kept seeing the photograph of Sheila. The medical examiner's office had tried, she was certain, not to make the picture any more shocking than it had to be, but they hadn't been able to hide the remnants of the tie around her neck. It hadn't been removed yet—the forensic investigators hadn't finished with her.

Something about the picture, besides the awful image of what had once been the face of a beautiful woman, was disturbing. It had teased at Kelsey all afternoon, but for the life of her, she couldn't figure out what it was.

Dane tapped softly at the door. "I'm taking the diary downstairs to read. All right?"

"Sure."

"You all right?"

"Yeah." She was quiet for a moment. "At least we know."

He was silent. "At least we know," he repeated.

He left, and Kelsey settled back in the tub. Her head

was pounding. For the longest time she just lay there, listening to the pounding. She decided it was her pulse.

The water grew cold, and she got out of the tub. She found clean underwear in her bag and slipped into one of Dane's T-shirts, which, despite her height, fell comfortably to mid-thigh. She wanted to lie down and let sleep dull the image of her friend that persisted in remaining in her mind's eye.

She lay down and closed her eyes, but when she did, she saw Sheila.

She sat up and noticed that Dane had taken the diary but not the pile of papers. Maybe there was something she had missed.

She lifted the pile of papers and started going through them again. She came to the drawing Sheila had done as an adult. Then she drew out the one she had done as a child. She frowned. They were poor drawings, of course. Sheila had never had the least interest in art; she had always been impatient whenever Kelsey had wanted to stop and sketch a scene.

She looked from one picture to the other. The female in both drawings was obviously Sheila. She had put the little mole on her left cheek in both drawings. But the man appeared different. In the second drawing he seemed straighter and heavier. Not fat, just heavier. As she puzzled over the pictures, she leaned forward. Her motion sent the pile of papers flying, dropping from her lap to the floor in disarray.

Softly cursing herself, she rose, then got down on her knees. The pictures had scattered on the floor, and some had slid beneath the bed. As she collected them, she hit one of the floorboards. To her astonishment, it moved.

Her first thought was that she needed to tell Dane he

had a faulty floorboard. Then curiosity got the best of her. As she pressed it, she saw that it could be removed. Dane must keep his private papers here. Or personal objects. Or...

It was none of her business.

A strange feeling settled over her, and she warned herself that this might be like opening Pandora's box.

She couldn't stop herself. She pulled up the floor-board.

Shock, like being squeezed by icy fingers, settled over her.

Then fear and amazement set in. She wasn't just see-ing Sheila's face in death in her mind's eye, she was seeing it in Polaroid color.

The first article in the space beneath the floorboard was a picture of Sheila. When life had just left her. Sheila's eyes were still open. Her lips were blue...her face tinged with blue.

And she was on the beach. Dane's beach. A corner of the dock could be seen at the edge of the picture.

Even if the picture hadn't shown her on Dane's beach, it would still have pointed clearly to Dane as the murderer. She knew what had been bothering her about the picture she had seen at the morgue.

She had recognized the remnants of fabric around Sheila's neck. The tie. It was Dane's tie. She knew it be-cause she had given it to him for Christmas years ago. She had given one to Joe, as well. It was a hand-painted tie. There were sea creatures moving through a back-ground of blues and grays. The ties had been special. She had labored over them for a very long time. Seeing it now, before the water and the muck had conspired to hide the pattern, it was obvious. So obvious.

Sheila. Dead. On Dane's beach. Strangled with Dane's tie.

Horror…fear…constricted her throat and every muscle for untold moments. She tried desperately to get her mind to function. She couldn't panic.

She had to get out.

She remembered the day she had first talked to Dane. How he had told her to go home.

What an idiot she was! The signs had all been there. Sheila had left the Sea Shanty with Dane. Sheila had slept with Dane the last night she'd been seen. Sheila's earring had been on Dane's floor.

Dane had killed Sheila.

And she, Kelsey, like a fool, hadn't wanted to believe it. He had been so convincing. He had gone to the strip clubs looking for suspects. He had pursued Andy Latham. Of course he had. He was going to see that the murders were pinned on Latham…

She forced herself to rise. She looked across the bed where he had left the .38 special that morning.

The gun was gone.

She picked up the receiver in the bedroom, then replaced it as carefully as her shaking fingers would allow. Dane was on the phone.

She looked around the room. He was a private investigator. There had to be another weapon around somewhere. She looked under the bed, then went through several of his drawers. She saw that she had left the board up and panicked anew, so she ran back and replaced the picture and the board.

She couldn't stop shaking. And she wasn't reasoning anywhere near as well as she should have been.

The picture was replaced. The board was replaced.

There was no weapon to be found. He would come up the stairs at any minute.

She would never be able to hide the fact that she knew he was a murderer. A sick murderer. He had taken a picture of his victim as a trophy.

She started for the door. She needed her purse and her cell phone. He was probably at the dining-room table, where he had set up his home office. That meant she had to go out the front door without being noticed. She could do it.

She was in a T-shirt, barefoot. No time to change, but she did need her shoes. Sandals, but better than nothing. The ground was strewn with crushed shells and pebbles. She would never make it barefoot. She slipped on her sandals and hurried to the door. Her purse was downstairs. She had left it on the table.

The table where Dane was undoubtedly working.

Her phone was in her purse. She needed her phone. No, she needed to get the hell out of there. She knew the way off the island. And she could run. She couldn't keep up with Cindy at the gym, but she was fit enough, and terror would give her wings.

Kelsey left the bedroom and moved to the top of the stairs. He wasn't on the stairway, at least. She started down, praying the old wood wouldn't creak.

At the foot of the stairs, she paused. Then she crept silently toward the rear, desperate to see where Dane was and what he was doing. If only he were in the kitchen, she could slip into the dining room and grab her purse.

She looked cautiously into the dining room. Dane was at the table, drumming the surface of it as he spoke on the phone in a low tone.

She saw her purse, just inches from his hand. His own cell phone was sitting right in front of him.

She bit her lip and backed away. She had to get off the island.

Kelsey turned and headed for the front door. As silently as she could, she turned the bolts. They seemed to snap open as loudly as a clash of cymbals, but she knew the sound was only in her mind. She opened the door, then closed it carefully, praying he wouldn't know she was gone until she was far from Hurricane Bay.

Dane heard the deep sigh on the other end of the phone line. Gary Hansen spoke patiently despite the sound.

"No, we haven't caught up with Andy Latham yet. Dane, everyone is looking for him. We've called the cops out in Collier County, as well. I talked to Jesse Crane, and his boys are looking in the Everglades. Trust me, every law-enforcement officer in the state is looking for Latham. We've got people working the airports, the train stations and the bus terminals, as well as the highways. They've set up a road block on US1 so that he can't get on to the mainland—unless he's already run that far already. If so, he can't get back on. Not with a car. And it's one damned long walk. Dane, do me a favor. Don't call every half hour. I'll call you. If you feel you have to call me, make it at least an hour between calls."

"You definitely have a man at the duplex?" Dane asked.

"I swear it, on my mother's grave, my father's grave...on the grave of every ancestor I've got. I'm responsible for the safety of the people out here. Don't you think this is driving me insane?"

Dane ran his fingers through his hair. "Yeah, Gary, sorry. It's just that…well, shit. I feel like he's out there, like he sees us but we can't see him."

"You're in your house, right?"

"Yup."

"Locked up tight, right?"

"Yup."

"You've got a gun, right?"

"On me, yup."

"And Kelsey's with you, and I have a guy at the duplex. Shit, Dane, go to bed. Get some sleep. They'll find him."

"All right."

Dane hung up. Sheila's diary sat in front of him. It told him so much.

It told him nothing he needed to know.

He rose. Here he was, being an ass again. Kelsey was up there, and she was devastated. Holding it together, but devastated. It wasn't a time for hot passion; it was a time to hold on to each other.

He walked through the house to the stairway and slowly made his way up to the bedroom.

It was empty.

"Kelsey?"

He walked to the bathroom door and looked in. No sign of her. Frowning, he went back to the bedroom.

"Kelsey?"

No answer. He ran downstairs, calling her name, tearing through every room. He went back upstairs, looking around.

Then he saw the pictures scattered on the floor. By the board.

He groaned aloud. She knew. She had to know. He should have told her from the beginning. He couldn't have told her from the beginning. And now...

He tore back downstairs. Her purse was on the dining-room table, so she didn't have a cell phone. She was hoofing it off of the island, certain she had been staying with a psychotic killer. The back door was still locked from the inside.

The front door had been opened.

And quietly closed when she left the house.

Dane tore out the front.

"Kelsey!" He shouted her name against the wind and the rain.

No reply.

Why would she answer him? In her mind, he was a homicidal maniac.

He had to find her. Not just because of what she thought. But because he had that feeling again. That feeling that they were being watched.

The cops hadn't been able to find Andy Latham. Which meant Latham was out there. Somewhere.

And so was Kelsey.

Kelsey ran down the road, cursing as the rain started again and the wind picked up, the trees dipping low. The private gravel road spat tiny rocks at her, and she nearly tripped over tenacious roots as she raced along. She could hear herself breathe. The pounding that had been her pulse seemed amplified. She had to keep looking back. She was afraid that if Dane was after her, she wouldn't be able to hear him. All that she would hear would be that pounding.

So far so good.

Then...

She could hear him. From a distance. He was shouting her name.

He had discovered that she was missing. And he would know. He would know what she had found.

She doubled her efforts, ruing the wind that whipped around her. She swore as the raindrops began to fall harder.

If she missed the fragile connection to the mainland, she would be swimming her way to safety. Something she could do, if she had to. But it was so dark, and the rain...

The rain was coming down so hard it hurt her flesh as she ran.

Suddenly she saw lights ahead of her. Strange lights. She blinked against the rain. They couldn't be Dane's Jeep lights, because the Jeep had been at the house, and these lights were coming from the mainland.

She kept running, waving her arms madly, wondering if the driver could see her.

The vehicle stopped. The lights were blinding. She shielded her eyes, ready to run to the driver's side for help. She blinked and saw through the rain. Saw who it was.

Andy Latham.

She stopped dead in her tracks, fear chilling her flesh with far greater speed than the rain.

But then she realized that she didn't have to be afraid of Andy Latham. Dane had murdered Sheila.

"Andy!" she said.

"Hey there, little girl. What are you doing out here? No matter. It's sure mighty fine to see you in that wet T-shirt. They say you're with some snooty ad agency up in Miami, but my, my, you could make some real money with that body. Oh, yeah. What are you doing running around in the rain?"

"Andy, I need to get off the island." Even though she was desperate, he still made her skin crawl. The rain was coming down in sheets now; she had to shout above it.

"Step right in, little lady."

"You can drop me at the highway," she told him. Despite knowing what she did about Dane, she was filled with apprehension, but it was too late to escape now. Andy was out of the truck. He had her arm.

He was wearing gloves.

He might be thin, but he was strong. He was dragging her, rather than walking her, around to the passenger side of his truck.

"You know, Andy, I think I'll just go ahead and walk," she said.

"In this rain? No way, Kelsey." There was a drawn out hiss as he said her name.

"Andy, let me go. I'll walk."

"There's thunder and lightning."

"I like the rain. I'm sorry for bothering you. Let me go. I'll just walk."

"No."

He had the car door open. She tried to wrench free, but his grip was unbelievably powerful. She reached out, clawing at his hand to get him to release her. She shrieked as she drew blood.

He reached into the car for something. In the rain, she couldn't see what.

Then it came crashing down on her head and it no longer mattered, as the gray light and rain faded away.

Dane took the Jeep, knowing that Kelsey would have to stick to the road if she wanted to get off the island.

The rain became blinding as he drove. He hunched forward in the seat, his bright lights on, trying to see ahead.

No sign of Kelsey, but...

He jerked the Jeep to a halt. Even in the rain, he could see the way the foliage was crushed. He hopped out, heedless of the rain, and walked to the left side of the road. Something had been in there. Though the rain was lashing the ground and making thick puddles of muck, he could see the tire tracks. A large vehicle had been parked in the bushes.

A truck.

Latham's truck.

Latham had been here now, right now, when Kelsey had suddenly run. How had he known she would run?

He hadn't. But he had been watching them. He had been watching them at the Sea Shanty, and he had known they were heading out to Hurricane Bay, so he had come here to wait. Maybe the rain even inspired his need to hunt, to kill. How the hell had he eluded the police?

It didn't matter. All that mattered was that he'd been here. And he had Kelsey.

Dane ran back to the Jeep for his floodlight. He was going to have to follow on foot. He would never be able to follow the tire tracks if he didn't.

* * *

Kelsey felt a rocking. She was lying on something soft but…smelly.

Her head hurt like hell. She wanted to touch it, but some instinct kept her from doing so, just in case she was being watched. She opened her eyes slowly and carefully. She swallowed back the scream of pure panic that came to her throat.

She was on a boat. A fishing boat.

She was lying on a bunk in a cabin. A small, tight, claustrophobic cabin. The bunk took up almost all the available space. She could hear movement on deck.

She gritted her teeth, trying to stop the rocking in her head and figure out if Latham was trying to move his boat out into high seas or if he had done so already.

She couldn't let him get out to sea. The wind was so high…the rocking would be worse if they were far out.

She tried to rise. Her head was spinning. As she sat up, she noticed the rack on the cabin wall, within arm's reach of the bunk.

It held a row of ties.

Silk ties, cotton ties, linen ties, black, patterned… even a cartoon tie.

Fear shot through her like a bolt of lightning. Andy Latham was the Necktie Strangler. Then what was the picture beneath Dane's floorboard?

She couldn't worry about that now. She had to find the strength to get off the boat. Where? Into the sea, into the mangroves…even though she probably didn't have the strength to swim two strokes.

She would find it.

She shimmied to the end of the bunk and rose. The sleeping quarters led out to a small galley and salon.

Tight, utilitarian, nothing more. She was dizzy. She brought her fingers to her head, and when she drew them away, they were red with blood. He had struck her hard.

She made it to her feet, though the room spun crazily. Some instinct for survival kept her from passing out.

Kelsey braced herself against the walls as she made her way out of the bedroom. Latham was still topside, cursing as he hauled in his anchor. Where the hell were they? She bit her bottom lip, fighting nausea and dizziness. She made it through the salon to the few steps that led topside. The rain had slackened to where she could see him. His back was to her.

Kelsey rushed from the door to the port side of the boat. Latham heard her just as she reached the edge and dived in.

The sea was dark. Pitch-dark, and cold from the rain and the thunderous sky above. Kelsey shot away from the boat. She surfaced, trying to look around. She could see mangroves around her. And a broken down old dock. Beside it, an overgrown path. She knew where they were. They were near the mainland, just before the road that led to Dane's...in good weather. The road would be flooding now.

She began to swim. If she could reach the trees and crawl ashore, she could elude Latham. If she could just...

A hand wound around her ankle. Pulled her under. She was choking. She kicked, scratched, pummeled...

He wouldn't let her up.

She wasn't going to be strangled. She was going to drown.

Gloved fingers threaded through her hair and hauled

her up. She took a desperate breath. Latham was swimming strongly, dragging her with him. She renewed her fight for freedom. His hand rammed through the water, catching her jaw.

For a moment she saw stars in the sea.

He had her. He was shoving her up. Up, over the bow. He was crawling up beside her.

She fell to the deck. Desperate, she made herself rise. She lunged for the side again. Latham captured her around the middle. He swore, ignoring the nails that tore into his flesh, heedless of the fact that he smashed her against the door as he pushed and shoved her back down the few steps to the salon. She began to scream.

Despite her efforts, he got her back into the tiny sleeping quarters, where he threw her on the bunk and reached for a tie.

Kelsey rose, screaming. He shoved her back.

"Kelsey…prim, proper Kelsey. I've always liked to play. But with you…we'll have to play after. And you won't know then. You won't care. You'll smile…and you'll like me then. Of course, you won't be able to whisper any sweet nothings in my ear, but—"

She rose in a whirlwind of motion, slamming both her fists into his face. He fell back, but she was trapped by his body, which was blocking the door. She tried to squeeze past him, and she nearly succeeded.

But then the cartoon tie came flipping around her neck, jerking her back.

Dane ran through the rain, following the tracks with desperation spurring his footsteps. He could barely see to follow, but he was grateful that Latham couldn't be that far ahead of him. The rain hadn't yet washed away the deep grooves the truck was leaving in the road.

He raced across the dirt and gravel path that would soon be under water and was back on the main island of Key Largo. After a hundred feet, the tire tracks suddenly twisted hard to the right. Dane followed.

Years ago there had been a road here. Now the movement of the vehicle had crushed through the dense brush, leaving a trail that was easy to follow. But how long since Latham had come through here?

The rain had slackened, but it was still coming down.

Dane suddenly knew where he was going. There had been a dock here once. A private home that had fallen in to decay over the years. The state owned the land but hadn't decided what to do with it yet.

But a beat-up old fishing boat could have been brought in and tied to what was left of the dock.

His heart pounding, he prayed that it would still be there.

That he was in time...

He burst through the last of the brush.

The boat wasn't at the dock.

He stared in gut-wrenching dismay.

Then he saw the boat, out on the water. He ran to the mangrove-tangled shoreline and crashed through the water until he could swim. He kept an eye on the boat, damning the waves that seemed to force him back with every stroke.

Kelsey fought. Even with the tie around her neck, she fought, bucking against Latham, desperate to kick, to claw.

They would know. At least they would know for

sure. She had scratched him and scratched him. She had drawn blood. They would find his flesh and blood beneath her fingernails…when they fished her body from the water. If they were in time, before the fish…

No…

She grasped at the tie around her neck. Latham jerked and struggled, trying to get her flat on the bed, determined to get her beneath him.

"No, you aren't like Sheila, are you? Heard today that she was dead, the little slut. Came to the end she should have come to. She was a born slut, you know. Like her mother. Cheating bitch. She didn't care what I did with her daughter, but then, the daughter didn't mind. Mother, daughter. You don't know what fun can be, do you, little girl?" Latham demanded. He was panting between his words. "Can't answer, can you? Got no breath. You go ahead. You struggle. I like it. I like that look in your eyes."

She kicked him. She had no breath and the room was spinning, but she kicked him. For an instant he lost his grip.

She desperately gulped in air.

He fell on her again. He had both ends of the tie, and he wound them tighter and tighter and tighter…

She would fight, fight, fight…

The cabin was growing dark.

Light, and life, were fading.

Something huge and wet hurled itself onto the bed. The constriction around her neck slackened instantly.

She gulped in air again, coughing as if she would never stop. Bodies slammed against her. She pressed against the cabin wall, still coughing. Her mind was numb. She was aware only of the bodies at first, flailing and thrashing around her. The boat was rocking madly in the high seas brought on by the storm.

Then Latham was jerked up. There was a tie around his neck.

Kelsey saw his eyes as he was jerked backward out of the cabin.

She crawled to the foot of the bed, then slid off it, using the wall for balance as she got to her feet. Dane was there. Dane had come to rescue her from Latham. They were still struggling, though Dane had the tie. He was dragging Latham away from her as Latham's fingers tried to ease the hold of the tie around his own neck. It must have loosened, because he got free and turned, heading up the steps. Dane was right on him.

Kelsey staggered after them. They were on deck together. Dane had the tie around Latham's neck again.

A huge wave struck, and the two men went crashing over the side.

Kelsey's cry was drowned out by the thunder that cracked almost immediately after the vivid flash of lightning that lit the sky.

She made her way to the port side, looking down at a dark sea.

"Dane!"

The wind whipped away her voice.

She saw a head, bobbing to the surface. A hand, reaching out...

Dane's hand?

Or Latham's?

She bent down, reaching over. Strong fingers grasped hers.

She pulled.

A body began to rise. Two hands gripped the hull of the boat.

She caught hold of them both as Dane Whitelaw struggled up and over the rail. Together, they crashed to the deck.

Chapter 18

Andy Latham's body washed up on shore three days later.

By then Kelsey had been out of the hospital a full twenty-four hours herself, and when the group met at the Sea Shanty, it was to celebrate rather than to mourn.

Dane had spent as much time with the police as she had healing, so once they were together, everyone started asking him questions, trying to get him to put the pieces together.

Cindy said, "My God…this is still so scary. So when we were kids, Latham was abusing his stepdaughter, and as the years went by, he started killing?"

"Unfortunately we'll never know for sure what happened," Dane told her. "I admit, when I reached the boat, I wanted to kill him. But I wouldn't have—except that it turned into a life or death struggle."

"Why would you have wanted to keep him alive?" Nate asked.

"Because he could have answered questions for us. No one knows when he started killing. There could be more victims in the waterways, in the swamps. We'll never know. And there are so many missing women out there. Families who will live with the dread all their lives but never have any kind of closure. He probably started off abusing Sheila, and then the violence escalated when she got older and broke free. No wife, no kid…and he probably always frequented strip joints and cruised the streets looking for prostitutes. Hector Hernandez believes he may be responsible for a number of unsolved rapes. And then he probably went from rape to murder."

"And he was watching us, all of us, before he attacked Kelsey," Cindy said. "It's possible that he walloped me with his crowbar that night, then ran off when he realized Nate and Larry were so close."

"Maybe. And maybe you just ran into the storm shutter."

"How did you know it was Latham so quickly, even before the police had him down as a suspect?"

"I knew it was someone who knew me," Dane said.

He looked across the table at Kelsey. She flushed. "He tried to frame Dane. Before he killed Sheila, he broke into Dane's house. He knew that Sheila had been there, so he went into Dane's place when he was at the Sea Shanty one day. He took one of Dane's ties, and he strangled Sheila with it. He watched Dane's schedule, and he saw Sheila when she left Dane's. Then he waited for Dane to leave again the next day, posed her on the beach and took a picture before disposing of her body."

"Then he left me to sweat, wondering where the next piece of evidence against me would turn up. The picture was left beneath my door," Dane said. "I didn't dare take it to the police. I couldn't afford to be arrested when I knew the real killer was still out there."

"Wow," Larry said. "So you knew she was dead all along."

"Yes. I'm sorry. I couldn't trust anyone."

"Have the police seen all this yet?" Nate asked.

"I've told Hector Hernandez," Dane said. "Problem is…the picture is gone."

Kelsey cleared her throat, staring at Cindy. "That's how I wound up with Latham. I found the picture under Dane's floorboard. He had it hidden. I was there and I stumbled on it. I could swear I put it back, but…anyway, we're searching for it. God knows, I was in such a panic, I might have held on to it and lost it somewhere while I was running. But it doesn't matter. Latham's not going to hurt anyone again, and that's what counts."

Dane said, "That's right. It's over. Thank God, it's over."

"And you're really all right, Kelsey?" Larry asked anxiously.

She nodded. "I'm fine." The bruises around her neck were going to stay a while, but that didn't matter. She was alive.

In fact, she was far more alive than she had been in years. She was home. And she was with Dane.

"We'll all think about Sheila, though, for years to come," she said.

"The only solace is that…" Nate paused, looking for the right words. "Well, like we said before. She was at peace. Sheila wasn't just running. She was miserable.

She had been miserable for years. She didn't know how to live anymore. Latham didn't just kill her when he strangled her. He killed her over the years. He killed her when she was a kid, bit by bit."

"Well," Kelsey told him, "we're going to try to do something for her. I was her beneficiary—a lawyer contacted me today. According to the terms of her mother's will, Latham only received money from the trust fund while Sheila was alive. At Sheila's death, the bulk sum came to me. So Dane and I have discussed it, and we thought the best thing to do was donate the money to an agency in Miami that cares for abused wives, children and runaways. We thought the best memorial to her would be to try to see that what happened to her never happens to another child."

"Bravo!" Cindy said. "What a great idea."

"Curious, though," Nate murmured.

"What's that?" Larry asked.

"That Latham killed Sheila. She was his meal ticket."

"I thought of that," Dane said. "I didn't realize it at the time, but that might have been part of the reason he was after Kelsey."

"Who would have thought Latham was smart enough to pull off everything he did?" Cindy murmured.

Larry shrugged and looked at Kelsey. "I take it you've decided that you're going to need more than a week's vacation time?"

Kelsey smiled ruefully. "I sent in my resignation, Larry."

"What?" Larry said, astounded. Then he looked from Kelsey to Dane and back again.

"Oh."

"I'm going to paint down here for a while," she said.

"Sure," Nate teased. "Paint. That's what they call it these days?"

They all laughed. "Seriously, I haven't done any real artwork since I took the job in the art department," she said ruefully.

"Shall I guess that you're not going to stay at the du-plex?" Cindy asked.

"She'll be living at Hurricane Bay," Dane said.

"Congratulations," Nate said. He lifted his glass and smiled at Kelsey. "Really. Congratulations. It took you two long enough to admit you want to be together."

"Thank you, Nate," Kelsey told him sincerely.

"It better be one good wedding—when you get around to it," Cindy said, adding the last hastily.

"Of course we plan on it being one good wedding," Kelsey said.

"You're not going to elope or anything?" Nate de-manded.

She shook her head, smiling at Dane. She was amazed that she could have lost an old friend and so recently have been near death herself, yet know such a strange, poignant sense of happiness. Sheila had done her the greatest favor in the end. She had brought her home. And to Dane.

She looked from Dane to Nate. "Actually we're going to go up and see my parents, and tell them, then come back and get married down here. And guess what else? My mom is pregnant. So Dane and I are going to go see them, then we'll arrange the wedding."

"Wow," Cindy said. "Your mom is pregnant?"

"Uh-huh. I'm going to have a baby brother."

"Wow," Cindy said again.

"That's great. Really great," Nate said.

"A toast," Cindy said. "To life."

"And friendship," Nate said.

"Hear, hear," Larry agreed.

They ate dinner together and were pleased when Jorge joined them. Marisa was with him, having given up her job at the club to work as a chef on Jorge's boat.

Kelsey was certain there was something going on there, as well.

It was late when they returned to Hurricane Bay. Dane locked the doors carefully, as he had done every night since Kelsey had been attacked.

Since he'd picked her up from the hospital, he had been treating her like glass. "Want me to run a bath for you? Need a cold compress for your neck?"

She shook her head, smiling. "I need you."

"Kelsey, he hurt you pretty badly. It's pretty late. You probably want to go to sleep."

"What I want to do is make love."

He eyed her for a long moment. "Careful," he said softly. "You know I'm easy."

"And good. Don't forget good."

"Naturally. So be careful what you ask for."

Kelsey wrapped her arms around his neck and kissed his lips. "I want good. Damn good," she told him.

Later she realized that he was still awake, staring up at the ceiling. "What's the matter?" she asked him.

"Something is still bugging me," he said.

"What?"

"What Nate said. That it was weird, Latham killing Sheila. She was his meal ticket."

"That is strange. Know what else?" Kelsey said. "It's hard for me to remember, because I'd been knocked on the head and I was busy trying to get away, but when

Latham talked about Sheila, it was as if he hadn't killed her."

Dane rolled onto his elbow, staring at her in the moonlight.

"What?" he demanded.

"Hey, you sound like the police. I can't remember exactly what he said. Something about he knew that she was dead and that she had gotten what she deserved."

Dane lay back down. She knew he was staring at the ceiling again.

Kelsey looked over at him. "Dane, he was the Necktie Strangler. We know it, the police know it. Maybe, in his warped mind, he didn't want to believe he killed Sheila. Maybe he didn't even plan to kill her."

"How do you not plan to kill someone—and have a stolen tie to strangle her with?" he asked quietly. "There's something else," he added.

"What?"

"The fish."

"The fish?"

He nodded in the shadows. "Andy Latham came over here the day of the barbecue with all those fish, convinced we were dumping dead fish on his property. Those fish had to come from somewhere."

"We're in the Keys. They could have come from anywhere."

"I know, but it's almost as if the fish were put there to make sure Latham would come after us. Or me. It's as if someone was trying to make sure Andy Latham would make himself a suspect."

"Then again," Kelsey said slowly, "maybe he caught the fish, then forgot about them until they rotted. He might have reached a point where reality and his psychosis were all mixed up in his mind."

"The whole thing still bothers me," Dane said. "Shit," he muttered. "I can't sleep. I'll go downstairs so you can get some rest."

She was immediately wide-awake.

"Don't you dare leave me. I'm not sleepy right now myself. And I can think of a perfect way to get some exercise and then relax."

"Kelsey, you're hurt. Are you sure twice is okay?"

"I never feel better than when I'm with you," she told him.

He wrapped her in his arms.

The call came early. Dane had just come downstairs, and Kelsey had made coffee. She had been staring out the window, basking in the sunshine.

"I love Hurricane Bay," she told him.

"Great," he teased, walking to where she stood and slipping his arms around her waist. "You're going to marry me for my island."

She laughed. "I love Hurricane Bay because it's an extension of you."

He wasn't able to reply, because that was when the phone rang.

He picked it up. Jesse Crane was on the line.

"Hey, Jesse," Dane said.

"Dane, let's have coffee."

"Jesse, you know I'm always ready to meet you. But I just woke up, and…why don't you come out here?"

"Dane," Jesse repeated firmly, "I need to meet you for coffee. Alone. I'm halfway there. I'll see you at the coffee shop at the base of the island."

Dane frowned. Apparently Jesse didn't want to spell anything out, but Dane could tell from his tone that it was important that they meet.

"All right."

He hung up. Kelsey was looking at him. "Who was that?"

"Jesse. Seems he needs to see me."

"Is he coming here? I'd love to see Jesse."

"No, I've got to go meet him. I'll be right back, though."

She smiled. "I'm not an invalid, Dane. I still have a little cut on my head and some bruises, but I'm fine. Take your time."

He still wasn't happy leaving her. Ever since the attack...

"I'll be right back."

He started out. Kelsey followed him to the porch.

"You know where the gun is. Under the bed, my side," he told her.

"I know where the gun is," she assured him.

He was still disgruntled, but he didn't ask her to come with him. Jesse had wanted to talk alone.

He wasn't going far, and he would be right back. He kissed her briefly, then left.

Kelsey walked out on the dock with her coffee. She loved to sit there, dangling her feet in the water the way she had years ago, as a child.

She found her eyes wandering to the beach. She bit her lip, recalling the photo of Sheila, posed there. The memory would haunt her for a long time. But she did love the property. Hurricane Bay hadn't caused the misery and horror—a man had done that.

On a whim, she went back into the house and picked
up Sheila's diary and the papers she had gathered. She
wished Sheila had said something more in the diary.
It was still disturbing, no matter what she had said to
Dane, to ponder exactly why Latham would have killed
Sheila when she was his source of income.

She started scouring the pages again, noting a few
she had skimmed over.

*Shopping with Cindy. Midget. I called her Midget
today. She got mad. It was her nickname when we were
kids.*

*I told her Midget wasn't bad. After all, the guys all
called me Boobs. And they did it in public.*

She isn't mad at me anymore.

*I wonder if Kels would be pissed if I called her Bub-
ble Butt today. I think I'm the one who made up that
name. Had to have something that went with Boobs.*

*Then there was He-Man. We liked to call Dane that.
He even got the good name.*

The entry ended. A few pages later, Sheila wrote:

*Another day at the bar. I called Nate Liver Lips. He
laughed and asked me if I'd heard from Web. I said
yes, of course.*

*He loves me too much. Even outright cruelty doesn't
seem to get through to him.*

"He loved you too much, Sheila. If only you had been
able to love him."

She glanced at the stack of papers again. The two
pictures still bothered her. The man in the second drawing wasn't Andy Latham. She was certain of it.

And it wasn't Dane. The man in the drawing had
dark hair. She frowned, studying the picture. She turned
it and looked at it from every angle. Sheila had scrawled

some kind of a border around the drawing. She tried to follow it. Was it just a border? It had the look of elongated writing.

She was so engrossed that she didn't hear the footsteps behind her. She jumped, dropping the diary, when she saw the shadow looming over her on the water.

Jesse was there when Dane arrived.

He must have driven like the wind.

Dane slid into the booth across from him. The waitress knew him and brought coffee right away.

"That's it, Sally, thanks," Jesse said.

Dane arched a brow. "This must be important."

"It is. They're going to reopen Sheila's case."

"What? Why?"

"Do you remember me telling you that there was something about the bodies that the police didn't tell anyone? Like a signature?"

Dane frowned. "Yes."

"The first two girls had the middle toe of the left foot removed."

"And Sheila's toe was there?"

Jesse nodded. "I wanted you to know right away. Because you're going to be in for another round of questioning. And I had to come here because...well, just in case any lines were being tapped or anything like that."

Dane felt a chill creep into him.

He jerked out of his seat. "I've got to go, Jesse. Kelsey's alone."

"Hey there," Larry said. "I just came to say goodbye. I'm heading back. We can't all retire and live the good life in the Keys, you know."

"Oh, Larry." She rose, giving him a hug. She stepped back. He was dressed for the office in a neatly pressed suit, silk shirt and tie. She smoothed the shirt. "I'm going to miss you. I'm going to miss working with you. But you'll be back. I'll see you again soon."

"What were you reading so intently?" he asked her.

"Oh, that. Sheila's diary. And some drawings of hers. I'm just…well, I don't know. I'm trying to make it all jell."

"Make what jell?"

"What Nate said yesterday. That it didn't figure for Latham to have killed Sheila, since she was his meal ticket."

"He was psychotic," Larry said.

"I know, but how do you explain the whole fish thing?"

"The fish thing?"

"The fish that Latham dumped here, remember, claiming we had dumped them on his property?"

"He was psychotic," Larry repeated.

"I suppose. We'll never know all the answers."

"Find anything in the diary? Or in those papers?"

"No." She laughed suddenly. "Sheila made me think of old times, though. She talks about us using our old nicknames." She made a face. "Remember, I was Bubble Butt. And you were Web. Weekend Boy. So you still have to be Web, all right? Come down often."

Larry stared at the diary.

"Want some coffee?" she asked him.

"Sure. Where's Dane? I thought I passed him out on the highway when I was coming here."

"Out. He went to see Jesse."

"Oh. Sure, I'd love coffee."

He followed her into the house. She walked straight to the kitchen, setting the diary and papers on the counter. "You know," she told him, "there's something else that's bothering me. Really bothering me," she said, pouring coffee from the pot. "When Latham was attacking me, he talked as if he hadn't killed Sheila. And did Latham really have the brains to take that photo and stick it under Dane's door? To break in and get a tie, then bide his time and watch the house?"

She looked up. Larry looked pale.

"Are you all right?"

"Fine."

She set a cup of coffee in front of him on the counter. She ran her fingers over the drawing, twisting it again to better see the strange border.

"It *is* writing, I think," she said.

"What is that?"

"A drawing Sheila made. Looks like a guy trying to hurt a woman. And you know, she had told Dane she was afraid. Larry, you're sweating. Are you okay?"

"It's a little warm. The suit, you know."

She took out the milk and sugar, and turned back. Larry was taking off his tie. As she walked back, she saw the paper from a different angle.

"Loosen your shirt collar, too, Larry," she said absently. Then she stood very still.

The first part of the border was definitely a letter. A *W* that swept over a third of the bottom of the page. She twisted the page around and saw that she had been right. Sheila had created a border out of letters. The first was a *W*. The second was hardly recognizable because it was so elongated in script. It was an *E*.

"Larry. Look at this. She was writing something to go with the picture."

She twisted the picture again. The last letter was a *B*. WEB. Weekend Boy.

She had written down Larry's nickname.

She looked up, instinct creating a warning chill within her. Larry didn't just look pale. He looked sick. She noticed the tie in his hand. The way he was knotting it.

The milk fell to the floor.

Larry stared at her, shaking his head. "I didn't want to do this, Kels. Really I didn't."

"Larry…no."

Why the hell hadn't Sheila just told her she was afraid of Larry? Because she worked with him, because she'd taken his side, and if she'd just had a chance to spend time alone with Sheila, her friend would have told her all the little reasons why.

"You know, Kels. I know that you know. I went through the house. I read the diary. There wasn't anything in it that pointed to me. I even went through those papers. I thought that…I thought that was one of Sheila's kid drawings. I never would have realized she was spelling my nickname. Not if you hadn't pointed it out. You never let go, Kelsey. You're like a determined little terrier. I should have realized that. Even without that drawing, you probably would have figured it out eventually. Found out how often I had been down here and seen Sheila. It's a good thing I came by."

"If I figured it out, Dane will, too."

He shook his head. "No. They'll think Dane did it. Naturally I'll get rid of that paper. And everything else points to Dane. Sheila slept with him the night I caught up with her, you know. I knew she would. And I knew when Dane would leave the house, so I knew when to bring her here and take the picture. And since he's already told them about the photograph, all I have to do is make sure they find it."

"Larry…why?" she whispered.

"Jesus, Kels, how can you ask that? I loved her, and she treated me like shit. She humiliated me. I was the only guy she wouldn't sleep with. And then there was Dane. He-Man, while I was Web. All my damned life. I couldn't stand it anymore. I had to kill her, so I did. And I planned it so it would look like the Necktie Strangler. Oh, Latham really was the Necktie Strangler. I thought he might be. He was such a sicko. But that didn't matter. I knew if I killed Sheila on Dane's property and took the picture, he'd have to go after the killer, and I knew I could count on him to find him. And he did. But…well, I didn't think Latham would talk to you while he was trying to do the deed. And I sure as hell didn't know about the trust fund—Sheila never told me anything. You can't imagine how I hated her."

"You're not going to kill me, Larry."

"I'm sorry, Kels. Honestly. As much as he's been a thorn in my side my whole life, I didn't really even mean to make Dane pay. But the way it's worked out… well, he's going to have to take the fall. For Sheila, and for you."

She shook her head. "No, Larry, come on, think about it. If you plead temporary insanity and tell the jury about your marriage, I'm sure they'll understand. If you kill me as well…Larry, don't be an idiot. Someone will figure it out. Dane will be back." She was trying to speak rationally. Trying to find an escape route as she spoke. She glanced at where he stood, and at the back door. "You're not wearing gloves," she pointed out. She was shaking inside, a continual "No!" wailing through her head.

Dane would be back.

But maybe he and Jesse had a lot to talk about.

It didn't matter. She wasn't going to let Larry kill her.

"No, I don't have gloves. I really don't want to do this, Kelsey. But this time I'll take the weapon with me," he said softly.

"Your tire tracks will be out there."

"So? I came to say goodbye. And then I found you. I'll call 911 right away."

Kelsey was still incredulous. She had worked with Larry for years. She had sympathized with him at his divorce.

She had slept alone with him in the other room in Sheila's house.

He took a step toward her.

Kelsey was terrified, but she'd fought for her life once already. She wasn't going to give it up now.

"Kels…" he said very softly, "I'll try not to hurt you."

She backed up against the counter. He followed.

She reached behind her, grabbed the coffeepot and brought it crashing against his head. He screamed as the glass and scalding liquid seared his flesh.

Kelsey shoved him hard. Then she began to run.

Dane burst into the house just in time for Kelsey to race into his arms.

Larry was flying after her.

Dane caught Kelsey and moved her aside, ready to meet her attacker.

To his amazement, Larry stopped and stared at him from a distance. Coffee stained his clothes, and there was a gash on the side of his head.

"So, you killed Sheila," Dane said softly.

"No...you killed her. That's the way it will look."

Dane pulled out his cell phone, staring at Larry.

Larry pulled a small gun from his pocket. "Don't! You're not the only one who knows how to use a firearm, Dane. Like this little piece? So small. It's usually a woman's gun. Fits into even a small handbag. But at close range...Dane, you're not dealing with Latham here. I'm not a madman. I just did what I had to do. Drop that cell phone. I'll hit you dead on in the chest if I fire now. And I will do it," he warned. Dane hesitated, slowly lowering the cell phone.

"They'll definitely catch you if you shoot us," he said.

"Let's go outside," Larry said.

Dane's eyes met Kelsey's. She stared at him and knew that he was silently telling her to listen...to buy time.

"All right," Dane said. "We'll go outside since you like to murder people on my beach."

"I'll shoot you right here, if need be. I know what you're doing, of course. Every second gives you a ray of hope, right, Dane?"

"Every second. But I know that you want every second, too. You're trying to figure out a way to kill us without getting caught. But you've blown it this time. Your prints are all over the gun. The cops aren't idiots."

"I can wipe off prints."

"They'll trace it."

"Don't be ridiculous. I bought this gun from Izzy Garcia. It can't be traced back to anyone. Let's go outside."

"Come on, Kelsey, let's walk outside," Dane said.

He prodded Kelsey before him. He followed her, and Larry followed him. Nervously.

"You know, Larry," Dane said, "you always were jealous of my beach. My property. My home. And, of course, my friendship with Sheila."

"Fuck you," Larry said angrily.

And in that moment he followed too closely.

Dane balked at the steps, slamming his body backward. Larry staggered. Dane turned, grasping him. He pinched his fingers into Larry's wrist, knowing the pain would cause Larry to lose his hold on the gun.

But it went off anyway, and Dane knew he'd been hit. In the leg. He could only pray that it had missed the artery.

Still, he forced his weight down on top of Larry's. He heard something crack. A bone. Larry's, thank God, not his.

But Larry was still struggling, reaching for the gun.

He didn't make it.

Kelsey dived in like a hawk. Suddenly the gun was in her hands, pointing down at Larry.

"One move and I shoot you dead! No, first I'll go for your kneecaps. For Sheila. But trust me, I *will* shoot," she said, and she meant it.

Dane knew he was losing blood. A lot of it.

"911, Kels, 911," he managed to say.

He was trying to remain conscious. He thought he must be insane. He could hear a siren. And then someone running.

Jesse. Jesse had followed him back to Hurricane Bay.

"I've got Larry covered, Kelsey," Jesse said. "Hurry up—call an ambulance. Fast."

Things hazed in and out. An ambulance came…and then a helicopter. Dane was being taken to the trauma center at Jackson Memorial in Miami.

He knew he was going in for surgery, knew he was being given blood.

And he knew when Kelsey was beside him, whispering to him.

"Don't you die on me, Dane. I love you. I need you. Oh God, Dane, we've both failed in many ways. But you never failed me. Don't you see? You never failed me."

He managed to open his eyes, though the sedation was stealing away what remained of his consciousness.

"I never will, Kelsey," he promised. Big words.

His eyes closed, and he was wheeled into surgery.

Epilogue

The wedding was at Hurricane Bay in November, when summer's edge had cooled but the days were still gloriously warm and the nights blissfully touched with the soft breezes of fall.

The groom still limped.

The bride was beautiful, and, despite the limp, the groom was incredibly handsome.

Nate was best man; Cindy was maid of honor.

Kelsey's father gave her away with the greatest plea-sure.

After the ceremony, the bride spent her time moving between her guests and her mother—and her new baby brother. Joshua Michael Cunningham was just a month old, but big and beautiful, and the bride's mother was so flushed and happy, she might have been the bride herself.

The partying afterward went on and on. It was midnight when the guests at last dispersed. Most of them. Kelsey's parents were staying. They had at last gone up to the master bedroom, where both Kelsey and Dane had insisted they stay with their newborn.

Kelsey and Dane planned to stay in his old room, down on the first floor.

Dane slipped his arms around Kelsey as she disposed of the finery she was wearing.

"This may be weird," he said.

"What?"

"Having your folks in the house. And we don't leave for the north and our honeymoon until tomorrow."

She turned to him. "But it's our wedding night."

He sighed. "I'm not as good when I have to be really quiet."

She laughed. "It seems like tonight, of all nights, you should get a chance to be really, really good."

"All right," he said. "I've got it."

"Oh?"

"There's a really beautiful boat docked out there."

Kelsey smiled. "I knew you wouldn't fail me," she said softly.

"As long as we live," he said softly. "I'll do my best to never fail you—in any way."

She stood on her toes and kissed him.

And whispered her reply.

Hand in hand they walked toward the boat. Then ran.

It was a calm night at Hurricane Bay. Even so, the old boat rocked beneath the moonlight.

* * * * *

Also available from Delores Fossen

HQN Books

Don't miss *Cowboy Heartbreaker*
the next book in the Wrangler's Creek series.

To see the complete list of titles available from
Delores Fossen, please visit www.deloresfossen.com.

A MAN WORTH REMEMBERING

Delores Fossen

To my sister, Linda Reeves, who taught me
many of life's most important lessons.

Chapter 1

Leigh realized she was being murdered.

She regained consciousness in the water. Cold, deep, dark water. It was above her, beneath her, around her on all sides. Smothering her.

Terror shot through her. She frantically tried to swim but couldn't. Her hands and feet were tied together. Water gushed into her nose and mouth. Her throat clenched. It hurt. She hurt. Her chest pounded as if it might shatter.

Someone had put her there. But who? She could just make out a milky image on the bridge above the water's surface. No face. No name. Just someone who obviously wanted her dead.

Inch by excruciating inch, she sank lower. She fought against the urge to surrender, to close her eyes and just give up so the pain would stop. No. She wouldn't give up. Couldn't. God, she didn't want to die.

Leigh twisted her body, using the last of her breath to try to stop her downward slide. She didn't succeed. The water coiled around her and sent her into a dizzying spiral until her feet dipped into the clotted mud at the bottom.

She didn't see the man before his arm snaked around her waist, but she felt his firm grip. It was a lifeline. Hope. Right now, hope and this man were all she had.

He stopped the mud from swallowing her up and began to haul her toward the surface. Leigh tried to help, but her wrists and feet were still bound. No matter how hard she struggled, she couldn't free herself.

Somehow, he got them out of the water, dragging her onto a muddy embankment. And then he kissed her. At least she thought that's what he was doing until she felt the air gust into her mouth. No. Not a kiss. Mouth-to-mouth resuscitation.

"It's okay," the man said. "You'll be all right."

He knelt beside her, his movements jerky but somehow controlled, and he got the ropes off her hands and feet. Every few seconds, his gaze darted around them as if he was watching for something.

Not something, she realized.

Someone.

After all, the person who'd try to kill her could return to finish the job.

She didn't have time to react to that terrifying realization. Her teeth began to chatter. Her body shook. She was cold and wet, and her head throbbed in pain. For that matter, the rest of her throbbed, too. But at least she was alive. Because of this man, she was alive. Too bad she didn't have enough breath to thank him.

He leaned over her to examine her forehead. It was

dusk, but what was left of the filmy sunlight allowed her to see him and his resolute expression. Did she know him?

No.

He was a stranger.

"You saved my life," she managed to say.

Water slipped off him and splattered onto her face. With the same gentle touch he'd used on her forehead, he wiped away the drops, letting his fingertips linger on her cheek.

"Yes. I did." He mumbled something else under his breath. Something in Spanish. And he shook his head. "I'd still like to have your butt for what you pulled, but we can get into all of that later."

She didn't understand what he meant. Exactly what had she *pulled*? She hadn't asked to be in that water. Had she? No, she was sure of that. This was no suicide attempt. She'd fought to stay alive.

"Who are you?" she asked.

Something she couldn't distinguish rifled through his eyes. "What the devil do you mean by that?"

"I'd like to know your name," she clarified.

He sat back on his heels and glared down at her. "Just what kind of sick game are you playing, huh?" She barely got out a denying shake of her head before he continued. "Believe me, it won't work." With each word he got louder. "I want answers. I *deserve* answers."

"I'd like some answers, too. For starters, please tell me who you are."

"Gabe," he said, hissing it out like profanity. "But you know that."

No, she didn't. She shoved her fingers through her hair to push the wet strands out of her eyes. Part of her thought she might recognize his name, the way he'd said it, but she couldn't be sure. Mercy, if her head would just stop pounding, maybe she could sort through all of this.

"Gabe Sanchez," he added after a moment.

Still nothing. But she *should* know him. Maybe she felt that because of his formidable expression and not because of any true recollection. "Well, thank you, Mr. Sanchez, for saving me. I thought I was going to die."

He sat there as drops of water slid down his face. He seemed oblivious to the water, to his drenched clothes. Oblivious to everything around them. Everything but her. He stared craters in her.

"You would have died if I hadn't been here," he assured her. "Someone shot you. When that didn't work, they clubbed you and threw you in the lake."

She gasped, horrified that someone would do such terrible things to her. "Someone shot me?"

"Looks that way. It's just a graze, but combined with that lump, you'll probably have one heck of a headache."

She nodded. She already had one heck of a headache so there was no *probably* about it.

"Who did this to you?" he demanded. "Who tried to kill you?"

He seemed angry with her, and she didn't know why. Worse, she didn't know why things didn't make sense. Who had done this to her? Why had she been in the water? And who was this stranger who expected her to have all the answers?

"I don't know." She touched her forehead. When she drew back her hand, she noticed the watery blood on her fingertips. She was injured but didn't even remember how it'd happened. God, how could she possibly not know that? "Did you see anyone before you jumped in after me?"

"Just a car speeding away. I couldn't make out the license plate." Vigilantly, he looked around them again. "When I saw the air bubbles in the water, I dived in."

Thank God he had. If not, she would without a doubt be dead. "Where are we?"

"Lake Pontchartrain." His narrowed gaze came back to her. "Are you trying to make me believe you really don't know?"

She glanced around her. All she saw was the sun setting on an ordinary lake. Other than that, it didn't look familiar. "Are we near Houston?"

"Houston?" he spat out. "We're just outside New Orleans."

Sweet heaven. Even with a multiple choice, she wouldn't have gotten it right. What the heck was she doing here?

"You honestly don't remember?" he asked.

"No." It was the one answer of which she was certain.

"All right, let's try something easy. What's the date?"

Again, she tried to concentrate. "Is it June something?"

He blew out a long breath. "Not quite. It's August twelfth. Okay. Here's a question that nobody gets wrong. What's your name?"

She opened her mouth, but nothing came out. Absolutely nothing. Her mind was a complete blank.

He stilled, his expression registering more than a little alarm. "You don't know your own name?"

She shook her head, trying to will away the dizziness that started to overpower her. "I have no idea." And she didn't. No idea whatsoever.

She was ready to panic, when it occurred to her that this had to be a dream. Yes, a dream. It was the only logical explanation. A full-fledged, mind-blowing nightmare. All she had to do was wake up, and she'd remember everything. Heck, right now she probably wasn't anywhere near this lake but in her own bed at home.

Wherever home was.

She blinked hard several times, trying to force a different scene to appear in front of her, but the nightmare was still there. And so was Gabe Sanchez. He stared at her, his dark, suspicious eyes filled with questions that she knew she couldn't answer.

So, with the taste of the muddy lake still in her mouth, she closed her eyes and let the dream take over.

Voices woke her. She caught a word here and there, but much of what she heard didn't make sense. Philip. Frank Templeton. Sanchez.

Gabe Sanchez.

The man who saved her. There were at least two other voices: a male and a female. All three used hushed tones, but they seemed to be arguing.

She forced her eyes open, even though the overhead fluorescent lights made her wince, and pain stabbed through her head. She felt groggy, almost drunk, but she finally managed to see the trio near the doorway. Sanchez, an attractive woman with pinned-up dark hair and a tall blond man.

The woman and the other man wore business suits in neutral colors. No suit for Sanchez. He had on faded jeans, a plain white T-shirt and a shoulder holster that had a pistol sticking out of it. There was a beeper attached to his belt loop.

She glanced down at her own clothes. Someone had dressed her in drab green surgical scrubs. And she was on a gurney.

"I'm not in ICU," she said to herself. "Or in an emergency room."

It looked more like a huge supply closet. There were several metal shelves crammed with boxes. A single window graced the far wall, and the blinds were closed, so she couldn't tell if it was night or day. Or if it was covered with bars. She was afraid it might have bars.

"It's what you have to tell her," the woman insisted.

Sanchez shook his head. "I won't."

The woman folded her arms over her chest and tapped her foot. "It wasn't a request. Now, what part of it didn't you understand?"

"The part where you started spouting Justice Department garbage, that's when, Teresa."

"You'd rather have her dead? Because that's what'll happen. Heck, it almost did, or have you forgotten that already?"

"I haven't forgotten anything. I'm the one who pulled her out of that lake." Sanchez mumbled something under his breath. Leigh only caught the *Jesucristo* part. "Hell, she almost died in my arms."

She lifted her head off the gurney. "Who are you people?"

The three rifled their gazes toward her, but they didn't say anything. She studied each one, trying to interpret their expressions and the snippets of conversation she'd heard.

She definitely didn't trust the blond man, and yet she

couldn't say why. The woman was no ally either. She didn't know what to make of Sanchez, but since he'd saved her from drowning, she would cast her lot with him if it came down to choosing sides.

It would, she feared, come down to choosing sides.

"Better yet," she amended when none of them answered her, "who am I?"

Gabe Sanchez walked toward her with an almost graceful ease. He was tall, over six feet, and muscular. His biceps strained against the cotton T-shirt. He had chocolate-colored hair that was short and neat. Efficient. Low maintenance.

When he got closer, she saw that his eyes were a deep blue. They, too, seemed efficient—his gaze swept over her with a minimal amount of effort. However, she had no doubt that he'd just given her the once-over.

The others trailed behind Sanchez, stopping when he did. They were friends. No, more than that. Or less than that. Maybe much, much less.

God, why was it so hard to figure out things?

"You still don't remember who you are?" Sanchez asked her.

"No. Why is that? What's wrong with me?"

"You took a hard hit on the head. It might take a while for everything to come back."

She touched the bandage on her forehead. There was indeed a lump under the gauze swatch, but she hadn't needed to feel it to know it was there. That was no doubt the source of her vicious headache.

"I have a concussion?" she asked.

Sanchez nodded. "And a few stitches in your forehead and on your ankle where the rope abraded your skin. The doctor examined you, but he doesn't think your memory loss has anything to do with the head injury. In other words, no brain damage. He said it was brought on by emotional trauma."

"Disassociative amnesia," she softly added. "How long will it last?" But she already knew. Like her aversion to the blond man and the woman, she just didn't know how she knew it.

It was Sanchez who answered. "The doctor's not sure. It could be hours. Or days."

"Or I might never regain my memory," she provided.

She lowered her head and tried to absorb that. She couldn't. It was impossible to understand anything while her thoughts whirled around like a tornado.

God, what she was going to do? She didn't know who she was, not her name, not her age. Nothing. She didn't know if she was still in danger or if she could trust anyone. She didn't even know what these people had to do with her.

But they knew.

They likely knew everything about her.

"What's my name?" she asked Sanchez. She wanted answers, and by God, she wanted them now.

"Leigh O'Brien."

That didn't mean anything to her. Only the water and Sanchez saving her meant anything. For all practical purposes, her life had begun the moment she realized she was drowning. That wasn't a comforting thought. "Where am I?"

"A private clinic near New Orleans."

So, they hadn't left the area. But it wasn't an ordinary clinic. She was sure of that. "Are you a cop?"

"No."

"Am *I* a cop?"

The room went deadly silent. "No," the blond man finally answered.

Leigh didn't like that hesitation. It sent a wave of panic through her. "Am I a criminal then?" And she braced herself for the answer.

These people might be here to arrest her for something she'd done wrong. Had someone tossed her in that lake because of a drug deal gone bad? An organized-crime housecleaning? What awful thing had she done to make someone want to murder her?

The blond man took a step forward, placing himself slightly ahead of the others. "You're not a criminal."

She allowed herself a short breath of relief. Just one. And got down to business. "Since these questions could go on forever, why don't you just tell me who you are?"

The three glanced at each other before the blond man said anything else. "I'm Wade Jenkins. People call me Jinx. Special Agent Sanchez and I are with the FBI. Agent Teresa Walters is an agent with the Bureau of Alcohol, Tobacco and Firearms—the ATF."

"FBI. ATF," Leigh repeated. "What about me? Am I some sort of agent, too?"

"You're a concerned citizen." The blond man burrowed his index finger into his eyebrow. "A concerned citizen with a rather large problem."

"Obviously," Leigh snapped. "Believe me, after everything that's happened, I can guess there's a problem. Now, other than a concerned citizen, who am I? If I don't work for an agency with initials, where do I work?"

"At a bookstore in Austin, Texas," Jinx answered.

"A bookstore?" A *bookstore*. That couldn't be right. Nothing about that felt right.

He didn't elaborate. "Exactly what do you remember about being in the water?"

A good question. Too bad she didn't have a good answer. "Not much other than Agent Sanchez saving me. Before that, all I remember is struggling and sinking deeper."

"Any idea who put you in the lake?"

She tried to force the answer to appear in her mind. It didn't work. She had no more answers about that now than she had when Sanchez had first asked her. "No. I have an image of someone on a bridge, but I can't make out any of the features. Someone wearing light colors. I don't suppose that helps you any?"

"No," Teresa Walters answered in a frustrated huff. "But your amnesia is only part of the problem. This might not be over. Someone might make another attempt to kill you."

Leigh swallowed hard. She hadn't considered that. Yet. However, after her adrenaline fatigue wore off, it would no doubt have occurred to her. Amnesia or not, she still had common sense.

She hoped.

Leigh turned her gaze to Sanchez. "Who wants me dead?"

He lifted his shoulder. "We don't know."

"Can you at least tell me what it involves? What—"

"The less you know, the better," Jinx interrupted.

"Maybe that's your way of looking at it, but I see things from a little different perspective than you do. Someone tried to kill me, and I think I have a right to know why."

"Jinx is right about this, Leigh," Sanchez spoke up.

"Even if we told you everything, it wouldn't make you safer. That's why we'll provide you with protection."

She shook her head, already objecting. "Now, wait a minute. I don't even know any of you, and you want me to place my life in your hands? How do I know you're not the people who tried to kill me, huh?"

"That doesn't make any sense," Sanchez answered. "If we wanted you dead, I wouldn't have pulled you out of that lake."

"But those two didn't pull me out." She pointed to Wade Jenkins and then to Teresa Walters. "The way I see it, I'm in a real mess here. What if some secret's trapped in my head, and you want me around just long enough to get it? What if you kill me the minute I tell you what you want to know?"

Agent Walters threw her hands in the air. "I give up. Let me know when you can talk some sense into her."

Leigh was about to tell the woman exactly what she thought of her when Sanchez broke in. "You can trust me, Leigh." The offer had not come effortlessly. It came with a scalpel-sharp glare.

"Why? Because you saved my life?"

He didn't answer, but after a moment Jinx did. "Not just that. You can trust him because Gabe Sanchez is your husband."

Chapter 2

Gabe could almost feel her gaze crawl all over him. He braced himself for the storm he was about to face. And there would be one heck of a storm when Leigh got going with her questions. No doubt about it.

"My husband?" she repeated.

He nodded but didn't add more than that. The details of their marital status were among a mile-long list of things he didn't want to discuss with her. Too bad he'd probably have to do just that before this was over.

"Is it true?" she asked. "Are we really married?"

He eased onto the edge of the narrow gurney and stared down at her. No sense standing for what would basically be an interrogation. "I'll answer that if you'll tell me the truth. Is this memory loss all an act?"

"No." Aggravation danced across her eyes. "I wish it were, because I can promise you I wouldn't be here. I don't like being here."

"Yeah, I know what you mean." Gabe made a sweeping glance around the room. "I don't care much for it myself."

Leigh made the same sweeping glance, and when she finished, their eyes met, coming together until they held. "Are you really my husband?"

Well, this was one part of the conversation that he obviously couldn't put off. Not that it surprised him. If their situations were reversed, he'd want to know the same thing. "Afraid so. You're not happy about that?"

"The jury's still out. It's hard to know if I'm happy about it when I don't even know you. So, how long have we been married?"

Ah, a test. He'd expected that, too. "Four years, six months." He paused, thinking. "And eighteen days."

He could have given her the hours if she'd asked. Gabe cursed himself. It didn't please him that he could recall something so painful in such detail.

"That long," she mumbled.

Yeah, that long. But half of that time she'd been gone. Now, here she was—right back in his life. It had taken him too long to get over her the last time. She'd turned him upside down and hung him out to dry. He didn't want another dose of that.

Even with the dye job, she hadn't changed much. A little thinner. And maybe there was something different about her expression. The old Leigh had been so self-assured. Not now though. There was a good reason for that. After all, someone had tried to kill her. That murder attempt no doubt had something to do with what had brought her back to him. Fate working overtime again.

Sometimes fate didn't know which end was up.

Well, he wasn't about to buy into anything that dealt with fate.

She continued to stare at him as if sizing him up. "Why didn't you say something earlier about being my husband?"

"There wasn't time. You were unconscious when I brought you here." He knew that wouldn't be the last of her questions, and he didn't have to wait long for her to verify that.

Leigh glanced at his hand. "Why isn't either of us wearing a wedding ring?"

Hell. The woman could certainly open old wounds. Gabe pulled the neck chain out of his T-shirt so she could see the simple gold band that it held. "I'm left-handed, and it catches on the holster. I'm not sure where your ring is. Maybe it slipped off in the lake."

Or maybe she'd thrown it away. He wouldn't put it past her. Obviously their marriage vows hadn't meant much to her. He couldn't say the same. And that was probably the only explanation he had for why he still wore his wedding ring. One thing was for sure, as soon as he got out of there, he planned to get rid of it. It was something he should have done months ago.

"I have to go," Jinx announced, the sound of his voice slicing through the heavy silence. "I need to up-date a few people about what's happened and try to figure out what we're going to do. Gabe, you wait here with Leigh."

Of course. Gabe hadn't expected it to be any other way.

"I should head out, too," Agent Walters added after checking her watch. She gave Gabe's sleeve a tug. "No improvising, all right?"

Gabe didn't concur either verbally or otherwise. Nor did he disagree with the woman who was coleader of this so-called task force. He just kept his rebellious thoughts to himself. "I'll walk you two out." He stood and looked down at Leigh. "Stay put."

Her unbandaged eyebrow winged up. "Do I have a choice?"

"No," he clarified over his shoulder.

"I told you to be nice to her," Jinx said the moment they were outside the door. "I told you to gain her trust."

Gabe wanted to laugh. "I don't perform miracles."

"No, but you will do your job."

Jinx's words hit him like a heavyweight's fist, even though Gabe had tried to brace himself for it. "And what exactly do you mean by that?"

"It means you'll protect her until we can make other arrangements." There was no hesitation in Jinx's tone, and that tone drew a clear line between their friendship and his role as Gabe's boss.

Gabe scrubbed his hand over his face. "It means you want me to be her bodyguard."

"If necessary," Teresa piped in. Jinx gave a nod of agreement.

It would be necessary. No doubt about it. That was the only way Gabe could see this playing out. Heck, if he hadn't been on the receiving end of this assignment, he might have even considered it a good idea.

There were just a couple of problems with this particular plan that Jinx and Teresa had come up with for him. It would mean he'd have to spend a lot of time with his wife. A wife he didn't want. A wife who didn't want him. But she was also a vulnerable woman with a killer after her.

Hell.

He'd do what the Justice Department wanted him to do, and then he was out of there. Leigh could go back to whatever the hell she'd been doing, and he would get on with his life. All he had to do was keep her alive, catch the bad guy and leave. Especially, leave.

There was no way he'd allow himself to be drawn back into her life. No way.

Leigh waited until Sanchez and the others walked out of the room. "Stay put," she said, repeating the terse order he'd just given her. "As if I had a choice."

In fact, her choices were extremely limited. Possibly even nil. She had amnesia, was hurt and didn't know where she could go to get out of danger. That didn't mean she trusted the three people who'd just left the room. Or that she believed them. She was almost positive they hadn't told her the truth.

It's what you have to tell her, Agent Teresa Walters had said before they knew she was awake. People didn't usually make remarks like that if they planned to tell the truth.

The whole truth, anyway.

So just what did the others want Sanchez to keep from her? She certainly intended to find out.

Realizing that she had to go to the bathroom, Leigh tossed back the covers and swung her legs off the gurney. She was achy, and her vision was spotty. There was a thick white bandage completely encircling her right ankle, and when she stood, the stitches pinched.

She made use of a pair of green flip-flops that were under the gurney and went in search of the bathroom. It wasn't hard to find. It was the only door other than the one through which her fearless protectors had exited.

The bathroom was enormous and had two vats filled with dirty linen and hospital-style gowns. The laundry chute was as wide as the bins, indicating the need to send plenty of soiled clothing to the laundry room. A regular clinic probably wouldn't have such a need.

So just what was this place?

Since she hadn't heard any traffic or sounds normally associated with a clinic, it was probably some secured area. Perhaps a military installation or maybe a safe house used by the FBI.

Now, just what did the FBI and an ATF agent want with a bookstore employee from Austin? Perhaps the books in the store weren't the run-of-the-mill variety. If so, she was obviously more than just a concerned citizen.

Leigh put that thought on the back burner when she noticed the mirror above the sink. She approached it cautiously, afraid of what she might see in her own reflection. And equally afraid of what she might *not* see.

Disappointment soon replaced the cautiousness. She didn't recognize a thing about herself. The face of a stranger stared back at her.

A troubled stranger.

Almost frantically, she studied her face harder, trying to force herself to see something familiar. She was pale and wondered if it was from the trauma or if that was her usual coloring. Perhaps a combination of both.

The skin surrounding the bandage was bruised—the purplish stain bled down to her cheekbone where someone had obviously hit her pretty hard. A blunt object was her guess.

Her features weren't prominent. Average. She certainly wasn't beautiful. Her hair was chin-length and cedar-colored, but since her roots were light brown, she figured that she wasn't a natural redhead. She checked in the most obvious place to verify her conclusion, stretching out the waist of the scrubs to look inside.

No. She wasn't a redhead.

She leaned closer to the mirror, suddenly puzzled by her eyes. They weren't the same color. One was dark brown; the other, pale green. She automatically reached toward the brown eye and removed the colored contact that had camouflaged her iris. So, her eyes were really green, and since she could see perfectly without the contact, she had to believe she'd worn them for cosmetic reasons.

Why?

Colored contacts. Dyed hair. She'd disguised her appearance. It made sense. Perhaps she'd been hiding because someone wanted her dead. Too bad the disguise hadn't worked. Obviously, someone had seen right through it and gone after her.

Leigh noticed the scar then. A puckered dimple on her right forearm. It appeared to be well healed, but she thought it might be a bullet wound. Or maybe her imagination was just working overtime. Just the sight of the injury, however, caused a sickening feeling in her stomach. It was yet another chilling reminder of her past she couldn't remember.

She finished up in the bathroom, returned to the room and got back on the gurney. A moment later, Gabe pushed opened the door and came in with a large disposable cup in each hand.

"Coffee," he announced. "I figured you'd need your caffeine fix by now."

Leigh didn't know about that, but the steamy brew smelled wonderful. "I'm a big coffee drinker?"

He nodded and glanced at one cup and then the other, apparently trying to decide which one was hers. He finally took a sip from one and grimaced. "Yours. Three sugars, just the way you like it."

She took the cup, knowing she would indeed like it. Odd. Why had sugary coffee felt familiar and not her husband?

Her husband.

As she'd done to her own face in the mirror, Leigh scrutinized his. Actually, he wasn't bad-looking. A little on the rough side, and the small scar on his chin only contributed to that image. His skin was a pale bronze, obviously a DNA contribution from the Hispanic heritage that his surname signified. The dark blue eyes, however, indicated some Anglo blood as well. All in all, it was a good mix that had produced an interesting face.

His eyes were…not bedroom eyes, even though it was the first description that sprang to mind. The dark lashes made them look half-closed, dreamy, but there was nothing *bedroom* about them. Those eyes meant business.

"Is the coffee all right?" Gabe asked when she took a sip.

"It's fine. So, you know how I like my coffee—that still doesn't mean I believe everything you've told me." Placing her cup on the table beside his, she glanced at her ring finger and noticed a faint line. Not necessarily from a wedding band. But it was possible. "Did I have any ID on me when you pulled me out of the lake?"

He stretched out his leg so he could work his fingers into the front pocket of his jeans. He fished out a single key. "This was tucked under the floor mat in the car. It had your fingerprints on it."

"It's for a car?"

Sanchez shook his head. "You left the keys to your rental car in the ignition. This looks more like a house key. Is it familiar?"

"No." It looked like a key, that's all. A key to a house, and she had no idea where that house might be. Austin, maybe, since that's where she supposedly worked. "You didn't find a purse or wallet on me or in the car?"

"I think the person who tried to kill you probably took it."

That was possible, which made her wonder if the attack was robbery related. But she didn't think so. She probably wouldn't be here if it'd been a simple robbery.

Leigh glanced at him. So far, he'd cooperated with her questions. Well, some of them anyway, but she had no way of knowing if what he'd told her was the truth or even part of the truth. Heck, she wasn't even convinced that the man was truly her husband.

"Why didn't you kiss me when you pulled me out of the water?" she asked. "If we're really married, wouldn't a kiss have been the husbandly thing to do?"

It happened so quickly, she didn't have time to protest or wonder why she'd issued such a stupid invitation in the first place. Gabe slipped his hand around the back of her neck and angled her head. His mouth came to hers. Touched. Brushed. And lingered.

Before he got down to business.

The kiss that followed was hot and clever. Slightly rough and a heck of a lot longer than it should have been. It certainly wasn't a husbandly peck. It had a slick veneer of all sorts of emotion, including some anger, but that didn't quite cover up the pure, raw attraction that sizzled beneath.

When he finally set her free, there was no doubt in Leigh's mind that she'd been kissed by someone who knew exactly how to do it.

Gabe looked deeply into her eyes. "Remember me now, *mi vida*?" he drawled, his tone a cocky challenge.

Actually, Leigh didn't, but she thought she might *like* to remember him. Too bad that kiss muddled her brain even more than it already was.

She pushed him away and turned her head toward the window. There wasn't much she could do about her erratic breathing, but she didn't want him to see the telltale bewilderment that had to be in her eyes.

"Look, I may not know who I am, but I'm not stupid," Leigh said crisply. "Other than the obvious thing of someone trying to kill me, something isn't right."

"Funny, it felt right to me." When her gaze came to his, he rubbed the pad of his thumb over his bottom lip and flashed her a grin that set her teeth on edge.

"I didn't mean that kiss. There has to be a reason why I have all these crazy feelings." Leigh aimed her finger at him when Gabe started to speak. "And I'm not talking about your mouth on mine. Why won't you tell me what's really going on here?"

Gabe dropped onto the gurney right next to her. "You'll be safer not knowing."

"I didn't buy that from Jinx, and I won't buy it from you. I could regain my memory in the next minute, and if I follow through with that asinine theory, I'll be in more danger than I am right now. Somebody wants me dead, and I don't think they care if I have amnesia or not."

He nodded eventually. "Okay. I'll give you the condensed version."

"Why not the whole thing?"

"It'll only muddy the waters, and it won't help you sort things out." He didn't wait for her to agree. "A little over two years ago you came across some sensitive information regarding a high-ranking government official named Joe Dayton."

Leigh gave that some thought. All right. What he said could be true. "I found this when I was working at the bookstore in Austin?"

The corner of Gabe's mouth kicked up. "No, you were working somewhere else at the time. And don't bother to ask where, because I won't tell you."

"Another of Jinx's orders, or did that come from Special Agent Walters?"

"Not Jinx. Not Teresa. *My* order. Like I said, it'll only confuse you more if I overload you with a bunch of facts that you don't need right now."

Leigh wasn't happy about it, but she'd take what she could get. Besides, on that point he might be right. "Okay, finish the short version. What about this Joe Dayton?"

"He was as dirty as they come," he answered after hesitating. "We didn't know if he was working alone or if what you learned would make you a target."

She shook her head, not understanding. "So, why did he wait two years to come after me?"

"You've been hiding all this time."

Finally, something made sense. But it was just the

beginning. She needed a lot more pieces of information for this puzzle to come together.

Gabe's pager began to beep. He jabbed the button to make the sound stop and sprang to his feet. In the same motion, he whipped out his pistol and reeled toward the door.

Leigh hadn't thought she could be any more frightened, but that did it. Her heart began to pound. "What's wrong?" she asked, getting off the gurney.

Gabe motioned toward the window. "See if anyone's out there."

She hobbled toward it, ignoring her stitches, and peeked through the side of the blinds. It was dark, and they were several floors off the ground, but she saw six cars in the parking lot.

"Nobody," she reported. But the words hardly left her mouth when four men exited one of the cars. "Somebody," she amended. "There are four of them."

"Watch the door," Gabe ordered and then traded places with her so he could glance out the window. "We don't have much time. We have to get out of here."

Leigh started out the door, but Gabe latched onto her arm and yanked her back. "We can't go that way."

"You're not suggesting we use the window?"

"No. They probably left someone to take care of us if we try that."

That was a chilling thought. *Take care of us.* In other words, kill them. "So, how do we get out?"

He didn't answer. Gabe grabbed a box from one of the shelves and pulled out another gun. It looked even more deadly than the one he already had. He checked to make sure it was loaded. It was. And he thrust it into her hands.

"What—" But Leigh didn't get a chance to protest. Gabe shoved open the bathroom door, pulling her inside with him. He held open the laundry hatch with his elbow and swung his leg into the opening.

"I'm going down first," he told her. "Count to ten and follow me unless you hear gunfire. If that happens, barricade yourself in here and shoot anyone who comes through that door. And I mean anyone. Understand?"

She nodded and examined the gun. "Do I know how to use this?"

"You know." He climbed into the duct. "Now, let's hope you remember."

Leigh hoped the same thing. "Let me guess—I learned how to fire guns like this at the bookstore?"

Gabe flashed her a dry grin and ignored her question. "There's no safety on that piece. If necessary, aim and fire. And Leigh? This time do as I tell you."

Before she could ask what he meant by that, he let himself drop. She kept her gaze on him until he disappeared into the tunnel.

"One," Leigh counted.

She stood there for a few panicky seconds, wondering again if she should trust him. And wondering if she should follow him. She really had no reason to trust him, but she wouldn't have any reason to trust those four men about to come through the door either. They no doubt wanted to kill her. She didn't know for sure what Gabe wanted to do with her.

So this was the proverbial rock and a hard place?

"Ten," she mumbled when she heard hurried footsteps in the hallway on the other side of the wall.

She climbed into the laundry hatch and let herself go. Moments later, she heard gunshots, but it was too late to stop her downward slide. Or anything else for that matter.

She was headed straight toward those deadly sounding shots, and there was nothing she could do about it.

Chapter 3

Leigh saw Gabe just before she reached the bottom—a split-second glimpse of a man prepared to kill. He was behind a concrete post about fifteen feet from the laundry chute. He'd assumed a classic isosceles stance with a two-handed grip on his pistol. Every inch of him looked primed to fight.

"Take cover!" Gabe yelled. Someone punctuated his command with a spray of bullets.

She torpedoed out of the chute, quickly rolled over the side of the bin and dropped. She landed in an unladylike sprawl on the concrete floor.

"I said take cover. Now!" Gabe yelled.

She was certainly trying to do that. Unfortunately, her body didn't want to cooperate. Leigh scrambled to her feet and with her flip-flops smacking against the floor, she ducked behind another of those concrete posts.

Should she try to get to Gabe? she wondered. Even with the obvious danger of someone shooting at them, she still considered the idea. It seemed a better option than being on her own when she didn't know what to do.

The next bullets that strafed across the floor put a stop to that notion. She had to stay put.

From her position, she couldn't see Gabe. There were more laundry bins, huge washing machines, industrial-size dryers and rows of metal tables. From the narrow view that she had, there were many places a gunman could hide.

Too many.

Besides, she didn't even know if there was just *one* gunman. She'd seen four men in the parking lot, and it was entirely possible all four were somewhere in the room, waiting for her to make a mistake.

If she called out to Gabe to ask him what to do, she might give away her position and force him to give away his. He probably wouldn't appreciate that. Sweet heaven. Another rock and a hard place.

"I'll take that," the man snarled. He snatched the gun from her hand and pressed it to her head.

Not Gabe. Someone else. One of the gunmen, no doubt. How the heck had he gotten so close? Leigh hadn't heard a thing. Of course, her heart was pounding so loudly, she was practically deaf.

Relying purely on instinct, she stabbed her elbow into the man's stomach and quickly spun around. Leigh used all her strength and rammed the heel of her right hand into his Adam's apple. She followed it with a left-handed jab to his mouth. He hissed and staggered back.

Leigh saw him clearly then. Too clearly. He was most certainly one of the men from the parking lot. There was no expression in his muddy-colored eyes, no emotion on his face. He latched onto her neck and roughly twisted her so her back was against his chest.

"Quit fighting me," he warned, shoving the gun even harder to her temple.

His voice was raspy, apparently from the blow she'd managed to deliver to his throat. That didn't give her much satisfaction. He towered over her. And he was solid. He could easily kill her with his bare hands. Of course, he wouldn't have to do something so menial since he had her gun and probably his as well.

"Let's do this the right way," the man yelled across the room to Gabe. "Depending on what you do, I can make this easy for her, or I can make it real slow and ugly."

Leigh didn't care much for those two choices. The man was no doubt talking about how he intended to kill her. "Step out where I can see you, Agent Sanchez," he ordered.

She wasn't sure what Gabe would do. Until she heard the thud of his weapon drop to the floor. He stepped out from behind the post and walked toward them with his hands tucked behind his head.

God. He was surrendering.

Her heart started to pound harder. She'd hoped he might be able to save them or at least buy some time so she could figure out what to do. But Gabe hadn't done that. Instead, he'd surrendered to a man who would probably kill them both before she drew her next breath.

"Who are you working for?" Gabe asked him.

"No one who's willing to bargain with you."

"Then how about we bargain? Before you say no, I think you should know the woman you're holding has plenty of money. I'm sure we can work out some financial arrangements that'd make it profitable for you to let her go."

"Save your breath," the man retorted. "I've got no plans to be a rich dead man, and that's what'll happen if I cut a deal with the likes of you."

Her gaze connected with Gabe's. There was a slight lift to his right eyebrow. For the first time, she recognized something in his eyes. Exactly *what*, she couldn't say, but he was definitely trying to communicate.

In a move that seemed both in slow motion and at a speed not humanly possible, Gabe's left hand whipped out from behind his head. He held another gun that he'd hidden. Something small and sleek. The fluorescent light licked the silvery metal and sent a flash across Leigh's face. Gabe aimed the gun directly at her.

She had no time to think, no time to react. She briefly, very briefly, considered that Gabe and his gun would be the last things she'd ever see. But what she couldn't figure out was why he wanted her dead, especially after he had saved her.

Gabe double-tapped the trigger. The shots cracked like enormous wads of chewing gum. Leigh felt warm spatters of blood on her cheek and waited for the pain or numbness to follow what was certainly a fatal head wound.

That didn't happen.

Instead, the man behind her slumped into a heap, the pistol he'd held against her temple clattering to the floor.

Her breath shattered, a noise coming from deep within her throat. Leigh's hands began to shake violently. Still, she kept her attention focused on Gabe, afraid to blink for fear he'd disappear before she could get to him.

Getting to him, she soon learned, wasn't even necessary. It seemed he made it to her in one step. She grabbed onto him and held tight.

Without breaking her grip, Gabe picked up the gun he'd tossed on the floor and placed the smaller one into the slide holster on the back waist of his jeans. He handed Leigh the other weapon that the man had taken from her.

"There's no need for you to see that," he said, referring to the body. He led her toward the door.

He was right. There was no need for her to see the man. That didn't stop Leigh from glancing back at the lifeless body and the perfectly centered hole in his head. Gabe had literally shot the man right between the eyes. The other bullet wound was only a fraction of an inch above the first one.

She pressed her hand to her stomach, hoping she didn't get sick. "He's dead?" she asked unnecessarily.

"He's dead."

"You could have shot me."

Gabe slightly rearranged his expression, apparently insulted. "I wouldn't have missed. Not ever."

Leigh prayed she'd never have to test his accuracy again. "Well, thank you. That's twice you've saved my life."

"Don't thank me yet. We're not out of danger. We have to get away from here first."

Leigh silently agreed. One man was dead, but there were at least three others who would probably be willing to do what their comrade had tried.

Gabe stopped when they reached a large metal door

at the end of the room and turned to her. "Here are the rules. Stay behind me at all times. I want us back to back, moving together. Got that?"

"Yes, I think so." Leigh hoped so anyway. She still felt woozy, and Gabe's quickly spoken instructions seemed jumbled.

"Rule two—you watch our backs, and I'll take care of anything that comes from any other direction." He tipped his head to her gun. "By any chance, do you remember how to use that?"

She eyed the weapon as if it was a foreign object. "Maybe."

Gabe repeated that, adding a soundless word of profanity. "All right. If you have to shoot, hold the gun level and brace your wrist with your left hand. That's a lot of firepower, and I don't want you dropping your weapon when you feel the recoil. Shoot to kill. Understand?"

Gabe didn't wait for her to answer, not that Leigh had anything to say about the abbreviated lesson on how to kill. He spun her around so they were back to back. He eased open the door and peered into the parking lot.

The alarm started almost immediately. It wasn't a typical security system that clamored loudly enough to be heard blocks away. It was a piercing hum, but it was certainly meant to serve as a warning.

"All right. Let's go," Gabe said. "Remember everything I've told you."

Leigh didn't know how he expected her to do that. She literally couldn't remember her name so how would she keep all the other things straight? Maybe she'd get lucky, and her instincts would kick in if she had to shoot.

The night air engulfed her when they stepped outside. It was humid, almost stifling. Even with the drone of the alarm, the place was eerily silent. No traffic noise. No birds. Nothing. Just the sound of their steps as Gabe orchestrated them away from the building.

Shoot to kill, he'd told her. That made sense because a wounded gunman could still have a deadly aim. She had to wonder if she could kill. Or if she'd ever killed before.

God, that seemed an awful thing not to know.

Gabe skirted along a row of shrubs, following the semistraight line until they came to a Dumpster. They ducked behind it just as the door to the laundry area flew open. Milky yellow light poured out into the darkness.

So did two armed men.

Gabe latched onto her hand and forced her to run. "Stay with me."

Shots shattered the near silence, sounding so close that Leigh didn't want to know just how close they were coming to Gabe and her. She lost count of how many times the guns fired, but they seemed to keep pace with her racing heartbeat.

Leigh hadn't remembered her flip-flops or her hurt ankle until they started to sprint. Not ideal running shoes, and the stitches tore at her skin. Somehow, Gabe managed to keep her on her feet, even when they left the pavement and darted over a patch of uneven ground.

The yard, such that it was, melted into a greenbelt cluttered with stubby trees and rocks. An eight-foot-high masonry fence was just beyond that. Gabe didn't ask if it was something she could climb—he just scaled it, dragging her like a rag doll with him.

When they reached the other side, she noticed the motorcycle. It was nestled between two scrub oaks, but not even the darkness could camouflage the chrome.

"We're riding that?" she asked in a frantic whisper.

"Yes." He slipped his gun back into his shoulder holster, straddled the leather seat and started the engine. "Keep your weapon handy. We just might need it before this is over."

She nodded. Somewhere behind them, close behind, those men were probably gaining ground. Still, she took the time to eye the motorcycle. "Do you have helmets?"

"No!"

It wouldn't do any good to point out that riding without helmets was dangerous. He'd no doubt point out that bullets and gunmen were even more deadly.

And he'd be right.

Gabe didn't try to alleviate her fears. He merely latched onto her wrist and hauled her on the bike behind him. Within seconds, he had the motorcycle rumbling through the night and away from the gunmen.

Leigh quickly learned she had to hang on or fall off, and the easiest thing to hang on to was Gabe. While still clinging to the gun, she wrapped her arms around his waist, pressed her cheek to his back and held on. And she prayed, hoping the God of whichever religion she professed would hear her. Right now, she needed someone of a divine nature on her side.

After all, she was with a man who killed as easily as he breathed, and Leigh knew all too well that he held her life—and possibly even her heart—in his hands.

Chapter 4

Gabe had a lot of questions. And too few answers.

That did not please him.

He was reasonably sure he'd lost the hired guns. Fairly certain he could remember his way down the dirt roads that snaked around the bayou. And he was hopeful he'd managed to save their lives. For the time being anyway. However, he wasn't at all sure what the heck was going on. Or who'd just tried to kill them.

Still, none of those things occupied his thoughts for long. It was the woman behind him that he couldn't get off his mind. His wife.

At the clinic, Jinx had ordered him to be nice to Leigh. But that was only the tip of the flipping iceberg. They also wanted him to lie through his teeth. He was supposed to tell her everything was all right between them. That they'd had problems in the past but had worked them all out.

Yeah, right.

Between the lies and being nice, he was also supposed to get her to trust him. Just like that. He was supposed to erase all the bad feelings between them and regain her confidence. He'd have an easier time forgetting that she'd ever been his wife.

However, it didn't matter if the task was impossible. The Justice Department expected him to give his all. Heck, he'd already done that.

And then he'd made it worse by kissing her.

That shouldn't have happened. What the devil had he been thinking when he put his mouth on hers? That was just it—he hadn't thought. He'd acted. Reacted. And much to his disgust, he'd even enjoyed it. He couldn't let it happen again, not with so much at stake.

Easy to say. Hard to do.

It was especially hard since she was right behind him. She had her arms wrapped around his waist— apparently holding on for dear life. No surprise there. Leigh hated motorcycles.

Of course, she probably hated him, too.

He wouldn't mention that to her yet. If she was faking this amnesia, then she already knew how she felt about him. If her memory loss was real, it would be a stupid time to remind her of their past.

Gabe drove nearly two hours before he stopped. Until then, he stayed on narrow dirt roads, using only the moonlight to keep him out of the ditches. When he finally found familiar ground, he pulled the motorcycle into a clutter of trees and turned off the engine.

"Any idea where we are?" Leigh asked, climbing off the seat. She massaged her backside and made a few sounds of discomfort.

He got off, too, and stretched. "Between Baton Rouge and New Orleans." Actually, they were still very close to New Orleans, but he'd taken the most circuitous route to get there. Hopefully, that had given Jinx enough time to get a few things under control. If not, then it would be one long night.

"Are we safe here?"

Gabe glanced around at the dense brush. "Hopefully."

"You don't sound hopeful."

He shrugged. "Guarantees are a rare thing in life, Leigh, but we're a heck of lot safer here than we were back at that clinic."

She stayed quiet a moment. "And you don't believe those men will follow us here?"

"No." Well, he was almost certain they wouldn't anyway. Getting to this particular area of the bayou wasn't easy unless a person knew the way. He knew the way. God willing, the gunmen didn't.

"So, is this the part when you tell me what's really going on?" she asked.

Gabe groaned. He didn't want to play a question-and-answer game tonight. *Keep her alive. Catch the bad guys.* Oh yeah, and, *Be nice to her.* At no time had anyone said a thing about answering her questions.

"You know what's going on," Gabe briskly assured her. "Some gunmen came after us, and we got away."

"There's more to it than that. How about letting me in on who those men are and why they want to kill us?"

"That, *mi vida*, is the big question of the day."

"Are you saying you don't know who's behind this?" She didn't wait for him to confirm that. "That breach of security at the clinic didn't happen by itself. And who's to blame for that, huh? Who was in charge of guarding the place?"

Gabe spat out some profanity. "The FBI."

Her mouth dropped open. "Your own people? Well, that's just great."

It didn't exactly please Gabe either, but the breach hadn't necessarily come from anyone in the Bureau, especially not from Jinx. It could have been an outside source. In other words, he still had nothing definite. Gabe didn't like that. He wanted something *definite*.

"Come on," he insisted. "We need to get moving."

"On foot?"

"Well, since there's deep mud ahead, and the motorcycle would get stuck, I don't see any other way." And with that, he took her gun, put it in the waist of his jeans and snagged her around the hips. Like a caveman claiming his woman, he tossed her over his shoulder.

"Hey! What the devil do you think you're doing?" Leigh complained.

Gabe began to walk, keeping the same pace he would have had she not been on his shoulder. "Carrying you."

She wiggled, squirmed and otherwise tried to twist her way out of his grip. "Put me down!"

"No can do. You have stitches in your ankle, remember? Now, let's see if I can recall basic first aid." He pretended to think about it. "By now, those stitches have probably worked their way partially loose, so you have an open wound. Add to that some of this sloppy, wormy mud, and I see the potential for a really nasty infection. What do you think?" He didn't let her answer. "I don't have time to take you to the doctor, so be still."

Just like that, Leigh stopped struggling, and her body practically went limp against him. "I suppose it's too much to hope that other than traipsing through a swamp, you actually have a plan?"

He made his way around a large cypress tree and its kneelike roots that stood almost a foot above the ground. "I have one, but I don't feel especially good about it."

Keep her alive. Catch the bad guys. Nope, he didn't feel good about that plan at all. It definitely lacked the necessary components for a successful mission.

"It'd be a heck of a lot easier if you just had your memory," Gabe let her know. "Are you sure you're not faking this amnesia?"

"No, I'm not faking it. You've already asked me that. Besides, why would I fake something like this?"

He could think of a reason. Leigh could be using the ploy so she wouldn't have to tell him why she'd really returned. "I don't have an answer to that one either, *mi vida.*"

She poked him hard on the back. "Don't call me darling."

Gabe grinned in spite of his rotten mood. Well, she remembered some of her Spanish anyway, along with remembering that she didn't like him to use that little term of endearment. And that's why he'd done it. Maybe he could work it into the conversation again. Numerous times. It might make him feel better if she was as annoyed as he was.

He stopped on a solid patch of ground, deposited Leigh on her feet and pulled back some low branches. Just as he hoped it would be, there was the truck hidden behind the curtain of Spanish moss.

"Thank you, Jinx," Gabe mumbled and opened the door on the driver's side. "I owe you another one."

"Jinx?" she asked. "What does he have to do with this?"

"He left this truck here for us, and he sent that warning over the pager to tell us those gunmen were in the parking lot." Gabe pulled down some moss and used it to clean the mud off his boots. "We'll spend the night here and head out at first light."

Leigh stared at him. "Here?"

"Yes, *here*." Gabe motioned for her to get inside. He slapped at a couple of mosquitoes that started to feast on his neck. "And hurry up before these things eat us alive."

She got in all right, after a loud huff, and she scooted toward the other side to get as far away from him as possible. Even then, they were practically shoulder to shoulder when Gabe joined her.

"Might as well get comfortable," he told her.

Her eyebrow arched. "You're kidding, right?"

Yeah. He was. There wasn't much chance of getting comfortable on a narrow seat with Leigh. Still, it probably wasn't a good idea to say that to her. It would only start another round of questions.

He pulled off his T-shirt and tossed it on the floor along with his holster and all three weapons. "We'll have to leave the windows up because of the mosquitoes, so it'll get hot in here. Wanna take off those scrubs?"

She gave him a look that could have withered a new fence post. "Not even if I were on fire and there wasn't a drop of water for miles around."

He chuckled and draped his forearm over the steering wheel. "Lie down."

She glanced at the seat. And then at his bare chest. "You want me to lie down?"

He rolled his eyes. "Hell. Leigh, we're married. And even if we weren't, we'd still have to get some rest. That means the seat or outside. I have no intentions of sleeping outside with the snakes and mosquitoes, do you?"

She looked out the window, apparently to weigh her options. Not that she had any options to weigh. She must have figured that out because without a sound, she lay on the seat. With her feet only inches from him, she let her hand dangle over the guns.

Gabe spun her around like a top and put her head right next to his lap.

With her eyes narrowed to slits, Leigh stared up at him. "Is there any particular reason you're treating me like a prisoner?"

"You bet. I know you too well. Right now, you figure you can't trust anyone but yourself. You wonder whose side I'm on. In the next hour or so, you'll start to think you need to get away from me, even at the risk of becoming gator bait. Well, until you figure out I'm the best thing you've got going, then I'm staying close. Understand?"

Her mouth twisted as if she'd tasted something sour. "Yes, I understand." She rolled onto her side, facing the back of the seat. Immediately, she made a strange sound.

"Now what?" he snarled.

"The seat smells like fishing bait."

Unfortunately, she didn't smell like bait, but it might have been better for him if she had. Since she was so close, Gabe couldn't avoid taking in her scent. The smell of the scrubs. Mixed with that was the hint of warm leather from the motorcycle seat. There was sweat, not stale and heavy, but just a hint. And beneath all of that was Leigh's own unique scent. Distinctively female.

And more than a little distracting.

It was a challenge, but Gabe had to prevent that scent from turning his brain to mush. He forced himself to remember what she'd done. It worked. Until she spoke.

"We don't get along very well, do we, Sanchez?"

He considered lying. A Justice Department slant on the truth. But there was something in her voice. A plea for the truth, and the truth was exactly what he gave her. "No. We don't."

She paused, apparently letting that sink in. "If our situations were reversed, would you trust me?"

Now he'd lie. Except it wouldn't really be a lie. Yes, their past had been, well, checkered. But if it were a matter of life or death, Leigh would come through for him. Gabe didn't have to guess about that.

"I'd trust you," he finally said. "Now, give it a rest and go to—"

"I hate being like this."

"Sorry, but it's the best I can offer under the circumstances. I promise, there was a time when you didn't mind sleeping this close to me."

"I'm not talking about that. Not entirely anyway," she added apparently as an afterthought. "I hate not knowing who I am or who you are. You could be an ax murderer, and I wouldn't know until it was too late."

She looked up at him. Gabe looked down and met her gaze in the moonlight. He didn't want to stare at her, but his body seemed to have a different idea. It was hard not to remember that this was a woman he'd once loved. A woman who'd loved him right back. Then, things had fallen apart.

And that was a whole set of memories he didn't want to deal with right now.

"I'm not an ax murderer," he heard himself say. "I gave that up years ago."

She actually smiled, briefly, but there was a frown not too far behind. "I know nothing about you or me except the few things you've let me know. I don't even know my middle name. I'm too scared to admit I'm scared because I don't know if I can trust you with that admission of weakness. I'm afraid you'll use it against me."

"Leigh." His voice was gruff. Then it changed. It softened. His hand was already on her hair. It was definitely intimate contact, but he didn't pull away. Gabe figured he would kick himself for it later. "Being scared doesn't mean you're weak. It just means you're scared. And smart. Stupid people are too stupid to be scared. By the way, your middle name is Ann."

"Ann," she repeated on a heavy sigh. "It doesn't even sound familiar."

Gabe said nothing. He leaned his head against the cool window and listened to the sound of her voice.

"I don't know what I was. Who I am. You don't know how frustrating that is."

Oh yes he did. Gabe knew a lot about frustration. After all, Leigh was right next to him, and more than anything, he wanted to touch her. Maybe even kiss her again. The old wounds stopped him. And the fact she'd probably slap him if he tried to do anything like that. She didn't know about the old wounds, but that didn't mean she trusted him.

"I seem to know a little bit about a lot of things," she continued. "Like I knew the clinical name for my amnesia, but I didn't know you. What was I, Gabe? And don't you dare say I worked in a bookstore in Austin, because I know that's not right."

He debated telling her since the truth would just create more questions. But without the truth, he didn't stand of chance of tapping into her mind to find out what had gone wrong.

"You were an FBI agent," Gabe answered. "The last year you were with the Bureau, you were part of the ERT, the Evidence Response Team."

"Yes." She nodded. Paused. And repeated it. "Now, that feels right."

It should. She'd been one of the best. "You resigned after all of this happened with the corrupt government official."

She pushed out a deep breath. Of relief, maybe. It didn't feel much like relief to Gabe. Her warm breath dusted his bare stomach. Not good. Maybe he should have risked roasting and kept his shirt on after all.

He inched slightly away from her. Not that he could *inch* very far without leaving the truck.

"So, I was working for the FBI and came across evidence against this official? Then what happened?" she asked.

"Things resolved themselves. At least we thought they had." He shrugged. "And then you disappeared."

Leigh started to come off the seat, but Gabe laid a hand on her shoulder to stop her. That would put her mouth much too close to his. He couldn't handle that right now. Best to keep as much distance between their mouths as possible. Another of those husbandly kisses was the last thing either of them needed.

"I think you left because of me," Gabe said, anticipating her next question. "We'd talked about a divorce." It was the truth, even though it was something Jinx and Walters had ordered him not to tell her. "It's late. We should get some—"

"You didn't know where I was all this time?"

Hell, she just didn't intend to stop. "Sometimes I knew," he admitted. "But I couldn't quite catch up with you."

"Was I ever in Houston?"

"Probably." And he made a mental note that it was the second time she'd mentioned that particular city. "You're originally from Dallas. Why? Do you remember something about Houston?"

"Not really. It's just a place that keeps coming to mind, but I can't associate it with anything. Houston might mean nothing." A moment later, she dismissed it with a wave of her hand. "I have to ask. Considering our marital problems, just how hard did you look for me during the past two years?"

"I looked," he said defensively. "You're the one who walked out. You didn't want anyone to find you."

"Apparently someone found me," she pointed out.

"Maybe. Or maybe you had no choice but to be found. Sometimes things play out that way."

She stared up at him. "What does that mean?"

"It means you need to get some sleep." Gabe yawned. Not a fake one either. It'd been a hell of a long day, and he was bone-tired. "Who knows? You might wake up tomorrow and remember everything."

She didn't disagree, but the little sound she made

wasn't one of hope. Still, at the moment, hope was about the best thing they had going for them.

Hope that Leigh would regain her memory.

Hope that those gunmen would stop following them.

Hope that he could, somehow, keep her alive.

Chapter 5

Leigh awakened slowly, trying to get her bearings before she moved or even opened her eyes. Her bearings, however, were wrapped all around her. She was on the truck seat cradled in a man's arms. Gabe's arms. Her face was buried against his neck, and his musky scent surrounded her.

This was not good. Not good at all. That scent went straight through her like a triple shot of whiskey. Not a memory, exactly. More like a feeling that what they were doing was right.

And wrong.

Quickly but not so easily, she unraveled herself from his snug grip so she could get to a sitting position. The moment she moved, Gabe did as well. He came off the seat, reaching for his gun in the same motion.

Their gazes collided. His eyes were still ripe with

sleep, and she saw some of the emotions that he'd kept so guarded, so under control the day before. The concern. The stress.

And other things she didn't even want to explore.

Leigh took a deep breath. Just who was this man that she'd once promised to love forever? She was almost afraid to find out.

Pulling herself away from that naked gaze, and from his partly naked body, Leigh opened the truck door and stepped out, careful not to put direct pressure on her wounded ankle. She made a sweeping glance around the thick cypress woods. The sun was just rising over a misty-topped bayou, and with the exception of a snow-white egret, they were alone.

Completely alone.

"Are you all right?" Gabe asked.

No, she wasn't. Reality was even harsher in the early-morning light than it had been in the darkness. She was in the middle of a bayou with a man she didn't know. She had no memory. And someone wanted her dead. Not the best way to start the day. Oh, and she was scared. Add to that a wicked headache and what felt like an overwhelming need for a cup of coffee, and it didn't seem she had a lot to look forward to.

Leigh leaned against the truck and tried to catch her breath. "So, what happens now?" she asked, almost afraid to hear the answer.

With catlike grace, Gabe slid off the seat and stood beside her. He brought his shoulder holster and gun with him, draping it over his arm. "We try to find out who's behind this and then get you to a safer place."

At least he seemed to think that was possible. She

wasn't so sure anymore. Maybe there were no safe places to go.

She glanced at him out of the corner of her eye. Still shirtless, the sunlight danced over his deeply tanned chest. And the jeans. God, the jeans. They gloved parts of him that she wished weren't so gloved.

Those were things she definitely shouldn't notice.

Still, it was hard not to notice and respond to him since he was an attractive man. Even if they hadn't shared a past she couldn't remember, that attraction probably would have still been there.

The attraction.

The emotions.

The uncertainty of their past.

Those things frightened Leigh almost as much as coming face-to-face with the person who'd tried to kill her. Eventually, she would have to remember what had torn Gabe and her apart. Leigh wasn't exactly looking forward to reliving any of that.

Gabe lifted the lid on the storage bin in the bed of the truck. Muscles flexed as he fished around inside and came up with two bottles of water. "I don't guess your memory returned overnight, huh?" He passed one of the bottles her way.

Leigh shook her head. No memory. Just a headache and an unwanted physical attraction to the man who leaned against the truck beside her.

She didn't plan to ask him to put on his shirt. No sense letting him in on the fact there was a whirl of emotions she didn't understand, or want to feel. Emotions that included a good old-fashioned case of lust. She might not remember Gabe, but her hormones sure did.

He took a long drink of water. "So, nothing about this place seems familiar?"

Leigh looked around again, hoping she'd missed something that would jar her memory. She hadn't. "No, should it?"

Gabe shrugged. "We spent our honeymoon not too far from here."

"We had our honeymoon in the middle of a bayou?" she asked, sure that she'd heard him wrong. It didn't seem the best of locations for that. Or maybe it did. If two people wanted complete privacy, it would be ideal.

Leigh quickly shoved that thought aside.

"We were in a cabin just a couple of miles away," Gabe added. "We didn't go there last night because it's a little too close to the main road." He stared out at the scenery, and Leigh could almost see the memories going through his head. Memories no doubt of all the things that couples did on a honeymoon.

Oh. Mercy.

It didn't seem a subject she should press, but it was also one she couldn't resist. After all, she'd spent two years with this man. "We were in love?"

She saw the muscles stiffen in Gabe's arms and shoulders. He put the bottle to his mouth, finished off the water and tossed the plastic container in the back of the truck. "Yeah. Once."

His answer wasn't just brusque. It was downright chilly. And that chill made Leigh want to know more. However, she didn't get a chance to delve any deeper into the feelings they'd once had for each other. The slight sound she heard caused her throat to snap shut.

Gabe obviously heard something too because without warning he caught onto her arm and shoved her to the ground. Suddenly, her face, and the rest of her, was in the moist dirt. He followed on top on her, sprawling himself over her back.

Pebbles and other assorted debris dug into her stomach and chest. Other than an involuntary groan caused by the weight of Gabe's body on hers, Leigh didn't even have time to react. She heard the gunmetal whisper against the stiff leather holster as Gabe drew his weapon.

All her fears returned in full force. Her heart started to pound. Her stomach twisted into a hard knot. God, she didn't want to die, and there might be nothing she could do to stop it. She couldn't even reach for her gun since it was inside the truck.

Leigh tried to look around, to see if there was any real danger. Maybe it was nothing at all—a sound made by some bayou animal or the morning breeze rustling through the trees. But she was almost positive an animal hadn't made that sound.

"I'd appreciate it a whole lot if you didn't shoot me," the man called out. "This shirt is new, and I don't want blood all over it."

With that calmly delivered, satirical remark, she felt Gabe relax. "It's all right," he assured her. "It's just Jinx."

Jinx. That didn't make her breathe any easier. Gabe seemed to trust the man, but Leigh wasn't about to dismiss that prickle that crawled up the back of her neck. After all, that breach in security at the clinic had happened on Jinx's watch.

Gabe lifted himself off her. Not easily. And not before his hand grazed the side of her right breast. Leigh pretended not to notice, but pretending didn't do a thing to stop her breath from shuddering. If Gabe noticed, he didn't say anything. Which was just as well. Instead, he caught onto her hand and helped her to her feet.

"What's he doing out here?" she asked none too pleasantly.

"He owns this place. And the cabin where we stayed on our honeymoon."

Leigh didn't have time to react to that, but she intended to give it some thought later.

"Gabe. Leigh," Jinx greeted, making his way through the ferns and jewelweed toward them. He stopped only inches away and pointed to the path that Leigh had already noticed. "I parked up there. No one followed me, but I covered my tracks just in case. By the way, glad you two made it out of that clinic."

"It took some doing." Gabe reholstered his gun. "Thanks for the heads up."

"No problem." Jinx's gaze raked over her. "So, did you get your memory back?"

"No."

Jinx didn't respond to that. He simply handed Gabe a plain black gym bag and a small cooler. "That means she can't help us with that little problem we discussed."

"What little problem?" Leigh asked.

"We were hoping you'd be able to tell us who tried to kill you," Gabe insisted.

As critical as that sounded, she was sure there was still a heck of a lot more to it than that. She doubted it was a coincidence that Jinx's comment had been vague.

Gabe set the cooler in the truck and handed the gym bag to her. "There should be some clothes in here so you can change. Those hospital scrubs are too noticeable."

He was right, of course, especially since the top had

spatters of blood on it. Still, she didn't think it was a change of attire that Gabe had on his mind. It seemed he was rather anxious for her to leave so he could talk privately with his friend.

Leigh accommodated him. Well, in a way. She stepped behind a large bell-bottom tree about fifteen feet away, but she kept her ear turned toward the men. Unfortunately, the breeze didn't cooperate, and she could only catch snatches of what they said. She heard something about Agent Teresa Walters wanting them to "come in immediately."

Without taking her attention away from the conversation, she went through the bag and found a phone, ammunition and a first-aid kit. There was also an envelope stuffed with cash. The only clothes were a pair of very short shorts and a cotton top. No shoes, which meant she'd have to wear the flip-flops a while longer.

Leigh snatched up the phone and turned it on. She'd hoped she would dial something automatically—a number so rote, so ingrained, that it would come to her in spite of the amnesia. That didn't happen.

Nothing happened.

Apparently, there was no critical phone number lurking in her memory. It was another dead end. That meant she'd have to try to get something out of Gabe and Jinx.

Not good.

She hadn't had a lot of success in that particular area. So far, all she knew was two years earlier she'd uncovered something dirty about a man named Joe Dayton. Now someone wanted her dead because of that.

Well, maybe.

And maybe it had nothing to do with Joe Dayton at all. Maybe something else had triggered these attacks.

Of course, Leigh had no way of knowing because everything was still trapped inside her head.

Frustrated, she tossed the phone back into the bag and peeled off the scrubs so she could change into the other clothes.

"Philip," she heard Gabe say, making the name sound like profanity.

"You think Leigh will know where he is?" Jinx added another question to that, but Leigh couldn't catch what he said.

"Maybe. She mentioned Houston in the message she left on my machine."

Leigh heard that part. Clearly. And again she felt that tug of familiarity. She didn't know anything about that message she'd left Gabe, but getting to Houston was important. Critical even. Too bad she didn't know why. Maybe it had something to do with this man named Philip.

So, who was this guy—a boyfriend? But that didn't feel right.

She bent down to pick up the shorts. And then she saw it. Or rather saw *them*. "Oh my God," she whispered.

Three thin, vertical scars were on her stomach, just above the top of her panties. The whitish lines were so faint, so threadlike, that she figured that's why she hadn't noticed them when she was in the bathroom at the clinic.

They looked like stretch marks.

That possibility caused her to reach for the tree for support. Stretch marks. God, had she been pregnant? Maybe. Leigh carried that out to its next logical conclusion—had she had a child?

Certainly Gabe would have mentioned something as

monumental as that. Wouldn't he? Leigh gave it more thought. Yes, he would have. There would have been no reason to keep something like that from her.

Well, unless he didn't know.

But that didn't make sense either. Like the scar on her arm, these didn't look fresh. Besides, a woman could get stretch marks for a variety of reasons—weight gain or just plain genetics. Those explanations were far easier to accept than the possibility that she had a child out there somewhere.

Far easier.

"Everything all right?" Gabe called out to her.

No, it wasn't, but Leigh didn't say that to him. "I'm almost done."

And the first chance she got, she intended to ask Gabe a few questions.

She pulled on the shorts, frowning at the fact that they fit like skin. There wasn't much of the waist-length top either, but since she didn't have a choice, she slipped it on anyway.

The men were still speaking in whispers when she came out from behind the tree. "I'm ready," she let Gabe know.

He was in midsentence, still speaking to Jinx, but the words seemed to freeze in his throat. Surprise rifled through his eyes. Then something else. Something smoldering, no doubt caused by the skimpy clothes. Gabe slid that smoldering gaze from her head to her toes, and that gaze did more than concern Leigh. It heated every drop of blood in her body.

"What's the plan?" she asked no one in particular. Best to move on from smoldering looks to business.

Gabe cleared his throat and motioned toward the

truck. "We put some distance between us and New Orleans. I need to get you to a safe place so we can start making a few inquiries."

That certainly sounded like a good idea. And while they were putting that distance between them and New Orleans, she would see what she could learn from Gabe. "Are we going to Houston?"

Gabe glanced at Jinx first. "Maybe. Eventually."

"What's in Houston, Leigh?" Jinx questioned. But it was more than a question. It was a challenge.

She shrugged. "You tell me. According to you, I'm just a bookstore employee."

The corner of Gabe's mouth lifted, but he quickly covered it with his hand.

There seemed to be some amusement on Jinx's face as well, but it didn't make it to his voice. "I don't think it's my imagination that you don't trust me." He didn't wait for her to confirm that. "Would it help if you knew I was Gabe's best man at your wedding?"

Leigh glanced at Gabe, and he verified that information with a nod. However, it didn't do a thing to change her opinion of Jinx. There was something about him, something she couldn't quite put her finger on. Something that caused that prickle to return to her neck. Still, it was best not to antagonize him.

"You and I want the same thing," she finally said. "I want to find out who's after me, and I want to try to figure out who I am. I'm hoping Gabe can fill me in on some more of the details."

It was subtle, but because Leigh kept her focus on Jinx, she saw him slip Gabe a warning glance. So, there were other things that Jinx didn't want her to know. Maybe those things involved the stretch marks that she just couldn't get off her mind, or maybe it involved the man named Philip. Perhaps Philip was the key to finding out what was going on.

Gabe opened the truck door and motioned for her to get in. "It's time to go."

Leigh was more than ready to leave, especially since she was sure Jinx wouldn't be going with them. She climbed onto the seat, and Gabe shut the door. He whispered something to Jinx before he joined her.

"Be careful," Jinx said to them as Gabe started the engine. "And if I were you, I wouldn't trust anybody until we have some answers."

Jinx obviously didn't include himself in that blanket warning, but Leigh silently added him to it. It was excellent advice, and she intended to take it. She didn't intend to trust anyone.

Chapter 6

"I have a question," Leigh announced. She drank some water and settled against the seat as if this would be a long-drawn-out ordeal.

Gabe figured it likely would be in just about every way possible.

"Just one question?" he asked.

"Well, actually, I have several, but I guess this is as good a place to start as any. Do we have a child?"

Gabe felt as if a bolt of lightning had hit him. He was almost afraid to find out what had prompted that question. "No," he quickly assured her.

"You're sure?"

He didn't even have to think about his answer. "Positive. Why'd you ask?"

She shrugged. "No reason. I just figured since we, uh, were married, there was a possibility we had a child."

"No. We'd decided not to have children."

He braced himself for yet more on the subject, but Leigh stayed quiet for several moments. Hell. What was going on in her head? Did she remember something, and if so, why had she remembered that particular piece of their past? That one issue had been the source of too many arguments to count.

"So, no baby," she mumbled under her breath. "Did I used to weigh more than I do now?"

Gabe glanced at her. "A little. What the heck is this all about, Leigh?" With everything else going on, he couldn't imagine that she'd be concerned about her weight.

She shrugged again. "I just got the feeling that I'm thinner than I usually am. I guess maybe a ton of stress is the ultimate diet, huh?"

Gabe thought maybe that was a smoke screen, but he didn't care. He was more than happy to let the subject drop. It wasn't a good idea for them to discuss anything about her body. It would only remind him that she had a body. A body that he was familiar with in every intimate kind of way.

"Okay. Here's something else I'd like to know," she continued a moment later. "Who's Philip?"

Gabe blew out a frustrated breath. Even though he'd known more questions would be coming, he didn't need this any more than a possible baby/weight-loss discussion. The traffic on the highway was light, but he wanted to keep his attention focused on their surroundings. That wouldn't be easy to do if he had to answer a lot of questions. Her clothes already gave him more distractions than he needed. Jinx was obviously trying to torture him.

The first problem was her shorts. They were snug in all the wrong places and showed practically every inch of her long, slender legs. The top wasn't much better, especially since she obviously wasn't wearing a bra. Gabe saw the outline of her nipples. Hard to concentrate on anything else when his mind kept going back to those.

However, Gabe forced his attention back on the immediate problem—Leigh's question. A question that he knew would just lead to others. "Let me guess. You eavesdropped on my conversation with Jinx?"

"I *overheard*," she corrected. "So who is this Philip? Is he the person who tried to kill me?"

Hell, he hoped not, but Gabe was almost positive Philip had no part in this. That didn't mean the man didn't have information, and with some luck, Jinx might soon know where they could find him so they could get that information. "No, he's your brother."

That improved her posture. Leigh barely got down the mouthful of water she'd just drunk. She obviously hadn't considered the possibility that she had family.

"I have a brother," she mumbled under her breath. "What about him and my parents? Certainly they're worried about me. I hadn't considered that someone might be concerned as to my whereabouts."

Oh, he was pretty sure there were plenty of people concerned. The right people. And the wrong ones. The problem was determining which category everyone belonged in.

"Your father died about ten years ago when you were in your first year of college," Gabe explained. "Your mother remarried some guy from England, and you haven't spoken to her in ages. But you and Philip—that's a different story. He's your only sibling, and I'm sure you've kept in touch with him. Too bad we don't know where he is."

"Yes, too bad."

She leaned closer. Too close. From that angle Gabe could see right down that skimpy top. He quickly turned away, but that one glance made his body clench. And beg. Gabe decided it was a great time to keep his eyes straight ahead.

"When we were still at the clinic and that man had a gun on me, you said that I had money," Leigh commented. "Any truth to that?"

"All truth. You're loaded. Your father invented some little gadget on an offshore oil rig. When he died, he left just about everything to you and Philip. Of course, Philip blew most of his on expensive wine, cheap women and there's-a-sucker-born-every-minute business ventures. When his inheritance was gone, he managed to talk you out of some of yours, but you still have plenty."

"So, I'm not broke. That's good."

It wasn't something he'd ever expected Leigh to say. She'd always dismissed her sizable inheritance, rarely tapping into it except for emergencies. But Gabe had to remind himself, again, that the woman sitting next to him wasn't Leigh. Not the old Leigh anyway. Even if she hadn't had amnesia, the past two years would have probably changed her in many ways. It had certainly changed him.

"Is having money important to you?" he asked.

She nodded. "It is if I need long-term medical care to help restore my memory."

So, that's all there was to it. Gabe didn't know why that made him feel better. Nothing about their situation—

except for the fact they were alive—should make him feel better.

Especially that outfit she wore.

Gabe took a deep breath and forced his attention back on the conversation. "I suspect if you hadn't had such unlimited funds, I'd have found you sooner."

"Maybe," she agreed. "If I have so much money, why was I working at that bookstore in Austin?"

Gabe smiled. The woman didn't miss a thing. "I believe you wanted to make us think you were working there. Jinx and I spent some off-duty time staking it out, but I never saw you in the place."

"Ah, I get the truth, finally." With that look of triumph on her face, she pressed her foot to the dash.

That wasn't the best place she could have put her foot. Nope. It caused the shorts to ride up even higher, and Gabe got more than an eyeful of her thigh. This might be his estranged wife, and a woman who didn't remember him, but his body had no trouble recalling why he'd been attracted to her in the first place.

"That's a good start," she continued. She was obviously unaware of the effect she had on him. If she glanced in the direction of his jeans, however, she just might see that effect. "But rather than me ask a whole bunch of question that you might or might not answer, why don't you tell me what's really going on?"

That encompassed a whole lot of territory. Territory that Jinx and Teresa didn't want him to cover, but Gabe wasn't so sure there was any reason to keep things from Leigh. After all, it was a long drive to the safe house, and recounting her life history might jog her memory. It would no doubt jog his as well, but Gabe figured he

didn't have a choice but to relive some of the things—
both good and bad—that had gone on between them.

Besides, he needed something to get his mind off
those clothes.

"Well?" Leigh prompted.

Gabe didn't pull any punches. "About eight months
ago, I stepped up my search to find you when I learned
someone was going through the Justice Department's
computer files to try to locate you."

Because she was so close to him, he heard her breath
hitch. "Who was doing that?"

"I don't know. But it's not just a hacker, nor is it
someone who's idly curious. These probes are specific,
calculated and thorough. And they specifically lead to
you. Or at least that's what they're trying to lead to. I
don't think the person was any more successful than
Jinx and I were, but they've been at it a lot longer than
we have. In fact, this person has apparently been searching for you since you disappeared two years ago."

Her tone took on a new urgency. "They've used my
name in these probes?"

"Yes, and your brother's."

"My God." Leigh touched her fingertips to her
mouth. "This person that's trying to kill me might go
after my brother, too?"

Hell. Just about all the color drained from her face.
That was something he probably should have waited
to tell her.

Gabe resisted the urge to reach out and comfort her.
But it wasn't easy. *Keep her alive. Catch the bad guys.
Be nice to her.* Getting involved with her again wasn't
on that list, and he wasn't about to add it either.

There wasn't much he could do about the physical

attraction his body still had for her, but there was a hell of a lot he could do to stop himself from getting emotionally involved with her again.

"I don't think anyone's after Philip," he let her know. Gabe gripped the steering wheel to make sure he didn't slide his hand in her direction. If he wasn't careful, he might take that *be nice to her* and turn it into an excuse to hold her hand. "I think they just wanted to use him to try to locate you."

"Maybe they were successful," she said softly.

Yes. And that was all the more reason to find Philip, so Gabe could make sure he was safe and stayed that way. "I think what's going on has to do with Joe Dayton, the corrupt Justice Department official that we talked about last night."

"The one you don't want to tell me much about."

It was on the tip of Gabe's tongue to deny that, but then he realized it was true. He didn't want to talk about Dayton nor about what had gone on right before Leigh left him.

Too bad it was necessary.

So, just how should he go about delivering what might be a bombshell? If she'd turned ashy at the mention that her brother might be in danger, what he was about to tell her certainly wasn't going to do anything to calm her fears. Still, it was vital information that she eventually had to know.

"Two years ago you came across some information that led you to Dayton," Gabe explained, trying to sound clinical. He'd just give her the bare facts and then hope like the devil it jogged something in her memory. "He was involved in a plot to sell huge quantities of weapons—items that the Justice Department had originally confiscated in various raids throughout the country."

"I see," Leigh said after several moments. "And Dayton's after me because I learned this information?"

"No. Dayton's out of the picture. He committed suicide a couple of days after you found the evidence. Unfortunately, he killed himself before we could learn where he'd stored all those weapons."

She didn't say anything. She sat there apparently processing that information.

"The one behind all of this is more than likely Dayton's accomplice," Gabe continued. He made the turn that would take them to the westbound highway and checked the rearview mirror to make sure no one was following them. "We never did find out who that person was. In fact, we didn't even know for certain that there was an accomplice. Not until some of those previously confiscated weapons showed up during an ATF raid of a militia compound about two weeks ago."

"You're sure the weapons were from Dayton's original cache?" she asked.

"We're sure. The weapons aren't of the ordinary variety, so we know what's out there. I'm talking some with biological and chemical components. Some are prototypes for weapons the FBI definitely doesn't want to see on the street. They're worth millions on the black market, and they're not easily moved because of the volume. My guess is they're still in the same storage facility where Joe Dayton originally had them placed."

She groaned softly, apparently grasping the motive of the person who wanted her dead.

"There's more," Gabe continued. "Those computer inquiries about you—they stopped a little over two weeks ago, at the same time those confiscated weapons showed up at the militia compound."

"I see." Yeah, she probably did. "So, the inquiries stopped because the person either found me, or he no longer needed to find me."

That's the way Gabe saw it, too, or maybe it was a combination of both. All he knew is someone wanted Leigh dead, and it was probably all related to the person making those inquiries.

"Is it possible that I know who Dayton's accomplice is?" she asked a moment later.

"I doubt it. If you knew that person's identity, you would have gotten it to me somehow." That was a stretch of the truth. Gabe hoped she would tell him, but he had no way of knowing that for sure. However, he was sure that Leigh wouldn't have kept that kind of information to herself. Despite their personal differences, she was a law-abiding citizen.

"Unless I was trying to protect someone," Leigh added softly.

Even though she had practically whispered it, Gabe didn't miss a word. "Why would you say that?"

"I don't know." She shook her head. "I'm not sure why that came to my mind. I certainly don't remember anyone that I'd go to such lengths to protect."

She might go to such lengths to protect her brother. But that didn't make sense either because Philip had no association with Dayton. At least, Gabe was almost certain that Philip didn't, and Gabe had been looking for that connection, any connection, for two years.

"So, we're right back where we started—again." Leigh put the bottle of water she'd been drinking from back in the cooler and rested her head against the seat.

"Joe Dayton's dead, and I don't know who his accomplice is."

"But that person might *think* you know something."

Just as quickly, she lifted her head. "Yes. Kill the messenger, and he'll kill the message."

"Something like that." Even though Gabe didn't like her choice of words. "Except there's another messenger."

Leigh turned to him. "What do you mean?"

"There was someone else, someone who was with you when you learned about Dayton's operation. During your search of an unrelated crime scene, you ran across a disk that detailed the proposed deal. The disk had a program virus that our systems didn't detect in time. The virus erased the data after it had been on the screen only a few minutes. You were only able to learn that the weapons were somewhere in Texas."

"That covers a lot of territory," she mumbled.

Loads. "Of course, you had no idea how important the information would be, or you would have tried other measures to remove the virus before you loaded the disk. You and a lab assistant, Frank Templeton, saw the information. No one else even got a chance to look at it."

She nodded and took it to the next logical conclusion. "Then what happened to Frank?"

"He disappeared about the same time that you did." And that might be the reason he's still alive. For that matter, he could say the same thing about Leigh.

"So Frank and I must have thought it was very important to keep our whereabouts a secret from everyone," she continued. "Including you." She angled her eyes in his direction. "Why would I do that, Gabe?"

His stomach didn't appreciate the question. It began to churn, and he could almost feel his blood pressure rising. It was one of the questions he would have liked to avoid, but avoiding it wouldn't make it go away. Still, if he told her everything, she just might jump out of the truck. She most certainly wouldn't cooperate with him.

"Joe Dayton was a friend of mine, and I didn't think he was guilty." There. That was it in a nutshell. Well, a sanitized version of a nutshell anyway. "That caused some problems for us."

She didn't say a word. She didn't have to. Leigh might have had amnesia, but he recognized that look in her eyes. She was trying to piece all of this together. Eventually, she would, with or without his help.

"And that's why you and I went our separate ways?" she asked.

He confirmed it with a nod, but that was all he intended to confirm about their breakup. Besides, there were other things about this that she needed to know. "For two years a lot of people have been trying to track you down and find out if Frank is still alive. We needed to know what else, if anything, you two learned from that disk."

"Well, obviously it was something that signed our death warrants. But I can't remember a thing, so you're back to square one."

"Not quite," Gabe explained. He checked the rear-view mirror and frowned. "Frank Templeton surfaced yesterday. Just as I was leaving my apartment to meet you at the lake, he called. He said he was coming in, that he needed protection and he wanted me to provide it."

"I take it that this isn't a coincidence—that Frank and I came out of hiding at the same time?"

"I don't believe in coincidences," Gabe said, looking away from her. He sped up so he could pass a big-rig truck. "Something made both of you come from underground. About the time I was fishing you out of that lake, he called back and left a message on my answering machine. He wants me to meet him tomorrow night at a safe house in Grand Valley, Texas. It's not too far from Beaumont."

"We're going to Grand Valley?"

"That's the plan." Gabe added some pressure to the accelerator and went around two cars. He didn't take his attention off the rearview mirror. "Frank Templeton doesn't have amnesia, Leigh. If anyone can give us answers…hell."

"What's wrong?"

"Someone's following us."

Chapter 7

Leigh's gaze shot to the rearview mirror. There was a dark blue car about thirty yards behind them. Just the sight of it sent the pulse in her throat hammering. God, had those gunmen from the clinic somehow managed to find them?

"How long have they been following us?" she asked. Leigh grabbed her gun from beneath the seat and braced herself for whatever was about to happen.

"About five minutes."

That was about how long it'd been since they got on this particular highway. Despite the rush of adrenaline that raced through her body, Leigh tried to force herself to concentrate. How could those gunmen have found them so quickly? She didn't care much for any of the answers that came to mind.

"Someone tipped them off?" she suggested.

Gabe didn't answer her. He gunned the engine, passing two other vehicles. The moment he got around them, he veered off onto the next exit. The truck wobbled and shook when Gabe forced it around the tight turn.

Leigh's grip tightened on her weapon while she watched and waited to see what the other car would do.

It followed them.

The profanity that Gabe spat out let her know that he was aware of that as well. He reached for his gun, moving it on the seat next to him.

"Get down," he ordered.

Leigh debated it. After all, if those men started to shoot again, she would likely need to return fire—if she could remember how to do that. But Gabe didn't give her a choice. He caught onto the back of her neck and pushed her down on the seat. "I want you to stay down!"

She did, begrudgingly, but only because she figured he must have some kind of plan. "What now?" Leigh asked.

"We lose them."

He sounded so calm and confident—and so vague— but she saw the concern that had a hold on the muscles in his jaw. If these were the gunmen from the clinic, then they wouldn't give up easily, and losing them on an open highway might be next to impossible.

Leigh lifted her head just slightly so she could check the side mirror. The car was right behind them, and she thought she could see two people inside. No sign of any weapons, but that didn't mean they weren't armed.

"Hang on," Gabe let her know.

She barely had time to grab onto the armrest on the door when Gabe twisted the steering wheel and sent the truck barreling onto a narrow side road. It sent her sliding into him as well. There wasn't much space between them, and her cheek collided with his thigh.

When she moved away, Leigh fished through the gym bag that Jinx had given them and took out the extra magazines of ammunition so she could place them in her lap. She prayed they wouldn't need them.

"Stay down," Gabe warned again.

She glanced in the side mirror to see what had prompted him to reissue his order. Leigh saw someone in the car lowering the window. Moments later, she saw the man's hand. And the gun that he held.

Before she could even bring up her own weapon, Gabe took another hairpin turn. She peeked over the dash just as the truck bounced its way onto a dirt road. Gravel pummeled the tires and undercarriage, and dust seeped inside, causing her breath to clog even more than the fear had done.

Gabe dodged a scrub oak, its scraggly branches slapping against the window. Without taking his gaze from the path ahead, he cursed.

"Should I shoot at them?" she asked.

"No. Not yet."

Leigh braced herself for the bullets that she was sure the gunmen would fire into the truck.

But that didn't happen.

She lost sight of the car when Gabe took the next two turns. He maneuvered onto a series of back roads and then cut through a narrow clearing that was lined with cedars and oaks. Whirling the steering wheel around, he circled them back in the other direction so they would face the car if it followed them. Just as quickly, he turned off the engine.

He didn't waste even a second of time. Gabe latched

onto his gun, brought it up and braced his hand so that he was ready to fire. Leigh did the same. They were shoulder to shoulder, but since Gabe was left-handed, it didn't interfere with either of their aims.

And they waited.

The minutes crawled by. One by one. Leigh counted off the seconds in her head.

But there was no sign of the gunmen.

Either those men had given up, or else Gabe had truly managed to lose them. Leigh tried to pick through the sounds in the woods. The breeze rattling the leaves. The few birds that they hadn't scared off. What she didn't hear was the sound of a car engine.

Oh, God.

That frightened her even more than if she had heard one. Did that mean the gunmen had stopped and were now circling around from behind? Or was it possible they were on foot? Obviously, Gabe had already thought of that because she noticed his gaze darting all around them.

It made her wonder if they'd been in situations like this before. Possibly. After all, at one time she'd been an agent, too. Perhaps they had worked cases together. That stirred something deep inside her. What exactly, she couldn't say. But even though the situation itself didn't feel familiar, the camaraderie, and the intimacy of it, certainly did.

Too familiar.

An image flashed through her mind. Not of gunmen or chases through the woods. It was an image of Gabe, naked. Beautifully naked. He had his hands on her. Their embrace was beyond intimate. The mental picture was so clear, so overwhelming, so erotic that Leigh gasped.

"What's wrong?" Gabe glanced around them, obviously looking for what had alarmed her.

"Nothing," she said on a rush of breath. "A memory, I think."

"Of what?"

She couldn't tell him. Leigh didn't even think she could get her mouth to say the words. She forced herself to think of the danger. The gunmen. It didn't completely wash away that image of Gabe, but it helped.

"How much longer do we wait?" she asked.

"Not long. If they were coming after us, they would have already done it." He started the truck again. "But cover us just in case. I'm getting us out of here."

Leigh didn't argue with that. She didn't want to stay in the woods any longer.

While Gabe maneuvered the truck through the path and back onto the dirt road, Leigh watched for any sign of the gunmen. It didn't disappoint her when she didn't see them, but it did create more questions in her mind.

"Why didn't they follow us, Gabe?"

"Maybe they didn't like the odds of coming at us head-on. I sure wouldn't have."

That made sense. Gabe had established high ground by the way he parked the truck, but high ground had merely given them a temporary advantage. It hadn't secured a victory. "That means they think they'll have a better opportunity to come at us later."

He made a sound of agreement. That didn't do a thing to ease the tension in her body. "So, is someone feeding them information as to our whereabouts?"

"Maybe," Gabe said quickly enough to indicate he'd

already given the idea some thought. "Or maybe they're just lucky."

Leigh didn't think luck had a whole lot to do with this. "Could Jinx or Teresa Walters have let these guys know where we are?"

"Not Jinx. He's on our side, Leigh. And it's Teresa's job to find that cache of stolen weapons. I doubt she'd want to see what could be her star witness dead, especially since this case could lead to a promotion for her."

"That theory only works if Teresa isn't Dayton's accomplice." Leigh silently added Jinx into that equation, too. And anyone else that had anything to do with Dayton. Leigh had no idea how long a list that would be.

"I don't have a good feeling about either Jinx or Teresa," Leigh continued. "For now I'd prefer they not know where we are."

Gabe didn't agree or disagree. He turned onto a paved road and sped up. "So, what exactly did you remember back there, huh?"

Great. Just great. Of all the things they could discuss, why would he bring up that? She checked to make sure no one was following them—not that it was necessary. Leigh had hardly taken her attention away from the rearview mirror. Still, it gave her a moment to try to figure out what to say. And after a moment, she still had no clue how to answer him.

"Was it about us?" Gabe asked.

Leigh nodded but didn't offer anything else. She took a deep breath when the same image flashed through her mind again. Good heavens, the man certainly had a beautiful body, or maybe she just had a good imagination. If so, then she also imagined that he had a tattoo on his right hip.

Gabe mumbled something under his breath. "All right, if you won't answer, I'll fill in the blanks. We had some bad times along with the good ones. *Very* good ones. Yes, we argued, but with the exception of the last argument, we always made up. And yes, we loved each other enough to stand in front of a priest and take vows that we swore we'd never break."

She was about to say that wasn't what she'd remembered—that it was nothing nearly as reverent as wedding vows and priests—but Gabe continued. "We had all the hopes, dreams and problems of any other couple in love. We cared for each other." He cursed. "And yes, damn it, we even had great sex."

Bingo.

He must have sensed that he'd hit upon something. Maybe it was the change in the air that suddenly crackled between them. Or maybe it was just the look on her face. For whatever reason, he gave her a considering glance.

"Great sex," he repeated, changing the inflection not from a comment to an assertion.

Leigh fought it, but the image stayed with her. The image of Gabe sliding his hands over her breasts. And lower. He touched her as if he knew every inch and every place of pleasure on her body.

He probably did.

And that was what Leigh had to push aside. She had no doubts that they'd had great sex, but it could have no part in what was going on now. They were in danger, and she wasn't even sure she trusted him.

"I won't get involved with you again," she said as if that answered everything. Now she only hoped her body understood the statement she'd just delivered.

"Are you trying to convince me or yourself?" he asked, that Texas drawl coming through and kissing each word.

The answer to that was easy.

Both.

Gabe didn't like the silence he heard on the other end of the line. Teresa Walters hadn't said anything for a full five seconds. He knew that's how much time had passed because he'd counted.

He didn't want to count much longer.

It wasn't safe to hang around the Tip-Top gas station since those gunmen might still be in the area. It'd been nearly an hour and over fifty miles of back roads since he'd last seen that dark blue car, but he didn't want to wait around for it to return.

With the phone cradled against his shoulder, he glanced up when Leigh made her way out of the bathroom. She didn't dawdle, and several times she checked their surroundings. Obviously, she wasn't ready to let down her guard either.

"What makes you think Leigh's getting her memory back?" Teresa asked, paraphrasing what he'd told her all those seconds earlier.

"I don't *think* she's getting it back," Gabe assured her. He finished filling the gas tank and replaced the nozzle. He'd already paid the attendant in cash and was more than anxious to get out of there. "I know she is."

It was a lie. Or better yet, a test. He'd wanted to hear how Teresa would react to such news. Besides, Leigh had remembered something when they were in the truck. Just what he didn't know, but he would bet a month's paycheck that it was raunchy and involved sex. The look on her face had said loads about what had crossed her mind.

"What has she remembered exactly?" Teresa went on. "Does she know where her brother is?"

"No idea whatsoever. But she wants to find Philip as much as we do. I don't suppose you've learned anything?"

"Nothing. I'm having someone check to see if he's with his mother in England."

The chances of that were slim to none. Philip disliked his mother as much as Leigh did. That's the last place he would have gone. Unfortunately, that didn't narrow down their search area nearly enough.

"How about Dayton's accomplice?" Teresa again. "Does Leigh remember anything about that?"

"Not yet, but I don't think we'll have to wait too much longer." Leigh joined him and got back into the truck. "Her memory's coming back pretty fast."

Leigh's eyebrow arched. When he was done with the call, he'd have to explain this game of cat and mouse he was playing with Teresa. Then he'd have to remind Leigh that in the grand scheme of things, they were still the mice.

"All right," Teresa said as if he was about to deliver a decree, "where exactly are you now?"

"In Texas. At a place called Ed's Café."

Leigh's eyebrow rose again, and the corner of her mouth lifted in a half smile. Maybe he wouldn't have to explain things to her after all. It had to be fairly clear that he didn't intend to trust Agent Walters with their whereabouts, but Leigh had said right from the start that she didn't trust Teresa either. Gabe wasn't as convinced as she was, but it didn't hurt to be cautious.

"It's a mom-and-pop place near the I-10," he added for Teresa's benefit.

Even as he told that additional lie, Gabe glanced at the sign that said Tip-Top Gas. *Louisiana Hospitality* was in fading red letters just below that. And the place wasn't anywhere near the interstate.

"See if you can find out who followed us, will you, Teresa?" Gabe asked, and he gave her the car's license-plate numbers. The *real* numbers. With some luck, and if she was so inclined, she might be able to find out who was after them. It was a long shot, but Gabe had gotten lucky with long shots before.

"Will do," Teresa assured him. "You stay put, and I'll have someone out to you in a couple of hours."

"Sounds good." Or it sounded like a trap. If so, it'd be a trap that wasn't anywhere near Leigh and him.

Leigh handed him a bottle of water from the cooler when he put away his phone. "That was Teresa," he let her know.

"I heard." She got some water for herself. "What will you do if it turns out that she's the one behind this?"

"Then I'll deal with her." And speaking of dealing with unpleasant things, there was something else he should have already checked. Gabe cursed himself for not handling the whole situation better. "I need to find out if you're wearing a transmitter."

The bottle of water stopped halfway to her mouth. "A what?"

"A tracking device that would allow someone to follow us. While you were in the bathroom, I checked my clothes and shoes. Now I need to check yours."

Alarm and maybe something else flashed through

her eyes. Gabe didn't want to hope that other flash was a result of what she'd recalled earlier.

"I'll check my own clothes," she let him know. "Why don't you go through the gym bag?"

"It's clean. Jinx put it together himself." Of course, she knew that, and that's why she'd suggested it. For whatever reason, she didn't trust Jinx.

"Why don't you check it anyway?" She put her water aside and felt around the pockets of her shorts. "So, exactly what am I looking for anyway?"

"A device about the thickness of a penny and a third the size."

He hadn't meant to watch her do a clothes check, but he rather liked the idea of watching Leigh run her hands over her body. It reminded him of the times she'd done the same to him. And vice versa.

She patted and felt around every inch of her clothes and finally shrugged. "Nothing."

"Hand me your shoes."

Gabe looked carefully at the flip-flops but saw nothing. He shook his head and handed them back to her.

"Maybe it's on the truck," she suggested. "Or maybe there isn't one at all."

The truck was out—Jinx would have already checked for such things, using the best equipment the Bureau had to offer. But it was possible those gunmen had just gotten lucky. Gabe, however, didn't want to rely on that. In fact, if he'd been thinking straight, he should have done this search the night before when they were in the bayou. It might have saved them that latest run for their lives.

He studied Leigh carefully, looking for possible hiding places. After all, there'd been a good hour where she was out of his sight when they were at the clinic. The doctor, MRI technician, Jinx and Teresa had all been with her at various times, and it was possible the doctor had been on the wrong payroll. Or maybe Teresa hadn't wanted to take any chances with Leigh getting away from her.

"Lean forward," he told her. Gabe climbed onto the seat next to her and reached for the bandage on her forehead.

"You think there's a transmitter in my bandage?"

"Only one way to find out." As gently as he could, he peeled off the tape. No transmitter, but there were some angry-looking stitches and a bruise covering a good portion of the side of her forehead. It turned his stomach to see that on her. It reminded him of the monster they were up against. A monster he very much wanted to deal with when the time came.

Gabe was actually looking forward to delivering some payback.

"What is it?" she asked, obviously seeing his alarm.

"Nothing." He quickly replaced the bandage and reached for her foot.

She gave him a puzzled glance. "So, why did you tell Teresa I'd gotten my memory back?"

Oh, that. He'd figured Leigh would want to know about that conversation, especially since he hadn't given her any warning about what he'd planned to say. "It wasn't a complete lie." As he'd done with the bandage on her forehead, he lifted back the tape and began to unwind the layers of gauze on her ankle. "Of course, I doubt you'd be willing to share with me exactly what you remembered, huh?"

"No."

It wasn't hard to see the deer-caught-in-the-headlights glaze in her eyes, and that told Gabe loads. "It was about sex," he concluded.

Her chin came up. "Is that all you think about?"

Gabe saw right through her—that insolent reply wasn't a very good smoke screen. There was a veneer barely covering the slick layer of emotions just beneath the surface. Something about that memory had shaken her.

But what?

And why the heck did he feel this overwhelming need to find out?

She must have sensed that she couldn't fool him because she glanced away. "I'm not even sure it was a memory. It could have been…something I saw in a movie."

He seriously doubted it. Movie memories didn't cause people to blush, and that's what she was doing. "Tell me about it, and I'll let you know."

Leigh hesitated. And hesitated. She began to nibble on her bottom lip. "Do you have a tattoo of a longhorn on your lower right hip?"

It probably wasn't a good time to smile, but Gabe just couldn't help himself. He nodded and continued to unwrap her bandage. "It's a relic from a trip that my uncle and I took to Mexico for my eighteenth birthday. The only way you could have seen that was if I'd been naked."

She nodded almost begrudgingly.

Gabe laughed before he could stop himself. "We were married, Leigh. *Are* married," he corrected. "Trust me, we got naked more than a couple of times. It doesn't surprise me that you'd remember one of them.

Just please tell me I was doing something memorable and not disgusting like drooling on my pillow."

Her mouth quivered as if she was fighting back a smile of her own. "You definitely weren't drooling. But I think maybe I was."

There was the sense of humor that he missed. God, did he miss it. It made him ache to know he'd gone so long without it. Without her.

Her eyes lifted to his, and he saw all the things Leigh was feeling. She obviously didn't want this heat simmering between them. Neither did he. Yet, neither of them seemed to have what it took to stop it.

There was a moment when he thought he could talk himself out of what he was about to do. That moment came and went. Then Gabe leaned in and brushed his mouth over hers. It sent a jolt through his body, and the memories of the taste of her came flooding back.

She didn't move away when his mouth came to hers again. Their lips touched. Barely. At first. But it didn't stay that way. Her mouth was warm and yielding. Gabe took it before he could stop himself.

Her scent curled around him. There were undertones of her arousal. Subtle. Yet not subtle to his own body.

Gabe hesitated a moment to see if she would stop him. She didn't. It was Leigh who deepened the kiss. Leigh who adjusted her position on the seat and wound her arms around him. The contact brought her right against his chest. He felt the softness of her breasts, and the hardness of her nipples, which were obviously puckered and drawn from the contact. What was left of his resolve went right out the window.

Lowering his hand, he slipped his fingertips over her

nipples and had the pleasure of hearing her moan in response. He was pretty sure he moaned as well.

"Leigh," he whispered against her mouth.

She gave it right back to him. She said his name. A whisper. A plea. An invitation. He couldn't accept it, of course, but with each passing moment, it got harder and harder for him to remember why they needed to stop.

He heard the ringing sound in his ears, but it took Gabe a moment to realize it was his phone and not his body's reaction to Leigh.

Hell. He'd obviously lost his mind. He had forgotten where he was and what had happened just minutes earlier. Here he was parked in front of a gas station kissing her. For about a million reasons, he shouldn't be doing that.

She made a sound of frustration that he understood all too well and eased away from him. Gabe did his own easing, knowing he had to put some distance between them.

Before he answered the call, he glanced around to make sure they were still alone. Thank God they appeared to be. The only person nearby was the attendant inside, who still had his face stuck in a magazine. Still, Gabe didn't plan to take any more chances with her life. He hoped the look he gave Leigh assured her of that.

He fished the phone out of the gym bag and brought it to his ear.

"Gabe? It's Frank Templeton." The man's voice was frantic and hardly more than a ragged whisper.

"Frank?" Gabe repeated. "How'd you get this number?"

"Jinx. I called him and convinced him that I'd talk to only you."

Gabe didn't know what to think about that. He hoped Jinx hadn't made a mistake by doing that. Of course, he did need to speak to Frank. He just hadn't expected it to happen over the phone. "Where are you?"

"I'd rather not say. I just want to make sure you'll be at the house tomorrow night?"

"I'll be there." Hopefully alone while Leigh waited in the truck. The only other person who knew about that meeting was Jinx, and Gabe wanted to keep things that way.

"Good. I have to talk to you. Listen, I can't stay on the line long, but you need to find Leigh. She's in a lot of danger."

Gabe certainly didn't need anyone to tell him that, but he played along, not wanting to send Frank deeper into hiding. "Why do you say that?"

"I don't have all the details, but I should have it worked out by tomorrow night. If you find Leigh by then, bring her with you so I can talk to her about that disk we found two years ago. I think that's what started all of this. And Gabe? Don't trust anyone on the task force. That's why I've been on the run. Somebody's out to kill me and maybe Leigh, too."

Oh, yeah. Definitely. But he wasn't sure that threat was coming from the task force. "Why would someone want to kill you?"

"I don't know. A cover-up maybe. I think it has something to do with those confiscated weapons that should have been destroyed and weren't. I have to go, Gabe."

Just like that, the line went dead. Gabe wasn't sure if the man had hung up voluntarily or if someone had cut his phone line. Either way, he obviously wouldn't get a chance to ask Frank a few more questions.

"Was that Frank Templeton?" Leigh asked.

"Yes. He's alive, but he sounds like a man who knows that he's in a whole lot of danger." Gabe turned off the phone and tossed it back in the gym bag. He couldn't waste any more time. He lifted Leigh's foot into his lap and continued to check the bandage for the transmitter.

Leigh leaned forward and looked into the gauze layers as well. "We're still meeting him tomorrow night, right?"

"Yeah." Hell or high water wouldn't stop that meeting. It would be dangerous, no doubt about it, but he didn't see another way around it. Frank probably wouldn't want to relay sensitive information over the phone. "This shouldn't come as a surprise, but Frank said you were in danger and that I shouldn't let you out of my sight."

Gabe figured that was advice he would most certainly take. It might significantly improve Leigh's chances of getting out of this situation alive.

Hurrying up his search, he continued to go through the bandage. He didn't find the transmitter until he got to the last of the gauzy layers. Just the sight of it made him curse. It was a chilling, hard reminder that he'd been stupid and that stupidity just might cost them everything.

Using the tip of his little finger, Gabe lifted out the tiny transmitter and inspected it. Too bad he couldn't send the device to the crime lab to have it checked out, but there wasn't time for that. In fact, there wasn't much time for him to do anything. He tossed it out the window and quickly started the truck.

"We have to put some distance between us and that thing," he let Leigh know.

He didn't waste another precious second either. He

pulled away from the gas station and sped up. Thanks to his lapse in judgment, he'd have to cover their tracks before he could even think about heading to Grand Valley. Gabe sure as heck didn't want anyone following them there.

"You mean I've been running around with that transmitter in my bandage this whole time?" She pressed down the edges of the tape that held the gauze strips in place. "Who put it there? And who had access to me before I regained consciousness?"

"Too many people," Gabe provided.

"Who?" she persisted.

"Well, the doctor and the technician who did your MRI." Gabe took a deep breath. "And a couple of times Jinx and Teresa were with you, too."

He was sure Leigh would have had an opinion about that. But she didn't have time to voice it. All hell broke loose.

A bullet came crashing through the back window.

Chapter 8

"Get down!" Gabe's voice echoed through the truck.

Leigh did as he said, dropping to the floor in a split second, but she had no intentions of staying down. Memory or no memory, she still had her instincts, and her instincts for survival were pretty strong. She certainly wasn't going to give up without a fight. She latched onto her gun and came up prepared to fire.

"Damn it, Leigh. I said get down."

Another bullet skipped off the roof of the truck, gashing through the metal. "Why? So you can be the sole target for whoever's trying to kill us? I'm not an invalid, so don't go all macho on me now."

She ignored his profanity-laced objection and stretched her hand toward the door. She rolled the window halfway down, all the while trying to stay low in the seat.

Leigh didn't know exactly what she planned to do, but she thought she might try shooting at the car tires. Using the small sliding window on the back was out—it had become a webby sheet of fractured safety glass when the bullet slammed into it. It was a chilling reminder of how close Gabe and she had come to getting killed.

"Climb over here and drive," Gabe snarled. "I'll return fire."

Leigh wanted to argue with that order, but she didn't want to try to win an argument at the cost of dying. It would only take one of those bullets to do either one of them in. Besides, she didn't even know if she was a good shot.

Gabe was.

He'd proven that back at the clinic.

Changing places was easier said than done, and they no doubt made clear targets while trying to do that. At Gabe's direction, she maneuvered her body across his, and he tried to slip beneath hers. They did all that while he kept his foot on the accelerator and while Leigh steered.

"Under different circumstances, I might consider this foreplay," he mumbled.

"You probably consider breathing foreplay," Leigh countered in a mumble of her own.

Gabe made a sound, part laughter, part frustration, all nerves.

There was another sputter of bullets. One of them took out a chunk of the mirror on the driver's side. Once Gabe was out of the way, Leigh floored the accelerator, watching the speedometer quickly go over eighty. The older-model truck probably wouldn't do much more than that, but she continued to press, knowing she had to put some distance between them and that car.

Gabe plundered through the gym bag and retrieved the extra magazines of ammunition. They were right where Leigh had placed them only minutes earlier. It wasn't quite an arsenal, but they could probably hold their own.

For a while anyway.

She glanced in what was left of the side mirror as Gabe aimed the gun out the window and fired several shots. Since they all appeared to be direct hits, and since the car windows didn't shatter, she guessed that the glass was bulletproof.

Sweet heaven. The gunmen had truly come prepared for a shoot-out.

"For God's sakes, Leigh, keep your head low," Gabe yelled when he glanced over at her.

"That's what I'm trying to do." She slid as deep in the seat as she could and took the truck around a sharp curve in the road. "Can't you shoot out their tires or something?" she asked impatiently.

"That's what I had in mind," Gabe said with equal impatience.

The barrel of a gun snaked out of the front passenger's window and rattled off more bullets. Gabe returned fire, and one of the bullets hit his opponent's weapon, sending a spark from metal colliding with metal.

Without hesitating, Gabe sent several rounds slightly farther to the right, and even with the distance between the vehicles, Leigh could see that he'd hit the gunman's shooting arm.

Gabe didn't let up. With the one gunman at least partially out of commission, Gabe leaned out the window and sent a barrage of bullets into the other vehicle. He must have hit something, or caused enough distraction, because the blue sedan clipped the ditch, the right tires dipping into some sloshy mud.

The driver swerved, trying to maneuver the car back onto the road. He wasn't successful. Gabe aimed his pistol at the tires and fired. And fired. And fired. The rubber on the tires disintegrated, unraveling until the driver had no choice but to grind to a stop.

Leigh didn't waste any time. She sped away, praying those men wouldn't get themselves out of that ditch anytime soon.

"Any sign they had backup?" She was almost afraid to hear Gabe's answer. The last thing she wanted was to go another round with yet another set of gunmen. Her whole body was a tangle of nerves and adrenaline.

"No. I think they were alone." But that obviously didn't make Gabe let down his guard. He kept his weapon aimed and his attention focused on the road.

"They must have found us by using that transmitter," she said more to herself than Gabe. "Or else Teresa somehow traced the call—"

"Teresa didn't put this attempted hit together."

"But you were just talking to her on the phone," Leigh pointed out. In fact, it appeared to her that Teresa was the most likely suspect.

"She wouldn't have had time to trace the call and dispatch someone that fast. These guys were right on our tail all along. My guess is they would have gotten to us even sooner if they hadn't had to navigate their way around these country roads. No. They had their orders long before I made that call to Teresa. That stop we made at the gas station just gave them time to catch up with us."

Gabe had obviously given it plenty of thought. Good. Maybe that meant he had a plan to put an end to this. Leigh didn't want to play hide-and-seek any longer with people who wanted her dead.

"Where to now?" she asked when she saw the sign for the approaching westbound interstate. It was the direction they needed to go to get to Frank Templeton in Grand Valley, but it would put them out in the open on a major highway.

Gabe never even hesitated. "We can't take the interstate, and we need to get off this road, especially since they know what vehicle we're in."

He turned around in the seat and reached out the still-lowered window to give his mirror an adjustment—probably so he could still do a visual check in case anyone else followed them. It was a reminder that even though she'd put some miles between the gunmen and them, they weren't out of immediate danger yet.

"So, where do we go if not to Grand Valley?" Leigh asked.

Again, he didn't hesitate. "I thought about the cabin back in the bayou."

It took her a moment to figure out what he meant. "You mean the place that Jinx owns?"

He nodded. "It might be safe there."

Safe, yes, in many ways. But Leigh remembered what Gabe had said about that cabin.

It was the place where they'd spent their honeymoon.

That shouldn't have bothered her. After all, this time they certainly wouldn't be going there to do honeymoonish things. They would be going there to get away from the gunmen. Still, there was something about the idea that made her pulse start to race again.

Leigh prayed it was racing because of the potential danger and nothing else.

"There's just one problem with going all the way out to Jinx's cabin," Gabe continued. "Tomorrow, we'd have a lot of miles to cover to get back to Grand Valley. Of course, we don't have to be there until midnight."

But it would mean a lot of extra time on the roads. Besides, for reasons Leigh didn't want to explore, she didn't think it was a good idea to spend the night there alone with Gabe. "Is there anyplace else we could go—a place that wouldn't involve Jinx?"

Or Jinx's knowledge of their whereabouts. Now, that was something Leigh didn't mind exploring. She really didn't want anyone to know where they were, but especially Jinx and Teresa Walters. If they went to his cabin, he might very well find out they were there.

"There is a place. A house." Gabe paused. Then he shrugged. "It's about fifty miles north of Houston. It's not that far from Grand Valley."

Houston. That got her full attention. There was a tiny flutter in her heart. A warm tingle worked its way from that flutter all the way to her stomach. "So, what is this place—an FBI safe house?"

"It's the house where I grew up."

The flutter got significantly worse. His home. "Your family will be there?" she asked hesitantly.

He shook his head. "My folks moved to Brownsville a few years back so they could help take care of my grandparents. I've got a brother, Reese, who's in the air force stationed over in Florida. My sister, Maria, is married and lives in Sacramento." He took a deep breath.

"Dad talks about selling the ranch, but he just hasn't gotten around to it."

Yet more pieces of her past that she didn't remember—she had in-laws. Apparently lots of them. Gabe's family. Leigh had been so preoccupied with various aspects of her own life that she hadn't thought to ask Gabe about his.

"So, we're both from Texas," she commented. "Then, how did we end up in New Orleans?"

He gathered up the extra ammunition and returned it to the gym bag. "We were both assigned there five years ago."

And that's where they'd obviously met. Fallen in love. Married. And then had fallen out of love.

Or something.

She glanced at him. He was still in a vigilant mode with his attention on the side mirror. She'd seen him like this before, of course. At the clinic and again that morning when Jinx came walking up to them in the bayou. But there was something about his formidable expression that made her go back for a second look.

And a third.

It was probably a weird hormonal reaction, but there was something appealing about that wariness. But Gabe didn't especially need to be on alert to be considered attractive. He was, well, hot. No doubt about it. It wasn't difficult for her to see why she'd been attracted to him in the first place.

Leigh cleared her throat. Best to put those kind of thoughts aside. Far, far aside. "How long will it take us to get to the house?"

"About four or five hours. We'll take the back roads so I can make sure no one is following us."

Of course, he'd want to make sure of that. She wanted

the same thing. She also wanted her heart rate to go back to normal, but it didn't seem as if that would happen in the next couple of hours. Leigh couldn't blame that entirely on the gunmen. It had plenty to do with that ill-timed, stupid kissing session that had gone on in the truck right before the bullets started flying.

Knowing she shouldn't put it off, Leigh broached the difficult subject. "We have to talk about that kiss—"

"Yeah, we do," he interrupted. "It shouldn't have happened."

She hadn't expected him to agree with her. Well, maybe she had. No one with a fully functioning brain could have thought that was a good thing for them to be kissing with all the danger lurking about. But she hadn't expected Gabe to voice that agreement so easily. After all, he was the one who'd started it.

Technically.

Admittedly, there was nothing technical about her participation.

"I'm sorry I let things go that far," she added. "I mean, it was just a physical response. And everything is all muddled up in my head." God, she was rambling. Why did her nerves suddenly feel so close to the surface? "I just didn't want you to read anything into it. Because I didn't."

He made a sound that could have meant nothing. Or anything. "Be honest, Leigh. Do you really think you could have done something to stop that kiss?"

Not that one, specifically. The heat of the moment had taken hold of her and hadn't been especially receptive to letting go. That didn't mean she would let the heat take over again. It was just a matter of her not letting herself get caught off guard.

Leigh took a deep breath, hoping it would help her come up with an answer to his question. It didn't. She settled for the easiest way out. "This isn't the right time for us to work out our personal problems, okay?"

"And you think by saying it, all of this heat simmering between us will just go away?" Gabe didn't wait for her to answer. "It won't, you know. Personal problems or not, it was there the first time we laid eyes on each other."

"Maybe, but even you should be able to see the logic in us not acting on this…heat."

"Of course I do," Gabe readily agreed. He scrubbed his hand over his face. "Look, I don't want to get involved again with you either."

That was exactly what she wanted to hear, but it made her throat turn to dust. She didn't even attempt to say anything. Leigh just kept driving while Gabe continued.

"When you left two years ago, I promised I'd never let myself care for you again." He mumbled something in Spanish under his breath. Definitely profanity. Leigh understood most of it, and it wasn't mild. "That's a promise I *will* keep. My job is to stop those gunmen from hurting you and find out who's behind these attacks. That's all."

"Yes," she agreed, a little alarmed that he sounded so adamant. And angry. She was just a job to him. Leigh had known that all along, but it was a shock to hear it spelled out for her. A few ill-timed kisses certainly wouldn't have changed that.

As if he'd declared war on it, Gabe checked the magazine in his gun. "Those vows that you threw away two years ago will just have to stay where you threw them because I don't intend to go there again, understand?"

All right. So, that was a little more honesty than she'd expected. Or wanted. "Then we agree. We shouldn't get involved again."

"Yeah, we agree."

For what it was worth, it seemed they'd reached a compromise. Sort of. But since his jaw muscles were battling each other, Leigh guessed that it wasn't an amicable one for him.

She told herself to leave well enough alone, but she didn't take her own advice. "Why did I leave you? Did I have an affair or something?" But Leigh knew it wasn't that. She just didn't know how she knew it.

"No affair," he confirmed several long moments later. He scraped his thumbnail over a ragged patch of leather on the dash. What he didn't do was look at her. "You came to me with information you'd learned about Dayton," he said slowly. "I'd known him for years. He was a friend. And I didn't think he was capable of doing something like that."

"But the proof—"

"I thought the proof was wrong, that someone had doctored the evidence."

"Certainly not me?" That didn't feel right either, but there was something about this explanation that stirred other emotions. Other sensations. Anger. Hurt. Pain. Betrayal. The emotions slowly began to unravel inside her.

"No. But I thought someone had," he explained. "You were equally sure of Dayton's guilt. A feeling, you said. A feeling I dismissed because I thought he was someone I knew and trusted."

In other words, Gabe had made a mistake. Leigh didn't need her memory to know he wouldn't have handled that well. But then, neither had she. "Did you confront Dayton?"

Gabe nodded. "He came to me and said he was innocent. I believed him. I told him that I'd do whatever I could to clear his name. I even went to Jinx and convinced him to investigate further before they brought Dayton in. Just the hint of impropriety would have destroyed his career in the Justice Department."

Okay. That probably would have happened. "Since I already believed Dayton was guilty, I suppose we argued?"

"We most certainly would have…if Dayton hadn't tried to kill you."

"He what?"

This time the profanity wasn't quite so muffled. "He tried to make it look a carjacking. He shot you in the arm and then chased you down an alley. Dayton would have killed you if a bystander hadn't stepped in. When he realized the game was over, he turned the gun on himself."

Leigh didn't remember any of it, but she could almost see those images in her mind and she could feel the raw emotions that went along with them. Not easy sensations to grasp.

"You nearly died because I trusted the wrong man." Gabe glanced at her, for only a second, before he turned back to the window.

This was probably one of the few times that amnesia was a good thing. Even though Leigh had hints of the horrible events that had gone on, her lack of memory forced her to look at them objectively.

"I was wrong to say you threw away your vows," he added several moments later. "I gave you a damn good reason to throw them away."

Maybe. But all the little pieces to this puzzle just didn't add up. She would have been angry and hurt that Gabe hadn't trusted her, but why would that have caused her to walk away from her job, their marriage and him?

There had to be something else.

But what?

Maybe it was simply that she knew Dayton did indeed have an accomplice, and she didn't want to take unnecessary chances with her life. But why wouldn't she have turned to Gabe or even Jinx to help her? One was her husband. The other, supposedly their close friend. With their combined FBI training, the three of them could have almost certainly flushed out an accomplice who might want her dead.

So, if her sudden, unexplained departure wasn't solely the result of the Dayton fiasco, then what had it all been about? And better yet—did Gabe know what had caused her to leave?

Maybe.

And if he did, why did he feel the need to keep it from her?

Leigh mulled those questions over while she drove toward the Texas state line.

Chapter 9

Gabe put the rest of their take-out chicken in the fridge and finished off one of the bottles of Mexican beer he'd found on the bottom shelf. Obviously, his folks came back often enough to keep the place stocked and clean.

The house was one big giant memory. Not all of it was good either. In fact, some of those memories were downright unpleasant.

Rather than reliving the past, he focused on the fact that it was a safe place to spend the night and trade out vehicles. He'd left his college clunker in the garage ten years earlier when he'd left for the FBI Academy. Thankfully, his father had seen to it over the years, and it started right up. Gabe just hoped the vehicle got them to Grand Valley so they could meet with Frank Templeton.

The old pipes in the house groaned and creaked when

Leigh turned on the faucet in the bathroom. Since the only bathroom was just off the kitchen, he had no trouble hearing the rattle of the shower curtain when she stepped inside the tub. He also had no trouble imagining how she looked with the water cascading down her naked body.

Of course, Gabe had an advantage with that particular image—he'd seen Leigh naked in the shower many times. Even in this one.

And on many occasions he'd joined her.

Cursing himself and his too-good memory, Gabe got himself another beer and sat down at the kitchen table. He'd have to tell his family, of course, about Leigh's return. He just didn't know what that telling would include. They knew little of Leigh's and his breakup, only that she'd left the Bureau to make her life elsewhere. Now he'd have to explain something he didn't have a real explanation for himself.

He took a long drink of his beer and stared at the ceiling. There probably wasn't one room in the entire house where at one time or another she hadn't told him *I love you*. In those days before the incident with Joe Dayton, Leigh had been generous with those three words. And they hadn't just been words. She'd meant them. It was impossible to fake feelings that ran that deep. Gabe knew. Because he'd said those words right back to her.

Riled at himself for remembering that, he took out his phone and pressed in the numbers for a call he should have made hours earlier.

"Who are you calling?" he heard Leigh ask.

He turned so quickly, he nearly fell out of his chair. She was in the doorway that led from the hall into the kitchen. Not naked, of course. She wore a robe she'd borrowed from his mother's closet. It was several sizes too large for her, but that didn't stop Gabe from noticing the way the sash cinched around her waist.

"Jinx," he answered.

Her eyebrow arched. "Why?"

"Because he'll want to know that we're all right. I'm sure Teresa's already contacted him so he'll know there were gunmen after us."

Her hair was still wet. It lay against the sides of her face and neck. When she stepped into the room, she brought the scent of her shower with her.

She smelled like gardenias. Something subtle but potent. The timing was lousy, but it went straight through him like wildfire. Of course, just being close to her had a way of doing that. The two years they'd spent apart had done nothing to diminish the raw passion she ignited within him.

Gabe didn't dare get up from that chair. For one thing, he couldn't. Well, not without settling down his own body first. But he also didn't need to be any closer to her. He decided it was a good time to make that call, so he pressed in the last of the numbers.

"I'd rather Jinx didn't know where we are," Leigh added.

Gabe was about to assure her, again, that they could trust Jinx, but he didn't have time because he heard his friend's voice on the other end of the line.

"It's me." Gabe paused, wondering what to add to that. "We're safe."

"Thank God. How bad did things get?"

"Bad enough. We're going to lay low for the night."

He glanced at Leigh. She still had that look in her eyes—the one that questioned his judgment. Maybe she was thinking about another man he'd trusted. Joe Dayton. A friend who'd turned out not to be a friend after all. But Jinx wasn't Joe Dayton. Gabe knew he could trust this man. Still, there was no reason to let anyone know where they were. That would perhaps give Leigh some peace of mind.

"We should make it to Grand Valley in plenty of time," Gabe continued. "You'll be there?"

"Wouldn't miss it. I'll stay back though. I don't want Frank to see me and get spooked."

That was a good plan. Gabe didn't know Frank Templeton that well, but he certainly seemed like the type who'd spook easily. Of course, in this case Frank perhaps had a reason for it. The same person who'd gone after them would likely go after Frank as well. If he or she could find Frank, that is.

"See you tomorrow." Gabe turned off the phone before Jinx could ask anything else—especially anything about their location.

Leigh leaned against the wall next to the refrigerator. "Thanks for not telling him where we are."

Gabe nodded and tipped his head to the beer. "You want one?"

"No, thanks. But I wouldn't mind another cup of that coffee." She walked to the old-fashioned drip coffeepot on the stove and refilled the earthenware mug she'd left on the counter. As Gabe knew she would, she added three heaping teaspoons of sugar.

Leigh drank several sips before she continued. "I found some clothes in that back bedroom that look like they'll fit me. If you don't mind, I'll borrow them for the trip tomorrow."

"Of course." They were probably some old things

Maria had left behind when she left home for college. Hopefully, the fit wouldn't be as distracting as the shorts and top had been. If so, he might have to borrow some blinders from the barn to keep himself from being too distracted.

"I noticed the pictures in your parents' room. I didn't recognized them," Leigh added almost as an apology. "But they look like nice people."

"They are."

She fidgeted with some chili-shaped salt and pepper shakers on the counter. "So, was this place part of a working ranch before your folks moved to Brownsville?"

When she pushed her hand through her hair, Gabe glanced at her. Her nerves were definitely showing. Hell, his probably were, too. There was nothing relaxing about this conversation.

"Yeah. There's about two hundreds acres total. The land has been in the Sanchez family for three generations. I think that's why my father is reluctant to sell it, even though none of the kids have ranching in their blood. I guess he figures either Reese or I will change our minds."

The room suddenly seemed too warm. Gabe got up and raised the window over the sink. The night air was more muggy than cool, and it began to spill into the room, bringing the scents of Texas with it. The pasture grass. The wildflowers. His mother's roses that were in full bloom. Even with all that, he could still detect Leigh's own unique scent.

Rather than stare at his wife, Gabe stared out into the darkness instead.

"There are four children in the photos in the bedroom," she said. "Two girls and two boys. I thought you said you only had one sister."

Hell. The woman sure could zone in on the worst of subjects. He bracketed his hands on the counter. "My other sister, Emily, died when she was just a kid."

"Oh." He heard the sympathy, and yet another apology in her voice. She cleared her throat and thankfully changed the subject. "Tell me about this house in Grand Valley where we're meeting Frank."

"It'll take us about a couple hours to get there." Thankfully, they had some time since they didn't have to meet him until the following night. Maybe nothing else would go wrong between now and then.

"There'll be guards?" she asked.

"There shouldn't be." He shook his head. "I have no way of knowing if Frank called anyone else, but it didn't sound as if he'd trust too many people."

Despite the fact he knew it was a stupid thing to do, Gabe looked at her again. Hell. How could anyone look that good wearing an old chenille robe? "Listen, I know the adrenaline might still have you pumped, but you need to get some rest. We'll have plenty to do if Frank comes through tomorrow night. If he can tell us who Dayton's accomplice is, then we'll have to get that information to someone who won't kill us just because we have it."

"Any idea who we can trust with that?" She drank more of her coffee.

"Jinx. He'll find a way to get it into the right hands. That's why I want him to meet us there. We'll have to get Frank out of the area tomorrow night. He won't be safe there very long."

"No, I don't suspect he will." Worry lines bunched

up her forehead. She set the coffee mug back on the table and slid the tip of her index finger around the rim. Gabe found the gesture, well, erotic. Of course, almost anything she could have done would have been erotic. He definitely had a one-track mind tonight.

Knowing he had to say, or do, something, he motioned toward the bandage on her foot. "How are the stitches?"

"As good as can be expected." She took a deep breath that forced her breasts against the tightly cinched fabric of the robe. "I changed the bandages and used some of that antibiotic cream from the first-aid kit."

"Good." And that was all he managed to get out.

Her gaze came to his. Slowly. As if she was fighting the moment as much as he was. There was a hint of panic in her sea-green eyes and something else, something familiar.

Something that immediately kicked his body into overdrive.

Gabe forgot all about her amnesia and the mess they were in. He forgot all about the hurt, the anger, the pain and the fact that just hours earlier he'd sworn never to get involved with her again.

All he remembered was that Leigh was his wife.

And he wanted her.

Gabe reached out and grabbed onto fists full of that god-awful robe and wrenched her closer. She didn't resist, didn't even mutter an objection. There were no more preliminaries, no long yearning looks, no soft caressing breaths. Just them. Two people who obviously needed each other.

Starving, he took her mouth—because it was his for the taking. He could feel every nerve in his body. And hers. The tension drummed through his pulse, slicing through him with both pleasure and pain. The sheer need he had for her nearly brought him to his knees.

Her breath caught when he turned her and backed her against the sink. Gabe wasn't even sure if he was breathing. Everything seemed to swirl around them.

"We should stop this," he somehow managed to say. "So, now would be a good time to do it…unless you want it to continue."

She just stared at him, her warm, moist breath hitting against a rather sensitive spot on his neck.

"Well?" he asked. "Yes or no?"

Leigh caught onto his shoulders and pulled him to her. "Yes."

She'd obviously lost her mind. She'd said yes. Yes! How could she have possibly said that? Still, Leigh kissed him as if he were the source of her next breath.

With the fresh, tangled emotions rocketing through her, she pulled back. Slightly. And tried to get control of herself. She saw something in the depth of Gabe's midnight-blue eyes that caused her heart to jolt. She saw the need and knew without a doubt that it was the same need reflected in her own eyes.

She pulled in her breath. This wasn't about passion, or sex. It wasn't the time for her hormones to start raging. Yet she felt helpless against the mighty force that had apparently already been set into motion.

Somewhere through the haze, it occurred to her again that she should stop and regroup. Things were spinning out of control.

"Gabe," she whispered. It was a warning. And a plea.

A fear. And a necessity. All of the things that she'd tried to tamp down rose to the surface.

And escaped.

In what seemed to be a burst of fire, his mouth came to hers, and he kissed her. It was rough. Almost punishing. But she knew it couldn't have been any gentler. The connection between them wouldn't have allowed anything less than what he gave her.

Digging her fingers into his shoulders, she snapped him to her so the hard muscles of his body pressed right into her. The fit was so perfect, so good, that her eyes watered. And her heart soared.

He didn't break the kiss, but Gabe fisted a hand in her hair and maneuvered her so that the small of her back pressed against the sink. Without it, and his arm to support her, she would have no doubt fallen.

He took his clever mouth to her neck, and then to the spot just beneath her ear. They'd obviously spent a long time kissing because Gabe seemed to know every pleasure point and erogenous zone on her body. He evidently remembered which ones would turn her to instant flames.

His lips brushed against her earlobe. It didn't stay a brush though. He flicked his tongue over it. Sucked it. Lingered with his hot, moist breath until she wanted to wrap herself around him and beg for more.

Still, she could have perhaps stopped at that point if it'd just been the kiss. It wasn't. While he continued the assault on her ear, he slid his hand over her throat. And then lower into the V-opening of the robe. His fingertips found her nipples and brought them to hard peaks.

"Yes," she whispered.

At the sound of her voice, he eased back and looked

at her. His eyes were hot and narrowed. The intensity should have frightened her, but she was beyond that. Beyond fear. Beyond reason.

She didn't even try to stop him when he reached for the sash that held the robe together. He undid it and eased one side off her shoulder.

"I'm going to kiss you there," he let her know, his fingertips fondling her nipple.

She heard the primitive sound claw its way past his throat, felt the slow, eating hunger in his touch. And she was lost. Willingly lost.

Gabe did as he promised. He lowered his head and claimed her breast, first one and then the other, much as he'd already claimed her mouth. Leigh leaned into him and let herself fall into the fiery haze of passion and need.

It was that need that sent her searching for relief. Leigh rubbed herself against him. Seeking. Needing something that only Gabe could give her. His thigh grazed the feverish center of her body, and the brief contact made her gasp.

That seemed to be the only encouragement Gabe needed to up the ante. He slid his rough, callused hand down her body and to her thigh.

"Don't look away," he insisted when she started to close her eyes. "I've waited a long time to be with you like this. I want to see what it does to you."

Leigh couldn't have refused if she'd wanted. She held his gaze, somehow. Even when he skimmed his hand to the back of her knee. He lifted it, positioning it, until it tucked against the outside of his thigh.

Still, she watched.

Her breath shattered when his hand began to move

again. He took his time. Inch by precious inch. Just his fingertips brushing over her skin as he made his way from her knee. To her thigh. And then to her stomach.

"Since the moment you came back, I've ached to touch you like this." His voice was hoarse and hardly more than a whisper.

Yes. She'd felt the same ache, even though she didn't have the words to say it. But Gabe knew. She could tell from the way he looked at her that he knew everything that stirred inside her body and her soul.

With that same torturous slow pace, he pressed his hand against her bare stomach. His fingers moved over the lacy panel of her low-cut panties. Leigh arched her back, and hips, to feel more of that touch.

"Say my name, Leigh," he told her, his voice thick. "I want to hear you say my name again."

"Gabe," she obliged. But then almost immediately, she went stiff. "Gabe…"

He must have noticed her reaction because he stopped. "What's wrong?"

She shook her head, already trying to move away from him. "I…"

"Tell me what's wrong."

She pressed her hands on each side of her head. "I remember something."

Only because she was looking at him did she notice the alarm that fired through his eyes. Just like that, the moment and the passion were gone. Those few words were obviously the slap back to reality they both needed.

"Did I try to call you a couple of days ago?" she asked.

He nodded. "You left a message at my apartment in New Orleans. You asked me to meet you at the lake."

Yes. That was it. That was the image that flashed into her head. Her on the phone…somewhere. And she was calling Gabe. "So that's how you knew I'd be there."

Gabe slowly pulled the sides of her robe back in place, stepped away from her and reached for his beer. He finished it off in one quick gulp. "I arrived just in time to see the car speed away. I was about to go after it when I noticed the movement in the water."

And she was that *movement* in the water. "Do you remember if I said anything else in that message?"

"I remember it word for word," he admitted. "You said you had something to tell me. That I should meet you at Lake Pontchartrain on the east end of the old Slidell Bridge so we wouldn't be seen. It's been closed to traffic for years. You added that if something should go wrong then I was to get to Philip in Houston."

"Philip in Houston," she repeated. Yes. That sounded right.

At first.

But then the prickle started up the back of her neck. The feeling that went through her made her feel on the verge of a panic attack. Something was wrong. Terribly wrong. "We have to get to Houston, Gabe."

He nodded and closed the window over the sink. "And we will, right after we've spoken to Frank."

Because her legs suddenly seemed wobbly, she sat down at the table. It didn't help. The panic attack seemed so close to the surface that she didn't know if she could control it. "There's something…about Houston." But what? Leigh tried to force herself to remember. "I think my brother might be in danger. All I know is that I *have* to get back to Houston right away."

Gabe sat down across from her and reached for her hand. Unlike his previous touch, there was nothing carnal about this. He obviously saw how close she was to losing it and wanted to comfort her.

"Listen, Leigh, if Jinx hasn't been able to find Philip, no one can. That means he's safe. If Frank can tell us who Dayton's accomplice is, then we have something to work with. We can get this person off our backs, and neither you nor your brother will be in danger."

Maybe. And maybe not. Still, Gabe was right about one thing. They did need to find out what Frank knew. It wouldn't do any good for them to go racing to Houston when she had no idea where in Houston even to look for her brother.

She pulled her hand from his and pressed her fingertips, hard, to her temples. "God, I hate this amnesia. There's something I'm supposed to be doing. Something important. I just know it. I *feel* it. And I don't have a clue what it is."

"It'll come to you. Beating yourself up won't help." He stood and pushed the chair back under the table. "Why don't you go to bed? You might remember something else after a good night's sleep."

Leigh didn't think she'd be doing much sleeping, but she did need to try. With a midnight rendezvous with Frank, it might be days before she got another chance to rest.

"You can sleep in Maria's old room," Gabe said, helping her from the chair. "It's at the end of the hall. I've already locked up, and I turned on the security alarm.

It's not state-of-the-art, but it'll give us enough warning just in case."

Just in case those gunmen returned. With the other things that had gone on, Leigh had almost forgotten about them.

She retrieved her gun from the table and stepped out into the hallway. "Where will you be?" she asked.

"I'll take the couch."

So he would be close to the front door, no doubt. In other words, he'd spend the night standing guard. "Let me know if you need some relief."

A short burst of air rushed out of his mouth. It was almost a smothered laugh. Leigh nearly laughed herself. That wasn't the best choice of words considering what had just happened between them. "I meant if you needed me to take a turn standing guard."

"Yeah." He paused. "I know what you meant."

No doubt. But knowing it didn't do anything to lessen the strain she felt between them.

She motioned toward the kitchen. "I'm sorry about what just happened, Gabe." It was paltry at best. But it was the only thing she could offer him at the moment. "I would say it won't happen again, but I'll save my breath."

"Good idea." He turned and walked into the living room.

She stood there and watched while he sank onto the sturdy, floral sofa. There was probably something else she should say to him. Perhaps a confession that she no longer doubted that they'd once been in love. But that would probably only make things worse.

It would for her anyway.

Leigh didn't need any verbal reminders as to how

deep her feelings for Gabe once were. Nor did she need to dwell on the fact that once her memory returned, she just might realize those feelings, that love, was still there.

Chapter 10

Leigh lifted her head from against the window when Gabe drove past the sign that announced the Grand Valley city limits. Finally, they'd reached their destination. They had taken what seemed to be the most roundabout route to get there, with Gabe meandering down one back road after another.

"Do you have any idea where this place is that we're supposed to meet Frank?" she asked, glancing around the pristine houses and shops that dotted the landscape. It wasn't a large town, but it seemed spread out.

"The house is on Outrider Street."

Since he didn't check a map or even look at the road signs, she figured Gabe had been there before. But then, it was an FBI safe house. She, too, might have visited it when she was still on the Evidence Response Team.

She glanced at the clock on the dash. It was still

nearly a half hour until midnight. Not a vast amount of time, but they'd already spent the entire day just killing time.

And trying to ignore each other.

Gabe had been far more successful at it than she had.

Basically, he'd just clammed up. When he did speak to answer one of her chitchat-type questions, he kept his answers to a bare minimum. In the five hours it'd taken them to get from his childhood home to Grand Valley, Gabe had really only passed on a few bits and pieces of new information. Leigh now knew that she was twenty-nine and, other than sugary coffee, she had a fondness for old Bogart movies, chocolate ice cream and reading murder mysteries. Not exactly a storehouse of information.

What he carefully avoided was any discussion about what had gone on the night before in the kitchen. Or any comment about their past relationship.

It was just as well. She had no idea what to say to him about those things either. It was clear that Gabe wasn't eager to resume a relationship with her, but he'd certainly had trouble resisting anything physical.

But then, so had she.

When Gabe slowed down the car, Leigh followed his gaze to the two-story house on Outrider Street. "That's it?" It looked like the dozen or so other houses that lined both sides of the street. Nondescript. A cookie-cutter image of the other houses around it. And that was probably why the FBI had chosen it.

Gabe nodded and drove right past it. He parked at the end of the block in front of a small park.

"Do you think Frank's already in there?" Leigh

glanced out the back window. She could easily see the house, but there weren't any lights on inside.

"Maybe."

But since he settled against the seat, that obviously meant he didn't intend to go in early. Maybe because it might scare off Frank, and maybe because he wanted to give Jinx a little more time to arrive.

"So, what's the plan?" she asked.

Gabe made himself more comfortable, stretching out his arm so that it rested on the back of her seat. It wasn't necessarily intentional. There wasn't much room in the two-seater car, and his arms were long.

"We wait, and when it's time, I walk to the house and go inside."

"That's it? It sounds too risky. What if someone used Frank to set a trap for us?"

"Well, I obviously won't knock on the door and wait for someone to invite me in. I'll go around back and get in without being seen."

Leigh didn't like that any better than the other part. "And what if Frank accidentally shoots you because he thinks you're someone else?"

Gabe lay back on the headrest. "He's expecting me. Besides, no one else is supposed to be here."

"You don't know that for sure. Jinx knows we'll be here. He could have told someone."

He angled his eyes in her direction. "We've been through this. Jinx is a decent guy. I've known him for years."

That didn't mean she would trust him. Leigh tried a different approach. "What if the accomplice is waiting inside?"

Gabe shrugged. "It won't change what I have to do.

One way or another, I have to meet Frank. I'll disarm the security system and hope for the best."

"Great day, this sounds like no plan at all. All right, Gabe, answer this one. After we get in and disarm the system, then what? Do we just pray that no one blows us away?"

He leaned closer and cupped her chin. "Let's get one thing straight right now. There's no *we* to this plan. *You* will wait here in the car while *I* go inside. I have no intention of taking you into that house."

This wasn't at all the way she thought things would be, and Leigh was sure her expression showed it. "But you're going in," she pointed out.

"Because I don't have a choice. I want to get in and out as fast as possible. I can't do that if I have to worry about you, too."

Was he right? Leigh had to concede that he might be. Frank possibly held information that could save their lives.

Or get them killed.

Either way, they had to know. And either way with the stitches in her ankle, she would be a liability to Gabe.

She huffed, frustrated at the conclusion she'd come to. "Why do you get to come up with the plans?"

"Because I don't have amnesia. When you get your memory back, you can come up with all the plans you want." He glanced at her foot. "How's the ankle holding up?"

"Fine."

He took two painkillers from the first-aid kit and handed her a bottle of water. "These might help."

She took the tablets, wishing there were such an easy

solution to the rest of her problems. "When we're done here, will we leave straight for Houston?"

"That depends. If Frank tells us what we want to know, then yes. But before we go driving all over Houston, I'm hoping Jinx will come up with an address for Philip."

Leigh hoped the same thing. There were too many hitches in her life right now—her brother's whereabouts and safety were just part of them. She could add Houston to that list. Just the mention of the place sent her blood pressure climbing. And then there was Gabe. When they'd worked through all those other problems, she would still have to figure out what to do about him.

The physical attraction was still there. The incident at the house had proven that. The heat still crackled between them even now. That meant whatever had happened to drive them apart, it hadn't destroyed the feelings they had for each other. Well, not all of them anyway. However, it had put a wedge between them that seemed to dissolve with each smoldering glance they shared.

If it'd just been those glances, Leigh could have dealt with it better. But it was much more than that. Gabe was someone she trusted. She no longer doubted that. That phone call she remembered making was one of the most important calls of her life, and she'd phoned the one man who could save her and her brother. She wouldn't have made that call to just anyone.

"You're sure quiet over there," Gabe said to her. "Are you thinking I owe you an apology for what went on back at the house?"

She nearly choked on the drink of water she'd just taken. "No apology. I was a willing participant."

Incredibly willing.

Leigh had already opened her mouth to delve into that can of worms he'd just opened, but Gabe spoke before she could. "It's time to go," he said softly. "I want to go over the rules."

"Rules?" she repeated. He'd made it sound as if they were back in elementary school. "Why do you get to come up with the rules?"

"They're like plans—my territory." He didn't even pause after that glib remark. "Keep your gun ready and stay put. I mean, don't move an inch. If and only if I signal do you come into that house."

"What's the signal?"

"I'll flicker the lights."

She felt her eyes widen. "And how will you manage that if someone's holding a gun on you?"

"*Mi vida*, the only time I'll flicker those lights is when and if the place is safe."

"So, I'm not supposed to come to your aid even if I can save your life?" Leigh asked.

"That's right. But don't worry, I'll be fine." He put his hand on the door handle, but he didn't open it. He hesitated a moment. Then, two. "By the way, if something does happen, Jinx will find you. He'll take you someplace safe."

That sent her stomach into a tailspin. "But you just said you'd be fine."

She would have added more, much more, if he hadn't kissed her. It happened so fast that Leigh didn't even see it coming. It didn't last long. Hardly more than a taste. He broke the contact and stared into her eyes. She was pretty sure she no longer looked argumentative.

"You said that complicates things," she pointed out.

And it did. Big time. She couldn't think her way out of a paper bag when Gabe kissed her.

"I know. What can I say—I'm weak. And I've gotta go."

With that calmly uttered remark, Gabe got out of the car and started toward the house. She kept her gaze on him, watching until he disappeared into the darkness.

Her fears certainly didn't disappear.

If something happened to Gabe… But Leigh couldn't even finish that thought. Instead, she forced herself to concentrate on something she could control—a backup plan of her own. If Gabe hadn't returned within fifteen minutes, she would say to heck with his rules. She'd go in after him. After all, those kind of rules were made to be broken.

The minutes crawled by.

She kept a close watch on the house, praying that everything was all right. But she saw nothing. No flickering lights. No shadows. No sign of life. It made the muscles in her chest tighten even more.

God, how many times had she sat through something like this? She didn't have a specific answer, but Leigh knew this wasn't a first. No, there'd been other cases, other assignments where she'd been in a position like this. Odd though, the potential danger didn't frighten her nearly as much as the thought of Gabe going in that house alone.

At the end of her self-imposed time limit, Leigh got out of the car, taking the gun with her. She didn't know exactly what she intended to do, but if she could get closer to the house, she might catch a glimpse of Gabe. That glimpse would hopefully be enough to reassure her that he was all right.

She walked toward the house, trying to stay focused on her surroundings. She didn't want another gunman sneaking up on her like the one at the clinic. Nor did she want a neighbor to see her skulking around and call the cops. A squad car with flashing lights wouldn't please Gabe or Frank.

Everything suddenly seemed quiet. Too quiet. And her instincts screamed that something wasn't right. Instead of staying on the sidewalk where she could easily be seen, Leigh went in the same direction Gabe had taken. She cut across one of the postage-stamp lawns and into a narrow greenbelt. Shrubs and mature trees dotted the area, providing her with an adequate hiding space.

She hoped.

A dog barked, and because it sounded nearby, Leigh froze. She hadn't thought her heart could race any faster, but it did. Was is possible she had a fear of dogs? Well, it didn't matter. This was no time to be neurotic. She had to make sure Gabe was all right.

She reached the house and flattened her body against the side so she could peek into the kitchen window. The only light came from the dim bulb over the stove, but it was enough to see things she didn't want to see.

Some kind of struggle had obviously taken place. A violent struggle. Broken dishes littered the counter. Chairs were knocked helter-skelter. What looked to be a bloody handprint was on the doorway leading into the hall. There was no sign of anyone, either wounded or otherwise.

"Please don't let that be Gabe's blood," she whispered to herself. But just the sight of it caused her breath to stall in her throat.

Speeding up her search, Leigh slipped around the corner and climbed onto the back porch that spanned the entire width of the house. The overhead light was out. Whether by design or chance, it didn't matter. The darkness cloaked her, and she hoped that was an advantage.

The darkness, however, didn't make it easy for her to move around. Groping blindly, she caught onto the arm of the porch swing and used it to maneuver her way to the door. A door that she prayed wasn't locked. Unlike Gabe, she didn't think she had any lock-picking skills. At least not skills that she remembered anyway.

It was obviously too late to consider something so critical, but it occurred to her that she might have breached some sort of perimeter security if Gabe hadn't disarmed it. Leigh didn't want to think about how quickly and how aggressively someone would respond to a triggered security system at an FBI safe house. It would no doubt be more than just squad cars with flashing lights. And maybe that wouldn't be such a bad thing.

After all, things didn't look secure by a long shot.

Leigh heard a sound come from inside the house—something like a swish, as if someone had blown out a candle. A shot fired from a silencer, maybe?

Oh, God.

If it had been a shot, then the struggle was still going on, and Gabe was probably right in the middle of it. Since he didn't have a silencer on his gun, that meant someone was shooting at him. Or at Frank. Either way, it wasn't good.

She forced herself to get moving and immediately tripped over something. Struggling to hang on to her gun and to break her fall, Leigh didn't have time to see what had snagged her foot. That is, she didn't see it until she hit the porch and came face-to-face with it.

The obstacle was a man.

He was on his stomach, unmoving, his face turned to the side. His eyes were blank. Lifeless.

Dead.

Choking back a scream, Leigh frantically searched that face to see if it was familiar. It wasn't Gabe. Thank God, it wasn't Gabe.

She scrambled away from the body, keeping her gun raised in case she had to defend herself. She bolted forward only to run head-on into something else.

Not something.

Someone.

Solid, strong arms suddenly clamped around her. A hand closed over her mouth before she could even call out for help.

And she was trapped.

Chapter 11

Gabe barely dodged the elbow that Leigh tried to ram into his stomach. He wasn't quite so successful avoiding the kick to his shin. Or the Muay Thai boxing move she used after that. She was in a fight-or-flight mode and had obviously chosen to fight. Too bad he was the one she was fighting.

"It's me," Gabe managed.

Leigh continued to struggle. She pivoted, and went after him again, but he managed to get a tight lock on her. It took several seconds for her mind to register what her eyes had already seen.

"It's all right," he said directly against her ear.

No, it wasn't all right, but it was the best he could offer her in the hopes it would settle her down. Her nerves were in a million pieces. Her body, a snarl of adrenaline, fear and relief. Gabe understood every single one of those emotions because he was feeling them himself.

"Gabe," she said as if just realizing who he was. She latched onto him and buried her face against his neck. "You're not hurt. Thank God."

"No." He wouldn't let himself be even remotely pleased with Leigh's concern for him. Nor would he let himself be too angry that she'd followed him to the house. Even with the stern warning he'd given her, he figured she would come after him.

"But that man—"

"He was dead when I got here." Gabe eased her around so she wouldn't be tempted to glance at the body. And so they wouldn't be seen by anyone who just happened to look out a window. He moved Leigh deep into the shadows of the porch.

With her breath racing, she pulled slightly away and met his gaze. When she spoke, there was some grit back in her voice. "And you went inside anyway?"

"I had to. I had to find out what was going on."

She shook her head as if trying to understand that. "Is it Frank?"

"No. I don't know who it is. Someone unlucky, that's for sure. I think Frank's still inside."

Her eyes widened. "You saw him?"

"I heard him," Gabe corrected. "At least I think it was Frank. Someone rigged one of the bedroom doors with an explosive device. I heard someone or something inside, maybe even a fired shot. But if I open the door, the whole place will probably go up."

"Sweet heaven." She pressed her fingertips to her mouth for a moment. The alarm, however, didn't stay in her eyes long. Her FBI training apparently kicked in, and Gabe could see she was trying to work things out. "What about going through the window?"

"There are metal bars. Security measures put in by the Bureau. I don't think we'll get through those without a key, and the key doesn't seem to be anywhere inside. My guess is the person who set those explosives made sure we wouldn't have an easy way to get into that room."

"Maybe Jinx is around here somewhere and has the key?" Leigh suggested.

Gabe shook his head. "I haven't seen him." Nor would he since he'd told Jinx to stay out of sight. Besides, he was positive that Jinx wouldn't have the key. It should have been in the safe, which meant someone had taken it.

"I was about to shoot a hole through one of the walls to try to get to Frank," he explained, keeping his voice in a whisper. "But then I heard you out here and thought someone was breaking into the place."

Leigh took a step toward the door. "Then let's go inside. I'll help you shoot through the wall."

He stopped her from taking a second step. Gabe caught onto her shoulder and held on tight. "I don't plan to start shooting at anything until I take you back to the car."

"The car is the last place I want to be." She gave a frustrated huff and mumbled something under her breath. "Gabe, I'll be in danger no matter where I am. At least if I'm with you, we can watch out for each other."

He gave that some thought. It sounded right, until he remembered the *least* safe place was inside the house. Well, maybe. Maybe there was no such thing as a safe place with Dayton's accomplice running around loose. A bullet was a bullet no matter where it was fired.

Gabe dodged her gaze and tipped his eyes upward to seek divine guidance. Or at least to get a grip on some common sense. Unfortunately, he didn't get either. "I'm positive I'll regret this," he heard himself say.

"Maybe. But if so, we'll regret it together." She raised her weapon. "Let's go."

Cursing himself and the mess they were in, he opened the door and stepped back into the kitchen. "Watch our backs," he reminded her. "I'll take care of anything else."

He led her through the L-shaped room, stepping around the overturned chairs and debris. "I wasn't in here when this happened," he let her know when he heard her start to mumble again.

"Thank God. Whose blood is that?"

Gabe glanced at the handprint on the wall before they went into the living room. "I don't know. Maybe the guy on the porch. Frank might have managed to get off a few shots before someone put him in that room."

"But why wouldn't they just kill Frank? Why go through all the trouble to rig that door so it would blow up?"

He didn't have time to answer her. The noise stopped him cold. There was a crash at the far end of the room. The glass exploded, the shards flying through the air toward them. Somehow, Gabe managed to haul her behind him.

And then he saw it.

A fist-size gunmetal-colored canister landed on the floor.

"Get out of here!" he yelled.

With hardly more than a glance at the canister bomb that was only a few yards from them, Gabe shoved her back into the hallway that led to the kitchen.

"What is that thing?" she asked. "God, is it a bomb?"

He grabbed Leigh and tried to get her to safety. He wasn't fast enough. They'd barely made it to the entryway of the kitchen when the deafening blast tore through the living room and the hallway.

The impact knocked Leigh to the floor, and Gabe followed on top of her with his body. Fragments of the canister flew through the air and pelted against the walls and ceiling. He thought of Frank trapped in that room. But there was no way Gabe could get to him. The place suddenly looked like a war zone, and his first instinct was to protect Leigh.

When the fragments stopped raining down on them, Gabe rolled off her. In the same motion, he forced her to her feet and got them moving into the kitchen. They'd hardly had time to take a step when there was another crash through the other window in the dining room. He heard a second canister land on the floor.

He pushed Leigh on the other side of the refrigerator, praying it would be enough to protect them. Gabe braced himself for the next blast.

He didn't have to wait long.

Like the first, the impact shook the house, and debris and glass shot everywhere. A chunk of ceiling just above their heads gave way. It would have crashed on them if they hadn't scrambled across the floor toward the back door.

Gabe forced himself to put a chokehold on his rage, but it took every ounce of his self-control.

Damn the person responsible for this.

Damn his twisted, evil mind.

And while Gabe was doling out damns, he added a harsh one for himself. He'd been a damn fool to allow Leigh to get anywhere near this house. To *this*. In doing so, he'd underestimated his opponent's capabilities, and it had almost gotten her killed.

That wouldn't happen again.

Knowing he had to get them out of the house before it collapsed around them, Gabe pushed Leigh toward the back door. Even in the dark, dust-filled room, he could see that her face was the color of skim milk. She wasn't just scared. She was terrified.

With reason.

Even if they made it out of the house, there was no guarantee that the person who'd fired those canisters wouldn't be waiting for them.

He knew that.

Apparently, so did she.

Unfortunately, it was a chance he had to take.

He shoved open the door and maneuvered himself onto the back porch just ahead of her. There was another crash of wood, metal and glass. Then another.

Gabe didn't wait around. "Run!" he ordered. He grabbed her arm and pulled her onto the back porch.

Probably because he didn't give her a choice, Leigh kept up with his pace down the steps and across the yard. Like Gabe, she kept her gun raised. And ready. He prayed it would be enough if someone fired at them.

"Where to?" she asked.

Gabe couldn't answer—he kept them running. Behind them, a vicious blast ripped through the house. The glass left in the windows burst outward, sending flames and jagged shards right out at them. The house exploded into a fireball. Black coils of smoke rose, smearing into the night sky.

Hell. If Frank was in that house, then he was a dead man.

"Keep running, Leigh!" Gabe shouted.

He caught a glimpse of the shadowy figure then. And the gun. It was drawn and ready to fire. Gabe pulled up quickly, trying to stop their forward motion, but he couldn't.

It was too late.

Chapter 12

Gabe must have seen the gun and the shadowy figure at the same moment Leigh did. He tried to step in front of her, but she wanted no part of that. He'd already risked his life too many times to save her.

He swerved toward the approaching gunman, and Leigh pulled up by his side, aiming her weapon as well. But it wasn't exactly the threat her body had braced itself for. Well, maybe it wasn't. It was Jinx, and he was making his way across the yard straight toward them.

Leigh didn't lower her gun even though Gabe did.

"Are you all right?" Jinx shouted over the noise of the fire and falling debris.

"What do you think? Someone just tried to kill us," Leigh icily informed him. And for all she knew, Jinx could have been the one to do it. Of course, she knew he was supposed to be somewhere in the area—Gabe had told her that. But that didn't give Leigh any reassurance.

Gabe caught onto her arm again. "We can't stay out here in the open."

He was right. With the men on each side of her, they began to run again. Where, she didn't know. Gabe didn't head in the direction of the car, which was just as well. It probably wasn't safe to go there.

"Did you see who fired those explosives?" Gabe asked Jinx. He stopped just behind a row of tall hedges near the street and looked around.

"No, but I think it must have come from one of those trees." He pointed to a cluster of towering oaks in the park area where they'd left the car.

Gabe glanced in that direction. "Yeah. The person probably climbed a tree and used some kind of modified artillery tube to deliver the canisters."

If so, that meant Jinx wouldn't have had time to fire them and then climb back down to run to the house. But Leigh wasn't about to buy that tree-climbing scenario. A modified artillery tube could be fired from anywhere, including the front lawn.

Gabe turned her toward him. "I need to get you out of here while I try to find out if Frank is still alive."

She was already shaking her head before he finished. "I'd rather stay with you."

"I can't—"

The sudden movement at the end of the row of hedges cut him off. All three shifted toward the person who rounded the corner.

"Mind telling me what the devil all of you are doing here?" Teresa Walters snarled. The woman looked harried. Not at all like the composed agent she'd seemed back at the clinic. Teresa gulped in her breath as if she'd just run a long distance.

"I might ask you the same thing," Gabe calmly remarked. "Did you just happened to be in the neighborhood?"

Teresa fired a tight glance at Jinx before she answered. "No, I was looking for you."

"Well, you obviously found us," Leigh confirmed. "I don't suppose you know who just tried to kill us?"

The other woman shook her head. "No. I didn't see anything or anybody."

If Gabe had any doubts if that was the truth, he didn't voice them. He tipped his head toward what remained of the house. "Frank Templeton might be dead in there. There's another body on the back porch, and you didn't see a thing. That's not a good endorsement for your skills of observation."

"I just arrived a few minutes ago," Teresa quickly assured him, obviously not bothering to address his sarcasm. "Now, perhaps you'd tell me how long you've been here and what happened?"

The sarcasm stayed in Gabe's voice. "Funny you should ask that. Leigh, Jinx and I arrived just a couple of minutes ago, too. No one answered the door, so we went inside to have a look around, and that's when someone started to shoot canister bombs at us. We were just about to call you and report it."

Teresa didn't look as if she bought that fish story at all. "Tell me what's going on, Gabe. Who's responsible for this?"

"I was hoping you could tell me," he answered. "Frank called and asked me to meet him."

"You actually saw him?" Teresa volleyed glances between Gabe and the house.

"No, but he asked me to meet him at midnight."

Leigh didn't want to put off the most obvious question any longer. "So why'd you come, Agent Walters?"

She didn't even hesitate. "The ATF had the place under surveillance, and when you showed up, they called me because I told them I wanted to talk to you. I got here as fast as I could."

Gabe took up where Leigh had left off. "And you just happened to be in Grand Valley, Texas?"

"No. I accessed your messages and heard the one Frank left on your machine in your apartment in New Orleans."

"But I erased that message," Gabe informed her.

Teresa shrugged. "There are ways, as you well know."

"Ways," Gabe repeated. "I guess you had to come up with plan B when I found that transmitter you'd planted in Leigh's bandage."

Leigh stared at the woman, waiting for her to deny it, but Teresa didn't deny anything. "That was my insurance that I'd be able to find you if you didn't follow orders. And I don't think I need to point out that I was right." She pulled out her phone. "Why didn't you and Leigh make your way to a safe house earlier?"

"But we did," Leigh said with sappy innocence. "We're standing in front of one now."

Again, Teresa didn't seem to react to that except to check her watch and take a surreptitious glance around the street where neighbors were starting to gather to watch the blaze. In the distance, Leigh could hear approaching sirens. Obviously, someone had alerted the local authorities. That didn't surprise her. Those explosions had jarred the entire neighborhood.

"I never thought you'd do something this stupid," Teresa mumbled. "You shouldn't have run from me."

"Well, someone didn't do a great job of providing security at the clinic, did they?" Leigh pointed out. "We had to fight our way past four gunmen and barely made it out of there alive."

"That was still no reason to stay on the run. Security failed," Teresa stated firmly, "and now we're trying to figure out why. We'll have answers soon."

"Forgive me if I don't hold my breath waiting for that to happen," Leigh retorted.

Teresa stared at her a moment. "We're on the same side, Leigh. Don't forget that."

"Are we actually on the same side? Because the lines are a little fuzzy here. Somebody is killing people and trying to kill others, namely Gabe and me, and all of that's happened while you and I are on the same flipping side. Makes me wonder if I'd be better off ending this association right now."

"You can't just *end* it," Teresa snapped. "You need protection, and I'm assigned to give it to you."

Leigh groaned. "I'd rather have a BB gun and a Boy Scout. I'd stand a better chance of making it out of this alive." She couldn't be sure, but she thought she heard Gabe try to muffle a laugh.

"You stand a better chance if you let me do my job."

"Once again, we don't agree. The only person I'm going to trust is Gabe. Got that? So you can just peddle your services somewhere else, Agent Walters. If you really want something to occupy your time, why don't you find out if Frank Templeton's body is inside that house?"

"I need to make a few calls," Gabe announced before Teresa could say if she would act on Leigh's suggestion. "And I need to get a closer look at the house."

Leigh was about to tell him that wasn't a good idea, but the look he gave her had her rethinking that. He obviously had something in mind and wanted her to play along.

"I won't be long," Gabe assured her. He pulled her aside and whispered the rest of what he had to say. "There's a silver car parked at the end of the street. Go there in a couple of minutes." He must have seen the look of uncertainty that went through her eyes because he gave her hand a gentle squeeze. "It's all right. I'll cover you until you're safe inside."

Leigh didn't like the idea of being left alone with Teresa, but then she could have said the same thing about making her way to that car. She just hoped that Gabe knew what he was doing.

When the men walked away, Teresa rifled through her purse and came up with a cigarette. She didn't light it but instead ran her fingers over it as if trying to decide if she really wanted to smoke it. "Gabe told me your memory was coming back," Teresa stated matter-of-factly. "Any truth to that?"

Gabe had said that to shake things up a little. It meant she, too, should stick to that story.

"I don't remember everything," Leigh answered. "But some key things have come back." Key things, if she counted the phone call to Gabe and the image of him naked. Pretty sparse pickings as far as memories went, but Leigh kept that part to herself.

"I suppose Gabe told you about all the problems you two were having before you disappeared?" Teresa asked.

Leigh looked back at Gabe. He was standing to the side of the house, his phone pressed to his ear. Jinx was making a call of his own. "Yes. We were talking about a divorce."

Teresa made a slight sound in her throat. "And do you know why?"

Leigh didn't think she cared much for the direction of this conversation. "Yes, I know. He made a mistake and put his trust in the wrong person, namely, Joe Dayton."

"Gabe told you that?" Teresa gave a heavy sigh and pushed back a wisp of hair that had slipped from her French twist. "He wasn't supposed to. He never sticks with the plan."

"I'm not absolutely sure, but I think I like that about him." Leigh added a dry grin because she knew it would rile the other woman.

Teresa snapped the cigarette in half and tossed it on the ground. "You're falling for him all over again, aren't you?"

Leigh stared at the cigarette for several seconds before she eased her gaze to Teresa. "Now, just why would that concern you?"

"Because I'd like to think we're friends."

Friends? Leigh didn't need her memory to know that wasn't true. "And why would you think that?"

"Well, I've known you for a long time now. We've even worked on some cases together."

"And this is leading…" Leigh gestured with her hand. "Where exactly?"

"Well, since you can't remember everything, I think it's only fair to warn you that Gabe hasn't always acted in your best interest. There were times when your marriage was rocky at best."

"Yes, I know. I'm still waiting for you to tell me where this is leading."

"It's not leading anywhere. I'm just trying..." But Teresa stopped and shook her head as if she shouldn't say anything else.

"Obviously. I think the term you're looking for, Teresa, is 'causing trouble.' You can save it. I already have more trouble than I can handle." Leigh turned and walked away.

She had no idea that Gabe had stepped up behind her until she heard his voice. "Anything wrong?" he asked.

"We have to talk," Leigh said softly. "But it can wait."

She saw an expression on Gabe's face that she had yet to encounter. Not quite anger but something close. Fury, perhaps. It actually frightened her, and she hoped this particular emotion wasn't aimed at her.

Gabe drew her away from Teresa. "There's been a slight change of plans. I just talked to Jinx, and we're getting the hell out of here, understand?"

She hesitated before giving a slow nod. "All right. Any idea how we're going to do that? I don't think Teresa will just let us leave without causing a fuss."

"Jinx will tell her to back off. Maybe this time she'll actually listen to him." He tipped his head to the silver-colored car parked at the end of the street. "That's where we're headed. Stay behind me."

Leigh nodded, but before she could take even a step, Gabe caught onto her arm. "Do you still trust me?" he asked.

She almost gave him a flippant comeback, but that tormented look in his eyes stopped her. Whatever was going on inside his head, it wasn't pleasant, and she thought its cause was more than what had just happened with the blast and the dead man.

"I trust you, Gabe." And she came up on her tiptoes and brushed a kiss on his cheek. To reassure him maybe, and maybe because she knew Teresa would see it. The kiss didn't stay on his cheek, however. Nor did it stay gentle and reassuring. With his breath coming out in rapid hot bursts, he gripped the back of her neck and captured her mouth in a searing kiss.

"Is there something else I should know about?" Leigh asked when he finally broke away from her. She couldn't imagine the situation being worse, but it was obvious that something had upset Gabe.

"We'll talk later."

That didn't do a thing to reassure her. God, what else had gone wrong?

"Wait a minute," Teresa barked when she saw them start to walk away. She covered the mouthpiece of her phone with her hand. "Just where do you think you're going?"

"It's all right, Teresa," Jinx called out. He came back across the yard toward her. Leigh didn't have to know specifically what Jinx was saying, but it was obvious that the woman was about to receive a dressing-down.

Gabe didn't waste any time. He led Leigh straight to the car, unlocking the vehicle with the remote on a key chain that he pulled from his pocket.

"Get in the back seat," he instructed. "And stay down. We'll leave just as soon as Jinx gets here."

She crouched on the floor but peered at Gabe over the seat. "Jinx?"

"He's coming with us."

Leigh didn't know how to react to that. She certainly

didn't want the man tagging along, but maybe Gabe needed him for something. Still, she didn't plan to let down her guard anytime soon.

"What the hell?" Gabe mumbled. With his gaze fixed on the passenger's window, he turned his weapon in that direction. "There's Frank Templeton."

Leigh popped up from her hiding space and saw him coming directly toward them. "He made it out of the house. I can't believe it."

The tall, red-haired man was hunched over and literally skulking his way around the other cars. To say he looked beleaguered was putting it mildly. His clothes were torn and dirty, and his hair tangled wildly around his face.

Gabe pushed the button to lower the window a fraction but didn't open the door. Leigh also noticed that he kept his hand on his gun. Not surprising. She wasn't in the frame of mind to trust anyone either. For all she knew, Frank could be the one behind this. He'd certainly had as much opportunity and motive as anyone else.

"Leigh," Frank said on a rise of breath. "Gabe found you. Thank God."

"Yes. Are you all right?"

"Not really. I was waiting in the house for Gabe, but someone tried to kill me."

"Yeah, I know. They tried to do the same thing to Gabe and me." She glanced around to make sure no one else was coming their way. "Listen, Frank, I don't have a lot of time to explain this, but I have amnesia, and I don't know what's going on."

He gave her a puzzled look, but that look soon turned to something more—alarm. "Neither do I, Leigh. That's why I wanted to talk to Gabe and you."

She shook her head, not understanding what he meant. "But why did you disappear if you didn't know what was going on?"

"For the same reason you did. It didn't take a genius to figure out that Dayton wanted us both dead."

"Dayton killed himself two years ago," Gabe reminded him.

"Yes, but he wasn't working alone. I knew Joe couldn't put together an operation like that on his own. Great day, we're talking three tons of weapons. Maybe more. It would have taken him years to siphon off that much without someone noticing."

Leigh had no idea the volume of weapons was that high. No wonder Gabe had figured the bulk of them hadn't been moved. Plus, they were hot goods. Probably every law enforcement agency would be looking for a cache like that. But in two years, only a few had surfaced.

Why?

An accomplice would have known the location of that storage facility. Well, maybe. Maybe Dayton hadn't trusted his partner with that kind of information. So, that meant Frank and she were possibly the only two people who even had a clue as to the cache's location.

And that made Frank a suspect.

Realizing that she very well could be looking at Dayton's accomplice after-the-fact, she wondered if she should just have Gabe arrest him on the spot. However, Frank was looking at her as if to decide the same thing.

"It's not me," Frank said firmly. "I had nothing to do with Dayton's plan. I didn't even see what was on that disk before it destroyed itself. Can you look me in the eye, Leigh, and say the same thing?"

"Absolutely."

"But how do you know?" he challenged. "You have amnesia."

"I don't need my memory to know that I'm not a criminal. If I'd seen something on that disk, I wouldn't have kept it a secret."

Frank kept his narrowed gaze on her as if trying to decide if he believed her. After a moment, he nodded. "Then someone else is out there. Someone who knows everything."

"Yes, and that person thinks we know the location of the weapons. He or she is willing to kill us to keep a secret. That's why it's important that you stay with us."

"I can't." His gaze cut to Gabe. "You need to get her out of here now."

"That was my plan. Jinx should be here any second. How about you? Where are you headed?"

"Someplace safe."

"Need a ride?" Gabe opened the door then, but it was more than just a friendly gesture. Gabe's body language and his raised gun made it seem more like an order. "We still have a few things to discuss."

Frank glanced at the drawn weapon and the still-blazing house. "I'll call you to set up another meeting. Someplace private. It's too dangerous for us to talk here." He started to move away.

"Wait," Gabe said in a stern whisper. "How can I reach you?"

"Don't know yet. I'm still looking for the accomplice, and I'm getting very close. Also, don't trust Teresa. There's something not right there." He raised his hand in a hasty farewell and disappeared into some shrubs.

"Shouldn't you go after him?" Leigh asked frantically.

"No. I won't leave you alone."

"But Frank might be able to tell us something."

"You heard what he said, Leigh. He doesn't know who did this. We'll just have to wait for his call. Besides, we're leaving."

Leigh craned her neck so she could look in the rearview mirror. It was Jinx. And from the look on his face, he was not a happy man.

Gabe climbed into the back seat with her, and Jinx got behind the wheel. "Let's get the hell out of here," Jinx insisted. "Now!"

Chapter 13

Gabe glanced behind him. Since Teresa wasn't in hot pursuit, he guessed she was still tied up with the call from the Bureau that Jinx had arranged. That call would buy them some time. Hopefully. But they needed to get away from Grand Valley and the safe house if they didn't want to get caught up in a full-scale investigation.

"Are you all right?" Gabe asked Jinx.

"I'm fine. Who was the man I just saw running from the car?"

Gabe met Jinx's gaze in the rearview mirror and gave him a you're-not-going-to-believe-this look. "Frank Templeton."

"Frank?" Jinx repeated. "I thought for certain that his body was somewhere in that burning house. I take it he's alive and well?"

"Alive, for sure," Gabe informed him. "I don't know

about the well part. He looked like hell. He said he still doesn't know who's doing this, that we shouldn't trust Teresa, and he'll call me to set up another meeting."

Gabe hadn't needed Frank's advice about trusting Teresa though. He had no plans to trust either Frank or her.

He checked the street behind them again. No sign of Teresa or anyone else. There was traffic, assorted emergency and law enforcement vehicles, but they were all headed toward the house.

Once they were away from the crime scene, he needed to have that talk with Leigh. She knew something was wrong. He could tell that from the side glances she kept tossing his way. Hell. Teresa had probably told her everything.

Jinx had just made it to the edge of town when his phone rang. Gabe was willing to bet it was Teresa, but he soon learned he would have lost that bet.

"Lieutenant Venegos," Jinx said to the caller. "Please tell me you have good news."

Gabe knew the name. Venegos was a Texas Ranger who often worked with the Bureau on high- and low-profile cases.

"Are you really all right?" Leigh whispered to him.

"I'm fine." She probably thought his somber mood had to do with their brush with death, but that was only part of it. "We have to talk," he let her know.

She nodded. Just nodded. That didn't do a lot to put him at ease. Damn Teresa and her big mouth.

"Our friend in the Texas Rangers found Philip about an hour ago," Jinx relayed when he hung up the phone. "He's safe. For now, anyway. He's using an assumed name—Tyler Wilkins."

Leigh moved to the edge of the seat. "My brother's in Houston?"

"No. He's living near San Antonio. Lieutenant Venegos tracked him down at the nightclub where Philip bartends. He didn't let Philip know anyone was looking for him."

"Did Venegos give you an address?" Gabe wanted to know.

"Yeah. Philip rented a place in the country, and the lieutenant thought it might be better for you to go there instead of the nightclub. He tried to call Philip's house, but he only got the machine. Some woman named Jenny recorded the message. Hopefully, I'll have more info on her before we get to San Antonio."

Gabe was sure Jinx would. By now, Venegos was probably tapping into every information source he had to help them. "Have you already assigned someone to tail Philip?"

Jinx nodded, but the eye contact he made with Gabe told him plenty. If the Texas Rangers could find Philip, the man needed protection. And fast. They had to get to Leigh's brother before someone else did.

Leigh settled back against the seat. "So now what—we just drive out to his house and surprise him?"

"You two will," Jinx answered. "You can drop me off at the field office in San Antonio so I can cover our tracks. I want to stop this information trail before someone else picks up on it."

She nodded, obviously understanding the need for that. "How long before we get there?"

"Four hours."

Of course, that wouldn't be a direct route, but Gabe knew it was necessary for them to cover their own tracks as well as Philip's. Fortunately, Jinx was very good at doing that.

Four hours. Soon they'd be able to see Leigh's brother and could hopefully stop anything bad from happening to him. Philip might also know where she'd been for the past two years, or better yet, he might know who was trying to kill her.

Gabe didn't dare hope for things to be wrapped up in a neat little package. If fact, he only hoped that Leigh could somehow forgive him for what had happened two years earlier.

He made another check of the highway before he angled his body toward her. "What did Teresa tell you back there at the house?"

Even in the dark car, he saw Leigh flinch. Maybe that was because of the abruptness of his voice. Or maybe it was because this was the last thing on earth she wanted to discuss with him.

After a couple of moments, she shrugged. "She was being catty, that's all. Did you two have a thing going, because she sounded a little jealous?"

"Tell me what she said," Gabe repeated, enunciating each word.

She cleared her throat and rubbed her index finger over her eyebrow. "Well, she claimed to be my friend and basically told me that you hadn't always acted in my best interest."

"And? Tell me everything, Leigh."

The fidgeting stopped, and she met his gaze head-on. "What is this all about?"

"Tell me what she said to you."

It seemed Leigh was about to clam up, but she huffed

and continued. "She was just trying to get to me, that's all. Listen, if you had an affair with her—"

"I didn't have an affair with her, and I want to know the rest of what she said."

"Gabe, this is ridiculous. What do—"

"Damn it, what did she say?"

She pulled back her shoulders. "About what?" Her voice rose to his level.

"You know about what. Now quit playing games with me. What the hell did Teresa say about the baby?"

Leigh felt as if he'd slapped her. The breath swooshed of her mouth. "Baby?" she managed to say. "What baby?"

But Gabe didn't answer. "Stop the car," he ordered Jinx.

Jinx glanced back at them. "Do I need to remind you that you're not out of danger?"

"Just stop the car, damn it! I need to talk to Leigh."

Jinx added some profanity of his own while he pulled onto the shoulder of the road. The moment he stopped, Gabe threw open the door, obviously ready to get out.

"Stay put," Jinx insisted. "But try not to take too long with this little heart-to-heart, will you? It's not a good idea to hang around here."

"What baby?" Leigh repeated the moment Jinx stepped outside and shut the door.

Gabe stared at her a long time before he answered. "*Our* baby."

She was absolutely certain she'd misunderstood him. That's why Leigh repeated those two words to herself. Our baby. Our baby.

"What are you talking about, Gabe?" But she was

almost afraid to hear what he had to say. "We have a baby?"

"No." Gabe cursed softly and looked away. "You thought you were pregnant, but it was a false alarm."

She almost asked for an explanation, but Leigh didn't need him to tell her. Images began to race through her head. Images of her standing in the middle of a room in a hospital gown, of her arm bandaged in a sling. Words followed those out-of-focus images. Words that wouldn't have made sense if Gabe hadn't just told her that she'd once thought she was pregnant.

"You shouldn't be out of bed," Gabe had said to her.

Leigh had just stared at him, her eyes filled not with tears but with anger. *"I heard what you said to Jinx. I heard every word. You didn't want me to have a baby."*

"I just wasn't expecting this. I thought—"

But Leigh had cut him off and moved into the hallway outside the room. *"I know what you thought. Well, don't worry, Gabe, you got your wish. There isn't a baby. The doctors did a test, and the results were negative."*

"My God, I remember." Leigh leaned her head against the window.

Almost afraid of what she'd see, she glanced at Gabe. He looked at if he'd just had a knife plunged into his heart. "How much do you remember?"

She wasn't even sure she could say it aloud. She took a deep breath. "The conversation we had in the hospital. You must have just found out that I wasn't pregnant."

"You were very upset," he said as if that explained everything. Gabe didn't even look at her. He stared out the other window. *"We* were upset," he added a moment later.

Leigh waited for him to continue—mainly because

she didn't have a clue what to say. Or do. This had obviously been a miserable time in their lives. The lowest of low points. Even now, it hurt just to recall those memories.

Gabe pushed his hand through his hair. "I didn't know that you suspected you were pregnant until the day before Dayton tried to kill you. You told Jinx, and then he told me."

She fired a glance at the man standing outside the car, but he had his attention focused on their surroundings. "Jinx?" she repeated. "Why would I tell him something like that before I let you know?"

"He's our friend, Leigh. I guess you thought you could talk to him about it. You asked him to keep it a secret. But he didn't. He came to me because he thought it was something I should know."

So, Jinx had betrayed her. Well, in a way. She hoped that was the only reason she had the feeling she couldn't trust the man.

"You overheard Jinx telling me," Gabe continued a moment later. "I didn't take the news well."

No, he hadn't. And just like the other images and past conversations, Leigh suddenly remembered that, too. "'I can't believe this,'" she repeated. "That's what you said to Jinx. 'I can't believe she'd do this knowing I'm not ready to be a father.'"

Gabe slowly brought his gaze back to her. "I did say that, yes."

"And then it turned out I wasn't pregnant after all." Leigh shuddered. There was one advantage to having amnesia. She was able to see the incident through eyes not clouded with so much emotion. Unlike Gabe. One look at his face and she knew he was experiencing an even greater pain than she was.

"Earlier, you said we'd agreed not to have children?" she asked.

"We'd agreed to disagree."

Oh. Leigh hadn't considered that angle. "And we had agreed to wait," she concluded. "Any particular reason, or do you just not like kids?"

"I like kids. A lot. It's just I've seen enough crime scenes and enough dead bodies to know just how fast life can end."

There was more to it than that. During their entire ordeal of running from gunmen and nearly getting killed, Gabe had shown absolutely no signs of weakness. But he was showing it now. Leigh figured she was getting a glimpse of a vulnerable side of Agent Gabe Sanchez that few people ever saw. It intrigued her. And made her ache.

"When I was eight, someone kidnapped my sister, Emily," he said softly.

"The one in the picture at your parents' house?"

Gabe nodded. "She was only eleven, and we were on our bikes less than a half mile from our house. A car pulled up next to us, and a man reached out and grabbed her." He snapped his fingers. "Just like that, she was gone."

Leigh barely managed to muffle her gasp. "My God. What happened to her?"

He kept his attention focused outside. "They found her body a week later in a dry creek bed. What they didn't find was the man who killed her. Every time you'd talk about wanting a child, all I could think about was losing someone I loved to a monster."

"I see."

And she did. From Gabe's point of view, having a baby would be like playing a game with stakes that were too high. There were tears in her eyes now, but Leigh hadn't been aware of them until she felt one spill down her cheek.

"I'm sorry about your sister. About Emily. And I understand why you didn't want to risk having a child of your own." She paused to collect her breath. "It's my guess that our disagreement about the pregnancy got all mixed together with what happened with Dayton. The truth is, I was probably as shocked about the possibility of being pregnant as you were. I'd just had a little more time to adjust to it than you had."

He looked at her then, his gaze combing over her face. "Is that what you remember?"

She shook her head. "I don't have to remember the incident to know that I probably didn't give you a fair shake because of all the mental junk I was going through."

For a while they said nothing else. He just looked at her, and Leigh just looked at him. In his eyes, she saw the swirl of emotions that had brought them to this point.

"I'm sorry," she let him know.

Surprised, he glanced at her. "Why are you sorry?"

"For the way everything turned out." She shook her head. "I don't even know if I'm the same person I was two years ago, but I suspect you haven't changed much."

"You're wrong. I've changed a lot."

And not necessarily for the better. She was responsible for that. She'd let the anger and bitterness drive her away from him. It didn't feel good to know that she'd been a quitter at one of the most important things in her entire life.

"I guess what I'm trying to say," she continued, "is that the things that brought us together five years ago are still there in full working order. The feelings. The connection. The people we are when we're together."

Gabe didn't say a word. He just stared at her.

She tried again. "I'm sorry about the argument, Gabe. Sorry that I left without trying to work things out with you. Sorry that I threw away what was no doubt a good thing. And I'm especially sorry that it took me all this time to figure out that I was wrong."

Leigh held her breath, and waited. She didn't have to wait long.

Gabe reached out and pulled her into his arms. Not for a kiss. Or even a hug. He just held her. And that was exactly what she needed from him.

Chapter 14

There wasn't a car in the driveway in front of Philip's house, but there was a huge Doberman sitting on the porch. The dog looked pretty territorial, and since they were about to invade its territory, Gabe hoped it didn't object too much.

"This might be just a weird case of nerves," Leigh said, staring at the porch as well. "But I don't think I like the idea of that dog being there."

"It's not a weird case of nerves," he assured her. "Not exactly anyway. You had a bad experience a couple of years ago. Some Dobermans came after you when you went to a house to interview a witness. You weren't hurt, but it scared you pretty bad."

"So, that explains why my heart feels ready to pound out of my chest. My body obviously remembers a lot of things my mind doesn't."

Gabe read a lot into that statement. Maybe too much. But it seemed pretty evident that Leigh still responded to him at least on a physical level. After the air-clearing they'd had in the car, he thought maybe she might start to respond beyond just the physical.

He wasn't sure how to feel about that. It was a lot to absorb, especially with everything else going on. He'd have to take it minute by minute and see how things progressed.

"We'll have to get past that dog to get inside, I suppose?" she asked.

Oh, yeah. And Gabe didn't think the fellow planned to move anytime soon. He wasn't barking. Yet. But he appeared to be growling. In other words, he was a watchdog, something he was glad Philip had. It might discourage anyone else from trying to get inside. Unfortunately, that left Gabe with one small problem— he had to find some way to get around the dog so they could get in. He didn't want to sit out in the open waiting for Philip to get home.

He parked the car behind an old barn. It was just a precaution, but he didn't want anyone to know they were there.

"I could carry you in," Gabe suggested when he saw Leigh still eyeing the dog.

"No, I can walk." But she thought about it first. And she latched onto her gun when they got out of the car.

Immediately, the dog shot to his feet. His posture was ready for combat, his teeth bared. A whisper-soft, feral growl rumbled from his throat. That put a dent in Leigh's resolve because she darted behind him. Gabe almost laughed. Here, she'd faced down gunman without so much as a whimper, and yet the dog terrified her.

"He'll probably be friendly once he realizes we're not burglars," he remarked as they walked up the steps.

As if to prove Gabe wrong, the dog chose that exact moment to growl. It was more of a perfunctory grumble, but it was enough to send Leigh crashing into him again. "It'll be all right," he murmured to both the dog and Leigh.

He cautiously offered the dog the back of his hand, but the canine didn't move from his position. Not right away. A few moments later, he stooped lower.

"Sit," Gabe firmly told the animal.

Thank God he listened. Within seconds, the canine's jaw relaxed, and he began thumping his tail on the porch.

"See?" Gabe said. "He's friendly."

From the grip Leigh still had on his arm, she probably didn't believe that. "So, how do we get inside? And please don't tell me we have to wait out here until Philip gets home."

He fished into his pocket and brought out the key. "This was under the mat in your rental car, the one with your fingerprints on it."

"And you think it'll fit this lock?"

"Only one way to find out." Gabe slipped the key into the lock and with one turn it opened. "Well, I guess you've been here before. Anything look familiar?"

She stepped inside, her gaze darting around the dark room. "Not so far. Can we turn on the lights?"

"We'd best not." Instead, Gabe switched on the small flashlight attached to Jinx's key ring. It didn't help much, but he didn't want someone seeing the light and getting suspicious.

The place was small, the living room and kitchen

bleeding together into one rectangular room. There was a hallway that Gabe soon learned led to two bedrooms. He quickly checked them out and found them unoccupied.

He breathed a little easier when he saw there was no sign of struggle. No sign to indicate that anything was wrong. Hopefully, that meant Philip was safe.

"Anything?" she asked when he came back into the living room.

Gabe shook his head. In this case, no news might be good news.

He picked up a piece of paper from the small table near the door. "'Jenny, I might be late,'" Gabe read aloud. "'I've got errands to do after I get off from work. Might not see you until breakfast. There are leftovers if you're hungry. Philip.'"

"So, we're alone?" Leigh asked.

"Seems that way."

He heard her pull in her breath. She put her gun aside on the table, shoved her hands in the pockets of her shorts and walked around the living room. He followed her gaze to every piece of furniture, to every knickknack. If she recognized anything, it didn't show in her eyes.

"There are no pictures," she mumbled.

No. Gabe had looked for that when he searched the place. Maybe Philip hadn't wanted to add personal touches because they'd been in hiding.

"I didn't see any women's clothes in the closets either," Gabe explained. He slipped his gun back into the slide holster on his jeans. "So, I guess it's safe to say you didn't live here."

She ran her fingertips over the back of the sofa while

she continued to walk around the room. "Maybe Philip can tell me where I do live. If he knows, that is. Maybe I kept it from him, too."

Gabe doubted that. The fact she had a key to the house meant she'd been in contact with her brother.

She groaned softly. "It seems so strange standing here, knowing I should recognize something. Anything. But I don't. With the exception of the few things I've recalled, the only past I know is the one I've made with you these last two days."

And with that, Leigh's gaze skimmed over him.

Something in the air changed. Not the smell of fear and danger that he'd practically grown accustomed to. No. This was a different sensation. A tangle of heat that could only happen between a man and a woman who'd been intimate in just about every way possible.

Gabe didn't even try to talk himself out of the step he took toward her. He reached out. And touched her cheek. Her eyelids fluttered down, and she moved into his touch, letting her lips brush against his fingers.

He could have just gone with the heat. He could have just taken the moment and pushed it until they ended up in bed. Or on the floor. But he wanted to give her more than some flash that was over before they knew what had hit them.

"We have other memories," he said to her. Gabe inched closer, careful to keep a fraction of space between their bodies. That was for his sake, not hers. If she touched him, what control he had left would go straight out the window. "Memories of the first time we kissed."

"Tell me," she whispered.

"It was in the French Quarter. I'd taken you out to

do the tourist thing. A date," he added. "I kissed you in the doorway of one of those voodoo parlors. Well, maybe it was more than just one kiss. After about ten or fifteen minutes, the owner said we should get a room."

She smiled, as he'd hoped she would.

"And the first time we made love—that's a memory, too," he continued. In fact, as memories went, that one was as good as it got. "It was on the back porch at my aunt Martha's house near Corpus Christi. A place not much different from this one." His gaze slid around the room before resettling on her. "And we were alone, the only two people for miles around."

"Like now."

"Like now," he confirmed. "Aunt Martha had put an old bed on that screened porch. I used to like to sleep there when I'd visit her. The place had a tin roof, and it was raining. Not loud, just a summer drizzle, but it made enough noise to blend right in with the sounds of that old bed. The springs were rusty and creaked a little each time we moved."

"Were the sheets white?" Leigh asked.

"I think so. Do you remember that?"

"Maybe." She shrugged, causing her breasts to brush against his chest. "Or maybe it's just wishful thinking."

Now it was his turn to smile. "My attention wasn't on the color of the sheets. It was on you, Leigh. Completely on you."

"White sheets," she repeated. "An old bed on a porch. Summer rain. Yes. I think I do remember that."

With that wistful look on her face, Gabe couldn't resist tasting her. He touched his mouth to hers.

"The place smelled like fresh peaches," Gabe's drawl brushed over the words. "So did we. We'd been picking them right before the rain started. Our clothes were wet by the time we made a run to the porch."

He might have said more, might have continued the seductive game they were playing if she hadn't caught onto his shoulders. That was all the encouragement he needed to put an end to the talking. He took her mouth instead.

Gabe latched onto a handful of her hair and brought her to him. The kiss was filled with all the fire and heat that had been simmering between them for days.

"This time, I'm not stopping," she mumbled. "I don't care what I remember."

That invitation was just what he wanted to hear. The sound he heard after that, however, wasn't.

Gabe cursed. "Someone's coming," he let Leigh know.

Outside, the dog started to bark.

Chapter 15

Leigh and Gabe unwound themselves from each other immediately and hurried to the window. A bright red compact car stopped directly in front of the house. They barely had time to grab their weapons before she heard someone walking up the steps to the porch.

"Is it Philip?" she whispered.

"Maybe. Don't make a sound."

She hadn't planned to do that, but it soon became apparent that if this was a would-be killer, then he or she was an inept one. The person made enough noise to wake the dead. There was a jangle of keys in the lock and a not-so mumbled string of profanity when the door didn't open right away.

"Get down, Toby," the man yelled. Not an angry yell, exactly. He sounded more annoyed than anything.

"Stop it. And don't lick my face, for Christ's sake. You got doggy breath."

"It's Philip," Gabe informed her. That realization, however, didn't cause him to lower his gun.

The door flew open, and the man walked in, still mumbling under his breath. He reached for the light switch but froze when he realized he wasn't alone. "Holy freaking hell! What are you two trying to do— scare me to death?" Philip pressed a hand over his heart. "How about letting a guy know you're in here before he comes walking in on you?"

Leigh couldn't manage to say anything, but Gabe greeted her brother. "Hello, Philip."

"Gabe." As greetings went, it was rather frosty, but Gabe's had been none too friendly either. "Well, I see you finally found her," Philip commented. "Not that it surprises me. I knew it was just a matter of time."

Philip tossed his keys onto the table and aimed his attention at Leigh. Even though the room was dark, she could still see the concern on his face. "Ever hear of a telephone, sis? It's an amazing invention that allows you to keep in touch with people who are worried sick about you."

Before Leigh could say anything, Philip put his arms around her and pulled her to him. "Now, start explaining," he said in a much softer voice that Gabe probably couldn't hear. "Just what are you doing here with Gabe? And I'm not talking about what you were doing immediately before I walked in. I can figure out that part. What I want to know is what you're *really* doing here with him."

God, where should she start? This wasn't a ten-second explanation. "We have to talk," Leigh simply said. She reached around him and flicked on the light switch.

"Yeah, well, that's what I had in mind, too. A long talk where you do a lot of expla—" His eyes lifted toward the bandage on her head. "What the hell happened to you?"

"It's a long story." She took a deep breath. "Gabe says you're my brother."

Philip stared at her a moment and then made a *yeah, right* sound. She looked at Gabe, silently pleading with him to help with the explanation.

He helped. Gabe spelled it out. "Leigh has amnesia. She doesn't remember much about her life."

Her brother volleyed confused glances between Gabe and her. "Is this some kind of sick joke? Because if it is—"

"It's no joke," she verified.

"Hell." Philip opened his mouth several times as if to add something to that. He finally leaned against the wall and blew out several quick breaths. "Is it temporary?"

She shrugged. "Hopefully. I've started to remember a few things."

"But not me?" Philip tapped his chest. "Not your own brother?"

"No, I'm sorry, I don't."

"But you remember Gabe—"

"No," Leigh interrupted. "I can recall bits and pieces, but I don't remember much about anyone or anything." She took a step closer. "Listen, Philip, how much do you know about what I've been doing for the last two years?"

"A lot. You're my sister, for Christ's sake."

"Then maybe you can answer a few questions. Someone tied me up and tossed me in a lake near New Orleans, and I wondered if you knew anything about it."

His eyes widened significantly, and he cursed. "Someone tried to kill you?"

"Yes. Any idea who might have wanted to do something like that to me?"

"No, of course not." Philip pushed his hand through his sandy-brown hair and made his way to the sofa so he could sit down. "Good God, are you all right?"

"I've been better." At least, she was pretty sure she had been.

Gabe maneuvered her to the chair in front of Philip. "Did Leigh say anything about going to New Orleans?" he asked her brother.

"No. When she came by the club in San Antonio where I work, she told me she had to take a trip, but she didn't say where she was going."

Leigh jumped on that right away. "I was in San Antonio?"

Philip nodded. "Of course. That's where you live. You have a house there."

A house. She finally knew where she lived. Leigh wanted to ask him more, but there were more important things to discuss. "I don't think I'm the only one in danger, Philip. I think you might be in danger, too."

"Yeah, I know. It's to do with those computer searches someone's making."

"You know about that?"

"Sure. That's all you've talked about lately. In fact, you said if you hadn't come back from your trip in three days, I was to call Gabe. I planned to call him this morning."

So, she'd made contingency plans. That meant she

had at least considered the possibility that something would go wrong. And it obviously had.

It seemed as if Philip was about to say something else, but the phone rang. He got up from the sofa and checked the caller ID box. "I'll take this call in the bedroom. Nothing critical. Just a friend. I won't be long."

Leigh actually welcomed his departure. She wanted a few moments to regain her composure.

"Are you okay?" Gabe asked. He pulled her into his arms.

"Not really. I have a headache."

"Maybe coffee will help. Come on. I'll make some." He led her into the kitchen and had her sit at the table. Gabe had no sooner reached for the coffeemaker when she heard another car outside. He pulled back the curtain and glanced out the window. "We have company. Get your gun."

Her heart sank. The emotional upheaval of seeing her brother had already drained her, and Leigh now had to force herself to respond to yet another threat. She snatched her gun from the table and faced the door. Gabe did the same.

"Did you see who it is?" Leigh asked. The dog started to bark again.

"It's a woman, I think. Philip's friend, Jenny. Hopefully."

Yes, Leigh hoped that, too. For a moment anyway. But the hope soon vanished, and what felt like the onset of a panic attack followed. She had no idea what this sudden surge of emotions was all about, but she didn't want Jenny to come through that door.

"Something's wrong," Leigh mumbled.

Gabe glanced at her. "Christ. You're as pale as a ghost. Take a deep breath."

"It won't help," she managed to say. She felt her throat tighten. "Something's wrong."

"Get in the bedroom with your brother. Now! I'll be in there as soon as I'm finished here."

The front door flew open, and because there wasn't time for her to get into the bedroom, Gabe pushed her behind him.

"He stripped off his clothes again on the way over here," the dark-haired woman called out.

She backed through the door and held open the screen with her shoulder. From that angle, she couldn't have possibly seen Leigh or Gabe. Nor did she immediately notice them. Leigh figured that's because the woman had a squirming, nearly naked child in the crook of her arm, and her attention seemed focused on putting a shirt over the child's head.

"I swear, Philip, this kid definitely takes after you," the woman continued. "Are you—"

She turned toward them, her startled blue eyes going from Gabe to the gun he had aimed at her. She reacted quickly, and in a clatter of motion, she tried to swing the child behind her and open her purse.

She wasn't successful at either.

"Who are you?" Gabe asked.

"A friend of Philip's. What have you done to him?" The woman's frightened gaze moved from Gabe to Leigh, and she let out a noisy breath of relief. "Thank God, Leigh, you're here. I didn't even see you back there. You scared me to death."

"Are you Jenny?" Gabe, again. Leigh couldn't seem to make herself speak.

The woman nodded. "And you're Leigh's husband, Gabe. I recognize you from some pictures she has at the house. I didn't know you were coming back with her. I wish I had. I nearly wet my pants when I saw you here with that gun."

"Sorry." Gabe lowered his weapon. "I didn't know I'd be coming. Things just sort of happened that way."

The child began to squirm again, and Jenny placed him on the floor. He broke into a run around the coffee table and stopped right beside Leigh.

"Hi," he said with perfect clarity, and he moved his chubby fingers as if waving at her. With the exception of a diaper, the child was naked.

He tilted his head, causing the loose, dark curls to bounce haphazardly. His wide green eyes held just a hint of mischief. That grin, however, held more than just a hint.

"He's a beautiful child," Leigh said softly, wondering if this was her nephew. But Jenny probably didn't hear her. The woman dropped onto the sofa and closed her eyes, undoubtedly recovering from the fright she'd just had.

Leigh couldn't resist touching those curls, but when she reached out, she remembered that she still held her gun. She quickly lowered it to her side and brushed her fingers through his hair.

The boy pointed toward the bandage on Leigh's head. "Ouchie. Boo-boo. Up, up." He held out his arms for her to take him, and Leigh did, after she put her gun on the bookshelf. She could only guess that he knew her well to go to her so easily.

"What's your name?" she asked, wondering if he was even old enough to tell her.

"Bitty bitty pider," he chattered, repeating the syllables so that they ran together. He gave her a wet, noisy kiss on the cheek.

The kiss made her smile. She didn't know why, but it seemed to be the exact thing she needed. It felt…right.

So incredibly right.

Leigh pulled in her breath and stared at the boy's face. Something was familiar. Something—

"He wants you to sing 'Itsy Bitsy Spider,'" Jenny clarified. The woman placed her purse and the child's clothes on the coffee table. "It's his latest obsession. He's already had me sing it to him at least three dozen times this morning."

Leigh wasn't sure she remembered the words to that particular song, but it didn't matter. Philip came barreling into the room.

Her brother gave each of them a wild-eyed glance before his attention settled on Jenny. "Did you tell them?"

"Tell them what?" Jenny asked.

"Tell *them*," Philip emphasized. He gave a series of awkward nods.

Jenny threw her hands up in the air. "I haven't got a clue what you're talking about. I just got here and found Leigh and her husband. Why didn't you tell me she was bringing him back with her?"

"They don't know, all right?" Philip practically shouted. "Leigh has amnesia." And with that, he turned to her. "I didn't want to tell you this way—"

"Tell me what?" Leigh hated that look of fear she saw in his eyes.

"Bitty bitty pider," the child repeated. He caught onto Leigh's cheeks with both hands and tried to force her to give him her attention. She would have if she hadn't instinctively known that Philip was about to tell her something she needed to hear.

"You honestly don't have any memory of this?" Philip asked.

"Of what? Just tell me what's wrong."

Philip gulped in a huge chunk of air. "He's your son."

It took several moments for those words to have any meaning whatsoever. It took even more time for Leigh to sort out that Philip had referred to the little boy in her arms. "My son. This is my son?"

"Your son?" Gabe put his hands on his hips and gave her a scalding look. "What the devil's going on here? You had a baby?" But he didn't wait for her to answer. His gaze swept in Philip's direction.

"*Your* son," Philip clarified. "Yours and Leigh's."

Chapter 16

Oh, God.

Leigh didn't have the energy to become hysterical. Nor the inclination. That probably had something to do with the child she held. Leigh felt only an odd sort of rightness. Something deeper and stronger than a memory. Love, definitely.

Immediate, unconditional love.

One glance at Gabe, however, and she knew he didn't feel that sense of rightness. He looked well past furious, and he was no doubt about to aim all that fury at her.

"Start explaining," Gabe said through clenched teeth.

She cleared her throat. "I take it you don't know about this?"

"No, and so help me, Leigh, you'd better have some answers. Is this my son?"

But Leigh guessed he already had the answer, and it

was a definite yes. The boy was a miniature version of Gabe. His hair, his coloring, the shape of his face. Her eyes, though, those green eyes were a genetic copy of her own. She didn't know why she hadn't noticed that when he first came through the door. Or maybe she had. Maybe that's what all those odd feelings were about.

"He's your son." Philip stepped between them. "His name is Houston Gabriel Sanchez."

"Houston," Leigh repeated. She immediately thought of the message she'd left on Gabe's answering machine. *If something goes wrong, get to Philip in Houston.* Except she probably hadn't said *in* but rather *and*. She must have wanted Gabe to protect her brother and her son.

Their son.

A son she obviously hadn't told him about.

Oh, God.

"All right, we have some volatile issues to discuss," Philip started. "I want everyone to take a deep breath and calm down."

Following his uncle's instructions, Houston took a loud, exaggerated breath and giggled. He gave Leigh another of those sloppy kisses, and despite the turmoil going on inside her, she returned it.

"I don't want to calm down," Gabe informed Philip. "I want answers. Now, I know Leigh can't remember why she'd mess me over this way, but you know why, Philip. Tell me why you two did this to me."

"I knew it!" Philip aimed a finger at his sister. "Leigh, I don't know how many times I told you this would blow up in your face. And was I right? Obviously." He fired his gaze back to Gabe. "You know how stubborn she can be. I begged her to tell you, and she wouldn't."

"Why wouldn't I?" Leigh asked, praying there was a reason she'd understand.

"Because you didn't think it was safe to come out of hiding. You made me swear not to tell him, or you said you'd disappear. Well, I swore to keep your secret and look where it got me, huh? Gabe is about ready to rip out my internal organs. And you know what, Leigh? I don't blame him one little bit for wanting to do that."

That prompted another round of the song from Houston.

Leigh suddenly felt sick to her stomach. Her son's cheerful song certainly wasn't congruent with what she'd just learned.

Gabe looked ready to yell, but the child must have stopped him. Gabe's mouth twitched. His eyes narrowed to slits. But still he didn't yell. "Leigh told me the pregnancy was a false alarm," he said to Philip.

"That's because the test at the hospital was negative. So, Leigh left thinking there was no baby. But she kept having these symptoms and finally went to another doctor. He confirmed that she was indeed pregnant." Philip huffed. "But before you jump down my throat, Gabe, I didn't know about any of this until almost a year later. Not until Leigh showed up here with Houston."

Gabe took one calculated step toward Philip. "And at that point you didn't think to call me to let me know that I had a son?"

"Of course I wanted to call you, but Leigh said she would just disappear again. And she could have, too. She was scared, Gabe. She said someone was trying to kill her."

And that was still apparently true. However, Leigh

didn't care much for the way she'd handled this situation. Obviously, Gabe didn't either.

She looked at her son's face. "I don't remember anything about him. I don't even know how old he is."

"Eighteen months," Jenny provided. "He was born on Valentine's Day."

That got Gabe looking in the other woman's direction. "I take it you work for Leigh?"

She nodded. "I guess you could say I'm a bodyguard-nanny. I was a cop for six years, and Leigh wanted someone who could protect her son if it came down to that."

So, according to Philip and Jenny, she'd been concerned about safety. Leigh had already known that, since she'd disguised herself, but it was a chilling reminder to realize she'd feared for Houston as well.

Gabe glanced around the room, his gaze landing on her. For a moment. That razor-sharp glare dismissed her and moved back to Jenny. "Do you, Leigh and, uh, Houston all live here?"

"No, we stay at the house in San Antonio."

"But your voice is on Philip's answering machine," he reminded her.

"Leigh had me do that because of those computer inquiries about Philip and her. Just a precaution, she said."

Leigh glanced down at her son, but Houston had his attention solely on Gabe. She saw Gabe glance at the child several times.

"Who?" Houston asked, pointing toward Gabe.

No one said anything, but their attention all turned toward Leigh. "It's Daddy," she answered, the word sticking in her throat.

It apparently stuck in Gabe's throat as well because

he didn't utter a word. Houston did. "Da-dee. Da-dee," he repeated and clapped his hands.

Gabe motioned for her to get up. "We have to talk. *Now.* Let's go outside."

"Here, I'll take him," Jenny offered, already holding out her hands for the child. Houston went right to her.

"You want me to go with you, sis?" Philip asked, obviously concerned about Gabe's mood.

Leigh shook her head. "Thanks though." She deserved anything Gabe dished out, and she didn't want an audience for it.

By tacit agreement, they went outside through the back door. Leigh didn't stop walking when she went down the steps and into the yard. She felt as if she would explode if she didn't keep moving, and if she had to look Gabe in the eye. She couldn't imagine what he was feeling right now, but it couldn't be good.

"You should have told me," Gabe let her know as they started down a narrow path away from the house. Thankfully, the dog stayed on the back porch and didn't try to follow them. Leigh didn't want to add the Doberman to what she already had to face.

Gabe kicked at a cluster of dandelion fluff, causing little white umbrellas to scatter everywhere. "You had no right."

"I know. I'm sorry."

He didn't seem to hear her. "How the hell could you do this to me?"

"I don't know." And Leigh really didn't know. If the same scenario played out now, she knew she would tell Gabe about their son. Even if he rejected her and Houston, she would have still told him the truth and relied on him to help her keep their child safe.

They reached a small pond and stopped under a cluster of live oak trees. It was a tranquil place with ducks and lily pads floating on the water. Somewhere in the distance, she could hear wind chimes. It was definitely too tranquil for the storm brewing between them.

"I don't care what your plans were," Gabe continued. "From now on, you *won't* cut me out of my son's life."

No, she wouldn't. Of course, he hadn't mentioned anything about wanting to stay in her life. It didn't surprise Leigh. This was, well, unforgivable. Unforgivable for Gabe. And for her.

"I'm waiting for an answer," Gabe insisted when Leigh didn't say anything.

Leigh slumped against the tree. "I have no intention of cutting you out of Houston's life again." She slid downward and sat on the ground. "Sweet heaven, you don't think I can justify what I've done, do you?"

"No." He had his fists clenched at his sides, and the veins in his neck felt ready to burst.

She shook her head. "I lied to you. I kept your son from you. What kind of person does something like that, Gabe? No wonder I have amnesia. I don't want to have to remember all the truly rotten things I've done."

That wasn't especially what he wanted to hear. He was spoiling for an argument and didn't want her to concede so easily.

Leigh looked up at him. "Well, say something. Anything. Go ahead and yell at me."

His fists clenched even tighter until he felt his nails dig into his skin. But he couldn't yell. This was a hurt, a wound, that cut all the way to his soul. Yelling wouldn't do a thing to fix that.

"I can see the pain in your eyes." Leigh's voice was the only sound around them. "I don't know how I can ever make it up to you."

"You can't," he snapped.

"I know." She caught her bottom lip between her teeth.

Gabe tried to hang on to the anger, but he felt it slip a considerable notch when he saw a tear spill down her cheek. He slowly lowered himself to the ground beside her. "I hate it when you cry."

She quickly wiped away the evidence. "Sorry." Leigh turned away from him. It didn't fool Gabe. He knew there were still fresh tears in her eyes. "What are we going to do?"

He wished like hell he knew. This wasn't a broken promise or a heated argument. This was his son. He'd lost a year and a half of his son's life, and all because Leigh hadn't trusted him with the truth. She hadn't trusted him to protect them both.

"I don't know a thing about kids," Gabe mumbled. That seemed the least of his worries, but it was a worry. Besides, it seemed less explosive than discussing the other aspects of this issue.

"Neither do I. I don't even know that song he likes. The song Houston likes," she corrected, emphasizing his name. "I don't even know why I named him Houston."

Gabe blew out a long breath. "Probably because that's where you conceived him. If I've done the math right, a little over two years ago we spent a couple of weeks in Houston working on a case. When we were done, we stayed an extra couple of days for a second honeymoon."

She wiped away another tear and glanced at him. "You don't doubt he's your child, do you?"

He felt the muscles in his jaw jump. "No. He's mine." He had no doubts about that. The only doubts he had were about Leigh. "He looks just like me."

"Yes. Except he has my eyes."

Gabe had noticed. He'd never be able to look into Houston's face without seeing Leigh's eyes. DNA sure had a warped sense of humor.

"So, what do we do?" she repeated.

He still wanted to yell and blast her with all the emotions that bounced around inside him. But he was too beat to do that. Besides, Houston added a new wrinkle not only to his personal life but to security measures. Right now, Gabe had to make that his first priority.

"We'll have to deal with all of this later," he let her know. "We can't stay here much longer."

"Yes," she mumbled and then repeated it. "But where will we go?"

"A safe house."

"I shouldn't have to remind you that wasn't the answer for Frank."

"Not an FBI safe house," Gabe corrected. "I have to find out who's trying to kill us. I can't do that if I'm worried about Houston's safety." And hers, of course. He was still too angry to add that part. "My brother has a place near Corpus Christi. He's not there this time of year, so we can use it. Shouldn't take more than a couple of hours to make sure it's safe enough for you and the others to stay there."

That quickly brought Leigh to her feet. "Gabe, I don't want to be tucked away in some house while you're out chasing bad guys."

"That's too bad. The rules have changed. One of us has to watch Houston. Whoever is after you could use him to get to us."

The color drained from her face. "You mean the way they tried to use Philip."

"Worse than that. Philip's a grown man and can take care of himself. My son can't."

My son. The words rang through his head, and Gabe wondered if he would ever be able to say that and not remember the pain Leigh had caused him. At the moment, it sure seemed like too much to hope for.

Leigh pressed her fists against each side of her head. "This would be so much easier if I just had my memory back. Then I might know who's behind everything."

That was true, but since they couldn't wait around for that to happen, Gabe had to go about this from a different angle. "Maybe I can figure it out some other way. There might be something at your house, some kind of information maybe that you've stored in your computer."

She seemed to give that some thought and then nodded. "Maybe. After all, I knew someone was making computer inquiries. I had to learn that somehow. Maybe I kept notes."

It was certainly worth a try. Eventually, they had to get lucky. "I need to work out some arrangements. And I need to call Jinx to let him know what's going on. Houston can stay with Jenny and Philip while you and I make a quick trip to your house. We'll take Philip's car." That way, it might throw off Teresa or anyone else who happened to have a description of Jinx's vehicle. "While we're in San Antonio, I'll have my father arrange for security at my brother's place."

"Yes," she said softly. "And Gabe? For what it's worth, I'm really sorry for not telling you about Houston."

It was worth a hell of a lot. One day, when the anger had faded some, he just might tell her that.

Chapter 17

Leigh hoped a quick shower and a change of clothes would clear her head so she could find something valuable in the information on her computer. So far, neither the shower nor the comfortable cotton dress had worked. She still couldn't find what she needed, but she continued to search through the information while Gabe answered the call that came in on his phone. What she saw on the screen in front of her didn't please her.

There were notes about the computer inquiries—dates and times when the records had been accessed—going back almost the entire two years since she'd disappeared. There was even a summary of the weapons that had been found a few weeks earlier in that raid of the militia compound. She'd apparently known those weapons were from Dayton's original cache. However, what was missing was any speculation about the identity of Dayton's accomplice.

In other words, another dead end.

Of course, she hadn't thought that she'd leave such sensitive information in a home computer, but Gabe had been right—it was worth a try. It was a good use of time while they waited for his father to set up security at the house in Corpus Christi.

She got up from the computer and stretched. "Nothing," Leigh mumbled under her breath. And that nothing just didn't apply to her computer files either. As she'd done at Philip's, she glanced around the room but didn't recognize anything about the place she'd called home for over a year.

Nothing.

To her brain, it was just a three-bedroom house in a somewhat modest subdivision on the north side of San Antonio. If it hadn't been for the upgraded security system and burglar bars on the windows, it probably would have seemed like the home of any other single mom with a toddler.

To her heart though, the house was much more than that.

It had become her hiding place. A place she'd kept her child from his father. What thought process had she used to reach the point where she would do something like that? Leigh didn't know and wondered if she would ever understand the actions she'd taken.

Behind her, Gabe was on his cell phone with Teresa. Leigh didn't bother to ask how the woman had gotten the number. She'd already learned that Agent Walters was capable of retrieving such things as phone numbers and messages. It was yet one more reason not to trust her.

As if Leigh needed another reason.

If it turned out that Teresa was behind these attempts to kill her, Leigh wouldn't forgive herself for not stopping the woman back in Grand Valley.

She heard Gabe mention two names. Men's names that she didn't recognize, but she knew from other parts of his conversation that they were names of the two people who'd died at the safe house. *Hired guns*, Gabe added. But he didn't seem to have the answer as to who hired them.

She left Gabe in the study and walked through to the adjoining family room. Something squeaked when she stepped onto the thick carpet, and the sound sent her heart racing. It took her a moment to figure out that it was her son's toy turtle. She automatically picked it up and tossed it into the nearby toy box.

Too bad the rest of her problems couldn't be solved so easily.

Gabe had only been back in her life a couple of days. Mere hours. And for all practical purposes, he'd been a stranger when he pulled her out of that lake. At first, she'd distrusted him, argued with him and fought the attraction that had immediately drawn her to him.

And somewhere along the way, she'd fallen in love with him all over again.

Leigh stood there next to her son's toy box and let that sink in. She was in love with Gabe. With her husband. Other than those who claimed love at first sight, this was probably some kind of record. It certainly didn't make things easier, especially since she had no idea if Gabe and she could even have a future together.

So, the real question was—what was she going to do about it? Or better yet, what would Gabe do about it?

Would he even consider forgiving her? Would he risk giving her another chance?

She turned and walked back through the kitchen to find him, but Gabe wasn't in the study where she'd left him. Leigh didn't panic. She knew he wouldn't leave her alone in the house. He'd probably come to the same conclusions she had about the information on the computer—that it wasn't helpful—and decided there was no reason to keep staring at the screen.

Leigh followed the hallway to the end and found him in Houston's bedroom. The walls had been painted sunshine yellow, and there was a double bed next to the crib. She'd likely spent many nights sleeping in her son's room, probably because she'd feared for their safety.

Gabe's back was to her, his gaze focused on something on the dresser. She glanced over his shoulder to see what had captured his attention. It was a photograph of Gabe.

"Thank you for that," he said without looking back at her.

"It seems a paltry substitute now. I must have been scared. I'm not trying to make excuses, because I know what I did was wrong. It was stupid not to trust you to protect us." Frustrated with his silence, and her own babbling, Leigh shook her head. "Look, I wish you'd just yell or something and get it over with. I know you're furious but—"

"Yeah, I am," he snapped.

She waited for more. But that seemed to be the sum total of what should have been a tirade. Gabe certainly had a right to a vent and rant.

"That's it? That's all you're going to say?" Leigh demanded. God, she was practically picking a fight, but she couldn't stand the silent treatment any longer. She deserved to be yelled at. "Will you at least look at me?"

He did. Gabe eased around to face her. And face her, he did. Leigh immediately regretted that she'd issued such a demand. There was something almost dangerous in the depths of those fiery blue eyes, and there was definitely something unnerving about the way he combed his gaze over her.

Gabe took a single step toward her, nearly halving the distance between them. The room suddenly seemed very, very small. And where had the air gone?

Leigh held her ground. Barely. "What are you going to do?" She felt her pulse sprint out of control. Not from fear. Not this. This was something that stirred deep within her blood.

His gaze never left hers. "Get on the bed."

She'd braced herself to hear Gabe say or shout almost anything. But not that. Certainly not that. Sweet heaven. The timing was all wrong.

Wasn't it?

Then, why did she feel that slow melting heat slide down the length of her entire body?

He caught onto her arm and maneuvered her to the bed. "Sit down. I want to check your bandage."

"Oh." That. Just that. Leigh tried to force herself not to be disappointed. Or scream. After all, the timing reeked for practically everything that had crossed her mind in the last thirty seconds. And a lot of things had crossed her mind.

Gabe stooped, pulled her foot into his lap and unwound the bandage. "When you get to my brother's house, you'll need a doctor to take a look at this."

"Of course."

"It seems to be healing," he continued. "But it wouldn't hurt to have those stitches checked."

"Sure." Leigh groaned when she heard her polite, clinical tone. It matched Gabe's to a tee, but it was nowhere near a match for what she was feeling inside. "If you yell at me, it might make you feel better."

He rewrapped the bandage and kept his attention focused solely on that. "Why are you so anxious to hear me raise my voice, huh?"

"Because I'm hoping it'll get us talking again. Really talking. And I don't mean this chitchat stuff either. I mean a real, pertinent discussion about us, and about our son."

Gabe looked up at her. And looked. She did her own share of looking and liked everything she saw. The man certainly had her hormonal number. Probably a conditioned response to all those times he'd made love to her. Or maybe she'd always reacted this way to him. It was like being micro-zapped with a lethal dose of testosterone.

"You want to talk, Leigh?" he asked, his words slow and deliberate. He kept his gaze fixed right on her while he tugged off the sandals that she'd put on after her shower. He let the shoes drop to the floor.

Gabe still had her foot in his lap, and with that same slow and deliberate pace, he slid his hand over the inside curve of her ankle. And he just kept moving up. Inch by inch. One unhurried caress at a time. His touch was hot, arousing. And effective.

His hand came to a stop at the back of her knee. "Well?" he prompted. "Is that what you want?"

Leigh tried to answer him, even though she had no

idea what to say. Leave it to Gabe to render her speechless. She settled for shaking her head.

"Know what I think?" he went on. That clever hand began to move again. Adding some slight pressure, he slid his fingers from her knee onto her thigh. He pushed up her dress along the way, baring her skin to his touch. "I think we could talk and yell until there's no breath left in us. But what would we accomplish?"

She shook her head again, aware of the instant energy that simmered between them. "Gabe—"

"It wouldn't accomplish much." He brushed his thumb over the little spot just above the back of her knee.

Leigh's breath shuddered. She shoved her palms against the mattress to keep herself from falling backward and just looked at him. His face, strong and angled. Handsome. Those intense eyes. The shape of his sensual mouth. His bronze-colored hand resting against the inside of her thigh.

He shifted his weight until he was kneeling between her legs, and he leaned in closer. Leigh felt his warm breath brush over her. He was nearly touching her panties. But not quite. It was that *not quite* that made her want to ask for more. Much, much more.

"I mean, what's there to say?" Gabe asked. "You feel the need to keep telling me you're sorry. Heck, I know that already. Just like you know when everything is said and done, we'll figure out a way to work through what's happened."

"We will?" she managed to say, though it had little sound.

He touched his mouth to the inside of her thigh. "We will."

She hissed when that touch turned to a full-fledged kiss. *Oh, my.* Her heart pounded. And she suddenly wanted him more than her next breath.

His hand went higher, bunching up her dress until both his hand and the loose cotton stopped at the juncture of her thighs. He lowered his head again. Paused. And snared her gaze once more. His eyebrow arched in what would normally be a questioning gesture. But there were no questions in his suddenly smoky eyes.

"What are you planning to, um, do?" she asked.

That dark eyebrow went up a notch more. "What do you think I'm planning to do?"

A few answers came to mind, incredibly satisfying answers, but he didn't wait for her to voice them. Nor did Gabe wait for her to brace herself for the erotic onslaught. He kissed the bare skin just below the edge of her white lacy panties. Slowly. Thoroughly. He nipped the tender flesh with his teeth. Leigh gasped and caught onto his shoulders.

And he didn't stop there.

Adding considerable breath, Gabe moved his mouth across the front of her panties. Where he lingered, and kissed, a while. Before making his way to her stomach. He circled her navel with his tongue.

"Did I make my intentions clear?" he asked.

She nodded, the movement of her head jerky and frantic. "Definitely."

"I thought so."

He reached out and slid his hand around the back of her neck—capturing her and her breath. Everything went still and hazy. Except for his face. His mouth came to hers.

Gabe took everything she offered him. Everything.

The kiss wasn't gentle, nor did she want it to be. It carried with it the years of want. Need. And desire. Leigh let herself be swept away.

He didn't stop or even slow down. Gabe, too, seemed to know exactly what would happen here, and he wouldn't ask for permission. He took those scorching kisses to her cheek. Her throat. His mouth moved over her as if he knew every secret she'd ever had. Maybe he did. Maybe that was part of the magic created between them.

Despite the horror of the day, and the uncertainty of their future, this was right.

Leigh pulled off his T-shirt and slid her hand down his bare chest. She felt the tight muscles, his warm skin, the rapid thump of his heart. It beat to the same rhythm as hers. And the memories of them together came flooding back.

The eager touches.

The long kisses.

Need that just wouldn't go away.

"Still want to talk?" he asked.

Leigh curved her arm around him. "No way."

Good. Gabe wasn't exactly in the mood for conversation either. Maybe later. Much, much later.

He snapped Leigh to him so he could feast on her mouth. He took. And took. But soon that wasn't enough.

"More," he demanded.

The slow, eating hunger that had always been there had a new urgency. This time he'd do something about it.

She fought with his jeans as he fought with her clothes. By default he won since her loose dress wasn't much of a barrier. He pulled it over her head and sent it flying across the room. Gabe took one look at her and nearly lost his breath.

Leigh sat there in front of him. Naked, except for the flimsy lace bra and panties. He could see right through those. And she was perfect. Absolutely perfect. The subtle scent of her arousal, and his, stirred around them.

"Do you remember how it was between us?" he asked.

The corner of her mouth lifted. "Remind me."

Oh, he planned to do that all right. That and more. Gabe slid his hand from the base of her throat to her bra. He opened the clasp and pushed the swatch of lace from her breasts. He didn't waste any time before he touched her.

A low sound rumbled in her chest. She grabbed onto his shoulders and pulled him even closer. "You're very good at this," Leigh let him know.

Gabe slid his fingers over her breasts. She felt like warm, wet silk. "*We* were always good at this."

"Really?" Her breath hitched when he captured her nipple between his thumb and forefinger. He gave it a gentle pinch. "Because I'm thinking this isn't a *we* kind of accomplishment here. You're the one who's doing the touching and kissing in all the right places. And trust me, you are very, very good at it."

He took her hand and placed it on his chest. "You're welcome to do all the touching and kissing you want."

She did. Somehow, Gabe knew she would. She watched his face while she ran her hand down his stomach. It was distracting, along with feeling damn good.

While he still had a little self-control left, he lowered his head and sampled her breasts. When his mouth closed over her nipple, she arched against him. Seeking more. And finding it.

It didn't, however, stop the downward progress of her hand.

She eased her nimble fingers right over the front of his jeans. Hell. That little maneuver caused him to see double, but he had no trouble seeing her wicked little smile.

"You're right," she assured him. "*We* are very good at this. Let's see just how good we can get."

The woman caught on too damn fast. He cursed and crushed his mouth to hers while she fumbled with his jeans. She finally succeeded in getting them unzipped. Leigh pushed them off his hips and slid her hand inside his boxer shorts.

Gabe managed a hoarse groan when she wrapped her fingers around him. What was left of his self-control shattered into a million pieces. He had to have her—now. He latched onto her hips and stripped off her panties.

He eased her back onto the soft mattress, ridding himself of the jeans and boxers along the way. Naked, he joined her on the bed.

"Now," she insisted.

Gabe very much wanted *now*, but he also needed to touch her. He needed to watch her respond to him in the most basic way. He slid his hands across her lower stomach and drew back her leg slightly so he could caress the inside of her thigh with his fingertips.

Leigh moaned. Her eyelids fluttered and threatened to close, but somehow she kept her focus on him.

"Gabe." It was a plea. And more.

He gave her back everything she'd just given him

with that promise he saw in her eyes. "Leigh. You're mine, understand? You'll always be mine."

He wasn't even sure she heard him, and there was no time for him to repeat it. Repositioning her, Gabe moved his hand and eased into that slick soft heat.

Leigh caught onto his shoulders and brought him even closer so they could complete the union. Her body adjusted, too.

She met his powerful thrusts, creating a rhythm between them that was unique but at the same time as old as time. He gave her exactly what she needed to coax her to fulfillment.

Friction. Pressure. Thrust after penetrating thrust.

He moved in and out, across the sensitive bud of flesh and deeply inside so that every inch of her body felt him.

Gabe felt her need rise and surged, coiling until it was no longer insistent but necessary. She said his name and added a mumbled plea, a primitive demand for completion. Driving faster, harder, deeper, he gave her what they both demanded. What they both needed.

When he could go no higher and take no more, Gabe did the only thing he could do. He surrendered. And took her with him.

Chapter 18

Leigh lay in his arms. Happy. Content. Peaceful. She was afraid to speak for fear of breaking the spell. She wanted to hold on to as much of the moment as she could.

One perfect moment. Well, several of them, actually. That thought made her smile. Yes, there were definite advantages to being naked in Gabe's arms. And having him naked in hers.

"Please tell me you're not having second thoughts," Gabe mumbled.

"No second thoughts."

"Good." He reached over, slid his fingers into her hair and pulled her mouth to his for another taste.

Leigh made a shameless sound of satisfaction and ran her tongue over her bottom lip to savor the kiss. "Since you kissed me in the clinic, I've always wondered about having sex with you—again. How it would be." She paused long enough to push his hair off his forehead. "And now I know."

"Not so fast." He gave his head a shake and eased right into his Texas drawl. "We didn't have sex, *mi vida*. We made love."

"And the difference is?"

"The people involved."

Leigh blinked. It wasn't an answer she'd expected, but it was certainly one she'd wanted. There was absolutely nothing about this that was ordinary.

He pulled her to him and kissed her again, a reminder of what was at stake here. Not that she needed such reminders. The reminder was there. It was something almost tangible between them. Emotion barely masked with a slick coating of fire. Nor was it likely to go away anytime soon. Everything they'd been through, all the disappointments and danger, hadn't been able to diminish it.

"You're thinking too much," he mumbled as if reading her thoughts.

Yes, she was. She didn't want to think about the challenges still facing them. Leigh didn't want reality intruding on this moment. Their moment. Gabe's and hers. Still, in the back of her mind, there was the doubt. The one question that she just couldn't seem to shut out.

What now?

Leigh settled deeper into Gabe's arms, knowing they had only a few more minutes before they had to get up. Since they hadn't been able to find anything on her computer, they'd need to get back to Philip's and get ready for the trip to Corpus Christi. She prayed Gabe's father would be as thorough with those security arrangements. She didn't want to take any more chances with her son's life.

She closed her eyes, and the image of Houston came to mind. Houston taking a nap on the quilt in the family room. She smiled at the serene memory.

But her smile soon faded.

Another picture slowly overshadowed that peaceful one. An image of murky darkness. Raw smells. And sounds that chilled her to the bone.

Leigh gasped.

"What's wrong?" Gabe asked.

She felt him move, probably so he could see her face, but Leigh wasn't able to answer him. The memories came flooding back in a jumbled heap. And the heap wasn't pleasant.

"The gun jammed," she heard herself say. But she didn't actually see a gun. It was the sound. That click. Followed by muffled profanity.

"What gun, Leigh?"

She forced her eyes to open to stop the speeding images, and she saw Gabe. As comforting as that was, it didn't soothe the storm inside her. "At the lake where I was supposed to meet you. I remember the gun jammed."

He studied her eyes for a moment. "Who tried to kill you? Do you know who Dayton's accomplice is?"

She shook her head to both questions. "I don't know." As painful as it was, Leigh closed her eyes again and let the images come. And they came all right. It was a deluge of everything that she thought she'd forgotten. "When I got to the lake, I could see a car down the shore. I thought it was yours. I parked behind it, but when I stepped out, I heard a shot and felt something graze my head."

Gabe cursed. It was no doubt as hard for him to hear this as it was for Leigh to relive it. "And then what happened?" he asked.

"I fell, and that's when I heard the click. The gun jammed."

He got to a sitting position and put his head against the backboard. "So, you're alive because the gun jammed."

That made her lucky. But it hadn't felt much like luck at the time.

"I must have passed out," she continued, trying to pick through everything and explain what had happened. "When I came to, I was already in the water. And you know the rest."

"Some of it," he corrected. He mumbled something under his breath. "I guess you called me because I thought I could help you find out who was making those computer inquiries. Or maybe because of those weapons that had surfaced. Too bad I didn't get to that bridge a couple of minutes sooner. I might—"

"I didn't call you just because I needed your help."

The next image that came into her head wasn't one of darkness and jammed guns. It was her making that phone call to Gabe.

"I called you from a pay phone so I could tell you about Houston." Leigh went on. "I'd planned to tell you everything. But then I thought someone was watching me. I got scared and rattled off that part about you meeting me. And that part about Houston. I knew you wouldn't know what it meant, but I didn't have time to explain."

He didn't say anything, but when Leigh looked at him she understood why. The news had touched him as much as it'd touched her. She'd planned to tell Gabe about his son. It was almost two years late, but there was some comfort in knowing she'd tried to do the right thing.

"Thank you," he whispered.

She nodded, not trusting her voice.

Gabe rubbed his hands over his face. "What else do you remember?"

Leigh sifted through the images, sounds and thoughts that were still going through her head. "Everything, I think."

"Everything?"

"Yes."

Leigh was almost afraid that the mere admission would make the memories go away again. But it didn't. She tested herself. She remembered her childhood. The first time Gabe had kissed her in the French Quarter. She even remembered the bed on the back porch at Aunt Martha's.

The sheets had been white. They had smelled of fresh peaches and rain.

She remembered Gabe's parents, the easy way they had welcomed her into the Sanchez family. She remembered giving birth to Houston. Holding him. Nursing him. And she even remembered the incredible guilt she'd felt because she believed the only way to keep her son safe was to stay in hiding.

"It's all there," she let him know. The happiness. The sadness. Her life.

Gabe hesitated a moment before he pulled her back into his arms. "Good."

He might have said more, might have even discussed where they would go from there, but the phone rang, taking away the rest of the moment.

"That'll be my father." He reached for the phone. "The house is probably ready."

Ready, as in they'd have to leave. She got off the bed and started to dress. It was just as well. Leigh was anxious to get back to Houston. Besides, she hoped there would be other times—in the very near future—when Gabe and she would make love again.

"Hell," Gabe said only moments after answering the phone.

Leigh stopped, her arm just partway through the sleeve of her dress. "What's wrong?"

Gabe didn't answer her, but she knew from his expression that something horrible had happened. He motioned for her to move closer to the phone.

"Please, God," she prayed. "Don't let anything be wrong with Houston."

With that prayer still fresh on her lips, Leigh leaned closer to the phone and heard something that turned her world upside down.

"I want to end this quickly," the mechanical voice continued. It was so distorted, Gabe couldn't tell if it was a man or a woman. It didn't matter. The greeting had been more than enough for Gabe to know this person meant business.

I have your son. And the others. They'll die if you don't do as I tell you.

Leigh had no doubt heard that part. Her gasp let Gabe know she didn't handle the news any better than he had.

"Who is this?" Gabe didn't figure he'd get an answer to that question, and he was right.

"Leigh should have been dead now. Put her on the phone. I need to speak to her."

"You'll speak to *me*," Gabe insisted. "What the hell do you want?"

"Put Leigh on the phone. I hate to be dramatic, but if you don't, your son will die right now."

He hadn't thought anything could scare him more, but that did it. Cursing the fact that he didn't have a choice, Gabe slowly passed the phone to Leigh. "This… person has Houston."

He watched the terror pass through her eyes. "How can that be?" She grabbed the phone. "What have you done with my son?" she yelled.

Gabe pressed his face close to hers so he could hear the person's response. It was a response that didn't give him much comfort. "The boy's safe. For now. Please help me keep it that way."

"Start talking," Leigh demanded.

"I have all four of them. Your son, Jenkins, your brother and the woman. They can't identify me. None have seen my face. All of them will be perfectly safe if you do as I say."

Leigh caught onto Gabe's hand and met his gaze. "What do you want me to do?" she asked the caller.

"I'll exchange you for your son. I promise to make it quick and painless, not like at the lake. Meet me at your brother's house. Park the car at the end of the road by the mailbox, put your hands on your head and walk toward the house. I'm giving you exactly one hour, Leigh. If you're even one minute late, I'll kill them all. And this time, I can promise you that the gun won't jam."

Because Gabe was so close to her, he saw the pulse jump in her throat. She almost managed to suppress the groan. Almost. But the groan was warranted. It was about a thirty- to forty-minute drive back to Philip's, and that was only if they drove as fast as they could. That gave them precious little time.

Still, when she spoke, Leigh kept the fear that Gabe knew she felt out of her voice. "Using my son wasn't smart. In fact, I'd say that was about the biggest mistake you could make."

"No, *you* made the mistake. By the way, if you're thinking about bringing Agent Sanchez with you, think again. If I see him within ten miles of this place, every one of you will die. Now, let me speak to him."

Leigh handed him the phone, but she didn't listen to the conversation. She hurriedly began to change her clothes, grabbing a pair of jeans and a shirt from the closet. With the phone cradled against his ear, Gabe dressed as well while the kidnapper rattled off yet more instructions. Instructions that would supposedly save his son.

And get his wife killed.

Gabe listened carefully, dissecting each word and each step of his orders. Before he could try to buy them some more time, however, the caller hung up.

He didn't waste any time with more profanity. "I'm supposed to leave now to find Philip," he relayed to Leigh. "He's tied up somewhere out in the middle of nowhere with an explosive device strapped to him. If I'm not there in an hour, he dies."

"Oh, God." Even though the horror of their situation was on her face, she didn't give in to it. "So, what do we do?"

Gabe thought about it for a moment, praying the fog would clear out of his head. Damn this person. He'd faced plenty of danger before but never when his wife's and son's lives were at stake. "This is all a ploy to separate us. Whoever's doing this won't let you just walk out of there."

"I know. For whatever reason, this person wants me dead."

He finished putting on his clothes, grabbed his gun and started for the car. Leigh was right behind him. He got them on the road, speeding toward Philip's, before he reached for his phone. "I'll call someone to go after your brother."

"But if the kidnapper sees you—"

"That won't happen." It couldn't happen. Gabe would just have to find a way around that.

He called the field office and explained everything so they would send someone to find Philip. It was a huge gamble. Philip might die simply because he wouldn't be the one to rescue him, but Gabe couldn't justify leaving Leigh and his son at the mercy of a killer.

"There's someone who wants to talk to you," the other agent informed Gabe.

"Who?" His first thought was the kidnapper had called the field office, but it wasn't the artificial voice he heard on the phone. It was Teresa.

"I listened in on your call to request backup," she let Gabe know. "I was already on my way out to Philip O'Brien's house so I could meet with Jinx. I'll see what I can do to stop this."

Hell. Couldn't he even manage to get a secure line to a field office? However, Gabe had too many other things to worry about without being riled about that.

"What'd you do—plant another transmitter so you could keep tabs on us?"

"No, but someone planted one in Jinx's car. I've been tracking you since Grand Valley. That's how I knew where Philip lived. I called Jinx when I realized where you were going, and he drove straight out to check on Philip and the others. When he didn't call back, I got concerned."

Gabe didn't even care if she was telling the truth. "This is none of your business, Teresa. Just stay out of it."

"Whoever took those hostages might be connected to Dayton's accomplice. That makes it my business."

Maybe. But he had priority. Because this was personal.

He hung up, ignoring her rather loudly spoken orders that he would cooperate. If he was wrong about Teresa, if she was truly the person behind the kidnapping, then he'd deal with her soon enough. But if she was just trying to do her job, then maybe she wouldn't get in the way of him stopping the kidnapper.

"Teresa knows what's going on?" Leigh asked.

Gabe nodded. "She says she's on her way to Philip's." He gave her the summary of what Teresa had told him.

"I don't like it." Leigh checked the magazine in her gun. "She could be lying about a transmitter being in Jinx's car. You think this is all just a ruse to make us think she's not the kidnapper?"

"Could be." He took out more ammunition from the compartment beneath the seat and passed it to her. "But it doesn't matter who we're up against. We still have to get onto Philip's property without being seen."

"Any idea how?"

"Once we're near the house, we'll leave the car," Gabe told her. "Then we'll cut through the woods and get to the house from the back."

"But the kidnapper will probably expect us to do that."

"Then we'll be careful." It was an inadequate postscript, but it was all Gabe could offer her. "We'll have to split up when we cut through the woods." He pulled off his watch and passed it to her.

"What's this for?"

"I can use the clock on the phone to keep track of time. That way, if one of us gets caught, the other will still have a chance to get to the house."

Leigh only nodded, apparently understanding what had to happen. One of them had to get to Houston in time. And it didn't matter what the cost. Damn. It was like sending his wife in front of a firing squad. It brought home too many painful memories. He felt as helpless as he had the day someone had kidnapped his sister.

"I'll take the side by the pond. You take the other," Gabe continued, trying to push the thoughts of his sister away. He tried to think of all contingencies. "If there's a trail, don't follow it. Stay in the brush and keep low. If you can, get to the house from the back or side, and if you make it that far, go in through the window."

"Okay." She took a deep breath. "You think this person is someone we know?"

"Could be."

"Maybe Frank or Teresa. Or maybe even Jinx?"

He didn't think it was Jinx, but Gabe couldn't rule out the other two. After all, someone had spent the past two days trying to kill them. "I won't ask you to change your mind about him, but Jinx is on our side, Leigh. I'd stake my life on that."

"Well, that's exactly what you're doing, isn't it? You're staking your life. Mine. And your son's."

Yes. He was. Gabe turned off the main highway and headed up the country road that would take him to Philip's house. Maybe it was the thoughts of his sister or perhaps the memory of Dayton's attempt to kill Leigh, but Gabe felt that tingle in the back of his head. It was a warning that something beyond the obvious wasn't right.

Hell.

He hoped he was right about Jinx. But hope suddenly didn't seem enough. Not nearly enough. He couldn't risk Leigh's and Houston's lives on hope.

"Don't trust anyone but me," he amended. "All right?"

She made a sound of contemplation. And then agreement. Leigh lay her gun on the seat and strapped on his watch. "What if we don't make it to the house on time?"

"If time is running out, I'll go in no matter what." Gabe stopped the car near a spot of heavy brush and stepped out.

Leigh got out also and looked at him over the hood. She swallowed hard. "In case I don't make it back—"

"Don't."

But she ignored him. "No, this is too important. If I don't make it back, let Houston know I love him. Okay?"

"Okay." The word nearly didn't make it out of his throat. There wasn't time for reassurance or even for a proper goodbye. Each second counted. Gabe had already started to sprint up the road when he heard Leigh call out to him.

"And Gabe? Just for the record—I love you, too."

She didn't give him time to respond. Not that there was time. She lifted a hand in farewell and disappeared into the thick woods.

Chapter 19

Leigh shoved away the low limbs of a hackberry tree and ducked underneath to run deeper into the woods. She'd left Gabe just minutes earlier. Six minutes, to be precise.

It felt more like a lifetime.

Streaky sunlight pierced through the thick overhead branches, so she could see where she was running. Barely. She'd already stumbled a few times. Thankfully, she had on a pair of sneakers she'd gotten from her house. If not, the flip-flops would have certainly slowed her down.

All around her were the smells of rotting leaves, mold and earthworms. It was Texas-hot, and sweat snaked its way down her face and back. Thankfully, she wasn't in physical pain. Her ankle was past the hurting stage. Now, it was just numb.

Things certainly weren't looking good. She had no real plan for Houston's rescue. Her son's abductor, however, probably had a well-thought-out scheme, one that no doubt included her death. And maybe Gabe's, too. But her own life meant nothing if she couldn't save them.

There were nineteen minutes left of the time the kidnapper had allotted her. At the pace she was running, she would probably make it to the house with twelve minutes to spare. Twelve very valuable minutes. It would give her time to consider her options and decide what to do. And she did have options, few that they were.

Of course, all scenarios were dangerous and could potentially end the same way—a deadly shoot-out with her child caught in the middle. Still, they existed, and that's what she had to concentrate on. Walking straight into the gunman's waiting arms was one way. She might get off a shot before he or she did.

Might.

And if not, then Gabe was her backup plan. She would gladly sacrifice herself if it'd give Gabe time to get to Houston.

She crossed a grassy hill and stopped at a gully not too far from the house. Because it hadn't rained recently, it was little more than a wide dusty ditch that made a beeline toward the barn. Using the thick cedars for cover, she peeked at the house, hoping to get a glimpse of her son.

Nothing.

The place looked deserted, and much too quiet.

The woods weren't quiet though. Overhead, some blue jays squawked. The wind agitated the leaves and branches. Her heart seemed to make the most noise of all—it pounded in her ears and throat.

Leigh moved closer, staying behind the trees for cover. The low, rumbling growl, however, stopped her in her tracks.

"Not now," she whispered. "Please don't let it be Philip's dog."

She fought against the instinct to run, and at the same time, she tried not to make any sudden moves. Leigh turned slowly in the direction of the sound. It was just as she feared. The dog inched his way toward her.

The animal's oil-black eyes immediately connected with hers. He growled again. She had no time to waste on this, and she couldn't very well fire a warning shot to get him to move away. To save her son, she had to get past that dog. And one way or another, she would.

"Sit!" she whispered.

The dog tilted his head, silently quizzing her. He still had his teeth bared though, so she repeated her command. This time he relaxed his jaw and sat.

Leigh quickly tried to level her breathing. She couldn't risk hyperventilation, nor could she risk being late. She checked the watch—time was running out.

A sliver of motion caught her eye. Whatever it was, it disappeared behind the remains of an old stone fence that meandered through the woods. If it was the kidnapper, then he or she couldn't have moved that fast with a child in tow. Especially not an active child like Houston.

So, where was her son?

In the house, maybe. But the kidnapper wouldn't have gotten too far away from the hostages. The person wouldn't have wanted to take a chance on losing a bargaining chip. That meant her son was probably close by. But where? And if he was close, then why hadn't she heard him?

Leigh quickly pushed that question aside. She already had too much to deal with without adding that.

"Leigh?" someone called out. The voice was hardly more than a whisper.

It was Jinx. *Jinx.* What in the name of God was he doing out here? The kidnapper wouldn't have just let him go.

Unless he was the kidnapper.

Every muscle in her body went stiff. "Where are you?" she risked asking.

"Over here."

He'd moved. His voice came farther from the right that time. Leigh moved, too. Toward him. It was a risk, since he might very well be the person who wanted her dead, but it would be more of risk to her son if she didn't face the kidnapper head-on.

"Houston's out here…somewhere," she heard Jinx say.

She'd figured that out already. Piles of leaves crunched with each step she took, and their sound probably gave away her position. There was nothing she could do about it. She only hoped it would work both ways, and that Jinx wouldn't be able to backtrack and sneak up on her.

"Teresa's here too somewhere," Jinx added.

Leigh had no time to react to that news. The birds suddenly became too quiet. She dropped to her stomach and listened. When she heard the snap of a twig, she rolled over and came up on one knee, prepared to fire.

Nothing.

However, she heard something else. A swishing

sound. Someone shooting a gun rigged with a silencer. But who was the shooter, and what were they shooting at?

She didn't like the answer that came to her.

"Please, not Houston or Gabe," she said to herself.

But it wasn't helplessness that she felt. Anger slammed through her, quickly replacing the fear. Raising her gun into the air, Leigh fired and yelled. The sound she made was nothing coherent, just something to divert attention from her husband and her son. She had no idea if it'd work, but she lowered her weapon to eye level again.

And waited.

She wasn't sure how much time passed. Probably mere seconds. She didn't dare let down her guard to check the watch Gabe had given her.

"Stay down, Leigh," Gabe shouted.

She almost panicked at the sound of his voice. God, she prayed he wasn't out in the open.

The bushes behind her rattled. Leigh reeled toward them just as a rock thudded to the ground only yards away. She spun back to her original position, cursing the fact that she couldn't cover all sides at once.

She saw someone race behind a tree. A man. She kept her attention on the spot where she'd seen him disappear, and soon he stepped out again. At first, Leigh thought she was seeing things, but she recognized the rusty-red hair and pencil-slim build. It was Frank Templeton. He had a piece of rope dangling from his left wrist. Had he been taken captive and managed to escape?

Hurried footsteps suddenly seemed to be all around her, so Leigh forced her gaze from Frank. She decided to hold position where she was.

As if obeying some silent command, the dog suddenly sprang to his feet, bolted in front of Leigh and disappeared into the brush. She didn't know whether to be relieved or not. Maybe the animal would attack the person who'd kidnapped Houston.

There was nothing muffled about the next shot. It blistered through the woods with an ear-piercing blast and came right at her. It clipped a small branch less than an inch from her head.

The next shot sliced across her arm and grazed her skin. Leigh dropped. Rolled to her stomach. And raised her gun to defend herself.

A flurry of activity was all around him. Gabe tore through the brush toward Leigh, who was still on the ground. He glanced at her for only a split second before he turned toward the direction of the shots and aimed.

"Are you all right?" he whispered.

"Yes. You?"

He nodded without taking his attention off their surroundings. He was well past being furious. How dare someone, anyone, take a shot at Leigh. Now, if he could just figure out who'd done such a stupid thing, then he would pulverize them. Unfortunately, time wasn't on his side. He had about eight minutes to figure it all out.

That eight minutes came sooner than he planned.

He saw Jinx emerge from a pocket of bushes about twenty yards ahead. Jinx apparently saw him too because he started toward them. His friend was armed, a sleek black pistol gripped in his hand. If this was a man Gabe shouldn't trust, then he needed to do something about it right away.

But what?

"Is Leigh all right?" Jinx called out.

Gabe didn't answer immediately. "No, she's not breathing."

The lie had barely left his mouth when Gabe heard the rustle behind them. Footsteps. Slow. Cautious. He hauled Leigh off the ground and spun her around so they were back to back, the same stance they'd used when they escaped the clinic. This time, however, he didn't order her to shoot to kill. He couldn't. He couldn't risk shooting their son.

It seemed the footsteps converged toward them at the same pace as Jinx's. Gabe knew they wouldn't have to wait long. Whatever would happen, would happen soon.

In front of Jinx, a flock of doves sputtered into the air and darted in all directions. Barking, the dog bolted forward to chase them. From his right, Gabe heard yet another person approach.

Teresa Walters.

He'd already seen Frank, so that meant all the players were in place. Knowing that, Gabe decided what he had to do.

"Get down, Leigh!" Gabe shouted.

Catching her arm with his elbow, he pushed her back to the ground and turned. The moment he saw the figure and where the person had the weapon aimed, Gabe fired.

"Oh, God." With her gun still ready, Leigh came up on her knee and aimed in the direction where Gabe had shot. Jinx raced to her side and did the same.

Frank stumbled forward just as his gun fired into the ground. With a bright red stain quickly spreading over his shoulder, he fell. He wasn't dead though.

And he had his gun aimed right at Leigh.

Grimacing, Frank went to fire again, but Gabe stopped him. He didn't want the man dead—yet—but he definitely intended to stop him. Gabe sent a bullet into Frank's right wrist. The second shot propelled the gun from his hand.

"I wouldn't if I were you," Gabe warned when Frank reached for his gun. He aimed right at Frank's head.

Jinx quickly retrieved the gun that Frank had dropped and restrained him.

"Where's Houston?" Leigh asked.

"I saw him. He's fine," Jinx assured her.

She nodded, obviously accepting his answer and turned to Gabe. "How did you know it was Frank?"

"He was the one person who *shouldn't* have been out here."

With all the worry about Leigh and Houston, it'd taken Gabe a while to figure that out. Jinx had already been on the scene, and Gabe had spoken to Teresa himself. That left Frank. There was no logical explanation as to why he would be in the woods behind Philip's house.

Fire flashed through her eyes, and Leigh whirled toward Frank. "Why did you do this?"

He actually smiled at her. "Because you knew where the storage facility was."

"I didn't." She shook her head and repeated it softly. "I had no idea. I only saw one word in the address—Texas."

"But I couldn't take that chance, could I? I knew you would eventually figure it out. I did, even though it took me nearly two years to check out every potential storage facility in the Dallas area."

Dallas. That was the piece of the address that Leigh

hadn't seen but Frank obviously had. That explained why the weapons hadn't shown up any sooner. It'd taken him that long just to locate them.

"How did you find Philip's house?" Gabe questioned.

"I put a transmitter in your car back in Grand Valley. I've been tracking you, waiting for my chance." He glanced down at the blood seeping through his fingers. "Guess I blew it, huh? You win this round."

"It wasn't a game," Gabe told him. He quickly turned to Jinx. "Where's Houston?"

"Nearby. I untied your brother—"

"Philip's here?" Leigh asked.

Jinx nodded. "And with Teresa's help, he should have Jenny and Houston free by now. I told them to wait until everything was over."

Gabe hoped this qualified as everything being over. But it didn't. One look at Frank, and he felt a hatred he hadn't thought he could feel. He realized he still had his gun aimed right at the man.

"I should just kill you," Gabe let him know.

Leigh stepped closer and slid her arm around Gabe's waist. "He's not worth it. When the ATF agents are finished with him, Frank will wish you'd put a bullet in him."

Gabe wasn't so sure about that. He could make things a lot more miserable for Frank than an entire task force of agents. However, he put those thoughts aside when he saw Philip, Teresa and Jenny walking toward them. Philip held Houston, but the boy squirmed to get down. With the exception of his diaper, his son didn't have on a stitch of clothes—Jenny had them in her hand.

Leigh moved at the same time he did, quickly eating up the distance so Houston wouldn't get a chance to see the wounded man lying on the ground. Leigh pulled him into her arms and pressed a flurry of kisses over his face.

"Not a scratch," she relayed to Gabe after she'd checked the child over.

He took his son and did his own inspection, but Houston seemed far more interested in giggling and singing that spider song than he was in his father's scrutiny. Houston pressed a loud, wet kiss on Gabe's cheek and wound his arms around Gabe's neck. It was pretty clear that Houston hadn't experienced any emotional trauma from the kidnapping.

Houston rattled off something that might have been actual words, but Gabe didn't understand him. One look at the child's face, however, and Gabe knew he had indeed understood. Houston smiled, a smile that melted away all the anger and fear Gabe had felt just moments earlier. A smile that touched the very center of his soul.

"Magic, isn't it?" Leigh whispered.

Gabe managed a nod. It was powerful stuff.

He put his arms around his son and wife and held on.

Chapter 20

"Well, that's something I thought I'd never see," Jinx remarked after he finished off a glass of ice water.

Leigh made a sound of agreement. Jinx and she were on the back porch of her house and had their attention focused on Gabe and Houston. The Sanchez males were on the flagstone walkway, Houston sitting next to his father. The little boy was trying to teach Gabe how to move his fingers to the now-infamous spider song. With Gabe's large hands, the motions looked absurd. And surprisingly tender.

It made Leigh smile.

"Special Agent Gabe Sanchez, a father." Jinx shook his head. "I wonder if hell really did freeze over. He always said that's when he'd have kids."

Leigh flexed her eyebrows. "Well, I didn't exactly give him a say in the matter."

"Still, he doesn't look upset. He looks content, if you ask me. And happy. Of course, he hasn't actually had to change a diaper yet." Jinx made a sound of mock contemplation. "Let me know when he does so I can give him grief about it."

She was just close enough to send the toe of her shoe into Jinx's shin. Not a kick. More of a friendly jab. "Careful, or I'll pass that chore on to you."

It felt good to joke around with Jinx. Now that the danger had passed, she wondered why she hadn't trusted him. Leigh figured it had something to do with the fact he hadn't kept that conversation confidential they'd had about her pregnancy. Still, she wasn't about to hold that against him.

"What are you two talking about?" Gabe asked. After giving his son a kiss on the cheek, he walked up the steps and dropped down on the porch swing next to Leigh.

"Diapers," Jinx readily supplied. "Hard not to look like a genuine wuss when you're changing a diaper."

"There's nothing wussy about my husband." And Leigh punctuated that with a kiss to Gabe's cheek.

With his dark curls dancing around his face, Houston toddled toward the back porch to join them. His hands bulged with rocks that he'd taken from the flower bed, and she could only guess that he had grand plans for them.

"He sure hates clothes," Jinx commented.

Houston had already discarded his shoes and socks somewhere near the birdbath—after he'd tried to drink some of the water from the somewhat dirty dish. His shirt lay near Leigh's feet. She hadn't even bothered to put it back on him after losing that battle with him twice. The only clothing items remaining were his denim shorts and diaper. She figured the shorts wouldn't last much longer either.

"Does he ever slow down?" Gabe asked, his attention focused on the boy who was busy climbing up the steps toward them.

Leigh grinned and snuggled deeper into the crook of Gabe's arm. "Never." It would be amazing to watch Gabe get to know his son.

Houston made it to them after a few somewhat precarious steps and began to arrange the pebbles on the toes of his dad's boots.

"Well, he sure doesn't look any worse for wear," Jinx went on. "But I was plenty scared there for a while. I can't believe I did something so stupid as to allow Frank to get near the house."

"How exactly did Frank manage to take all of you hostage?" Leigh asked. Since the FBI had only been gone less than an hour, this was their first chance to talk. She hoped Jinx could fill in some of the sketchy spots.

"Because I was stupid, that's why." Jinx shook his head in disgust. "I'd just arrived and didn't hear him come up behind me. He was wearing a ski mask and shoved a stun gun into my ribs. Then he drugged me. By the time I came to, the four of us were already tied up, and none of us knew who'd done it."

That wasn't an image Leigh cared to dwell on so she pushed it aside and concentrated on the rest. "I'm just thankful he didn't hurt any of you."

"And we were lucky that he separated us. I managed to get away while he was checking on the others."

Yes, and that explained why Frank was out in the

woods behind the house and why he had that rope in his hand.

"It'll all be in the report," Jinx continued. "But Teresa got Frank to tell her what happened at the house in Grand Valley. Frank wanted to kill you two, but he wanted to make it look like you were just caught up in the wrong place at the wrong time. The two dead men were his hired guns that he eliminated so he wouldn't leave any witnesses."

"But how did he know I'd be on that bridge?" Leigh asked.

"He followed you. Frank was the one who'd been accessing records right and left. He got lucky and located Philip. He said he'd been tailing him for a couple of days before you showed up at the nightclub to tell your brother about your trip. Frank just followed you from there and then apparently accessed the message you'd left on Gabe's machine. That's how he knew you'd be at the lake."

Houston climbed up into Gabe's lap, oblivious to the serious conversation that was taking place around him. He grinned and pinched his father's nose.

Jinx took a deep breath before he continued. "But Frank sure took a chance by following you to that bridge to meet Gabe. Gabe could have seen him. And almost did."

"I've been thinking about that," Gabe explained. "Frank called me just as I was about to leave to meet Leigh. He tried to keep me on the phone, using every stall tactic in the book. Thank God I hung up on him, because my guess is he was already near that bridge waiting for Leigh then."

Leigh pulled in her breath at hearing that. How close she'd come to dying. But it was over. It was finally over.

Jinx got to his feet. "I guess it's time for me to head out. You three probably need some time alone." He reached down and goosed Houston's bare stomach. The boy laughed and wiggled out of Gabe's lap. He returned to his rock-piling activity. "By the way, Leigh, if you ever want your job back, I'm sure that can be arranged."

She hadn't had time to think of anything like that, but it sounded like a good offer. "I believe I'll take you up on that in a month or two. Right now, I really just want to spend some time with these guys."

Jinx nodded. "All right. And Gabe, when I'm gone, you can give Leigh that kiss you've been wanting to give her. Just remember, you've got a pair of little green eyes watching you." He tipped his head to Houston, who was trying to pick grass bits off his blueberry-size toes.

"We'll keep any activity G-rated," Gabe assured him.

Jinx gave them a yeah-right look before he left.

Gabe angled her chin and kissed her. It definitely wasn't G-rated, but at least no clothes were removed.

"I love you," she let him know.

"I love you right back."

The easy way that he said the words brought tears to her eyes. "I can't believe I almost threw all of this away," she whispered.

"I wouldn't have let you do that. Ever."

Yes. She could see that now. What they had wasn't something that could be discarded. After all, she'd fallen in love with Gabe not just once, but twice.

Gabe reached into his pocket and pulled out a ring. But Leigh soon realized it wasn't just *any* ring. It was her wedding band. "I found it on your dresser," he explained. "I thought maybe you'd start wearing it again."

She smiled. "Definitely."

He slipped it onto her finger, adding another of those hot kisses.

Houston pushed his way between them and lifted his arms to be taken. "Up, up."

Leigh reached for Houston, but Gabe beat her to it. He scooped up his son and planted a kiss on the boy's cheek. Houston giggled and slipped his rather dirty, sticky hands around Gabe's neck. The hug he gave his father was hard, long and apparently satisfying to both, because neither of them seemed to be in a hurry to end it.

There was no doubt in her mind that this was right. She finally had the answer to the question that troubled her. Where would they go from here?

Anywhere.

Everywhere.

Leigh knew it wasn't so much the destination that was important but the fact she'd be making that journey with Gabe and their son.

* * * * *

We hope you enjoyed reading
HURRICANE BAY
by *New York Times* bestselling author
HEATHER GRAHAM
and
A MAN WORTH REMEMBERING
by *USA TODAY* bestselling author
DELORES FOSSEN

They were originally MIRA® and
Harlequin® Intrigue stories!

❖HARLEQUIN®

I N T R I G U E
Edge-of-your-seat intrigue, fearless romance

From passionate, suspenseful and dramatic
love stories to inspirational or historical,
Harlequin offers different lines to
satisfy every romance reader.

New books available every month.

www.Harlequin.com

Get 2 Free Books,
Plus 2 Free Gifts -
just for trying the Reader Service!

"I had nowhere else to go." Her words came out in a rush. "I was so worried that you wouldn't be here." She burst into tears and slumped as if physically exhausted.

He caught her, swung her up into his arms and carried her into the house, kicking the door closed behind him. His mind raced as he tried to imagine what could have happened to bring her to his door in Gilt Edge, Montana, in the middle of the night and in this condition.

"Sit here," he said as he carried her in and set her down in a kitchen chair before going for the first-aid kit. When he returned, he was momentarily taken aback by the memory of this woman the first time he'd met her. She wasn't beautiful in the classic sense. But she was striking, from her wide violet eyes fringed with pale lashes to the silk of her long blond hair. She had looked like an angel, especially in the long white dress she'd been wearing that night.

That was over a year ago and he hadn't seen her since. Nor had he expected to since they'd met initially several hundred miles from the ranch. But whatever had struck him about her hadn't faded. There was something flawless about her—even as scraped up and bruised as she was. It made him furious at whoever was responsible for this.

"Can you tell me what happened?" he asked as he began to clean the cuts.

"I…I…" Her throat seemed to close on a sob.

"It's okay, don't try to talk." He felt her trembling and could see that she was fighting tears. "This cut under your eye is deep."

She said nothing, looking as if it was all she could do to keep her eyes open. He took in her torn and filthy dress. It was long, like the white one he'd first seen her in, but faded. It reminded him of something his grandmother might have worn to do housework in. She was also thinner than he remembered.

As he gently cleaned her wounds, he could see dark circles under her eyes, and her long braided hair was in disarray with bits of twigs and leaves stuck in it.

The night he'd met her, her plaited hair had been pinned up at the nape of her neck—until he'd released it, the blond silk dropping to the center of her back.

He finished his doctoring, put away the first-aid kit and wondered how far she'd come to find him and what she had been through to get here. When he returned to the kitchen, he found her standing at the back window, staring out. As she turned, he saw the fear in her eyes—and the exhaustion.

Colt desperately wanted to know what had happened to her and how she'd ended up on his doorstep. He hadn't even thought that she'd known his name. "Have you had anything to eat?"

"Not in the past forty-eight hours or so," she said, squinting at the clock on the wall as if not sure what day it was. "And not all that much before that."

He'd been meaning to get into Gilt Edge and buy some groceries. "Sit and I'll see what I can scare up," he said as he opened the refrigerator. Seeing only one egg left, he said, "How do you feel about pancakes? I have chokecherry syrup."

She nodded and attempted a smile. She looked skittish as a newborn calf. Worse, he sensed that she was having second thoughts about coming here.

She licked her cracked lips. "I have to tell you. I have to explain—"

"It's okay. You're safe here."

Don't miss
COWBOY'S REDEMPTION by B.J. Daniels,
available May 2018 wherever
Harlequin Intrigue® books and ebooks are sold.

www.Harlequin.com

HARLEQUIN™

INTRIGUE

EDGE-OF-YOUR-SEAT INTRIGUE, FEARLESS ROMANCE.

Save $1.00

on the purchase of ANY Harlequin® Intrigue book.

Available wherever books are sold, including most bookstores, supermarkets, drugstores and discount stores.

Save $1.00

on the purchase of any Harlequin® Intrigue book.

Coupon valid until August 31, 2018.
Redeemable at participating outlets in the U.S. and Canada only.
Not redeemable at Barnes & Noble stores. Limit one coupon per customer.

52615623

5 65373 00076 2 (8100)0 12352

® and ™ are trademarks owned and used by the trademark owner and/or its licensee.

© 2018 Harlequin Enterprises Limited

HIBJDCOUPBPA0418